About the Author

Mark Hayden is the nom de guerre of Adrian Attwood. He lives in Westmorland with his wife, Anne.

He has had a varied career working for a brewery, teaching English and being the Town Clerk in Carnforth, Lancs. He is now a part-time writer and part-time assistant in Anne's craft projects.

He is also proud to be the Mad Unky to his Great Nieces & Great Nephews.

Four Roads Cross

The Tenth Book of the King's Watch

MARK HAYDEN

www.pawpress.co.uk

First Published Worldwide in 2021 by Paw Press
Paperback Edition Published
December 01 2021

Cover Design – Rachel Lawston
Design Copyright © 2021 Lawston Design
www.lawstondesign.com
Cover images © Shutterstock

Paw Press – Independent publishing in Westmorland, UK.
www.pawpress.co.uk

ISBN: 1-914145-03-8
ISBN-13: 978-1-914145-03-2

For Jen & Richard

Who have waited patiently

for many years

to get their own dedication.

FOUR ROADS
CROSS

A Note from Conrad

As usual, there are new people to meet and new magick to discover in this book. In a slight change, Mr Hayden has put together a list of all the new people in this book only and put it on his website.

Also available on the website are some new maps to help you find your way round some of the more obscure places I have to visit.

You can also find a full list of everyone in the previous stories and a glossary of magickal terms on the Paw Press website:

www.pawpress.co.uk

And now on with the story.

Thanks,
Conrad.

1 — *Anniversary*

'I didn't know if you'd come, my lord. May I offer you a drink?'
I stood up from the camp chair and bowed low. The Allfather nodded, his wide-brimmed hat dipping and showing nothing of his face yet. He took off his billowing grey cloak, and it seemed to fold itself into a bundle without any help from his hands.

Under the cloak, he was well wrapped in black outdoor gear that looked a lot more expensive than mine, and was perfectly suited to a cold evening in December. It also had the little plastic ties from where he'd ripped off the price tags. The gods do not often shop, but they do love a wind-up. He sat on his cloak and removed his hat, and as he did so, there was a rush of displaced air that moved the fallen leaves: the phantom had just become physical. His long, thin face, deeply etched with lines turned to me, and his one eye froze me to the spot.

'Where else would I be on the anniversary of your recruitment?' he said with a smile that reminded me of a hungry Mannwolf. 'Inkwell bitter would be most welcome, thank you.'

I had a gallon jug and two tankards on a tray, perched on the lip of the Clerk's Well, now all lit up by the LEDs that Myfanwy had installed as part of the Great Garden Makeover last summer. I'd drawn the beer myself, straight from a barrel at the Inkwell's craft brewery. Reynold had been most upset when I told him it really did have to come from an untapped cask.

I filled the tankards, placed Odin's on the well edge and stepped back. 'You honour my house, Allfather.'

He raised his tankard. 'You have honoured me, Lord Guardian. Please sit.' We both drank, and I nestled back into the camp chair.

'Tell me, Mister Clarke, how have you found the last year?'

'Challenging, my lord. Rewarding, yes, but most definitely challenging.'

He nodded and drank more. 'You have invited me here either for your answer or for your boon. Am I right?'

'An answer, my lord.'

When he released me from being his bonded agent, the Allfather had given me a gift – the troth ring on my right hand. He had also promised an answer and a favour at a time of my choosing. The first anniversary of my entrance to the world of magick seemed as good a time as any.

He drained his tankard and accepted a refill. I'd barely touched mine. 'I was going to see you anyway, after your trip to Ireland, but I think we have both been busy.'

I'd half expected him at Yuletide, and I'd had a visit from murderous Fae instead. Since then, I've been doing what any self-respecting hero would do: getting ready for Christmas.

He looked into his beer, then looked up. 'Before you ask your question, let me tell you a story. It is as I heard it, and as I lived it, but some of it I was not present for. Do you remember why I recruited you?'

It was a bit like asking *do you remember the first time someone shot at you*. Of course I did, so why did he ask? He must be expecting a different sort of answer. 'I remember what you *said*: to pay a debt to Hledjolf the Dwarf. On reflection, I'm not sure that was the whole truth, my lord.'

He gave a low chuckle that vibrated the fillings in my teeth and set my titanium tibia throbbing.

'Ever the diplomat, Mister Clarke. I think that you have seen enough to understand more of the truth now.' He ran his hand over his nearly shaved head. 'We do not call ourselves *gods* in our own tongue. The best translation that I can offer you is *Elderkind*. It covers a multitude of those such as me.'

He had pronounced the word with a short *i* in *kind*, like the German *kinder*. Children. He could see that I'd registered the connection, and he continued, 'There is some thought that the original was *Elder Children of the Sun*, but that makes no sense to me. What I can tell you is that the sun was not shining the day I fell on Vígriðr.'

Vígriðr, the Battle Plain, the site of Ragnarok. The battle took place on a higher plane than this one, as you might expect, but it had a mundane correlate: the village of Wednesfield in the Black Country. Two or three of the chronicles kept by monks during the tenth century refer to a solar eclipse that lasted for hours accompanied by a great storm. You can only find those chronicles in the Esoteric Library now, and any astronomer will tell you that England saw no total eclipses during that century.

No one who has looked into this properly contests the basic facts: Odin – and many other Elderkind – died on Vígriðr, and chunks of the Allfather's Imprint were scattered across the wider field. In the eighteenth century, Niði the Dwarf re-forged him. Somehow.

The Father of War drank and continued. 'When the Dwarf woke me, I was weak. I was partial and I knew little.' His hand moved towards his eye patch. 'This was not the only part of me missing. I was not ungrateful to the Dwarf, but he would not tell me why he had brought me back. Not at first. Only when I was … complete did he reveal that I was to search for his stolen book. The one you call the Codex Defanatus.' His gaze had dropped to his ale, and when he looked up and smiled, my buttocks clenched like a vice. 'I told him it didn't work that way. More beer.'

I poured, and while I did, he lifted his hat and set it spinning with his finger. Then he took his finger away, and the hat floated in mid-air like a silent drone, quivering and ready to zoom off at any moment. I tried to swallow and failed. The hat jiggled from side to side, then gracefully descended and settled back on the well rim. I'd been watching it, and nearly jumped out of my skin when he spoke. 'Cigarette?'

He was offering me a battered packet with the Spanish Excise sticker on them, like the one in my pocket. I tapped my coat. Empty. I took one, afraid to speak, and he repeated the gesture of one year ago – lighting it with his thumb.

'Keep them. They're yours.' I dropped the packet in my pocket and somehow managed to sit back down and swallow some beer. 'Misdirection,' he said. 'Your younger sister is a natural at misdirection, and so are you, in your own way. Not even I knew that you had shipped the Dwarf over to Ireland. The Morrigan certainly didn't, a point she made to me quite forcefully at Yuletide.'

The thought of the Allfather and the Morrigan having a domestic over the Yule log was something my mind instantly rejected as blasphemous. 'Th..thank you, my lord.'

He carried on with his story. 'I told Niði that I was not his bloodhound, but that I would grant him a boon. In another life, I helped him escape the Balkans and travel north. I have no more understanding of his kind now than I did then, and no more than you. He took my boon like a token, and passed it to his kinsman, Hledjolf. You will have to ask Hledjolf himself why he waited two hundred and fifty years to claim it, and why he chose finding the thirteenth Witch as his prize.'

I like that word: *Elderkind*. I think I prefer it to *gods*. The trouble with the Elderkind is that they never answer one question without leaving you a bigger one. I could see Hledjolf hoarding his favour for centuries, and the Allfather was right: choosing to cash it in on the hunt for a lost Witch seemed like a very bad deal on the surface.

'Why me?' I asked.

His eye glinted as if we were by a log fire and not a bank of LEDs. 'Is that your question, Mister Clarke?'

'No, my lord. Just my vanity colliding with my insecurity.'

'Hah. Your mother screamed in fear when you were born. I don't blame her: your house was encircled by the Elderkind, and the Morrigan was keeping watch at your door. You got your spark of magick from her, as I'm sure you know, and she was a brave woman that night.'

'She still is.'

His smile verged on human this time. 'And she had Rachael in hospital. I don't blame her. I kept my eye on you from time to time during your life. Less so after you became a man. Until the accident. When your helicopter plunged to the ground, the rope of Fate was loosened.' A gnarled white finger pointed just above my right eye socket. 'The magick was starting to come on its own already. When Hledjolf pressed me for help, I decided to take a risk with you.'

'For Abbi Sayer, or for the Codex?'

'That book was made, hidden, locked and stolen all while I slept. I know that it was not ordained that you should find it. I know that there were many paths that did not lead you to Galway. That much I have seen, and that much you will have to take on trust or waste your question. Take your time before you ask, but not too much today. I must go soon, and I will finish that draught before I do.'

I emptied the jug into his tankard – I'd only had half of my first – then settled down again. 'Thank you, my lord. You have been generous with your wisdom. My question has not changed, though, and it is this: What stake did the Morrigan have in the Codex that she became involved in the first place?'

He drained his beer and stood up. With another theatrical swirl, the cloak was around him again and the hat was back on his head. He placed the tankard on the tray and came round behind me, putting his hand on my shoulder. Not in the least scary. Merely totally terrifying.

'When the Elderkind talk of each other, we know of it. Our ears really do burn, as you say. Ask me another question on another day. Go well, Mister Clarke.'

The fire of Lux on my shoulder stopped burning, and I didn't need to look up to know that he had gone.

I breathed out slowly and opened my magickal senses. All I could feel was the throb of Lux from the well and the baby Ley line that I'd drawn down to the Gift of the Eldest.

'You don't know, do you?' I said to the cold air. 'Because if you did, you'd have told me regardless of whether she could hear your answer.'

The flap of wings in the darkness beyond the lamps could have been an owl, or it could have been a raven. His or hers.

'Twas the night before Christmas, when all round the house … total chaos prevailed.

Dad gave me a baleful look when I returned to the kitchen with an empty jug. 'How many people did you say you were meeting, Son?'

'Just the one, Dad. A thirsty one, yes, but he was on his own.' I left a pause. 'He's not someone you say no to.'

Dad smiled. 'So Rachael's suggestion that you'd gone to drink on your own to avoid helping out is just a slander is it? Hmm?'

'Yes.'

As if to prove me right, Mina and Myfanwy appeared in the doorway, both looking anxious. 'Did he turn up?' said Mina.

Myfanwy knew full well that he'd turned up. That garden is hers more than it is mine now, and the presence of the Allfather would have been like a lighthouse to her. 'How did it go, then?' she asked.

'*Inconclusive*, is the best word, I think.'

'Hmph,' said Mina. 'Typical. You are needed for decorations, and your mother wants to know where the angel has gone. Call me when you're ready to deck the tree.'

I headed to the hall and muttered to myself. 'Where do angels always go? They go to sodding Spain, and if they've any sense they stay there.'

Christmas at Clerkswell, at least this year's version, has been cooked up by Myfanwy and then seasoned by Mother and Mina. As usual, I was doing what I was told, and so was Rachael, and she looked like I felt. I found her closing the dining room door behind her with a grumpy look on her face.

'Good. You're finally here,' she said. 'I can last another hour, then I'm going to the pub in search of a husband. I'd try to turn Mike if it didn't mean having Reynold as his ex.'

'Mother on your case again?'

'This is the twenty-first century, Conrad. I am a successful professional with a great future. I should not be defined in my mother's eyes by my relationship status. I'm only twenty-eight, for God's sake! Anyway, I blame you. All this bloody talk of weddings is your fault.'

I put my hand on her shoulder. 'Has Mina been threatening you with the peach bridesmaid's dress again?'

Her brows knitted like an impending thunderstorm, and I'm sure I saw lightning flash in her eyes. She knocked my hand off her shoulder and brushed her top to remove Conrad contamination. 'You have no idea,' she

13

sniffed, and having had the last word, she headed for the drawing room. I opened the dining room door and went to see what was really going on.

Mother does worry about Rachael, and while she should really be worrying about Rachael's high-stakes career, she doesn't know enough about it to worry productively, so she gets on Rachael's case about her love life whenever there's something bothering her.

For Christmas dinner tomorrow, there will be thirteen guests around the table. Yes, you read that right: thirteen. It's a good job that none of us are superstitious or believe in the supernatural. Hah. The usual suspects will be joined by Ben's family, his two widowed grandmothers and Miss Parkes, our old school headmistress. I thought that Myfanwy had bitten off more than she could chew, especially as she's having a bit of a do with morning sickness at the moment, but Mother and Mina are determined to make it work.

Myfanwy had decided to put the main tree in the hall this year, and she'd secured a magnificent specimen to take advantage of the height available. The only problem was that, being a Druid, she'd gone for the live option, and the fir had arrived complete with root ball; it now sits in a huge builder's bucket, which Myfanwy has decorated like a witch's cauldron. As you do.

The tree has been adorned with lights, baubles and Welsh ornaments (spoons really are a thing, it seems), and now all it awaits are the Elvenham heritage pieces, and they were what Mother was poring over.

They covered half the dining table, and stretched back well over a hundred years. Naturally, I sought out my own contributions, and the first was a morbidly obese snowman in modelling clay from primary school. The Year 5 teacher had fought a constant battle against Miss Parkes' Calvinist attitude to Christmas, and Super Frosty was my blow in the struggle to defend Yuletide. What? Of course I'd given him a name.

The other was from the Christmas after my eighteenth birthday, twenty years ago now, and it was the month I handed in my RAF application. The decoration was plastic, tacky, and it showed Father Christmas flying a helicopter. I'd looked for Santa in a Tornado (the strike jet of the time), but my luck was out – and no, I didn't see it as a Sign.

I was holding Chopper Santa when Mother looked up and pulled a face at him. I know it's not the most tasteful ornament, but still…

'The fairy's in the loft,' I said. 'If the Villa Verde has a loft, that is. Don't you remember? You took it with you last year. You said that if Christmas was going to be in Spain, you'd still have the fairy.'

'Did I?'

'You did. I think you were worried that I'd sell the place and chuck everything in a skip.' She blinked, and I could see that she wasn't far from tears.

She and Dad had arrived on Tuesday, and Ben had had to collect them from the airport because I'd had my latest near-death experience the night before at Birk Fell. Mom didn't know about that one (nor about the Birkfell Pack), but Rachael had told her all about Ireland. Oh yes.

'Conrad, for once in your life, don't be deliberately obtuse. You're worse than your father. I was worried about *you*. I was worried about what you'd got yourself into, only now I discover that it's ten times worse. A hundred. Who were you meeting tonight? Mina and Myfanwy were worried sick while you were out. I thought Myfanwy was going into labour when the clock struck five.'

'Do you really want to know?' I asked. Mother's attitude to magick is one of horrified rejection. She knows it exists (unlike Father), but she won't have anything to do with it. A bit like her attitude to Brexit and its potential impact on their lives in Spain: she knows it's going to happen, but she refuses to think about it.

'Is he dangerous?'

'Not to me. He's ... You could say he's a sort of sponsor.' I put Chopper Santa down in the cleared space in front of her and risked putting my arm around her waist. 'You know that we'd have come to you in San Vicente, don't you? Myfanwy would have been looked after by the Thewlises. We're really glad you came, though. This is going to be a ...'

'Don't! Don't you dare say that this is going to be a *magical Christmas*.'

Oops.

The tears were coming now; reluctantly, as if her tear ducts were out of practice. She pointed at Chopper Santa. 'It's his fault.'

Okay. That was cryptic even by her standards. 'Him in particular or Santa Claus in general?'

'Him. You brought that hideous thing into the house just after your father had got back from his first trip to San Vicente. The one where Sofía was conceived. One of the main reasons for us coming to England is that she's gone home to Spain for Christmas.'

Oh. Oh dear. I wanted to say *I thought you were okay about her*, but I couldn't find the right words, so I gave her a squeeze instead. She understood.

'It was fine here, and fine there, while it was just her and your father getting to know each other, but someone's blabbed. I blame the Bloxhams.

It's all over San Vicente that Mercedes' daughter is also *Señor Clarke's* daughter.'

For once, I think that our ancestral enemies, Stephen and Jules Bloxham, are innocent. For one thing, they don't know anyone in San Vicente; for another, there's been a truce of sorts since it became clear that the women's cricket team couldn't function unless Elvenham Grange and the Manor House co-operated. My money was on Mercedes or Sofía herself.

That, however, was not my problem. 'How do you feel about her coming for New Year?'

'I'll put on a brave face. I've had a lot of practice.' My arm was still round her waist, and she slipped hers around mine. 'Do you know why I stayed with your father? Monte Carlo, that's why. Do you remember going to Grandma Enderby's when you were about six?'

I remembered Granddad Enderby taking me out on a boat. It was blissful, and there'd been cake when we got back, so that would be Grandma. 'I do.'

'Your father took me to Monte Carlo. I'd worked out a system to beat the bank at the Casino.'

Of course she had. Her first in maths from Cambridge made this a credible enterprise, even if it was doomed. How do I know it was doomed? Because they picked me up from Lincolnshire in a battered Ford Granada instead of flying me out to their new yacht on a private jet.

'Do casinos employ Mages?' she asked as a way of putting off the rest of the story.

'Sort of. The ones that aren't owned by the Fae have Wards built in. Even if the security staff don't know why, they know enough to have a quiet word with people who use magick.'

'Makes sense. You know what he did? He let me sit there for *six hours* while I lost a year's salary. Then he took me to a private dining room in the most expensive restaurant and presented me with a pair of antique diamond earrings as if I'd won a fortune instead of putting us on the breadline.'

She left me to draw my own conclusions about that, and picked up a flat square of tissue paper. She carefully unwrapped it and revealed a wooden star, painted blue and complete with fixings for the tree. 'Why has your boss sent this? And I do know that it's a Star of David and that she's Jewish.'

I rubbed my chin and gave it some thought. 'It's her way of saying, "Your family is important to me, and so is the Lord." The two triangles: the inner and the outer, the hidden and the revealed. Something like that.'

Mother patted my hand and moved away, placing the Star in the middle and hiding Chopper Santa behind her last gift from her own mother, a hanging Blackpool Tower. 'Whatever, Conrad. So long as the Star isn't a joke or an insult, that's fine. Hannah Rothman's Star can top the tree this year. Now, shall we begin? You put that half on the tray and bring them through. I'll go and round up Mina and your sister.'

My job was to hold the tray while Mother and Rachael hung the ornaments, with assistance from Mina, who slowed down the whole process by asking questions about every piece and making mental notes of the stories that went with them. ('From my brother who owns the car dealership. That really is their logo, I'm afraid.') Mina only went quiet when the other two dug a hole in the soil and buried an especially tasteless bauble bearing the image of the infant Prince William.

Rachael saw the look on Mina's face and whispered, 'Dad's mother.' Mina's eyes bulged a little, but she said nothing.

My mother waited until she was hanging a tiny white Greek church before she detonated her bombshell. She showed Mina the church and said, 'Tenth wedding anniversary trip to Greece. Our first child-free holiday after he came along. You went to cub camp didn't you, dear? Thought so. Now, tell me why you two have made an appointment to see the vicar next week.'

'How...?' said Mina.

I knew exactly *how* (it's a village thing), so I said, 'Because we knew she'd be busy over Christmas and didn't want to trouble her this week.'

'I don't know how you put up with him, Mina,' said Rachael.

'It's a labour of love,' replied my fiancée. It was an endorsement of sorts, I suppose.

Mother had ignored this exchange and waited implacably for a response, holding the plaster church by its thread as a reminder of her question, and she was looking at Mina for an answer.

'We were going to tell you later,' said Mina nervously. She raised her voice. 'Alfred! Could you come here, please?'

If my father has a magickal talent, it's Hiding in Plain Sight. How he'd got into the dining room without me seeing him is a total mystery. 'Everything okay, you lot?'

Mina reached out and took my hand. 'We want our wedding to be as inclusive as possible, and that is why we want the legal marriage to take place in Saint Michael's, early on the Monday, to be followed by other ceremonies through the day.'

'Oh,' said Mother. 'I see.'

Rachael had known about this, but couldn't resist making her dig in front of our parents. 'Nice one, Mina. You get to wear a white dress after all!'

Mina lifted her nose. 'It will be ivory, as I'm a widow.' Having made sure that Raitch had got the message, she grinned. 'It's really so that I get to see Conrad in uniform. The pictures will look amazing, so long as he keeps his cap on.'

Dad gave me a fatherly wink, and was about to say something when Mina switched back to serious mode and shook her hair out to look him in the eye. 'Alfred, I do not know if my brother will be able to come, and if he can't, will you be on stand-by to give me away?'

'Of course I will. It would be an honour, though I hope that Arun can make it. All this sounds like a good reason to celebrate.'

'Yes. What? Of course. I mean, what?' said Mother.

'We are going to the Inkwell at eight,' said Mina. 'We have a table reserved, and a sharing platter on order.'

'But...' said Mother.

'Ben is coming shortly to help Myfanwy, so all of that is in hand.'

'Excellent!' said Dad. 'Wonderful idea, but how in the Devil's name did you get a table for Christmas Eve?'

'The water contract's up for renewal,' I supplied. 'They brewed a batch with Severn Trent's finest last month, just to show that they don't need the Clerk's Well. All the customers except Old Tom said that it was off. Mike is now being very nice to me.'

Mother thrust the Greek church into the branches. 'We'd better get a move on then.'

She picked a hand-painted robin off the tray (one of Rachael's), and I coughed quietly. 'There's something else I need to explain,' I said. 'I got sacked last week.'

2 — New Year's Resolution

Mother didn't offer to come and collect Sofía from the airport, but she did cancel an outing to be there when Dad and I got back, and she stopped running around long enough to give her husband's love-child an air kiss, ask if she'd had a good flight and was it true that she did magic tricks?

I felt for her – Mother, that is. It's one thing to be accepting and non-judgemental in theory; the reality can be very different. I don't want to generalise, but if I said that the wider public sometimes wondered why Mother hadn't kicked him out, and sometimes wondered why she hadn't kept him on a tighter leash, you'd get the picture. Thankfully, in England anyway, Sofía's existence was the least unusual thing about life at Elvenham, and Mother's old friends just pretended that everything was normal.

Sofía does do magic tricks – and magick ones as well. That night, she did some absolute stonkers to entertain the house, including shuffling and dealing all thirteen spades to Mother. As she stared in disbelief at the cards in front of her, Mother fingered her earring. It was an antique diamond, and it could have come from Monte Carlo. Who knows? I wasn't going to ask, was I?

When she slowly nodded her head, accepting that Sofía had done something awesome, I think the overriding emotion in Mother's face was *satisfaction*. Satisfaction that Alfred's child wasn't going to be a disappointment.

I got the other side of the story an hour later, in smoker's corner. We'd had the official version of Sofía's Christmas in the car coming back from Birmingham, and I asked a more pointed question. 'What was it like to go home after your first term at Salomon's House?'

She made a face. 'I could kill Mamá sometimes. She wants the world to know that my brother is a Dragonslaying Inquisitor, and in Spain, the world of magick has the world of gossip on speed dial. I love Pápa, and I am proud to be Sofía Clarke in London, but I do *not* like it when Creepy Pablo from the grocers calls me Señorita Clarke. Poof. Sorry.'

'I…'

'No, I am not sorry, because now you have made it worse. My friends all start messaging me: is it true? Is Conrad dead? Has he been put in prison? Has he really killed the Great Queen of Ireland? Dio knows what they will say when I get back to London.' She stubbed out her cigarette violently and looked me in the eye. 'Why did you really do it, Conrad? I have a right to know the truth.'

'I told you. The Clarkes created this mess, and one of them had to sort it out.'

'And that is it?'

'Pretty much. Rachael said she'd have done the same, but she'd have tried to do it less violently.'

Sofía had already lit another cigarette without realising, and looked at it in surprise. 'Then I shall have to think very hard about being a Clarke in future. I did not sign up for this.' She paused. 'Perhaps I say that Mamá is a liar and that you are not my brother.' She laughed. 'What are you going to do with yourself?'

'And now *you* sound like Mother.'

She gave me the evil eye and shivered in the breeze. 'It is going to get colder, yes?' I nodded. 'I still want to know what you are going to do.'

I wanted to tell her, but only Mina could know my plans until they became public knowledge. 'I'm going to fly Chris and Kenver around the countryside for a while, and I'm really looking forward to the next *Fiesta del Fuego*. How's it coming along?'

We started drifting inside. 'Good. Mamá was impressed.' She stopped to share a sibling smile. 'For once she thinks that I am not a lost cause, and I think that all mothers are the same, no? Mamá even helped me with a truth trick. It will be a great finale.'

Sofía doesn't really know anyone in the village except us, and she spent most of the time in Erin's old Scriptorium, practising for her show, with Rachael's help in the afternoons.

Mina won over the vicar when she made it clear that we wanted a simple, traditional service at ten thirty on the Bank Holiday Monday. The vicar was all smiles when she realised she could fit in a shift at the hospital later in the day. These days, of course, country vicars are no longer figures of landed leisure. They either have a whole cluster of parishes, or a proper job, or a rich husband. Ours is a nurse. (And no, I have yet to come across a vicar with a rich wife).

New Year's Eve was muted, because we were saving ourselves for the next day's racing at Cheltenham. Besides, after the epic (and entirely successful) Christmas Dinner, most of us were beginning to yearn for simpler fare. Unlike Mother at Monte Carlo, I made a decent profit from the on-course bookmakers, and before we knew it, Sunday had rolled round, and the next day was Monday the fourth of January, time to go back to work. For those of us who had jobs, that is. I didn't have a job, but I did have a Sunday morning video call booked with my potential new employer.

'Hi Saul,' I began when the screen came to life. 'Good Christmas?'

'Good enough for a rest,' he replied.

The Chief of Clan Skelwith, Gnomes of Lakeland, was wearing an expensive looking shirt. You can't buy Gnome shaped dress shirts off the peg, and this one fitted him perfectly. I felt underdressed and hoped that this wasn't going to be a formal interview.

'Congratulations on your elevation,' I said with a smile. 'Does this count as your first day at work?'

'I wish. Where has it gone?' he muttered, searching for a paper on his desk.

Saul Brathay has been Chair of the Langdale-Leven Union for some years now. The unions of the Lakeland Particular are autonomous political bodies who run magick in Cumberland, Westmorland and Lancashire over the Sands. They usually, but not always, follow the rules of the Occult Council, and they are subject to the Cloister Court. What they are not subject to is the King's Watch.

Instead of the Watch, they have nine assessors, one for each union, and one Chief Assessor who answers to the Grand Union Council. As of New Year's Day, the President of the Grand Union is Saul, and he wants to give me a job. A job that currently does not exist.

He found the paper and looked back at the camera. 'On Christmas Eve, the Sisters of the Water in Ulverston detected a Summoning down the road in Swarthmoor.' He glanced at the paper, grunted, and put it aside. 'There being no assessor in Furness, they sent it to Philippa. When she did nothing, not even sending an acknowledgement, they sent it to me. It was the first thing in my inbox on New Year's Day, even before the polite congratulations. This can't go on.'

The current Chief Assessor is Philippa Grayling, and our paths crossed during my investigation into the death of a Mage called Harry Eldridge. Grayling and her assessors failed spectacularly, and the Assessor for Eden is currently awaiting trial for attempted murder. My murder.

Saul's answer to their problems is me, an option made possible because I am in a historically almost unique position: fired by the Watch, but still the anointed Guardian of the North, anointed by Nimue and appointed by her as a Bearer of Caledfwlch.

'Have you thought of a suitably grandiose title for yourself?' asked Saul.

'I thought *Commissioner of the Lakeland Watch* sounded good. The assessors could be re-titled as Lakeland Watch Officers.'

He stared at me for a second. 'Don't mess around, do you?'

'It's a big hint.'

Saul's long-term plan is to make the assessors accountable to the Watch – still independent, but subject to outside scrutiny. 'We'll keep the *Watch* part quiet,' he said with a sour face, 'and go with Lakeland Commissioner. I've had a word with my daughter.'

'Oh?'

Saul has five living daughters that I know of, and none of them have a direct hand in the clan's affairs. That doesn't mean they aren't important, though…

'Do you remember the Windermere Haven Hotel?'

I nodded. The hotel had furnished me with a temporary LZ for the Smurf. 'I do, but I never met … Grazia, is it?'

'Grazia and Gloria Brathay-Whitfield. Grazia said that you could have either the Lake Suite or the Lake Cottage. That's the accommodation on offer, and this is the rest of the package.'

He named a salary that was well in excess of my remuneration as an RAF wing commander, and I might get a Service pension on top if I was lucky.

'Sounds good,' I told him.

'You haven't heard the catch yet,' he said with a grin. 'We both know that you'll need a magickal partner in practice, don't we? In theory, though, you only need a part-time admin assistant, so you'll get an allowance of eleven thousand for that. You can find the difference yourself.'

'Understood.'

'Good. Now the hard part: the politics. The Grand Union meets on the second day of the festival, and I want this sewn up in advance.'

'Of course.'

'Your interest in the turf will make that part easier.' He held up three elaborate Enscribed invitations, edged in blue, gold and silver. I could tell that they were magickal because I've watched Erin at work often enough to recognise Enscriber's Regular Hand. And the late Harry Eldridge was one: I had to study his notes. Saul put down the stiffies. 'There's one for each of the Chases, and the Greenings will expect you at the market beforehand.'

'Market? Diarmuid never mentioned a market.'

Saul snorted. 'Nor would he. Only interested in the racing, Diarmuid. The unions began as gatherings for trade, don't forget, and every union has one, and this is ours. At least I don't have to organise this year's. It's held in the grounds of the Academy and starts at noon on the Tuesday. Grazia is expecting you on Monday night, and I'll leave the tickets with her. And George and Sapphire will join you that night for dinner to bring you up to speed and explain who you need to schmooze. I'll be down at Waterhead all day tomorrow making sure that my son has sorted the courses and that my successor hasn't made a balls of the market magick. Any questions?'

'I take it that the tickets have a plus one?'

'Of course.' The grin was back. 'I'll let you decide which of your women to take.'

You can go off a person very quickly, you know. I gave Saul a bland smile and we finished the call.

From behind my laptop, Mina stood up and glared at me. 'I can see why you didn't say anything this time, but I have noted that you let him get away with saying that. Next time, remind him that you have many female associates and even female relatives, but you only have one *woman*.' Having made her point, she came round and leaned on my shoulder. 'Do you think you need a Mage with you? Erin would jump at the chance, and she'll be going anyway. I suppose.'

I bent my neck down and kissed her hand. 'If I thought there was danger, I wouldn't go. It should be fun. Cold and probably wet, but fun.'

She squeezed my shoulder. 'There is a lot to do before then, starting with our farewell Sunday lunch. Can your father really cook a roast dinner on his own?'

'He can, and then we're off to Kernow. At least we won't have to put up with Maggie Pearce's driving.'

3 — *Take Off*

The weather gods were kind to us on the way to Pellacombe, and the roads were empty – driving down to Cornwall on a Sunday evening has its advantages. Even so, it was a long trip and well after seven when we arrived at the seat of the Mowbray family and handed over the one-way hire car to their driver to deal with. We won't be needing it tomorrow.

The Clarkes and the Mowbrays have become rather entangled of late, both with and without the capital *E*. I'd led the hunt for Lord Mowbray's killer, and since then I'd saved the life of his younger daughter, Morwenna, and together with Eseld I'd gone to Ireland in search of answers about Morwenna's condition, and that was only the latest way our fates have become entwined.

On the drive down, Mina had broached the delicate subject of my relationship with Eseld. Shall we say that it goes well beyond friendship.

'We are inviting all the Mowbrays to the wedding,' she'd said. 'Will Morwenna come?'

I didn't comment on the *we* in her statement. *We're* past that stage. 'Morwenna's a fighter. In a few months, she might be more recovered, and if she travels with Lena…'

'Hmm. I have decided that Eseld should be one of your ushers. It's where I would expect to find your RAF comrades, if you were still on speaking terms with them, and that's what Eseld is: a comrade.'

She'd said it with an air of finality that meant she wasn't expecting a comeback or comment. And she was right (as usual). Eseld has been a comrade in arms, and I'm lucky to have someone who appreciates that. Mind you, the rumour from Rachael that Eseld is seeing someone doesn't hurt.

And talking of Rachael, she's one of the reasons we've made the trip tonight. As well as being Eseld's friend, she's trying to convince the whole family to join her new enterprise. Before Rachael discovered magick, she'd been looking after the Mowbray fortune for a wealth management company, and when the estate was split on Lord Mowbray's death Rachael decided to leave her employer, and she wants the Mowbrays to jump with her.

I wouldn't say that my trip to Ireland had been a pre-condition for them joining her, but before it only Eseld had signed on the dotted line.

Kenver Mowbray, Master of Pellacombe, was waiting for us under the grand stone canopy that projects from the front of the house, and he looked more relaxed than the last time I'd seen him. Inheriting the bulk of the Mowbray Estate at nineteen had been a big shock, and he had been struggling under the weight of expectations, of loss, and of what had happened to Morwenna.

His siblings were arranged behind him. Cador is the eldest, mundane and a rising star in the legal firmament; he looked cold and anxious to get back inside.

Eseld had a big grin on her face, rather at odds with her country tweed outfit (very lady of the manor), and she was carrying a riding crop as if she were about to indulge in a little light S&M.

And that left Morwenna.

It was hard to read her expression, and if I had to pin it down, I'd have said *regret*. What for, I had no idea.

'Welcome to Pellacombe,' said Kenver, rather formally. 'Our doors are always open.'

I stepped forwards and gave his hand a firm shake. 'Thank you, Kenver. Good to see you again,' and that was the cue for a more informal round of hugs and kisses.

Mina held Morwenna's hands and asked how she was. The poor girl had had most of her vocal chords ripped out and could barely whisper without using magick the last time we met. She swallowed hard and said, 'Better thanks. I can manage a few sentences on my own now.' She let go of Mina's hands, breathed through her nose, and when she spoke again, it sounded completely normal. Slightly out of synch with her lips, but completely normal. 'Lena says that I should be able to scream properly by the time I'm due to give birth.' She patted her bump-to-be. 'The twins are fine, by the way, because I know that was your next question.'

Kenver started to lead us inside, and I was last, next to Eseld. With supreme subtlety, she placed a very local Silence, used the whip to administer a playful swat on my backside and gave me a dirty wink. 'You just wait,' she said. 'I've got a present for you.'

I said nothing.

We soon found ourselves heading towards the family wing, where a roaring fire waited. Mina shed layers of clothing on the way and said to Eseld, 'The outfit almost suits you. Is there a good reason for it?'

'Virtual staff meeting at Salomon's House this morning. I wanted to try out a new look for the new term.'

Mina sniffed. I didn't believe Eseld either.

My love now had an armful of clothes and thought about dumping them on Eseld, just to make a point, then changed her mind and put them on a chair against the back wall. A wise move in my opinion.

We turned back to the group, and everyone was still standing. 'There's supper next door,' said Kenver. 'Shall we have a drink first?'

'Can you?' said Eseld to me.

'One very small one, thanks.'

'Good.'

Drinks were served and we were invited to sit on the comfy two-seater, with the Mowbrays opposite. Kenver swirled the vodka tonic round his glass and wondered where to begin.

The family drawing room at Pellacombe was re-decorated by Lord Mowbray's fiancée in a very designer-y cream style, presumably as a way of stamping her mark on the place. Kerenza is now doing time for conspiracy to murder; whether the court took crimes against interior design into account, I've no idea. What I could see quite clearly was that redecorating was not Kenver's top priority, and underneath a truly spectacular coat of Christmas varnish, Kerenza's cream was still there.

'That tree is lovely,' said Mina. 'Did you decorate it, Morwenna?'

'Nothing else to do,' she answered, flicking her eyes to Kenver. 'But thanks.'

Kenver finally made up his mind to speak, and lifted his glass. 'To the new year and to new beginnings.'

We drank the toast, and he took a deep breath. 'Where are we? I mean, I know the Fair Queen is dead, but where does that leave Morwenna?' Morwenna looked down at her ginger ale.

'She'll hate me for asking,' continued Kenver, 'but are you sure it's finished, Conrad? Is Eseld right that it's all down to the Ahearns, and Cliodhna in particular?'

'Yes. When Princess Lussa died, the rest of her People fled to Ireland and made peace with the new Queen.' I shrugged. 'If Morwenna's grandmother – Cliodhna – was working on Mull, there's no trace of her now and all debts are paid or void.'

'Do you think we can all move on?' said Kenver.

I locked eyes with Eseld. We both had unfinished business with Cliodhna, but it was so far down our to-do lists that she gave a slight nod.

'Please,' I said. 'Rachael may kill me if we don't.'

Morwenna had remained silent up to now. She put her hand on Kenver's shoulder, and I'm sure that something magickal took place between them. He would do almost anything for her, and it finally seemed as if they were all in agreement.

Kenver lifted his glass again. 'To peace and friendship.'

This was a big moment, and he knew it. The Clarkes were now as close to being allies of the Mowbrays as we could get without having it written in blood. There was calm for a second, and then Eseld jumped up, brandishing the whip.

'Good,' she announced brightly, turning and picking up a small box wrapped in expensive gold paper. 'Merry Christmas, Mina. Merry Christmas, Conrad.'

She handed Mina the golden gift and presented me with the whip. 'I got it made specially to go with your Enchanted saddle. The whip should help you use it properly.'

I got a flash of Lux from the riding crop. It quickly subsided (there being no horse at hand), and then all eyes were on Mina as she unwrapped the gift. Inside the heavy paper was a flat, square jewellery box stamped with a fat golden brazier: the mark of Ginnar the Dwarf. Mina looked up. 'Is this magick?'

'The box, no, but the contents are.'

Mina lifted the lid. Inside was a single bangle, of platinum, and studded with bright blue stones. No gem is naturally that shade or that shiny. It was the bright sky of Mowbray blue.

'Before you say something polite,' said Eseld, 'take it out, put it on your tunic and rub the stones.'

Mina lifted the bangle and placed it on her (mostly) red tunic. She rubbed the stones, then flinched when they turned bright red and the bangle turned gold. She did it again with her black leggings, and black went the stones.

'Put it back in the box,' said Eseld. Mina did so, and without contact with her skin, it reverted to blue and silver. 'I spoke to Rachael,' added Eseld. 'She told me that almost all your jewellery is red or green. Or gold, obviously. I thought this might count as *something blue*. For the wedding.'

Mina stared at the bangle for half a second, then slowly closed the lid. She took the box in her right hand, stood up and wrapped her arms around Eseld, leaning up to kiss her cheek. She said something in an Indian language and gave her an extra squeeze. When she sat down, she smiled and added, 'Some people will do anything for an invitation. I have the *save the date* cards in my case. You are *all* invited.'

'And you are invited to eat,' said Kenver.

Over a cold buffet, we caught up on gossip and rumours, avoiding the topic of the Mowbray Estate because Kenver said that we were going to video conference with Ethan later. After coffee, Eseld and I headed on to the

27

terrace. 'Are you still on the guest list for Saturday?' she asked. 'Despite your fall from grace?'

Eseld is the third partner in Sofía's *Team Gitana*, and Saturday will see them return to the Cherwell Roost. 'Technically, I was never on the guest list in the first place,' I replied. 'The invitation was addressed to the Peculier Auditor + 1. That would be me.'

We lit cigarettes, and she asked what the hell I was going to do now that I'd been sacked. 'I've got something in the pipeline. Up north.'

She nodded, content to do without details for the moment. 'Now that the dust has settled, do you still think it was worth it?'

'Yes. I couldn't ignore what we'd discovered, and any other approach would either have failed completely or been fatal to someone else. Someone like you.'

She nodded again, more finally this time, and then rubbed her arm. 'I wish I'd worn a long-sleeved blouse under this.'

'Go on, Es. Tell me the real reason you've raided the dressing-up box. Again.'

'Bugger off. It's your fault anyway.'

'So Mina keeps telling me. I won't let it go, because Mina will assume I know, and you don't want me to make it up, do you?'

'Ha Ha. I wore it because I had a preliminary video call with the family therapist this afternoon. I wore it to keep her guessing. And because it's uncomfortable.'

It sounded exactly like Eseld. Her shoulders had come up and her head had inched forwards aggressively. I tried to be sympathetic. 'How did it go?'

She stubbed out her cigarette and turned on the heel of her shiny black stiletto. 'I did it, okay? I'm not going to give you a running commentary.' She clicked towards the drawing room. 'And then I called … And then I really did have a staff meeting. Oighrig's staying in Galway for a few extra days.'

We were back inside and headed to the media room, a space I'd not visited before. Other rich families would call it the home cinema: there were a dozen comfy reclining seats, some in pairs, facing a giant screen.

Cador was still fiddling with a laptop, and Mina was whispering to Morwenna. She straightened up and raised an eyebrow at me. I shook my head and muttered, 'Later.'

I sat next to her and took her hand. The new bangle was already on her wrist, glowing redly. 'Morwenna says that I shouldn't wear it for extended periods where there is no background magick or it will give me a headache.'

'What did you say to Eseld?'

'It was a Sanskrit blessing. She…'

The screen flashed and the image of Ethan and Lena appeared from their home at Kellysporth in North Cornwall. They had been to Pellacombe for Christmas, then gone back for New Year. They looked very happy, and swapped greetings with Mina and me before Ethan cleared his throat and said, 'Over to you, Cador.'

Cador had been as full of life as anyone over supper, and he has a wicked sense of humour when it comes to Mina's boss, Judge Bracewell, but whenever the topic of conversation is magickal, he watches and says nothing. 'Thanks, Uncle Ethan,' he began with a smile. Ethan Mowbray is now the Staff King of Kernow and can't decide whether to reign or resign. Calling him *Uncle Ethan* was the mundane Cador's little joke. The lawyer turned to focus his courtroom gaze on us. Me, specifically. 'The reason we didn't push for Rachael to come along, Conrad, is that some of what we've decided has to stay in this room. For now. Okay?'

'Of course.'

'Thanks. We've thought about this long and hard, and the easiest part of the decision was to transfer all our real assets to Rachael's new company.' He smiled. 'I've already messaged that part to her so as not to completely ruin her evening.'

I smiled back. 'I'm sure she'll be very grateful.' Mina dug her nails into my palm. Hard. Oops. I'd forgotten that Cador has been trying to get Rachael into bed for a couple of years now (she never sleeps with clients, apparently). 'And so will Alain,' I added quickly. The nails drew blood this time.

'Stop digging, Conrad. You're deep enough now,' observed Eseld.

'Moving on,' said Cador without a trace of shame. 'We've also decided to amend Dad's dispositions. When he made them, he didn't know what would happen to Morwenna.'

'You could say that my priorities have changed,' said Morwenna in her mundane voice.'

'Mine too,' added Eseld. 'Which is why we're changing Dad's will.'

'Can you do that?' asked Mina, with more curiosity than outrage.

'Yeah,' said Cador. 'If all parties agree, it's legal under Occult law. Pellacombe and Kellysporth stay as they are, as you might expect, but everything else moves one to the right. A Mowbray game of pass the parcel, if you like. You remember the house at Nanquidno, that was supposed to go to Kerenza? Now she's in jail, that's going to me. I'm giving Mowbray house in London to Eseld, and she's giving the Predannack estate to Morwenna.'

I turned sharply to Eseld. She had a lot of horses there, and it had been as close as she got to a home. She looked down before she spoke. 'Morwenna wants to stay in Kernow. I don't think I do, any more.'

'I'm getting cash as well,' added Cador. 'To even things up.'

'But they're not even, are they?' I said.

'They are as far as Rachael is concerned. What I'm going to say next is the confidential part.' He paused. 'Ethandun is going to Eseld. It's occluded and was never in the mundane estate.'

Ethandun is a ruined castle in Wiltshire, once the palace of a king. When Lord Mowbray thought his missing daughter was coming home as a red-hot Mage, he'd wanted to found a new college of magick with her as its director. Mowbray College, of course. He'd put a substantial sum of money in trust for that to happen, as well.

Morwenna spoke, using her Enhanced voice. 'I might run Mowbray College one day, but I can't set it up. Not with so little magick in me and not even a voice to call my own.'

I turned to Eseld. 'Is that what *you* want?'

She blinked a couple of times. 'I'm gonna repeat what I said to them on Boxing Day, when we thrashed this out. *I haven't got a fucking clue what I want.* I'll start the renovations on the castle, and make my mind up no later than summer next year. At Ethan and Lena's wedding.'

'You're a witness to this, Mina,' said Cador. 'Because Dad set up the Mowbray College trust while he was still alive, it's been lodged with the Cloister Court. We can't just tear it up and pocket the cash. Nor do we have to jump in and fulfil its mission. This is our official declaration that it's in abeyance, pending a decision.'

'I understand.'

'Thanks. There'll be something for you to sign at the end. Anything else, anyone?'

'Not from here,' said Ethan. When no one else spoke up, he said goodbye and disconnected.

We got up and started to leave. It had been a long day for everyone, one way or another, and we all fancied an early night. As we got undressed in the guest suite, Mina asked me about Eseld.

'She says she wore that outfit to wind up the family therapist, and I believe her: there's no more formidable armour than a double row of pearls and a tweed jacket.'

Mina leapt under the duvet. 'This bed is just as comfortable as I remember. Hopefully there will be no ghosts tonight. That's not all she's up to, is it?'

'No. She's definitely up to something. Or someone. Now come here and shut up about Eseld, or I'll be the one getting jealous.'

Kernow arranged a special goodbye for us the next morning. The weather front had blown off to the north east, and the Smurf gleamed in the sunshine on Lamorne Point. The humans had also come to say farewell.

Leah Kershaw had brought baby Arthur, and Mina almost looked broody when she peered at the well-wrapped bundle. Almost.

Leah had come to give me another severe warning about looking after her firstborn - the helicopter. Her mother had come across the estuary with us, and I'd discovered that she was now full-time Steward of Pellacombe. 'I've told Mowbray that I'm doing it for five years max,' she announced. 'In three years, I'm going to start shoving alternative candidates under his nose.'

She'd said that in a loud voice, so that Kenver (now promoted to "Mowbray") could hear her. In a real sign of maturity, Kenver responded by saying, 'So long as they're good looking.' What? Of course it was maturity: three months ago, he'd have gone red and turned away.

I'm not saying that he's there yet, as Eseld quickly told him. 'No point, kid. You've got no chance. Bye, Jane.'

Before I started the engines, the Ferrymistress's husband handed over the tablet computer with pre-flight checks completed, and Leah gave me a final Christmas present – if you can call it that.

'It's a Bluetooth enabled alcohol detector. You have to take one before flying, and the result is logged.'

'What are you trying to say?'

'That you're a good pilot and that the world should see the evidence,' she replied sweetly. I blew into the device, and it came up as close as the machine's tolerance would have to zero. Hah.

It was a fairly full load today, what with all the luggage and four passengers. At least they were all experienced flyers. There wasn't a single complaint when we caught up with the weather front near Winchester and I had to take the Smurf under the clouds for a bit, and ATC wanted me to take a fairly big detour around the Heathrow approaches.

Eseld headed straight off when we disembarked at the London Heliport, and I waited with Mina for her lift. She spent a long time combing out her hair in the lounge and announced, 'After that flight, I now know why you are going deaf. I am going to miss you. There they are. Quick, let's kiss.' So we did.

There was a large 4x4 in the drop-off zone outside, and we did a quick swap: Chris Kelly's bags for Mina's luggage, and the man himself for Mina. Not a fair swap in my opinion, even if Chris is a good friend.

This was going to be a busy week. Eseld was on her way to welcome Sofía to Mowbray House. Even Rachael was moving in there for the week so that they could practise the Fiesta ahead of the weekend. Mina was due in court tomorrow, but she was spending tonight with Tamsin Kelly out in Richmond. As well as having a girly night in, Mina was going to assess the eldest Kelly daughter's suitability as a flower girl. And then tomorrow, Mina had a difficult job: interviewing Karina Kent for the post of Madreb to my pack of Mannwolves in Lakeland. Assuming that Karina survived the court martial this morning.

Chris Kelly, Earthmaster of Salomon's House, is also Kenver Mowbray's tutor in the science of magickal engineering: creating and maintaining the arteries of Lux that flow through Albion's Ley lines. They were having an intensive week before term started, and I was their pilot. After a quick nicotine break, we were back in the air: next stop an exposed hillside in the Derbyshire Peak District.

'Don't tell Leah where we're landing,' I said over the intercom. 'It should be okay for a quick drop-off.'

'Pick somewhere drier,' said Chris. 'We need to set down for a bit. We don't mind the walk.'

I swept around the moor above Derwent reservoir and saw somewhere suitable. It looked like a rendezvous point for the fire services who'd been dealing with the horrible moorland fires last summer. When we'd landed, I shut down the Smurf completely.

'Get your coat and your dowsing rod,' said Chris. 'You're coming with us.'

I frowned. 'Why?'

'You need to see some proper Ley work if you're going to get your doctorate. It's only a mile and a half from here, and I'll Ward the Smurf before we go.'

Chris is a good friend, and I owe him. Part of paying it back is submitting to his plan for me to become a Doctor of Chymic at Salomon's House. I simply don't have the magickal talent (or the inclination) to pass the first degree, the Fellowship, but I am a Master of the Art. This rather honorary qualification allows me to study for a Doctorate in my only strength: Geomancy.

It was a pipe dream, of course. I had already chalked up a few easy passes in the Part I course, but I'd never be able to submit a dissertation at the level required. Still, if it keeps Chris happy…

The Earthmaster has even longer legs than me. He is also a mad runner and doesn't have a titanium tibia. His idea of "A mile and a half" would see him fail the RAF navigation test, that's for certain. By the time we reached the Node, we were wet, dirty and I was knackered. So was Kenver, but he doesn't have much experience at Grinning and Bearing it, so I let him moan on my behalf. When he'd finished, I added, 'So long as you can organise a taxi back to the Smurf, I'm not bothered.'

'Eh?'

'Pilot hours,' I said with a straight face.

'I … You're winding me up, aren't you?'

'Maybe, maybe not. What's the job, then?'

'The Network…' Chris started, then stopped. 'You tell him, Kenver. Imagine he's a client.'

'I … err … You know about the Network, right, Conrad?'

'I've read Chris's book. It was riveting.'

'Tell me about it.'

'Less of your lip, Mowbray. I'll have you know it's one of the most borrowed books in the Esoteric Library.'

Kenver looked mutinous. 'Only because it's so flipping expensive and because no one wants to own a book they're never gonna read again. You should write a second edition with guides to waterproof clothing in it. I still can't feel me feet, and Dad always got us chauffeured up to the site.' He looked at me. 'Or dropped off there. This is your fault.'

'I've missed this,' I said.

'What?' they asked in unison.

'Never mind. I take it the reservoir has something to do with me standing on top of this hill.'

'Yeah,' said Kenver. 'Chris, tell him what it was like before. You must have been here then.'

Chris took the bait. 'How old do you think I am! That reservoir was built in 1947.'

Kenver grinned. 'I know. Serves you right for dragging me over that bog.'

'Shall we get on?' I asked. 'Pretty please?'

Chris took over properly this time. 'This is the most southerly of the Trans-Pennine Ley lines. It was rudely interrupted by the reservoir and my predecessor had to decide whether to re-route the line or bury it so deep underground that the water wouldn't affect it. He chose to bury it.'

'And the bliddy thing breaks down every Yuletide,' muttered Kenver. 'And every Midsummer, but that's a nice day out.'

Chris had already taken off his rucksack and removed some of his tools of the trade. He also had a plastic wallet full of papers, which he offered to Kenver. 'This is a blank tender document for fixing it permanently. Salomon's House is going to seek bids when the new Warden is elected, and I think you should bid for it.'

Kenver stared at the wallet. 'Do you really think I'm ready?'

'Let's find out shall we?' He thrust the wallet again, and Kenver took it. 'You can put Conrad down as your assistant if he's still unemployed. Even if he isn't. And he can start by finding the Node.'

'Every day's a school day with you, Chris,' I half muttered as I took out my dowsing rod, now no longer known as Maddy.

A year ago (ish), I chose a willow wand as a gift from the Witches of Lunar Hall. It was inhabited by what I thought was a Memory – the lingering thoughts of a woman called Madeleine. It turned out to be her full Spirit, and no, I have not been given a satisfactory explanation for that. Last spring, I was joined by another Spirit, who took possession of a Border Collie pup. That Spirit turned out to be Madeleine's father, and again, it was not a coincidence.

They are both gone now, who knows where, and the dowsing rod is back to being a powerful Artefact that helps me sense the flow of Lux, especially in Ley lines. Just how powerful I was about to find out.

Chris had wisely stopped us a hundred metres from the actual Node. Good job. If I'd opened my Sight on top of it, I'd be on my way to hospital. Again. And Leah Kershaw would be trying to retrieve the Smurf. Again.

'I need to practise my levels of sensitivity,' I said. 'And the Node is on top of that rise, over there.'

Chris frowned. 'What do you mean, practise your sensitivity? This is Geomancy, not Geo-therapy.'

I waved the wand. 'You don't look at arc welding without goggles. That sort of sensitivity.'

'Oh. Right. Put the rod down on the grass, and when you pick it up, reach inwards for your magick leg, then calibrate.'

I ignored the inaccuracy and did what he said. Number 498 on the list of Mysteries is my titanium tibia: specifically, how it turned into a store of Lux that I can control, a bit like the top of a vacuum flask. I did what he suggested, and it was an excellent idea. I know exactly how much Lux is stored there, and with that as a calibration level, I opened my Sight further. Much safer. With a nod, I led the way to the Node and took a good look at it. The others had been here several times before and focused on getting ready for the repair.

I really have read Chris's book, and it's not as bad as Kenver makes out. Either that or I'm getting very old. When I detected twin, parallel tracks heading north west towards Glossop, I couldn't help being the teacher's pet. 'Roman,' I said. 'Original?'

Chris nodded. 'Standard Gauge. There was a Roman continuation due south, but that's long gone. What else can you see?'

The line to Glossop throbbed with suppressed power, suppressed because it would normally flow east south east, towards Sheffield, but that link was broken and the Lux spooled around my feet with nowhere to go except on a branch line to the south, towards Castleton. I reported that, and Chris put his hand on my shoulder.

'I think you can find the nub, Conrad. That's the hard bit. It's where the line's broken off, and I'll give you a clue: it's not where you'd expect.'

He removed his hand and stepped back, whispering something to Kenver as he retreated. Right. Here goes.

Wand firmly in my left hand, I plotted a counter-clockwise path round the Node, then closed my eyes. I started just to the left of where I thought the direct line would run and moved away from it.

I've never dowsed a Node before, but something did seem different this time, and I only found out what had changed when I cracked open an eye to check for mundane trip hazards. It was very different because I could actually *see* the Lux as well as sense it. Very faintly, and a very muddy brown, but I now had a visual perception I'd only been capable of before via Maddy herself.

Not that it helped. I kept going for a while, and apart from the open channels to Glossop, I got nothing. Until I realised that there was a definite boundary to the swirling energy: something was stopping it leaking into the wet peat. As soon as I realised that, I caught a really tiny glimpse of blue, like crepe paper, at the edge of the circle. Interesting. And diametrically opposite the route under the reservoir, I found a thickening of the wall, a solid point of magick. 'Here,' I announced.

'What have you found?'

When I told him, Chris was thrilled. 'Excellent, mate. You've got it. The blue stuff you can see is what we do. It's crystalline Lux, like using ice to make a channel for water.'

'Chapter Nine, if I remember rightly. I skimmed that one because I thought it would be beyond me.'

He smiled. 'And it probably always will be. That's why me and Kenver get the big bucks for standing up to our arses in mud.' He pointed to the distant acres of water down the valley. 'The other end is physical. A Dwarven Artefact with an Anchor point. Kenver and I are going to reach out to it and draw a line back to here. You can watch.'

I blinked and stuffed the dowsing rod in my belt. 'If it's all the same to you, Chris, I seriously think I'd better not. I'm already getting a headache, and I really do have to be firing on all cylinders to fly. I'll head off back to the Smurf, and you can call me when you're done. Perhaps next time.'

His face was full of concern. 'Of course. Do you think you can still fly us to Dumfries?'

It was already heading for darkness, and we were staying in a Scottish hotel tonight, ahead of tomorrow's jobs. 'No problem. And thanks, Chris. Thank you very much.'

Chris put on a serious face. 'No need to thank me. Knowing that you've just passed two more elements of Part I is all the thanks I need.'

'By the gods of Kernow, he talks bullshit sometimes,' observed Kenver.

I hitched my rucksack. 'That's the weird thing about growing up, Kenver: discovering that something can be both true and bullshit at the same time. See you soon.'

4 — *The Power Behind the Throne*

卐

'Are you sure you don't want fortifying before you go out?' asked Tamsin Kelly, waving a bottle of gin in my direction.

'You are a Rākshasī, Tamsin, tempting me. Did we not drink enough last night, never mind the night before?'

She considered the bottle as she stood on one foot, poised elegantly in front of the marble-topped island in the middle of the biggest kitchen-living space I've ever seen in real life. If only it weren't hidden from mundane sight, it would be in every interiors magazine going, and Tamsin would be pictured in it, glowing healthily after a run along the Thames. For those reasons, I should be consumed with a jealous rage, but I am not. I am sorry for her. Today and every day. And not just because she is married to Chris Kelly; for that she only has herself to blame.

'Perhaps not. I've got work to do,' she said, returning the bottle to a well-stocked drinks cart. An actual cart that can be wheeled outside or hidden away. Her socks padded over the marble tiles (with underfloor heating), and she flopped at the other end of the settee. From a distance, she looks like a young woman with an enviable figure. Close up, she looks like she's barely more than a child. The truth is neither of those things.

Tamsin Pike was born forty-three years ago, was a leading Mage in her field and had been married to Chris Kelly for ten years when she was told she was dying of cancer. Tammy was some sort of magickal therapist, and one of her own patients, Melody, called to say that she had taken an overdose of a seriously fast-acting poison, and that she was alone in the house. Tammy was riding her bike on the way to somewhere, and she says that she could do nothing for her. In one of those decisions that you can't explain, Tammy turned her bicycle into an oncoming lorry and projected her Spirit across London. She erased everything that was Melody Richardson and became a thirty-seven year old woman in the body of a fourteen year old girl.

'Are you sure you don't want to come back here tonight?' she asked hopefully.

I raised my eyebrows. 'You are forgetting that I know the nanny's day off is tomorrow. Siona deserves her time off.'

'Worth a try.' She stretched out her legs and stopped short of resting her feet on my thigh. They may have a cleaner, but no house with three children under five is ever truly clean, as I could see from the soles of her feet. She knew better than to get stains on my new kameez.

I slapped her toned calf (not at all jealous), and said, 'Besides, you have homework. Those nurseries will not select themselves. I shall be back on Friday morning.'

She sat up, effortlessly bending from her abdomen, and took my hand. 'Thanks, Mina. You don't know what this means.'

Unfortunately, I knew exactly what it meant to her. After Melody became Tammy, she was ostracised by the world of magick. Totally. Melody's parents conducted a vicious campaign of harassment against her and Chris, and Tammy was pregnant with Amanda two weeks after her "sixteenth" birthday.

Since then, Tammy has barely left the house, partly because she was afraid, and partly because she looks like Chris's daughter when they are together. She used to take little Amanda away with Chris and pretend to be the nanny. Her children have never been to nursery, which explains why Amanda had never talked to a "brown person" before she met me.

Tammy's life changed last autumn when she started studying with the Fae Queen of Richmond, and now she feels brave enough to put them in a nursery part-time.

I squeezed her hand in return and reached for my phone, which had just had an incoming message. It might be Conrad, saying that they'd arrived at Inverness. I have been checking the weather constantly since Monday, and I did not like the look of the forecast for the Highlands. Not at all.

It was him. *Safe. Another hotel on the list for our Grand Tour. This one has an Indian Room, but I'm staying in a room called Balmoral. I'd miss you too much in the other one. C.*

'They've arrived,' I said to Tammy. 'Did you not get a message?'

'Oh, yeah. Sorry. I was distracted by the gin bottle. Besides, they've got Conrad to keep them in line.'

I was still holding my phone, and another message came in, this time from Hannah. I had to peer at the screen to make sure I wasn't seeing things. To prove it was real, I read it out loud. 'Change of plan. Meet at the Kernow Room, Waldorf Hotel. Trust me. Hannah.' I looked up. 'What is Eseld up to now, I wonder?'

'Could be Cador,' suggested Tammy. I gave her the look. 'Okay, it's Eseld. I thought you were playing nicely with her.'

'I am, but she is incorrigible. We'd better leave soon, hadn't we?'

She swung her legs down and moved her hair away from her face. It's still long, but a good six inches shorter than when we first met. 'Do you think Siona would mind if I joined you for dinner? Might be fun.'

'Yes, she would mind. She has already agreed to do extra hours tonight. Where did I put my dupatta?'

We loaded my cases into Tammy's car and we set off towards central London. It was kind of her to give up a couple of hours just because I had too much luggage for an Uber and had a new outfit to preserve. Then again, I had put the girls to bed last night so that she could do the Big Shop. On a whim, I checked the Waldorf website and decided to book myself in. Why should Conrad be the one to stay in swanky hotels all the time? Not only that, I could wear my new sandals instead of waterproof boots.

Because we'd budgeted time to go via Notting Hill, I was early and checked in to my room. And that meant I got some quality Facetime with Conrad.

We ticked off the items on the list: his day next to a loch, my day in court, news from Elvenham (none) and news from Birk Fell.

'Erin has reported in,' he told me. 'Karina arrived safely and has been introduced to the pack. All going well so far. I get a huge sense of *reserving judgement* from Erin, though.'

'This is not surprising. They have a lot of history. It's a good job that Erin doesn't have the emotional energy to bear grudges. We shall see for ourselves at the weekend. Is it going to rain?'

'This is January in Lakeland. What do you think?'

'Hmmph. Your room is bigger and better than mine, and you're getting it free,' I sniffed.

He snorted with laughter. 'I bet your room has got two things that mine hasn't: a functioning heating system and you.'

'And me what?'

'Just you. Your room has you in it; this one does not.'

Aah. How sweet. I pressed my finger towards his lips on the screen.

He leaned in towards his camera and dropped his voice to a whisper. 'My room does have good soundproofing. We could…'

'Don't! I have to have dinner with Hannah in twenty minutes. And probably Eseld, too.'

He gave me an evil grin. 'Hold the thought, then. Unfortunately, I have to be sober by 0800 tomorrow, so no drams of single malt by the peat fire for me. Give Hannah my love, and give any other guests whatever emotion you think appropriate.'

When I descended from my poky attic space, I spent a long time looking for the Kernow Room. Surely it couldn't be magickally hidden could it? No, it was hidden round an awkward corner and through a staff door because it's not used very often.

'Please tell me that I'm not the first,' I whispered to my guide.

'No, ma'am. The other lady arrived ten minutes ago.' The nice concierge knocked once and opened the door for me to go through.

Hannah looked pleased to see me, and gripped me in a big hug. The last time we'd met was the day she handed Conrad his dismissal notice. 'Good to see you, Mina. That blue really suits you.'

She stood back and held my hands, then looked down. 'Mina! That ring is … Wow.' She looked up. 'The diamond didn't…?'

'It did. And the rubies.'

She squeezed my fingers and let go. 'It's very Rani. Very you. Very Conrad, too. Look, I'm sorry about the change of venue.'

I had a good look at Hannah, who had clearly come straight from Merlyn's Tower, and then the room. 'Hannah-ji, you are looking well. Unlike this room.'

Conrad had told me that the room was "A bit bland." The rooms at HMP Cairndale have more life in them, unless you are a devotee of faded etchings and beige carpet. Literally the only splash of colour was the shield with a white boar's head on a Mowbray blue background.

She looked around as well, as if this was the first time she'd noticed it. 'Yeah, well, it's private. We won't be interrupted, spied on or eavesdropped in here now that I've set the Wards. That's why old Tusky on the wall is so bright. Did they really do a whole roast wild boar for Ethan's coronation?'

'I'm afraid so.'

'Eurgh. Let me get you a drink.'

I stopped her moving away. 'First put me out of my misery. When is Eseld coming? Why is Eseld coming?'

She snorted. 'I wish she was. At least then we'd be guaranteed a good time. One way or another.' She paused to mull over that idea, then shuddered. 'I couldn't bring myself to text. I told myself it was because you wouldn't turn up if I did, but I knew you would anyway. I didn't text you because I wanted to put off spoiling your dinner as long as possible.'

My mind was now full of alarming and disturbing possibilities. She shook her head slightly. 'It's Michael Oldcastle,' she said. 'He insisted on doing this in person. And now you really will need that drink.'

It was like expecting a spicy samosa and being given a lemon to suck instead. The Reverend Michael Oldcastle stays away from the Cloister Court, so I have not met him, but Conrad (and Vicky, and Hannah and everyone I've spoken to) says that he is a sanctimonious prig of the highest order. Unfortunately, he also pulls most of the strings that will decide Conrad's immediate future.

When he brought down the Fair Queen in Ireland, Conrad broke no laws. You do not have to declare a Dwarf when you go through customs. Telling Niði who had robbed him was not illegal. The United Irish Inquisition could not charge Conrad with *Conspiracy to commit Fairycide*, as his lawyer put it. Instead, they lodged a formal complaint with the Duke of Albion, the nominal head of magick in Britain.

The King's Watch is a Royal Peculier – hence Hannah's title. Since George III (or was it II? I? Whatever George). Since the 1700s, the King or Queen has left it to the Duke of Albion and a few key players to choose the Constable, the Deputies, and generally watch the Watch. There is a Latin phrase for this, but I do not care. Accountants don't like Latin phrases. Since the 1950s, they have been known as the Oversight Committee.

If Sir Roland Quinn were still Warden, I suspect that none of this would have happened, but he is now with us in Spirit only, and until the new Warden is elected, the Deputy Warden is having his moment in the sun.

The Committee had received the Irish Inquisition's complaint, and Oldcastle had insisted that Conrad be dismissed as Deputy Constable. The rest of the Committee (except Hannah) had agreed with him, and because it is a royal appointment, Conrad has no comeback and no appeal. With a stroke of the Duke of Albion's pen (she didn't attend the meeting), Conrad was no longer Deputy. And now they are beginning to regret it.

First of all, Nimue laughed in their faces. The Nymph who watches over Albion said that she was quite happy having Conrad as Lord Guardian of the North, and she even confirmed his appointment as bearer of that sword whose name I can't pronounce in Welsh. Excalibur. You know the one I mean.

And then Conrad also refused to resign and pointed out that he was still a Wing Commander in the RAF and licensed to carry firearms by the police. I was so proud of him when he did that, even if it did put me in an awkward position with my Matron of Honour.

If the Committee sends Conrad to a court martial, they will lose control and risk being embarrassed. Nor do they have any say in his firearms licence, and that's why Hannah has been trying to broker some sort of compromise.

She poured me a large glass of wine and topped up her own from a different, kosher bottle, and that reminded me. 'What are we doing about food, Hannah?'

She grimaced. 'You two are having the private dining menu, I am having kosher takeout. It'll all arrive together, but yours will have been individually cooked, and mine will have been lovingly shoved in the microwave. Eseld says the fish is always fresh, which is a good job because it's that or beef. Sorry.'

I glanced at the menu. 'When is he coming?'

'He's due now, but he'll be late. Shall we sit down?'

There were chairs that matched the beige carpet. Comfortable, though, if you're Conrad's height. I kicked off my sandals and curled up.

'How is he? Trip going well?' she asked.

'He is flying helicopters, staying in the best country house hotels and enjoying the bachelor life. And no one is trying to kill him. Of course he's enjoying it. And he sends his love.'

'And he no doubt has a plan for his future.'

'He does. Depending on this meeting, of course.'

'Of course.' Her voice rose in pain. 'Why did he do it, Mina? Why didn't he leave it to me to sort out?'

I nodded slowly and said, 'He did it for the same reason you are eating kosher takeout. It is because that is who he is. When you strip everything else away, that is what you have left.'

'What about you? Wouldn't you have rather he left it to me?'

I shook my head. 'For the same reason, no. I love him for who he is, and he let me deal with Pramiti on my own.'

She looked down. 'Of course. Sorry.'

Hannah had left her scary wig on the dining table, and I could see it over her shoulder. She took off her headscarf without thinking and I flinched away. When Hannah realised what she'd done, she went as red as her wig and held out the scarf. To me. 'Would you?'

I got up and went behind her, accepting the scarf and trying to remember how she liked it done. This meant that I had to look down on the wounds, on the titanium plate that stands in for part of her skull and the wisps of white hair that she must hack off with scissors. 'Is that too tight?'

'Perfect. Thanks. Sorry. Top us up, would you?'

I didn't need topping up, but Hannah did. I was half way to the drinks, padding across on my bare feet, when there was a knock on the door and Oldcastle was shown in. Damn. Now I would look even shorter than I normally do. From the other end of the room, I heard Hannah swear.

'Good evening,' he boomed in his pulpit voice. 'You must be Mina Desai.'

'Namaste, Reverend,' I responded, bowing low. When I stood up, he didn't offer to shake hands with me, for which I was both insulted and relieved. They looked rather sweaty.

Michael Oldcastle is a large man. He was wearing all black except for his dog collar, and his loose black shirt didn't hide his love of the great Christian festivals – especially the Christmas pudding, the chocolates and the cake. And probably the port.

A waiter was lingering at the door, and guess what? After a brief glance at the menu, Oldcastle ordered the beef. When he did, Hannah gave me a slight shake of the head, so I said nothing. I was going to let her lead tonight.

Oldcastle accepted a large gin and tonic and immediately tried to take over by leading us back to the comfy chairs as if he were the host. I don't know whether that's because he's a priest, a man or because he's obnoxious.

He was about to sit down when he noticed my sandals on the floor in front of the chair and swerved to the one with Hannah's bag on it. Foiled again, he had to make do with the one at an angle. At least he waited for us to sit down first.

That didn't stop him taking over as soon as his well padded backside had hit the fabric. 'You didn't go on the ill-fated mission, did you Mina?'

I smiled at him. 'No, Reverend, I was at work, so Conrad took a holiday on his own.'

Hannah jumped in. 'I think that what Mina is trying to say is that Conrad was on sick leave at the time, and what he did shouldn't be construed as a *mission*. Isn't that right, Mina?'

I smiled at Oldcastle and blinked like the little woman I can be when I need to.

'Quite,' said Oldcastle. 'Did you have a good rest over Christmas, Mina?'

He clearly wanted to enjoy his dinner and keep me in suspense, and that was not going to happen, despite Hannah giving me a warning look. Oldcastle has a low opinion of me, so I decided to confirm his prejudices. 'We had as good a Christmas as we could, Reverend, but I was so worried about what would happen. Sometimes I didn't sleep. I am really anxious to move on with our lives.'

Hannah gave up playing it straight and decided to join in. 'Yes. We could all relax if we heard what you have to say.'

'Of course.' He folded his hands and rested them on his stomach. In his head, he probably thinks that this makes him look like a wise Buddha. It doesn't. It makes him look like a pompous windbag.

'I have had long conversations with some of the other members of the Committee,' he pronounced. No doubt these conversations were fuelled by large quantities of gin that someone else paid for. 'I was particularly struck by what the Vicar of London Stone said to me.'

No one in our circle knows the identity of the Vicar of London Stone except Hannah, and she refuses to say. All we know is that on a day-to-day basis, Hannah answers to another woman.

Oldcastle left a suitable pause for us to be impressed, then continued. 'After a lot of prayer, she thinks that we should remember our Christian duty of charity.'

I could tell straight away that Hannah had had enough now. Telling a Hindu and a Jew that charity is a Christian thing did not go down well.

'We also have a duty to promote peace and work with all the creatures that God has put amongst us. If Nimue wishes Mr Clarke to guard the North, then we should work to support this. Within the law, of course.'

Hannah gave a feral grin. 'In other words, the Vicar of London Stone has had the same thought as me: that she wants him out of sight and out of trouble.'

I doubt very much that Hannah wants Conrad out of sight. That way she can't shout at him. I didn't say that, though.

'As you say, Hannah. We would like to make an offer: Conrad can transfer to the RAF Reserve and keep his Veteran's pension with no proceedings against him, provided he gives a written assurance that he will keep the King's Peace.'

I breathed a sigh of relief. This was what we wanted, and for once I could speak for him with full authority. 'He has already given his word on that matter.'

Hannah decided on a strategic lie. Conrad never puts his word in writing. 'I already have the piece of paper in the safe,' she announced. 'Tennille can process his transfer effective next Monday. To the future. Whatever it may bring.' We raised our glasses, and I hadn't set mine back down before the food arrived.

We had got what we wanted, and by unspoken agreement Hannah and I avoided discussing dietary differences. Now that his mission was over and he had something disgustingly bloody in front of him, Oldcastle actually seemed rather interested in what Conrad had done, and I didn't mind answering questions. The more the truth is out there, the better. Not the *whole* truth, of course. No one wants the *whole* truth.

We got rid of him by virtuously declining dessert and leaving him the option of eating sticky toffee pudding on his own or making his excuses. His appetites clearly have some limits, and with a sigh he put the menu down and made his excuses. I'll say one thing about him: his hands actually weren't sweaty, and he didn't try to crush my fingers when he left.

'Do you know what the Keeper calls him?' I said when the door was firmly closed.

'Don't tell me. I don't want to know. What I do want is another drink. You look like you could use one, too.'

'Oh yes.'

As Hannah sat down, I got in first. 'Thank you so much for that. You need to know what Conrad's cooking up.'

She narrowed her eyes. 'Is it going to make me track him down and stab him?'

'No. He wants to work with Clan Skelwith to bring the Particular under Watch jurisdiction.'

She jerked upright. 'What!'

When I'd told her what he was up to, her first question was, 'And this definitely came from Saul Brathay?'

'Oh yes.'

She sat back. 'I wonder what the old goat is up to.'

'Don't worry, I am constantly asking the same question. Conrad is too inclined to take him at face value. I think his defenestration from the Watch hit him harder than he realised.'

'Please tell me that *defenestration* is his word. I couldn't be Matron of Honour for a bride who uses words like that.'

I spread my hands in supplication. 'He does have a huge problem, of course. He needs a magickal partner.'

'And the Clan aren't choosing for him?'

I shook my head. 'He wouldn't have been interested if they were. What are your plans for Cordelia?'

'I was coming on to that. You know she's back at Middlebarrow, right?' I nodded. We had heard from her. 'She's told me, off the record, that if Conrad is up to something, she'd quite like to work with him. Just for a bit.'

'Oh?'

'She can't do it on the books, of course, but I could second her. Unpaid, obviously.'

'That is very good to hear.' I reached down to find my bag and checked the time on my phone. 'Do you mind if I text him now? Unofficially?'

'Be my guest. I'll get more wine. Oh, you haven't finished yours.'

I had barely started. While Hannah reached for her bottle, I sent the message. When I'd finished, I told her that Karina was in post at Birk Fell.

'Good. I hope it works out for her. It's not going to be a quiet life up there, but I'm beginning to think that girl was not born to enjoy a quiet life. Unlike me. I was born to have a quiet life, but Hashem has never seen fit to let me fulfil my destiny.'

'Perhaps now the Codex is buried under a hill in Ireland, things will settle down?' I suggested.

'We can only pray.'

'In that case, we should ask Reverend Oldcastle to join in. His prayers seem to all come true.'

She coughed into her glass. 'Don't! I have to work with him *and* London Stone, don't forget.'

'Then shall we talk about the elephant in the room? The large, bright blue turbo-charged elephant?'

'You mean that bloody helicopter.'

'The King's Watch has a six month lease on it,' I said.

From the look on her face, you'd think I'd just made an offer to buy her nieces. She pointed her finger at my chest. 'If you do not get the Mowbrays to cancel that lease, I will contact the Royal Artillery or whoever and I will ask them to supply me with an anti-aircraft missile.' She paused. 'It's Warded against them, isn't it?'

I smiled sweetly. 'I couldn't possibly comment. What I can say is that Conrad is hoping to come to some sort of deal with the Union where they lease it part-time and he flies Kenver and Chris around occasionally. If not, I'm sure that we can sort something out. Now, shall we go somewhere more colourful? I do not want to discuss my wedding in here.'

'You and me both. Look, before we go, I've got something else to say. Do you want to finish the bottle?'

'I am saving myself, so this will do.'

Hannah looked at the waistband of her denim skirt. Kosher takeout can be just as stodgy as the gentile version. 'Diet starts on Sunday. Definitely.' She put down her almost empty glass with a thump. 'Cora's been on my case.'

'Oh?'

Dean Cora and Hannah used to be civil to each other. Since the Codex became a live issue, they have become a lot closer, and since Cora withdrew from the Warden election, they have become closer still.

'Cora heard that you're going to Cherwell Roost at the weekend, and she knows all about this little party we've had tonight. She asked me to ask you if there were any chance, any chance at all, that you or Conrad or both of you could have a word with Heidi Marston.'

This I was not expecting. Cora's friend Selena Bannister is standing for Warden, as is Saffron's cousin, Heidi Marston. Both of them are senior figures at Salomon's House and neither of them is expected to win: that ticket goes to Lois Reynolds from the Manchester Alchemical Society.

I took a drink to hide my surprise. 'What on earth for?'

'Because Selena thinks that Lois Reynolds is dangerous, that's why. If Doctor Reynolds puts her plan into action, she'll destabilise the world of magick completely. And even if she fails, the unholy row will have the same effect.'

'You may be right, Hannah,' I said. 'But Heidi will only say that Selena should withdraw first, and then she will laugh at us.'

'I tried.'

And I tried to smile. 'What I will do is talk to Lady Hawkins. If I can. Perhaps she feels the same way, even with family loyalty?'

'Would you do that?' said Hannah. There was too much hope in her voice for me to dash it.

'Of course. And we will try to get the Mowbrays on the case, too.'

'Thanks. That means a lot. Now let's go and get a proper drink and you can tell me why I have to go to a church and have *five* different outfits for one weekend.'

I stood up. 'Thank you for what you've done for Conrad. And for me. Now and in the future.' I retrieved my bag. 'And you will need a lot more than five outfits, Hannah-ji. That is just for the ordinary guests.'

Cordelia disconnected the call and went back into the Middlebarrow Haven kitchen. The heating in the rest of the house *was* switched on, but at such a low level that all it did was stop the place actually freezing. If you wanted warmth, it was the fan heater in your room or the kitchen, and given that the kitchen had company, it was where they spent most of their evenings.

Evie Mason, part-time housekeeper to the Haven, was staring into space with the proverbial blank piece of paper in front of her, searching for inspiration. Her eyes focused again. 'You're looking a lot happier, Cordy,' she said. 'Good news, I take it?'

Cordelia gave a quick flash of a smile to show that the good news was provisional only. 'I hope so. That was Conrad.'

'Let me guess: he's up to something. So long as it doesn't involve a secret mission to a foreign country, it should be good.' Evie paused, and a thought struck her. 'That's it! He's not really been sacked, he's been transferred to the ultra-ultra-secret Black Ops division of the Watch for foreign missions.'

Cordelia's imagination conjured the image of Conrad Bloody Clarke in black camouflage gear, limping around France and trying to be inconspicuous.

'What?' said Evie. 'What's so funny?'

'Nothing. No, it's a bit closer to home than that, but it is confidential for now. Sorry.'

'Fair enough. Could you top me up?' Evie lifted her mug and offered it for a refill. The mug had been Cordy's gift to her at Yuletide, and it said, *Do not annoy the writer. She may put you in a book and kill you off.* 'How is he?' added Evie.

Cordelia weighed the cafeteria sized teapot and found it wanting. She put the kettle on the Aga and turned round to lean her back against its warmth. 'How do you think? You know, there's something wrong with us.'

'I know there is. What in particular?'

'The man's been sacked, taken himself off on a jolly round Albion in a helicopter and we're *still* talking about him. We need to get a life, Evie.'

Evie turned round. 'We do. If you can find me a job which pays better than this one *and* has accommodation thrown in, I'll take your hand off. And who's the one after a job with him anyway? Tell you what, we're going to Manchester this weekend and I am going to show you a good time. No buts.'

The thought of Evie's Good Time made Cordelia quake in her flock-lined Rudolf slippers (from her daughter), and she turned away to stop the alarm showing on her face. The whistle on the kettle meant she didn't have to respond directly to Evie's suggestion.

Tea made, Cordelia took it over and sneaked a peek at Evie's piece of paper. It wasn't totally blank: at the top, three titles had been written and all of them had been crossed out. *Blades at Dawn, Inside the Circle* and *A Night with the Elf King* had all been rejected. Cordy put the tea down and said, 'I'm going to the spring.'

'You're mad. It's fucking freezing out there.'

'It is, and I shall pray to the Goddess to send you inspiration while I shiver.'

'Shut up and go.'

Suitably wrapped and insulated, Cordelia carried the steaming mug through the night and down to Nimue's spring in the woods. The tea was nearly cold by the time she got there, and she placed it on the grass to lose the last of its heat: it was an offering.

She prayed, and she did indeed ask the Goddess to send inspiration to Evie, but that wasn't the main focus of her devotions. She tried and tried to find the calm space within her where dwelt the Goddess, so that she could ask for her guidance. If Conrad got his new commission, and if she joined him, it would mean committing herself to the search for Raven.

Down in Wells, Rick's arms were open and waiting for her to come back to the family she'd effectively walked out on, spurning their love and their needs to chase the dream. The dream of Raven with her mighty soul burning brightly and her huge arms, bigger and stronger than Rick's, ready to wrap her up and carry her away.

Christmas at the Old Rectory in Somerset had shoved in her face exactly what she'd been missing. She'd slept in the spare room, and Rick hadn't harassed her once. She shivered at the memory of her daughter's tears when she left before New Year, only it wasn't a memory: she'd done the coward's trick of leaving while Rick had taken the kids to the cinema in Weston-super-Mare. Her imagination had supplied the tears, they were a cruel gift.

She stood up, and her right knee cracked painfully. She rubbed the joint and offered a supplementary prayer: *Spare me from the Mage's Curse.* It was instinctive and forgotten immediately when she saw the two lights approaching. What did Lucas want this time?

Lucas of Innerdale and two other Spirits (and where was the third tonight?) had been visiting Cordelia on-and-off since she first went to the

Particular. Lucas had left the mortal world some time in the Victorian era, and the world had thought itself well rid of him. A hundred and more years later, he had returned in the form of Conrad's Familiar – Scout. Now he was free again, and he was determined to win Cordelia over.

The Spirits kept telling her that the Queen of Derwent *must* be the one who had bound Raven's Spirit. It was as plain as the nose on Mina's face that the Spirits had their own agenda with the Fae, but Cordelia had no one else who either knew or cared about Raven.

As the balls of light approached the spring, they drew Lux from it and took human form – Lucas had been the only one who'd shown himself up to now, but tonight he was joined by a woman wearing a Victorian hunting gown and coat, stiff top hat in place.

Lucas bowed. 'Well met, my lady. I hope that we have not disturbed your devotions.'

'No. Not that there was much to disturb.'

'May I present my wife, Helena of Eden.'

Cordelia nodded to the glowing horsewoman. In her assumed form, Helena looked thin to the point of emaciation, and to Cordy's shock, she was looking her in the eye. Well, Victorians were generally shorter than us, weren't they?

It had been a long time since the Spirits had visited her – well before Yuletide. Was this just a catch-up? Lucas guessed her thoughts and said, 'The Dragonslayer has been absent for some time. We hear he's abroad in his thunder chariot.'

The last line was delivered with a grin. Lucas knew damn well what a helicopter was. Heavens, he'd flown in the Smurf often enough when Conrad was in Cornwall. When Raven was still with her.

'He's coming back soon. Back to stay. Probably. The Gnomes want him to drain the swamp.'

Lucas rubbed his spectral chin thoughtfully. 'As we thought. And does he want you by his side?'

'Yes, but I don't know whether I'll join him. There are other places I could be.'

Lucas looked to his wife, and she nodded back to him. 'We have seen something. Something in the Echo.'

'Show me.'

The two Spirits stood either side of the spring and raised their arms. Between them, Lux flowed out of the ground, and an image formed. An image of stones, of grass and of distantly surrounding water, all seen from a bird's eye view. She didn't recognise it.

Under their control, the centre shifted, the view descended and the illusion of daylight faded until it focused on a tall, glowing stone. Cordelia opened herself to the image, and the focus shifted to one side of the stone, and then she saw it: the vortex. At the heart of Raven's being had been a vortex which hid her true nature and which hid it so deeply that Raven couldn't see herself there.

'It's a fake,' said Cordelia. 'A cheap shot. You knew Raven well enough to have done this yourselves.'

Helena spoke for the first time, her words a whisper in the night. 'Aye, we did know her, but look more closely.'

Cordelia stared into the swirling image of Raven's Self, trying to untangle the visible colours and failing to get a grip because she couldn't find the familiar hints of violet that had been visible, like the radiation around a black hole. But they weren't there. Instead, there was a green…

'This isn't Raven!' she said. 'What is this?'

'Another creature, trapped like she is,' said Lucas. 'And there may be more.' The couple collapsed the image, and Helena collapsed herself, too, becoming once again a ball of light. Lucas continued, 'Don't take our word for it. Visit the Fae lands at Furness and see for yourself. Make it part of your mission. You know how to call us.'

'Wait! How did you…'

They were gone, away from the grove and the spring. A distant flash from towards Chester winked a little closer, then shot off. There was a fourth Spirit out there, a big rainbow globe of power that the Innerdales were scared of. Had the rainbow globe scared them off, or had they left deliberately, so that she couldn't ask more questions?

She realised that her hands were shaking violently and that the shivers were spreading up to her shoulder. She spilled the cold tea when she picked up the mug (she was supposed to carry it back intact), and she tried to jog back towards the warmth of the Haven but her legs wouldn't work properly. She settled for a fast walk and went straight into the kitchen without taking her boots off.

'Oy! Mucky!' said Evie indignantly.

Cordelia grabbed a clean mug and poured luke-warm, stewed tea into it. She took a long swallow and breathed out. 'Sorry. I'll clean it up in the morning.'

'Are you okay?'

'Yeah. Just remind me not to meditate outside in January, okay?'

Evie grunted and wrote something down. A few minutes later, Cordy felt safe enough to start stripping off layers. She dumped them on a chair rather than go back to the unheated utility room, then she looked at Evie's masterpiece.

Mashed carrot & swede

Sweet potato chips

Fat-free Fromage Frais????

Cordelia tapped her finger in the blank space. 'Don't forget wooden floor cleaner. Your mum will have a fit if you wash the floor in that other stuff. I'm going for a bath and an early night.'

Evie lifted her phone. 'Got a message from Saffron Hawkins. She's got some family do on this weekend, so she'll be coming up on Monday. I'll make cocoa in half an hour.'

'Cocoa. I'm not sure I can stand the pace, Evie. Don't let anyone say the King's Watch don't live life on the edge.'

5 — Fun and Games

I heard him coming. Well, I heard them all coming – you can't miss a helicopter landing in the field next to you. I didn't go and meet them, because I'm not the hostess, and only the bravest of the brave would try to usurp Lady Hawkins at Cherwell Roost. As you all well know, I don't mind the odd Dæmon, but I'm not up to taking on the magickal aristocracy.

I did go out of the cottage, though, grabbing my coat and leaving Saffron to sort through the food delivery. I went up to the fence that borders the meadow in front of the grounds to the Big House and watched Conrad execute a smooth landing.

Lady Hawkins and her husband, Rupert Thornhill, walked through the gardens as the rotors slowed down. They were in position by the gate when the doors opened and the passengers got out, with Mina in the lead. I couldn't help but smile to meself as I imagined the argument that would have gone on this morning:

'If we land in a field, I will get muddy and I do not want to meet Lady Hawkins with muddy feet.'

'I'll drop you at the service station and you can hitch a lift if you want.'

I sometimes think that Mina and Conrad are pretty much the definition of the irresistible force and the immovable object. The score so far was Object 1, Force 0. At the end of the day, it would probably be a tie. It usually is.

Mina waited until Chris and Tamsin Kelly had caught up with her, and Conrad appeared last. They made their way to the gate and I watched the namastes, bows, handshakes and hugs play out. A few seconds later, the girls were heading for the big house while Chris and a Rupert took a buggy to get the luggage.

Conrad did what he always does: his duty. It took him another few minutes to finish shutting down the Smurf, and then he finally looked across at me and waved. He picked up his personal case and limped over the grass to the fence. I was getting bloody cold, so I retreated to the porch of Saffron's cottage.

With his usual determination, he clambered over the fence, shook out his leg and came up to me. When he was nearly here, I spoke up. 'So what's it like to be up at the big house, eh? Alright for some. As usual.'

'I'm glad to see the chip on your shoulder is still in good condition.'

'Hey! I'll have you know that I'm a well-balanced person. Chip on both shoulders, me. How is it that even though I'm going out with one of the Hawkins, I have to slum it at GG's place in Oxford, while you get sacked from the Watch and still get treated like royalty?' I gave him a stare, just to let him know I was letting him off the hook this time, then let him give me a big Uncle Conrad hug. We both squeezed extra hard because we had a lot to say, and sometimes you can only say it with a hug.

Since the last time we'd met in person, a lot has happened. He's been to Ireland and been dismissed, while I've been promoted to Constable's Adjutant and got meself a boyfriend. Oh, and we've both nearly died. Him more than me, but that goes without saying.

'Is he here?' asked Conrad, looking over my shoulder.

'Jay? Nah. He's having lunch with Georgina and bringing her over later. I think he didn't want to be outnumbered the first time he met you?'

He raised his eyebrows. 'What have you been telling him?'

'Give the poor bloke a break, Conrad. He had to put up with the full Rani Desai Interrogation on Thursday night. I had to work extra hard to make up for it on Friday. I ...'

He held up a hand. 'Stop! I do not want to know what my adopted niece gets up to in the bedroom. Besides, from what Mina tells me, you didn't exactly leap to protect him from the Rani Onslaught.'

'Why should I? I was enjoying meself way too much, and Mina found out more about him in two hours of conversation than I have in a month, and I've been shagg ... dating him. Even when I did that thing he likes, he didn't tell me that he'd once had a fling with Eilidh Haigh. Then again, when your ex girlfriend once led a criminal conspiracy, it's not something you boast about to the woman who got stabbed by her associate. At least now I know why he didn't ask about the scar after the first time we...'

He put his fingers in his ears, and said, 'My hearing's getting worse, you know.' When I'd stopped laughing, he took them out and put on a serious face. 'Mina will come over for lunch when she's sorted the room. Could you get your woolly hat and come for a walk?'

'Aye, give us a sec.'

Saffron was waiting inside the door, ready for her own reunion with him, and looked really cut up when I said that he wanted to talk to me alone. When I'd got something warmer on, I went out and hissed, 'Say hello to Saff first.'

'I was going to.'

I stood aside and watched them catch up. It didn't take long because Saffron only had a thin top on, and Conrad didn't want to get her floor dirty. A few seconds later, we were off down the track that led away from the house, and he'd got his fags out. When he stopped to light one, I stopped to think.

'Have you been here before, 'cos it looks like you know where you're going. I certainly don't.' And then it dawned on me. 'You've studied the map, haven't you.'

'Mmm. This track leads to the back of the Wetlands centre. Should be private.'

It was, and we found a sheltered spot, near the water but away from any bird watchers. There was plenty to see out there, if you know about birds. No ravens, though, and that's the main thing.

'What's up, Uncle C?'

'Since I started on this journey, people keep telling me I've changed. Literally. When the Warden died, you said he changed my Imprint. When Nimue drank my blood, I got something in return, and when I did the same to the First Daughter, something *really* changed. It started in Ireland, when I found I could see the bottom end of the spectrum when I plane shifted. And now when I dowse, I can see Lux for the first time. A sort of muddy brown.' He turned to look me head on. 'I want to know what's happened, Vic. Am I still your Uncle?'

He looked as concerned as I've ever seen him. If I had to guess, I'd say that Mina had no idea about this. I felt like a doctor about to open the envelope with the test results. 'Hey, you'll always be me uncle. That's a fact, and if there was anything really different, I'd know it as soon as we'd hugged just now. Do you really want me to take a look? A proper look?'

'Yes.'

'Right. Take off your Artefacts. And open your shirt.'

A creature's Imprint is a bit like a spider's web drawn by a three year old with a big box of multi-coloured crayons. Or at least that's how I see it.

A human grown-up is a complex thing, and their Imprint is just as complex. Yes, I can see your DNA, because that's at the centre of who you are. Right at the centre of every cell. Beyond that, it gets a bit complicated.

There was a lot of pressure on me to train in Medical Imprimatism from some people, and I've always stuck up for Cora Hardisty because she supported my decision not to, and she got people off me back when I told them. At that time and that age, I did not want to trail round cancer wards learning to recognise corrupted DNA outbreaks. It's a long programme, and you have to feel something of the pain every time you look. If that makes me a bad person, then so be it. Maybe that's why I joined the Watch, to make up for it.

The reason that you need training is because we're all a soup of DNA. Every virus circulating in your body, every one of the billions of bacteria in your gut, and even the demodex mites that live on your face (yes they do) contribute to a smorgasbord of life. You have to learn to filter all that out.

That's just the core. You also see other parts of people as a sort of tube-map. I can see a painful joint as a flash of colour. Conrad's disaster of a leg is like an old map of the British Empire – lots of it is coloured red. And then the intangible bits. The personality. They're there, but not even the gods can truly understand them, otherwise I'd have a permanent job in the courts acting as a one-woman jury.

The one thing I can do is spot where there is, or has been, active intervention by magick or trauma. The one and only time I got a good look at Mina (we were both drunk), the shadow of her smashed face was a dark place in her Imprint that I did not want to go. So. That brings us to Conrad.

When I'd finished looking, I lifted my hand off his hairy chest (lots of mites. Ugh), and ran it down his strong flinty cheek.

What! I did what?

I snatched my hand away, just as his eyes were about to pop out of his head. I coughed and stepped back. 'Just checking. Yeah. Don't worry. All good.'

'Are you okay, Vic?'

I was *so* not okay. Before starting, I'd forgotten that Conrad isn't actually my blood relative, and it's easy to get a little too close to someone. Just for a second. I decided to take a leaf out his own book and tell a straight out lie. 'It came as a bit of a shock, that's all, and I wanted to check some of the fringe areas.'

He looked worried now. 'What for?'

'For Gnomish attributes. Hey, calm down, I said it's all good, didn't I? It's just that the First Daughter's blood must have had more of a reaction to you than normal. You now have an even stronger connection to Mother Earth than you did before, that's all. You're still You. End of.' I scratched under my woolly hat. 'Mind you, there's more Mowbray there than I'd have thought. Saving Morwenna must have strengthened your bond with Eseld, that's all. And don't worry, there's a corner of Conrad that will forever have a Banyan tree growing in it. Would you mind if I touched your forehead for a second?'

His eyebrows drew together a fraction, and he lowered his head a little so that I didn't have to stretch too far. What I was about to do had nothing of Salomon's House to it and was very much Old School magick. I placed my fingers in the little depression just above his eyebrows. Legend has it that this was once a third eye and that magickal Sight is propagated just around there. I don't do this very often, but if I really, really look, I can look straight into your Third Eye. I don't do it very often because it allows you to look back at me. I've never done it to Conrad before because I knew that his Third Eye was stuck fast and closed. Not any more.

It was like he was dreaming. In a very light sleep. The lids flickered and opened a fraction. A bright, pure light, like sunlight on ice, shone back at me through the lashes.

I took my fingers away and couldn't wipe the grin off me face. 'You have changed,' I told him. 'You're starting to look like a proper Mage.'

'And you have royal blue hair.'

'I have what?'

'When you touched me, your hair turned royal blue. That's it.'

Oh. No one's ever seen that before. Not even me. It was probably an illusion or a projection from his unconscious. 'Can we go in now? Mina and Saff will be wondering where we've got to.'

'Mina won't. I'll catch up with you.'

I left him to his thoughts and his tobacco and headed back to the warmth of Saffron's cottage. The wine was already open, and Mina was curled up on the settee, letting Saff get on with it: she'd picked up that this was something that mattered to Saffron, even if our hostess hadn't done much more than turn on the oven and sign for the delivery.

I grabbed a glass and took the other couch. For now. 'How was last night chez Kelly?'

'Fun. The boys were a bit tired after their week, but it was good. With the lights down low, it almost looked normal.'

I shivered. I doubt I'll ever get used to seeing Chris get all handsy with Tamsin. At the last Fire Games, the Edwardian dress and the formal atmosphere discouraged that sort of thing, and I was glad that it would be the same again tonight, which meant I'd be squeezing into those white jodhpurs later. 'Are you getting changed here or in your palatial suite up at the house?'

Saffron laughed first, and Mina shot her a bruised expression. 'You knew, didn't you?' said Mina.

'Yeah, but I didn't want to spoil the surprise. Will he be long?'

'No,' I said. 'What surprise?'

'There was a leak in the north wing last week,' said Saff to me, still highly amused. 'Two of the guest rooms are out of action, and with the Geldarts as guests of honour, the Peculier Auditor and the Earthmaster got bumped to the old servants quarters on the top floor.'

'No!'

'Yes. It's been done up, though. Has heating and everything.'

'But it doesn't have a proper mirror or dressing table, and neither does Tammy's. Not only that, Saffron has a hairdresser coming.' She paused and looked at my barnet as if the attentions of a professional would be wasted. Actually, she's right. I was having a military plait to go with the uniform. 'Would it be okay if I invited Tammy to join us here? If it's a problem, I can say that there's no room. After all, you do have a magick mirror.'

Saffron didn't hesitate. 'I wouldn't leave her to have her corset laced by Baldy Kelly. She deserves better.'

'Thank you.' Mina looked at the door. Still no Conrad. 'Have you got a second?'

Saff looked confused. Mina sat up and patted the cushion next to her. Saff glanced at the kitchen timer on the counter and sat down. 'What's up?'

'It's about the wedding. Specifically, the bridesmaids.'

Saffron shook her head. 'Not a problem. I wasn't expecting to be asked.'

I knew for a fact that she was. Since I started dating Julius, Saffron and I have become proper friends, and being a bridesmaid at the Royal Wedding was something she secretly really wanted. Royal Wedding? What else would you call it when a Rani gets married? Don't tell her I said that, though. Please.

'Of course you must be a bridesmaid,' said Mina. 'A very special bridesmaid, in fact. For the church.'

'The church? What about it. Vic told me that's where you're tying the knot, but what's special?'

Mina put her hand on Saffron's. 'Could you be security? I know that we have enough magickal power to start a small war coming to the wedding, but I don't want to have to worry. Just from dawn until we get back from church, could you do that for us?'

Saffron didn't know whether to be flattered or annoyed. 'And after church?'

Mina's mouth twitched. 'Princess Birkdale has accepted her invitation, but will not go near the church, of course. She will be bringing her own security.'

I mentally took off my regimental cap to Mina. This would actually be a very high profile wedding.

'One condition,' said Saffron.

Mina grinned. 'Don't worry. You do not have to wear uniform. Unless you want to.'

'Am I interrupting something?' said Conrad from the doorway.

'No,' said Mina. 'But you are letting in the cold.'

There was a lot of catching up to do over lunch, and Saffron had a bone to pick with Conrad. A dinosaur sized bone. I'm not saying that me Mam is right *all* of the time, but when she told me that you should always be careful what you wish for, she was spot on.

Saffron had wished for a new Watch area. Her first full-time Watch had been Mercia, and she hated it. What she really wanted was London, and our budding friendship was nearly nipped out when Hannah made me Constable's Adjutant, because I got to be based in Merlyn's Tower, supporting and co-ordinating the other Watches to take some pressure off the Boss.

This had all come about because Hannah had lost her Deputy, and in the fallout, Hannah had promoted Xavier Metcalf to become Watch Captain of Mercia and given Saffron the new posting she had wished for, but it wasn't London, was it? Instead, she got the Marches, with the Palatinate as cover.

'This is your fault,' said Saffron to Conrad. 'Why am I stuck out in bloody Shropshire and cleaning up your mess in Lancashire? It was your idea, wasn't it?'

She said it as banter, but there was an edge that Conrad tried to deflect. 'As you pointed out, Saff, I was sacked.'

'But the Boss listens to you! I bet she asked you how to sort things with you out of the way.'

He snorted. 'You don't know her very well then. I did lobby on Cordelia's behalf, which is why she's assisting you in the Palatinate. In case you'd forgotten.'

And this was something else that bothered Saffron. 'I can't be her supervisor! She's like, old, and she's got two kids. And she used to be at Glastonbury.'

He shifted in his seat and his eyes flicked to Mina before he responded, a sure sign that he was up to something. 'It may not be for long. I'm sure that Cordy will be striking out on her own soon. If you ask nicely, I'll even let you stop at Middlebarrow Haven.'

Saffron glared at him, and Mina changed the subject. Apart from that little disagreement, it was like old times again, and before we knew it, the clock said that it was time to move. The hairdresser would be here soon.

As we helped clear up, Saffron said something about the guests tonight, and I remembered a message I'd had from Conrad. 'Why did you want to know if Stew...'

'Oww, my leg!' he said, lurching towards me and hanging on to me arm. He also leaned in and whispered something. 'Later, eh? ... Oww. Sorry.'

What on earth could Conrad want with Stewart McBride? And more to the point, was he trying to keep it from Saffron or from Mina?

An awful lot of what I'm about to tell you depends on whether you've read the horribly embarrassing story of the first Fire Games. The one where I nearly ended up homeless and dead but actually made money and got Jay's number. That one.

Tonight was all about Team Gitana's magickal entertainment: the Fire Games, or Fiesta del Fuego as they prefer to call it, what with Sofía having Gypsy blood and all that. Sofía is the magician, and Rachael is her glamorous assistant (her choice of words).

Rachael is also the business manager (surprise surprise), and she put together a package to sell the night as Edwardian Glamour. Rich people do love to dress up, and the Hawkins are no exception. They even have their own dressmakers, and Tilly had run up a beautiful blue gown for Saffron. She was wearing it again, with different accessories, and Mina was doing the Full Indian. As she pointed out, Edwardian dress for her would just mean no artificial fabrics. Because I don't have a private dressmaker, I'd been to a costume hire shop and rented the uniform of a cavalry officer. And that left Tamsin.

Last time, she'd worn white. A big mistake. It made her look like an Edwardian débutante and even more like Chris's daughter when she stood next to him. This time she'd opted for something heavy and dark. Much better.

By the time the hairdresser had finished winding gold chains through Mina's hair, Saffron had shared some of her stash of Myfanwy's special cannabis and we were ready to party. Oh yes.

The Hawkins own three golf buggies, and all of them turned up to take us to the ball, driven by Conrad, Chris and Edward Thornhill, Saffron's mundane brother. The first Fire Games had been mostly a Hawkins affair, with Chris and Tamsin as the principal guests. I did not count. Not really. This time I was in the odd position of being a plus one to Julius Hawkins, and I was right happy when I saw that he'd turned up and was waiting by the entrance to the function room.

Julius – Jay – is a cousin to Lady Celeste Hawkins. He's an Enscriber by trade and has the special quality of being almost normal. Unlike his relatives. He is very thoughtful and has the sort of hair that you want to run your fingers through while you feel his big shoulders with your other hand. He only lets me do that on special occasions. I haven't felt like this about someone for a long, long time.

'You do realise you've got a silly grin on your face,' said Saffron as the buggy drew up.

'I don't care.' And I didn't.

He handed both of us down from our carriage, and I gave him a squeeze. 'I am so glad to see you,' I whispered.

He looked bemused. 'I thought these were your friends.'

'They are, but they're a terribly bad influence. Your job is to stop me embarrassing myself.' I drew back. 'Right. Time to meet the gang.'

Jay and Conrad shook hands vigorously, as befits Edwardian gentlemen in their finest tail coats, and Conrad said, 'You first, Julius.'

'Sorry?'

'You can be the first to say *I've heard a lot about you.*'

'Right. True, though.'

'And this is Chris and Tamsin Kelly.'

That made seven of us, and it was immediately obvious that Saffron was on her own. I let go of Jay and drew Saff in to the conversation while we waited for the female footman to get in position to introduce us inside. 'Go on then,' I said to Jay. 'What's she wearing tonight?'

'Who? George? The same. With white gloves this time. And she's had some replica Edwardian spectacles made.'

'I don't know how you can work for her,' said Saffron. Being GG's part-time amanuensis and assistant is the closest that Jay's had to a real job. 'Here we go.'

'The Earthmaster and Tamsin Kelly,' announced the footman. Game on.

Of course we were late, and the main guests had already descended the dramatic staircase to be presented. I know very little about the Geldart family because they are from Yorkshire and none of them were at Salomon's House when I was an Aspirant. According to Saffron, they're older, almost as rich and nearly as powerful as the Hawkins. Lady Hawkins has them down to

Cherwell Roost at least once a year, and it was a big one-up to our hostess that she had put on the Fiesta as entertainment. If it all worked.

I had no wish to upset things by making a scene in front of the Geldarts, so I stuck to Jay and avoided them. This meant that the biggest misfit in the room immediately latched on to us.

Georgina Gilpin is Heidi Marston's daughter, not that you can tell by looking. In heels, GG is taller than Conrad and thinner than Mina. And blind as a bat without her glasses. Perhaps she wasn't wearing them when she commissioned a light green dress that makes her look like a sapling. Once you get past the visceral hatred of her mother, the total lack of social filter and the braying voice, she's actually as mad as a hatter. Lovely, but mad as a hatter. When we're alone, I'm allowed to call her *Gina*. It doesn't happen very often, so I'll stick to *George*. She calls her mother *The Progenitor*.

'I hear you were summoned,' she said to me. 'Jay tells me that Celeste had you to Kensington.'

'True enough.'

'Did you pass muster?'

Jay has a perfectly good mother of his own in Northampton, but she's mundane. Lady Hawkins considers herself guardian of all the Mages in her family, including Jay, and she summoned me to their *place in town*, also known as Kensington Roost. Yep, it's as posh as it sounds.

'She was lovely. Helpful, even.'

'Not surprised,' said George. 'You're a top class Mage, Vicky, and you're from good peasant stock. Helps freshen the gene pool.'

See? I told you she had no filter. You get used to it after a while. Even Jay wasn't bothered.

She looked around from her great height and spotted Conrad. 'I can see the Dragonslayer, but not Mina. Where is she?'

'Next to him,' said Jay. 'Look for the bright red saree and the bling.'

'Bloody hell, is that her? She's tiny.' They were trying to disentangle the various Geldarts, something I hadn't managed. George blinked at them and looked quite wistful. 'It's a shame he chose someone so short,' she mused.

'Instead of someone freakishly tall like you?' suggested Jay. He can be cruel sometimes. George's love-life is almost as remarkable as her mother's, something that they do have in common.

'Precisely,' said George. No filter and no shame either. 'What's he like in bed? Do you know?'

Jay let go of my arm and grabbed George's firmly. 'Let me introduce you, then you can ask him yourself.'

I cringed inwardly. She just might, you know. I followed in case someone needed rescuing and because I was fascinated. Like watching Formula 1 to see if anyone crashes.

She didn't ask him. What she did do was become totally entranced by Mina's engagement ring and collection of Artefact jewellery. Before I realised what was happening, Conrad had detached me and was steering me across the room.

'What's up?'

'Stewart McBride is over here. I need a word with him.'

'How did you recognise him?'

'His picture's on the college website. Can you help me out here? This has to stay secret, but it's really important.'

What the hell? What could Conrad want with Stewart?

Dr Stewart McBride is Reader in Political Philosophy at Harwood College in Oxford. He's here because he's married to Celeste's mundane brother, Solomon Hawkins. There was no sign of Solly, and Stewart cast a shrewd (and rather dirty) look over Conrad. Did he lick his lips, or was that my imagination?

He's also been very nice to me, and gave me an extravagant double air kiss. 'How are you, my dear? Still looking gorgeous and commanding. I hear you've put a spring in young Julius's step and no mistake. I hope you're not playing tonight?'

I shook my head firmly. 'No chance. Sofía has given her word that she will never let me gamble again.'

'Good,' said Stewart, turning to Conrad. 'And you can't play either. Are you here to network?'

'In a way. I'm here to help people sign over their assets to Occult Estate Management.'

It was true. Conrad would do just that for Rachael. It was also a blind for something, I could tell that, and so could Stewart. 'Very honest of you, Conrad. And while you're here, recruit some people for your campaign?'

Conrad smiled. 'I don't run campaigns. I'm just a tradesman, but you're right, I do have an ulterior motive. How much would it cost to sponsor a seminar at Harwood College?'

That came out of left field and no mistake. Stewart looked just as puzzled as I felt. 'Any particular topic?'

Conrad didn't blink. 'Yes. A seminar on the implications of big data for democracies, jointly presented by Doctor Stewart McBride of Oxford and Doctor Arun Desai of MIT.'

Oh. Mina's brother.

Stewart took it in his stride. 'I can see that you're serious, but why? I've never heard of such a thing.'

'I know. Will this go no further?'

'Of course.'

'As you may have heard, we're getting married in May.'

'It has been mentioned.'

'Mina's cousin is coming from India, but she's a woman. Mina really, really wants a man to walk her down the aisle and give her away. My dad will do it, but she wants her brother. Unfortunately he's not returning her calls. He rather thinks that she brought shame on the family.'

Stewart couldn't decide whether to dive in for the gossip or be respectful. He opted for the latter. 'Is that irreversible?'

Conrad rocked his hand from side to side. 'Mina turned up to their mother's funeral handcuffed to the Indian version of the King's Watch. And I'm the second Englishman she's getting married to. The first was a crook.'

'So's the second,' I added. 'In case you were wondering, Stewart. But Conrad's never been caught.'

'Mmm,' said Stewart. 'I'm not surprised. Do you think this improbable plan will work, Conrad? You could spend a fortune and he could thumb his nose at you.'

'I've spoken to his wife,' said Conrad. 'She's desperate to see her parents in London. The seminar will get the project over the line. Simple as that.'

Stewart took another look at Conrad, this time with his academic cap on. Metaphorically speaking. 'Will Doctor Desai embarrass the college?'

'According to my sources, he's a rising star in his field. Just don't expect him to be charismatic in public. Not everyone has your flair, Stewart.'

'Indeed they don't. Flattery will only get you so far, by the way.'

'Far enough. Do your due diligence and get back to me. Sooner rather than later. Here's my card.'

Stewart looked at the card and put it away. 'Who will be the front for this? I presume your name will be conspicuous by its absence?'

'The Talpa Foundation will be the proud sponsors.'

'Leave it with me. I think they're collecting the money now, so it won't be long.'

We headed back into the crush. 'That was a lovely gesture,' I said. 'But she's bound to find out.'

He shook his head. 'Yes, she will. But only when it's a *fait accompli*. Will they have chairs in the games room? My leg is playing up.'

6 — Truth or Dare

The drinks and pre-game socialising had all taken place in a big, rather empty room that Solly Hawkins rents out for functions. Yes, you can actually get married there, so long as you don't want to get married on a Saturday: Lady Hawkins does not want the hoi poloi interrupting her weekends. You can also attend one of the chamber music concerts, if that's your thing. It's not mine.

Refurbishing the old dining room also meant installing proper toilets. Asking the bride to use a chamber pot behind a screen is not a good selling point. I needed to go, and was heading for the facilities when Mina swept up to me, grabbed my arm and propelled me into a cubicle.

'Can you put a Silence on us,' she hissed.

'I can,' and I did. 'What's up?'

She leaned against the cubicle wall and closed her eyes. She lifted her hands, bangles jingling, and rubbed her temples for a second, keeping her fingers well away from the elaborate eye makeup. She was still for a moment, and I was reaching out to comfort her when she came back to life with a smile.

'The world of magick is in for an interesting time,' she announced. 'Did Saffron or Julius not tell you why the Geldarts are here?'

'Party?' I suggested hopefully.

Mina has perfected the art of looking down her nose at people even though the only person shorter than her is Niði the Dwarf. It helps that she has such a beak of a nose. Again, don't tell her I said that.

'Rich people do not gather at each others houses for fun,' she declared, then waved her hand. 'Not that I will ever be materially rich unless I dump Conrad and marry Kenver Mowbray.'

'And you think Eseld would let that happen? It wouldn't be a horse's head in your bed, it would be your head in a horse's bed. Why are we even talking about this?'

'Because Hannah asked a favour of me. Not Conrad. Me.' She shook her head. 'I have just tried to convince Celeste to talk Heidi out of standing for Warden.'

'What? Noooo. You're joking, aren't you?'

'I wish.'

I took my cap off to her. That took balls, that did. No wonder she needed a time-out in the Ladies. 'No joy?'

She gave a hollow laugh. 'It gets worse. Celeste invited the Geldarts to get them to drop Lois Reynolds and back Heidi. Celeste has decided that whatever reservations she has about her cousin, family comes first. The Geldarts have decided that backing the Yorkshire candidate takes priority, so it was a case of thanks, but no thanks.' She bobbed her head around. 'Don't tell Conrad, okay?'

'No. Course not.'

She closed her eyes and breathed in, then slowly out. 'So that's that. We can just sit back and enjoy the show now. Do you want me to hold your jacket while you go three rounds with those jodhpurs?'

If you've read about the Fire Games before, you'll know what to expect. If you haven't, here's a quick introduction, and because I wasn't going to be playing tonight, you don't need all the details.

We gathered in the drawing room, all darkness, candles and log fire, and in the middle, two rows of chairs facing each other. At one end are the Field and the Bank, two tables where the magician does her stuff. There's a lot of theatrics and even a rabbit called Pedro, but the real action is a series of Trials. Sofía will do what looks like a magic trick, and she'll do it three times: once or twice with magick and once or twice with sleight of hand. The two teams then bet on which is the odd one out.

Teams. That was next: selecting the teams. When I'd played, there had been no non-playing spectators. Tonight there were a few – all the mundane guests plus Conrad, Mina and me. Oh, and Saffron, but she had a job to do. The other difference was that Lady Celeste was going to play instead of being Hostess. That job fell to Eseld, and she was welcome to it because it was going to be Hawkins vs Geldart, with a sprinkling of Kelly to keep it sweet.

Conrad put his hand on my shoulder and whispered, 'Would you mind getting the drinks, Vic? I want to grab that chair before someone else gets it.'

'Aye, nae bother.'

The favoured drink is Fire Punch, and boy does it pack one. Tonight I could indulge quite happily without risk, so I queued up and found myself next to Stewart again. 'Do you fancy a side bet?' he said with a snarky grin. 'My money is on the Hawkins, because they don't mind getting caught cheating. I think Mama Geldart would rather die than be shown up.'

'You know them better than I do, so no thanks. If you know what Chris and Tammy are doing here, I'd be interested to find out.'

He looked at me curiously. 'The odd couple? Didn't the Clarkes stay there last night? Weren't you all getting changed at Essy's place? I thought girls didn't have secrets like that.'

He meant Saffron when he said *Essy*. Don't ask. 'Aye, well, that's the thing. Tamsin thinks that they've been invited for themselves.'

Stewart can be as camp as Christmas when he wants, and he was about to say something catty, then stopped himself. 'But Mina and Tamsin really are friends. Am I right?'

'Aye. Up to a point, like. The difference is that Mina knows exactly why she and Conrad are here.'

He nodded slowly. 'I've told you before that I'm rarely allowed near the magickal people. Celeste doesn't trust me not to be mischievous.' His eyebrows did a little dance. 'With some justification, I must confess. Now, I did hear some other names mentioned. And places. Kenver Mowbray and the Danelaw both came up a few times, specifically Worksop and Mansfield. Make of that what you will. How many glasses of punch can you carry?'

Three was the answer, which was enough. The players in the Fire Games had theirs brought on trays by the maids, who when not dressing up and serving drinks, are Aspirants at Salomon's House. They were going to be locked out soon.

'Cheers, Vic,' said Conrad. He sipped the fiery concoction and looked for somewhere to put it down. 'One of those is going to be enough for me, I think. Here we go.'

There was a burst of light from the candles, a magickal sound effect, and Eseld Mowbray swished into the room to great applause. Chris and Tammy were declared captains, and they began choosing teams. This was not because there was any doubt about who was on which team, but there had to be some mechanism for keeping Heidi and George as far apart as possible. Tamsin was leading Team Hawkins, and she picked Heidi first. Politically astute, perhaps, but it meant that GG would be on the end, hemmed in by Bertie, the Devious Hawkins from Worcestershire.

I call her Devious because she lives in a great house and has no visible means of support. Now that Saffron was no longer Watch Captain for Mercia, perhaps I'd order Xavi to investigate. Perhaps not. I had told Jay in no uncertain terms that he was not George's minder and someone else had to stop her betting her house on Green in the fourth Trial.

The staff withdrew, the doors were closed, and Saffron set the Wards around the room. Eseld did something I don't understand, and the centre of the room became a little island of Mowbray Blue in a sea of Hawkins Purple.

In magickal terms, that is. Mina and I linked arms and moved to somewhere with a better view. Eseld sat down and spoke up. 'Let the games begin.'

Conrad had chosen his chair so that he could watch his sisters. That was all he really cared about, and they both did a brilliant job. Sofía is a natural performer, and Rachael a great foil. Between them they had the players eating out of their hands, and Sofía's magick was even better for the practice she'd done over Christmas.

Through most of the Trials, neither family got the edge, and no one lost their shirt. The first real drama came in the fourth Trial, the cup-and-ball trick where I'd embarrassed myself spectacularly. So had George, to be fair, but she could afford it. I started to watch through me fingers. I couldn't bear it.

Sofía did the old trick with three different coloured balls and three cups upside down, only with a magickal twist. When the Trial was set, the two teams turned to each other to decide which colour to bet on.

'I say it's green,' said George emphatically. I closed my fingers and contemplated putting a Silence on.

And then Mina dragged my hand away. 'This should be fun!'

'Your idea of fun is very different to mine, pet.'

'Don't be ridiculous,' said Heidi. It sounded like her patience was running out. 'Anyone can see that it's red.'

'I think your mother is right,' whispered Bertie. It was the wrong thing to say.

George shot right back. 'I don't have a mother, and the colour is green.'

By now, the Geldarts were agog, and Jay had his head in his hands. Talking of hands, was that Tamsin's? On Heidi's? It was too quick to see properly, and too dark, but Heidi cleared her throat loudly and said, 'Perhaps I'm wrong. I'm happy to go with green.'

'Did I just hear that?' said Mina.

'I think you did.'

She nodded, confident that she knew something I didn't, and added, 'They're both wrong. It's blue.'

'And what, Oh Rani, do you base that judgement on?'

In a movement that only I saw, she shimmied her hair, her saree and her bangles in one sinuous, sensuous shake, as if she were practising for later. 'Because they are both wrong, that's why, and the universe will send them a message to that effect.'

'You are so full of shit sometimes.' Did I mention that I'd had a few glasses of Fire Punch?

She looked up at me and grinned. 'Twenty pounds at two-to-one says I'm right.'

'You're on.'

The Geldarts had gone for red, but neither team was willing to risk too much. Only a few hundred quid. Rachael placed the platter with the tokens on the Bank, and stood back for Sofía to make the Declaration. As she did so, she looked across the room to me, and gave me a big wink.

The candles flared. Blue it is. 'You owe me forty pounds,' said Mina. 'I shall collect on the hen night, which you are in charge of, by the way.'

'What? How come?'

'Because part of it is on Shabbos. Make it something suitable for Hannah on the Friday and something wild thereafter. You have Leah Kershaw and the Smurf at your disposal.'

'Erm, thanks. I think. Right. Did you have inside information about the Trial just now?'

There was a break, and Mina gathered her saree, ready to move. 'Sofía doesn't always like being a Clarke, but she's embraced the motto. She would never give anything away. Rachael too.'

She sashayed off before I could point out that she hadn't answered the question, and I dashed to see Saffron and co-opt her to Project Hen-night.

The final third of the Games started as a real triumph. Two new tricks that really had me going, one of which got Sofía a standing ovation. How on earth she got Pedro the rabbit to do *that*, I have no idea. And that brought us to the finale.

Sofía swished her gypsy skirt and came round the tables to parade along the two rows of players. As she moved, she gave them the patter. Her English is very good. Good enough to know what people expect a Spanish gypsy to sound like, and a good showman always gives people what they want.

'My mother is what you call a *Diviner*. She can see things that I cannot. Perhaps you can, too. But can she really see the future, or is it just that she can see inside you, eh? Like when I try to go party when I am fourteen, she stop me at the door and says, "Sofía! Where are you going?" "To Elena's house," I say. "Go to your room now!"'

Sofía paused to ride the laugh. 'Could she see the future, or could she see the bottle of vodka in my bag? A good mother, like a good magician, never gives away her secrets. Unlike you. You are going to give away your secrets to me. Right now.'

She swept back to her place at the Field, and I heard someone say, 'Does she know about you and the Gnome?' I think it was from the Geldart side, but I can't be sure.

Sofía took charge again. While she'd been parading around, Rachael had set up the props on the Field: a velvet bag, three envelopes made of heavy paper that looked like Enscriber's Parchment, one of each game colour, and a deck of cards. Large cards. Tarot cards.

Sofía's mam is a Diviner. She can use the cards to see things in the Sympathetic Echo that I can't, and neither can Sofía. Where on earth was she going with this?

She picked up the cards and fanned them, showing the faces to the audience. They were the common Rider-Waite cards that all Mages are familiar with, even if they never use them. She peeled off the Major Arcana and put the others to one side. 'I need three volunteers. It does not matter from which team. You must choose a card which is personal to you. One with a secret. If you think you can keep the secret from the eyes of La Gitana, then raise your hands!'

A good half a dozen hands went up. They'd been on the punch, too. Sofía picked up the envelopes and handed them to Tamsin, to Georgina and to one of the Geldarts, and older guy who she called Ricardo.

'These envelopes are good,' said George. 'Completely opaque, but with a key inside. Have a look, Jay.'

'She's right,' said Richard Geldart. He held up the tiny piece of paper from inside that would take whatever key the Mage put on it. 'Exquisite workmanship. Where did you get them, Señorita?'

'A friend make them,' said Sofía, with a glance at Conrad. That would be Erin, then. I wonder if Erin had anything to do with the Tarot cards? Worth keeping an eye on them. She handed Richard the Major Arcana and said, 'And these?'

He fanned them, checked them and looked round the group. 'Completely mundane, and as far as I can see, unmarked in any way. Straight out of the packet.'

'Gracias, Señor. Turn your back from me, choose one and place it in the envelope.'

Richard didn't hesitate. He swivelled around, took a card and held up his envelope. Rachael stepped forwards, holding the velvet bag.

'Very good,' said Sofía. 'If you would be so kind, make your seal, pass the envelope to our Hostess, the cards to Señorita Hilpin, and place the key in the bag.'

He looked puzzled, until he realised that *Hilpin* was Sofía's deliberate Spanish pronunciation of George's surname. In a few moments, Eseld had three envelopes, the bag with three keys and the balance of the Tarot cards on her side table. Sofía swished over and swirled her shawl, collecting the envelopes and passing the velvet bag up to Eseld.

'In this bag,' said Sofía, 'are the keys to the envelopes. Please, choose one at random and place it in my palm.'

She stood to one side of Eseld, holding out her palm and doing something to the rings on her hand that made them glint and sparkle in the candlelight. Eseld waggled her fingers, dipped them in the bag and chose one of the rolled up pieces of paper that held the keys. She placed it in Sofía's hand, and no one could have seen which colour she'd been handed. I presume that she was going to use that key to unlock one of the envelopes and use her Sight to peer inside it.

Sofía closed her fingers and closed her eyes. 'Very good. Now the Trial begins.' She went back to the Field and placed the envelopes on the table. She pointed to the red envelope, and Rachael took it back to Richard Gilpin.

'Señor. Can you confirm that this envelope is undamaged?'

Richard gave it a good feel, and while he did, Sofía came over. 'Perfectly sealed,' he announced.

Sofía came up behind Rachael, who was still in front of Richard, and placed her hands on Rachael's shoulders. 'Take it back and tell me what you see.' This was real bravado, this. Everyone in the games would know that Rachael had not a trace of magick in her, except maybe in the shoes. Heels that high would go well with an anaesthetic Work for a long evening.

Rachael took Richard's envelope and ran her fingers over it with her eyes closed. 'I'm getting three figures … I'm getting youthful energy.' She paused to look at Richard and raise her eyebrows. 'I'm getting a dirty weekend in Florence with…'

'Stop!' commanded Sofía. 'Enough. It is the Chariot, is it not, Señor Ricardo?'

Richard had the look on his face, the one which said, *I've been conned, but I've no idea how.* He broke the seal on his envelope and showed the card to the players. When he sat down, the Geldart matriarch leaned over to have a strong word with him. He just grinned.

Tamsin had chosen The Hermit, and was vaguely accused of cheating in her exams at Salomon's House, and Georgina had chosen The Moon, and a confession of spending a month in the sídhe of a Fae Queen. Even from outside the circle, I could hear Heidi muttering, 'In her dreams, perhaps.'

Three cards, three revelations, and I hadn't a clue how Sofía and Rachael had done it. She'd used the magickal key to see inside one of the envelopes, but the other two? Not a Scooby. The two teams would now bet on which envelope had been breached.

The Geldarts, led by Chris Kelly thought they knew something, and they bet a lot of money on Green almost immediately. Green, of course, was George's envelope. Team Hawkins was less certain, and only matched about half of the other team's money. They went for red – Ricardo's card.

As the bets were being placed, I heard George saying, 'They know something. I'm telling you they do. They've got inside information.'

'Don't be silly,' said Bertie. 'Celeste has eyes like a hawk, and she couldn't see a thing. You've been wrong about absolutely everything else this evening, and with those glasses, I'm surprised you could see your own card, never mind what the other team was doing.'

'You just wait,' said George, flopping back and folding her arms.

When Sofía made the Declaration, it was green. Hands were half way to applauding when George stood up and pointed to Team Geldart. 'They cheated. They cheated at least three times, I'm telling you.'

Heidi exploded and stood up to face her daughter. 'Sit down you stupid girl! You're making an exhibition of yourself and you don't know what you're talking about. Of course they didn't cheat. Are you seriously suggesting that one of the Bloody Clarkes has taken a bribe?'

'Not them. Her.' She pointed to Eseld. 'Chris Kelly didn't need to bribe the gypsy when he's been shagging the Hostess for months.'

Have you ever seen a whole room cringe? I have. And I joined in. All eyes flew to Chris, but instead of looking at George with fury or his wife with innocence, he looked at Eseld. With concern all over his face. Ohhhh Shit.

'You bastard!' screamed Tamsin, and she threw down her chair, lifted her dress and legged it towards the doors. Saffron stood up, panic on her face, because those doors were locked and Warded.

Tammy didn't even break stride. She Plane Shifted, right in the middle of Cherwell Roost, and disappeared from sight. Bloody hell. Those lessons from the Fae have paid off big time.

Into the stunned silence came the ringing smack of flesh on flesh. Heidi had back-handed her daughter, broken her glasses and sent George stumbling backwards into her table. She tripped and collapsed in a heap.

Mina rushed towards the doors, which Saffron was struggling to open, and everyone else stared at their chosen object of dismay. Take your pick from: the exit, the collapsed body of Georgina, Heidi, and the (alleged) lovers.

The only two exceptions were Jay and Celeste. Jay looked at me, and pointed to George. We both started to move towards her, and Celeste stood up to speak. She paused a moment while we checked George for serious injury, then she forced a smile and looked at Chris Kelly.

'I take that you're not a cheat? At least not at the Fiesta del Fuego?'

Typical bloody aristocracy: putting their stupid entertainment ahead of everything else. Jay was helping George into a sitting position, and I was holding her hand, more to stop her lashing out at her mother than anything.

Chris sat down and shook his head. 'I wouldn't insult you like that, Lady Hawkins. Nor would Ezzy.'

Ezzy? They've definitely been shagging in that case.

Celeste turned like a lighthouse and looked at Sofía and Rachael who were almost huddled together. Conrad was behind them in the shadows, arms folded, his face a blank.

Celeste cleared her throat. 'Lest we forget, tonight we have been treated to the most spectacular magickal entertainment I can remember. We on our side are going to donate *all* our tokens to La Gitana and her glamorous assistant, and I personally am going to match that. Bertie? Would you?'

Everyone stood up and gave Sofía huge applause, and the Geldarts joined in with a very generous tip.

'Let's get her out of here and into the fresh air,' I said to Jay, and we heaved Gina on to her feet. Over Jay's shoulder, I could see Bertie berating Heidi in the corner, probably under a Silence. We only just made it outside before Gina threw up.

The final scene of the drama took place a couple of hours later in a sheltered corner outside the house, between the function room and the Orangery. It was liberally provided with ashtrays and infra-red heaters, and I was headed there because Mina had come up to us and asked Jay, 'Where do the smokers go?'

'I'll show you,' he replied, and I followed. I wasn't gonna miss this, was I?

There was no sign of Eseld, but Conrad and Sofía, now in civvies, were deep in conversation. As soon as Sofía saw Mina approaching, she touched Conrad's arm, kissed his cheek and made an exit almost as sharp as Tamsin Kelly's.

'Tell me you didn't know, and tell me truly,' said Mina to Conrad.

A lot was hanging on this. Conrad had Eseld at his side in Ireland, and he'd just been flying around Albion with Chris. If anyone was going to know, it would be him.

He lifted his right hand, and the Troth ring glinted with Valknuts. 'As the Allfather is my witness, I neither knew nor suspected anything I haven't told you.' He lowered his hand. 'And that's the last time I'm doing that.'

Mina flinched back. She'd been with Tamsin over at Saffron's cottage for ages, and it looked like Saffron wasn't going to be sleeping in her own bed tonight. 'I ... I'm sorry. It wasn't for me, it was for Tammy. She has no one except me, and she needs to know that I knew nothing.'

Conrad gathered her up and gave her a kiss. Out loud, he wondered, 'Then how did Georgina Gilpin know? Any ideas, Vic?'

'That was my next question,' said Mina. 'But you don't have to answer. Either of you.'

'No, we don't,' said Jay.

'Aye,' I echoed. 'You can't fix everything, Mina.' I sighed. 'As it happens, she got it on a staff night out at Salomon's House, and she got it from someone who'd come across them at it in the Warden's Parlour, would you believe. Gina won't say who told her.'

All three of us turned to look at Conrad. 'And Chris?' said Mina.

'He says that he and Eseld are in love, and that he was going to tell Tamsin when she'd finished studying with the Queen of Richmond.'

'The old, old story,' I said. 'I'll leave my wife, but not just yet.'

Conrad laughed. 'Eseld is not the sort of person you mess around. Not if you want to keep your manhood intact.'

Mina considered this. 'Probably true. How is Georgina?'

'Sore. This isn't the first time she's embarrassed the Hawkins, but it's the first time that Heidi got physical. There's going to be an apology from both of them behind closed family doors in the morning, isn't there, Jay?'

He looked at me curiously, as if he'd seen a side of me he'd never suspected was there. 'Do you tell them *everything*? This is none of their business.'

Mina put one arm through Conrad's, one arm through mine, and waited until I had hooked up with Jay. 'We share everything outside the bedroom,' she announced. 'And talking of bed, before we go, I think we deserve a nightcap.' We started walking towards the hidden door, the night air suddenly freezing away from the heaters. Mina continued, 'And Vicky tells me that you know where the key to the wine cellar is, Julius. You lead the way.'

7 — *Market Forces*

We arrived at the Windermere Haven Hotel in a triumph of synchronised autopilots – mine in the Smurf and Mina's in the BMW's Satnav. Note that I didn't say we arrived at the same time, just that we'd synchronised it. Mina wanted to get there second, after I'd shut down the helicopter. That way, she wouldn't have to stand around in the cold. Mina does not like the cold in the same way that Dwarves do not like the sunlight. Well, almost.

Grazia Brathay was waiting for me on her own, at the edge of the field, sheltering behind some trees. When I strode across the grass, she emerged and stood tall to greet me with a greeting she probably wouldn't perform if her wife weren't indoors with her feet up.

'Well met, Lord Guardian. Welcome to our home.'

I bowed. 'Well met, Daughter of the Earth. It is an honour to be received in a home blessed by the Mother.'

She followed that with a handshake, and ushered me towards the hotel. We hadn't got there before Mina swept up in the car. A couple of minutes later, we were unwrapped and sitting in the owners' parlour, drinking tea and getting to know each other.

Gloria Whitfield needed to put her feet up, because judging by the size of her bump, she'd very soon be run off them by their new baby.

'How did you meet?' asked Mina while Grazia poured the tea.

'I was a guest,' said Gloria. 'Come up from Essex for a joint celebration with the Sisters of the Water.'

'It was love at first sight,' added Grazia. 'At least it was for me.'

'Me too,' added her wife, after adjusting her position on the couch.

'So this was your business before then?' said Mina, looking around the cosy parlour towards the rest of the grandly Gothic hotel.

'That's right,' said Grazia, smoothly moving to ask, 'And you? How did you meet?'

'Murder and money-laundering,' said Mina. 'As you do. So what is the difference between the Lake Suite and the Lake Cottage?'

'Self-catering,' said Grazia with a mystified frown. 'I'll show you in a minute. Was someone actually murdered?'

'Oh yes. My first husband. Do you know whether it's a boy or a girl yet?'

And the tennis match continued for another twenty minutes until Gloria decided she'd had enough and played the ultimate change-the-topic card by asking me to tell her about the Dragon. Could have been worse: she could have asked about the Fair Queen.

'Save that for tonight,' said Grazia. 'Let's explore.'

The Windermere Haven wasn't built as a hotel, it was some mill-owner's palace by the lake, and had been (badly) converted in the nineteen-twenties, then again in the twenty-first century by Skelwith Gnomes. The Gnomes had done a much better job: after all, it was for the Chief's daughter, wasn't it?

What the hotel didn't have at the moment was a full-service dining option. There simply weren't enough guests over the winter. There was breakfast every day if you wanted it, and lunch hampers if ordered in advance (for the walking holiday brigade).

When it came to choosing our new home-from-home, Mina reluctantly turned her back on the pale earth tones and stunning view of the Lake Suite for the rather damp convenience of the cottage. At least the cottage has two bedrooms and a galley kitchen, even if it is tucked away in the woods. It also has an open fire. We moved in and whacked up the heating.

Just before we got changed for dinner with the Brathay-Whitfields, Mina got a call from Tamsin. She put it on speaker and asked how things were going.

'The bastard won't talk to me. He actually got his po-faced stick-up-her-arse mother to ring me about the kids. Can you believe it!'

'Are the girls still with the Foresters?'

'At least one more night. His mother says she won't bring them home until we've calmed down. Bloody woman's got a nerve. Do you know what, she even threatened to send a minion to collect Siona and take her up there.'

Mina shot me a look of alarm. Without taking sides, I could see Oma Bridget's point of view. I wouldn't be keen to send my grandchildren back to Earth House the way things were at the moment.

A sigh came over the air, and some of the outrage subsided suddenly. 'You know I'll have to move out sooner or later, right? This isn't our house, and he really does have to manipulate the Ley lines from here.'

'Then you should use the extra day to start looking for somewhere to live,' urged Mina.

'Yeah. Part of me wants to get out and move on and take him and the Bitch for every penny they've got, and part of me knows that as soon as I move out, he'll be giving her a key and moving her in. The bastard won't tell me a thing. Won't tell me when it started, where they did it or who else knew. Are you sure you can't get the Great Geek to tell you how she found out?'

Mina recoiled from the use of Georgina's unpleasant nickname and scratched her head. This was not the first, or the tenth phone call since yesterday morning. Mina had only escaped during the day today by lying and saying that she was in the air with me and therefore unable to take calls.

Tamsin really was all alone in the world. Her mother died a while ago (of the same cancer that killed the original Tamsin), and Mina is the only person who fully accepts who she is. Tammy set off again, and Mina drummed her fingers for a few seconds before pressing the mute button and saying, 'Ganesh forgive me for this.'

When Tammy paused for breath, Mina nipped in. 'Here is what you are going to do. You are going to reclaim your future, Tammy. Tomorrow morning, bright and early, you are going to get into Chris's Range Rover – which is now your Range Rover, by the way – and you are going to drive up to Henley in Arden with Siona. When you have collected your gorgeous children from their grandmother, you are going to set your Satnav for Elvenham Grange, and you are going to let Myfanwy look after you for a few days.'

There was a pause. 'How did you talk her into that?'

Mina waved her hand, even though Tammy couldn't see it. 'She needs practice with small children, and she needs to see how useful a nanny is.' It goes without saying that Myfanwy has no idea about this yet.

When it became clear that Mina was not going to rush back to Richmond, Tammy embraced the idea and rang off to go and talk to Siona. Mina sighed and looked at me. 'Any more news on your side?'

I sat down next to her. 'Chris and Eseld are not *my* side.'

We'd had this conversation yesterday as we relocated to the Particular. I was determined not to let Chris and Tamsin's separation force Mina and I to take sides. Not only do I need Chris as an ally, forcing a wedge between me and Eseld would also force a wedge between me and Rachael. That was the last thing I wanted.

Perhaps not the last. Forcing a wedge between me and Mina would be the nightmare scenario. Mina got that, of course, but it wouldn't stop her doing everything she could to fight Tamsin's corner.

'No,' I said. 'They're keeping their heads down until Wednesday.'

'Ah yes. The new term at Salomon's House. I would love to be a fly on the wall of the Senior Common Room on Wednesday morning. I have had one message, though. From Erin. She has got some sort of work emergency and has left Karina in charge at Birk Fell.'

I frowned. 'Yes. I got that message, too, but as Pack Guardian, I'd expect to get it.'

'Don't be dense. Your message did not include the diplomatic rider.'

'No. What rider?'

'That she will be too busy to start on our wedding invitations for a few days. Erin said, diplomatically, that if we revise the guest list, could we let her know?'

And there it was. The elephant at the wedding. Mina said yesterday that if Tamsin couldn't face being in the same marquee as Chris and the Mowbrays (any Mowbrays), then the others would be disinvited. Yes, it was extreme, but just because Tamsin has no friends, that shouldn't mean she should suffer.

I was not happy about this. I had my own ideas on the subject, but until I'd had a proper talk to Chris, I was keeping them to myself.

Mina stood up. 'This is only the beginning of the tunnel. There will be many dark days before there is light. For all of the people involved. I shall wear black tonight.'

'No you won't,' I said. 'You will wear the new red kurti with the golden peacock on it that's lying on the bed.'

'I was not being literal, and you know it. Now go and make tea while I check the hot water.'

George Gibson is third in Clan Skelwith, and from what I can gather, he is a rising star in the Gnomish firmament (if you can come up with a suitably subterranean metaphor to replace *firmament*, then let me know). I've dealt with him a few times before, and he's always been straight with me. Or as straight as the Clan allow him, which is good enough.

Just before we left the cottage, I got a message to meet in the bar, not the private apartment. We found out why when we discovered Grazia serving drinks to thirsty customers while Gloria perched uncomfortably on a bar stool.

'I've been let down at the last minute,' said Grazia. 'There is literally no one else to do this. Do you really need me at dinner?'

'Erm...'

'I'll cook. Don't worry,' said Gloria.

Mina looked at the swollen ankles appearing from under Gloria's skirt and gave her a game smile. 'I have a better idea. One second.'

She turned and whipped out her phone. At the same moment, a rather perplexed George Gibson appeared, along with his wife, Sapphire. As soon as she spotted me, I knew where she got her name from: the brightest pair of blue eyes I've seen in years riveted themselves on me and didn't let go.

We shook hands, and I was starting to explain the situation when Mina ended her call and apologised. 'Change of plan. We are going to the Oak Tree, if that's okay with you.'

'I have got to do you. Both of you. Separately and together,' said Sapphire with an urgent intensity that sent Mina's eyebrows into orbit.

'You're a photographer, aren't you?' I remembered out loud.

'Yes. Portraits. Way too many landscape people up here.' She paused. 'The Oak Tree. Isn't that the place Harry Eldridge had going on the sly?'

'It's run by his widow now,' I said with some force. 'Zinaida Zinchenko, together with her brother, Anatoly. The food's good, especially in winter.'

'Is there room in your car?' said Mina. 'We should be able to get a taxi back.'

We offered to take Gloria with us, but she gave a huge smile, politely declined and headed off upstairs. Grazia looked most relieved, and said to call her if we couldn't get a taxi.

Sapphire is around my age, or perhaps slightly older, and has hair that is even blacker than Mina's. All the better to bring out her eyes. Most disconcerting. My spies tell me that she had a son before she was thirty, to go with the four living daughters. During the short trip to Ambleside, she asked a lot of questions about Zina, and I got the distinct impression that George doesn't share much with his wife. Perhaps they both work long hours.

We got a warm welcome at the Oak Tree. And free Ukrainian spirits. Before we were shown to our table, I discovered that Matt is no longer around so much. 'He has gone back to work,' said Zina. 'Perhaps now he will not scare off the customers. He is so sad-looking all of the time.'

The Union Assessor for Ambleside – and all the lands around Windermere – is Matthew Eldridge. Harry Eldridge was his younger brother, and Matt was devastated by Harry's death. As soon as Matt discovered that his brother had a 'secret' family, he considered it his duty to look after them. I put the quotes around 'secret' because it's the first instance I've come across of a mundane life being hidden from the magickal world; usually it's the other way around.

Harry and Zina had a daughter, Lara, and the last time we came it was obvious that Matthew was falling for his brother's wife. It was not reciprocated, and I hope for both their sakes that going back to work is a reality check. For complicated reasons, Harry is also the father to Morwenna Mowbray's unborn twins, but that's a headache for another day.

We got to know the Gibsons a bit better over dinner, and I was right: they don't talk much about work. Every time I tried to get on to the subject of my future, George asked about my past. Or Mina's. Sapphire started to get interested when I told them about the Noble Queen of Galway. Yes, I said, I would try to get Sapphire an introduction.

'That would be awesome. Imagine how many people would come to an exhibition called Eight Queens of Albion.' Her eyes got even wider, and I was beginning to suspect magick was at work. 'And you have the Pack, don't you? The Werewolves of Birk Fell.'

George, Mina and I winced in unison. 'Mannwolves,' I corrected. 'Yes, I do.'

'Mmm,' said George. 'I heard you've got a new live-in Madreb there.'

Karina has been there less than a week. How on earth he knew about it is one of the many mysteries that can only be explained when you understand that even in the mundane world of Lakeland, everybody knows everybody. In the magickal world it's ten times worse.

'Yes, that's right. Karina Kent. She's worked with me before and has excellent outdoor skills.'

Mina couldn't help herself. 'She would be an excellent subject for you, Sapphire. She is young, wild and totally in tune with Nature. She also carries a huge hunting bow with her most of the time.'

Sapphire's eyes went to the middle distance. 'Bow in hand, surrounded by wolves on the snow. In black and white, of course.' She snapped back to the restaurant and looked at me. 'Where are they, exactly? Do I need to make an appointment?'

'I think she needs time to settle in, don't you?' I turned to George. 'Between Karina and Erin, the Pack are in very good hands. They'll play their part when they're ready.'

'Erin,' said Sapphire. 'She's working with the Sextons, right?'

In despair, Mina ordered us to skip dessert and sent me out to the smoking shelter with George. He began with a take-it-or-leave-it suggestion for my new title: Commissioner of the Peace. I took it.

There was a lot of detail in Saul's plan, and a lot that would prove controversial in Particular politics; even one year ago, he wouldn't have dreamed of suggesting it. One year ago, he didn't need to. There should be nine assessors in the Particular, one for each union; currently there are four vacancies and no candidates. No wonder things need to change.

To get his plan through the Grand Union council, Saul needs five unions to vote for him. He has two votes in his pocket, and it's up to me to secure the other three at the Waterhead Market and festival and do so on the first day, ahead of the Grand Union meeting on the Wednesday morning.

George gave me a lot of background and inside information, and when Mina stuck her head to ask how long we were going to be, I finished off by saying to George, 'It has been suggested that the Unions voting for me would be like turkeys voting for Christmas.'

He stood up and shrugged. 'It took a hundred years for the Grand Union to be formed because no one wanted to give up their independence. They only pulled together when it looked like there would be a national magickal power base. Same now: unity against Lois Reynolds and all her plans. Are you sure we can't give you a lift back to the hotel?'

'No thanks, George. I'll see you at the market.'

We waved goodbye on the front steps, and Mina almost climbed inside my coat to get away from the cold. 'Don't ever leave me alone with her again. That woman talks like a man.'

I knew I was going to regret it, but I asked anyway. 'What do you mean?'

'She asks questions but never listens to the answer because she's thought of a better one herself.' She gave me a squeeze that could have meant *you're not like that*. That's how I'm taking it. 'I had two missed calls and a message from Myfanwy. She will do it, but I think she needs more money.'

'Don't we all. Here's the cab.'

One of the first things that the Grand Union did after its creation was to found a school: the Waterhead Academy. It's still the only all-Entangled school in England, and up to the age of sixteen, Mages are in the minority. At the end of Year 11, the non-Mages and the Gnomes go elsewhere, and the Mages join the exclusively magickal School House.

The new school buildings have a huge car park at one side, next to the stand of trees that separates the mundane from the magickal. The car park was nearly full when we got there on Tuesday morning, and the path through the trees had been stripped of its magickal protection. Mina grumbled for the umpteenth time about holding an outdoor market in January, pulled on her overgloves and followed me to the small gazebo that guarded the path. I stopped dead when I saw who was taking the tickets.

'Happy New Year, Lord Guardian,' said Liz Skelwith-Swindlehurst, Daughter of the Earth and detective sergeant all rolled into one roly poly frame. She is also the boss of Erin's boyfriend, Barney Rubble.

I was going to bow, but Mina sailed straight past me and gave Liz a hug. 'How is the leg?'

'Much better, thanks. It still aches, but it's getting there.'

'Do I need to show my ticket?'

'Yes, but not to me. I'm only holding the fort for a minute. We all get roped in for the Winter Market. Oh, here she is.'

A girl of about eighteen jogged down the path, hair streaming behind her.

'Where've you been?' said Liz. 'You said ten minutes, and it's been nearly half an hour. You get your proper break later.'

The girl didn't look happy at being called out in front of strangers, and her mouth worked for a second before she apologised to Liz, blaming her mother for the delay. I didn't believe her, and I don't think Liz did, either.

The girl had been glancing at us while she spoke to Liz, and had clearly worked out who we were. When she'd said her piece, Liz got off the stool and shook her leg. I knew that gesture well: you think that shaking it will make the pain go away. It doesn't. Liz had picked up a knife wound at Yuletide when she was visiting the Pack. She stood aside and said, 'This is Iolanthe Preston. Her mother's just taken over as Chair of the Langdale Union.'

Mina made namaste, and I shook hands. 'Conrad Clarke. You weren't in Harry's last poker school, were you, Iolanthe?'

She looked very surprised, but held her grip. 'People call me Io for short. No, sir, I was barred because I broke the school rules.' She blinked once, twice, and looked at her feet for a second. 'Is it true what Mum said? That you got them all?'

'Near enough.'

She nodded slowly and pouted. It was totally unselfconscious, but deep down, Io knew that nature had given her big, statement lips, and she had become used to expressing herself with them.

'Would you like to see my ticket?'

'Yah. Yes please. Thanks.'

She ran her fingers over the stiff card and blinked again. 'Mister Eldridge made these. We all helped him in class. It was just before he died. Thanks.'

'Come on,' said Liz. 'I'll show you which mulled ale stalls are worth visiting. Barney should be here soon.'

We set off down the path, and I said, 'How's your new boss settling in?'

After months of dithering, DCI Tom Morton had decided to take the job of running Cairndale Division CID. He was on a year's secondment to start with, and last week had been his first in the job.

'He's getting up to speed,' said Liz. 'I've tried finding out exactly what the history is between you two, but he's very close lipped about it.'

'Between us three, actually,' said Mina. 'We all go back a fair way. What do you think of Elaine?'

Liz gave us an appraising look. 'It's hard to fit in when everyone knows you've only arrived because the Sheriff asked for you, but I think she's a good copper.'

We emerged from the trees and stopped to take in the view. The School House has a beautiful setting – it's about a hundred metres from Windermere, and the architect had made sure it created its own atmosphere. You'd think that a school of magick would reject the clichés of Gothic style, but no, they had embraced them and maxed them out.

The grey granite looked like it had been hewn from the surrounding fells, the windows were tall and narrow, and from the two visible corners, turrets kept a watch on the market. I glanced left, to where Harry had lived on a houseboat. It was gone now, and the jetty was home to a coal barge (where had *that* come from?) and the apron sported three smoking forges, two manned by Gnomes and one by a group of humans. Between the School House and the water, a village of tents, marquees, gazebos and shelters had sprung up, connected by roads made of event matting to protect the sodden grass. There was a fenced off area of extra-strong matting at the far end where the action would switch to tonight when the racing began.

The first tent we passed had the Langdale-Leven Union logo on the board outside, and two more teenage girls inside. That would be where Iolanthe had been lurking, then. One of them looked away before I could see her face, and the other one smiled at us. I nodded back, but Liz didn't linger for introductions. We rounded a canvas corner and stopped to admire the heart of the market.

I knew it was the heart because here was their version of a Troth Ring: a large anvil mounted on a block of wood and radiating Lux. At either end of the anvil were glowing braziers with irons sticking out of them, and a variety of Gnomes, humans and Fae gathered in knots around the open space. Right next to the larger brazier, Saul Brathay was deep in conversation with Matt Eldridge and a tall woman. Matt saw me and waved, and Saul looked up, too. Liz pointed to a stall and mimed drinking, then started to lead us around the crowds.

All the stalls facing the anvil seemed to be food or drink (and mostly drink), and if I hadn't had a cooked breakfast, I'd be salivating wildly. When I glanced back at the customers, almost all of them were sneaking glances at us.

'Good job I'm not undercover,' I whispered to Mina.

'For once, it's not you,' she replied. 'Can you see a black face or a brown face here? Did you see one in Ambleside on the way over?'

'Here,' said Liz, stopping at a large tent with a big awning and several open wooden barrels. 'Conrad, Mina, can I introduce my cousin Daisy? Puts the Ale in Langdale, she does.'

A harassed Daughter of the Earth rolled her eyes at Liz and quickly shook hands before shoving three tankards at a boy no more than fourteen. 'I'll put them on the Clan tab shall I, Liz? Good. See you later, Mister Clarke, Ms Desai.'

The young lad dipped all three tankards into a barrel and headed to the brazier with Liz in pursuit. We followed and watched the lad place the tankards on the anvil before he used tongs to take an iron from the fire and dip it quickly in each of the tankards. He shoved the iron back in the brazier and pointed to the tankards. 'There you go. Thanks.'

I glanced over my shoulder, and a queue was forming at the tent. No wonder he was too busy to hand them out. We took our drinks and made a toast to Good Health and New Beginnings. The beer was good stuff, and just warm enough to keep the cold at bay.

Liz checked her phone. 'Barney's arrived at the car park. See you later.'

'Thanks for the drink,' I replied.

I could see Saul waiting to talk to us, so we joined him. There were more introductions, this time to Victoria Preston, the new Chair of the Langdale-Leven Union. 'We've just met your daughter,' I said. 'Iolanthe.'

A guarded look came into Victoria's eyes. 'And?'

'And nothing. She checked our ticket and made polite conversation. I think we saw her classmates in the Union tent, too.'

'Willow and Persephone,' said Victoria. 'They're … never mind. You'll have so many new faces to meet, I won't bore you with the next generation. Saul says you've got a meeting with the Greenings.'

'I have.'

Matt stepped forwards. 'I'll take you, shall I?'

'And I'll take your empties back,' said Saul, relieving us of our tankards. 'You'd be amazed how many of these we lose. Good luck.'

Matt pointed a way through the stalls, heading towards the school. He didn't say anything at first, and I amused myself by peering at the stalls beyond the centre of the market. None of them had doors or flaps open, and all of them were Warded to stop prying eyes looking in. What they did have was boards outside.

'I take it they are not supposed to be blank,' said Mina, pointing to a large board outside a medium marquee. Medium by wedding standards, that is; compared to most in the market, it was huge.

'It says *Eden Wards Guild*,' I supplied.

'And it does what it says on the tin,' added Matt. 'They aren't all from the Eden Union, but the Eden Guild have the best freelance Warders in the Particular.'

While we watched, a woman emerged, wearing the characteristic robes of Witches who have dedicated themselves to the Goddess. She smiled and headed off to the square, lifting the hood of her cloak to keep off the wind.

'Do I need to learn all the coven sigils?' I asked, pointing to the elaborate design on the back of her cloak.

'Not unless you're planning to shoot them,' said Matt. 'The basic design is common to all the Sisters of the Water and they make individual embellishments. It's quite common for Witches to move within the Sisterhood, so they don't waste time doing local coven embroidery.'

'For the record, I wouldn't shoot someone based solely on their cloak,' I said. 'They would be guaranteed to have borrowed it.' I also made a mental note to find out more about the Sisters of the Water. I knew the basics – that they were an offshoot of the Daughters who had been independent for generations, but beyond that, they were a bit of a mystery.

We stopped in an open area which was far too exposed for Mina's liking. 'How do you feel about having a new Commissioner, Matt?' I asked. Best to get it out of the way now.

'It's the only reason I came back to work,' he said. 'And yes, it is personal. I'd rather become a mountain guide than work for the Grayling ever again. And you've more than proved yourself to me, Conrad.'

Matt was in a fragile state underneath his granite stoicism, and I couldn't lean on him completely, but having him on my side was a prerequisite for this. 'Thanks, Matt.'

'We were in the Oak Tree tree last night,' said Mina.

'Everything okay there?' he asked with a frown.

'Perfect, thank you. Zina seems on top of things again.' She smiled at him, and he tried to smile back.

'Yeah, well, there's only so much Ukrainian food a man can eat. Back to dinner for one now.'

'I thought you shared cooking with your apprentice,' I said, to try and keep the conversation going.

'She moved on at Christmas. A better offer came up in Cockermouth. Much better for her. Have you been to Cornwall recently?'

'We have. Morwenna's doing well, and so are the twins. I've been thinking,' I added. 'You should go down there, Matt. And soon. Now that Kenver is on the road, she could use some company, and you could get to know her for who she is now, not the illusion that Harry fell for. She's been through a lot.'

'Thanks. I've been thinking the same myself.' He gave me a sideways look. 'A lot depends on whether the new boss will give me any time off. I think the Greenings are free now.'

He'd been looking at something over my shoulder, and took us off the straight path to a line of tents that sheltered a small farm. Or that's what it looked like. A large section of grass had been divided into pens, and inside them was a selection of wild and domesticated animals: fine stags, sturdy ponies, fat sheep, hairy wild boar with sharp tusks, and, in a special pen, a family of grey wolves. They were looking hungrily at all the other animals, and for a dark moment I wondered if they were Mannwolves, then stopped myself. They weren't big enough, and besides, that would not happen. Not here.

'Alex and James are in here,' said Matt. 'I'll introduce you.'

'Do you really need me for this?' said Mina. 'That beer was nice enough, but in this cold I will need the ladies *very* soon. And I am not using that thing,' she declared, pointing at the portable toilet.

'I'll take you to the civilised option,' said Matt. 'We use the School House.'

'Thank you. And after that, there is another stall I would like to see.'

'Of course.'

Matt walked in front of the largest gazebo and called out. The darkness within shimmered and vanished to reveal a very well appointed home-from-home with several camp chairs arranged around a coffee table, the whole lot standing on rugs. At the back of the tent was a unit with flasks and bottles, mugs and glasses. As ever up here, the two occupants knew who we were without an introduction. Matthew made them anyway, for our benefit, and I added another family from the magickal aristocracy to my tick-list: the Greenings of Grizedale, or as they now preferred to be known, the Greendale Trust.

Matt began with the woman, a redhead in her forties with equestrian thighs and a windswept complexion. 'This is Alex,' he said. 'She's the Principal Trustee, and this is the Chair, her uncle James.'

He was a much older, slighter version of his niece, and had a well-practised professional smile. 'Can we do first names in private?' he asked, and when we agreed, he pointed to his niece. 'I'm the only one who gets to call her Alexandra, by the way. What do you think of the market?'

'I'm looking forward to exploring it further. Not that I have any need of what's on sale.'

'Still less do I,' said Mina. 'And if you will excuse me, Matthew wants to show me something else.'

Matt and Mina left us alone, and my first look out was to the animals. 'I take it the horses are in stable?'

'They are,' said James. 'You'll see plenty of them at the races or at the auction on Thursday if you've the stamina. Let me show you round.'

A younger version of Alex but with James's darker colouring was showing somebody the wild boar, and James set off in the opposite direction. 'That's my daughter, Iras. She looks after the bloodlines and her twin – Charmian – is the trainer. I don't want to cramp Iras's style, so we'll leave her be if that's okay.'

'Of course. Charmian and Iras. They sound familiar?'

'Shakespeare. Cleopatra's handmaids. Their mother was nicknamed Cleo. We'll start with the wolves.'

I wondered why he'd moved swiftly on from the subject of his girls' mother, and added a mental note to the ever-growing list of questions.

'I've heard about your pack,' he said when we reached the wolf enclosure. 'What's it like being their Protector? You're the only human with that role whom I've come across, Conrad.'

'It's a bit like being a company captain in the Army, I imagine. A lot of people under your command instead of the one or two I'm used to in the RAF – or the Watch. So I've done what any good captain would do: appoint the best lieutenant and sergeant major I could find.'

He considered that for a second. 'Except you're not a captain, are you? A captain has a colonel or a general to give them orders, and you don't. That was a good dodge, though, and I take your point about the responsibility. This lot don't answer back.'

I decided to throw him a bone, if you'll forgive the canine image. 'Honestly, James, I have no idea what to do with the pack in the long term.

You can rely on one thing, though: whatever I decide will be in their best interests.'

'As you see them.'

'And didn't you do the same for Charmian and Iras?'

He glanced at his daughter with a smile. 'Fair enough.'

I turned to the wolves and changed the subject. They had neither cowered nor approached us when James came over, and I asked, 'I know why I've got a pack. How come these are here?'

'Only the Fae get to hunt with Mannwolves. We offer our domesticated pack as the next best thing, either on our own lands or for hire. There are only a few couple.'

I looked more closely, and the wolves seemed as content as you'd want. They weren't afraid of the fence that kept them in, and there were no signs of mistreatment. I turned from the predator to the prey, and James continued his tour, moving quickly now that a cold wind was blowing.

The most famous of the Greendale Trust livestock (other than horses) are the wild boar, and James took great pride in showing me a grizzled boar with a back-off look in his eye. 'It took us a week to round him up from the forest, even though he's getting on now. Like me. He's got four notches on his tusk, has old Mowbray over there.'

I could hear the smile in his voice when he said it. The Mowbray family animal is, of course, the wild boar. 'Did Arthur Mowbray know about his namesake?' I asked.

'He tried to make out that we'd stolen our first boar from them, generations ago. Claimed the Mowbrays have the oldest boars in Albion. Shall we go in?'

There was no heating in the shelter, but there was hot tea, served by another alumna of Harry's poker school: Jocasta Greening, daughter of Alex. She placed my mug down and bobbed her head, and I asked her what Harry had been like as a teacher. It was telling that she looked at her mother before answering.

'He was good. He didn't pretend to be "Down with the kids" like some of the younger teachers. We miss him.'

When Jocasta had gone, Alex asked if I'd met Iolanthe.

'Yes. Why?'

'Because Iolanthe is the girl you don't want your daughter to be friends with. Unfortunately, Jo thinks that Willow and Perci are stuck in the mud. Literally. It's been an uphill struggle to get Jo interested in the family business, I'm afraid. Cake?'

'This is lovely. Is there a Daughters of the Earth bakery? There seems to be a lot of them about.'

She snorted. 'Tell me about it. We have more children of Gnomes per square metre up here than we do sheep. No, this is from Brysons in Keswick.'

Cake consumed, we got down to business. It wasn't an interview, exactly, it was more like the questions you'd ask a candidate in an election. I really have no hidden agenda here. I just want a job where I can do some good, I suppose, and I think that the Watch under Hannah Rothman is a force for good, so that's what I told her, including a gentle reminder that failings in the assessors had allowed the Ripleys to keep an illegal pack of Wolves and murder Harry Eldridge.

Alex looked at James when I said that, and James responded. 'Would anything have stopped Sura Ripley?'

'It would have stopped her keeping the pack.'

Alex looked like she'd sucked a lemon and bitten her tongue, all in one unpleasant move. I got the feeling she was going to come back to that point.

There was only one question that I didn't give a straight answer to. Alex told me that she'd heard the true story of Ireland from Saul Brathay, then asked, 'What do you *really* think of the Fae?'

I pointed to the School House, where Mina had been heading. 'I think the same about the Fae as I do about Indians. You can't judge a people – or *the* People – like that. I love Mina, but I can give you the names of several Hindu Priests I will strangle if I ever meet them.'

James didn't have much to add, but he did listen very carefully. When we got up to shake hands at the end, he announced that Saul would get the vote from the Vale of Coniston Union, and then Alex said what she'd bitten back when we discussed the Ripleys.

'You know that Stella Newborn is a close friend of the current Chief Assessor?'

'I had heard.'

'Stella said you threatened to burn her house down.'

I didn't know whether the fact that the Greenings were talking to the Ripleys was a good thing or not. The Ripleys of the Eden Valley are not huge, but they are important. When I first met Stella Newborn, I was on the hunt for a Dragon's egg, and I didn't know then that she was from the Ripley family.

'I did more than threaten,' I said. 'How do the Ripleys as a whole feel about the proposal?'

'They are still licking their wounds. Stella has told me that if I support you, the Eden Union will abstain. Good luck tonight,' she added. 'You'll need it.'

Tonight, I was meeting the Fae Queen of Derwent. Alex wasn't wrong. I would need a lot of things, luck included.

8 — Novice

I found Mina by using my highly honed tracking skills. That and a text message saying *Where are you?* She was at the Ambleside Gallery.

On my last visit to the Particular, I'd stumbled into a jewellery boutique run by several Daughters of the Earth in the town. I was beginning to see Alexandra Greening's point here.

Mina emerged from the tent and looked very pleased with herself. 'I have just commissioned a ruby threaded head piece for the evening of the wedding.'

'I'm sure it will be your crowning glory. Anything else you want to see?'

She shook her head. 'I think we should find a nice place for lunch and get warmed up before tonight.'

'You don't have to come.'

She set off towards the distant trees. 'The last time I let you meet a Fae Queen on your own, it didn't end well.' She looked up. 'For her, I mean. Will there be a nice warm fire I can shelter by?'

'Or we could commission a hot water bottle harness for you.'

'Hmm. How did it go with the Greenings?'

I started to tell her, and finished as we arrived at Zeffirellis restaurant, part of Ambleside's independent cinema venue. 'This will do,' she said. 'It looks warm inside.'

And that was more than could be said for the paddock that night. Even I would have welcomed a hot water bottle harness, and I made a mental note to top up my thermal layers in town tomorrow.

In a race at a normal race course, the horses and riders go round the paddock for the punters to get a good look at them before placing any last minute bets. Parade finished, they trot on to the course and get ready for starters orders. Things were different for the Chases because the start is a long way away.

The world famous Grand National is the longest mundane race in Britain – four miles and two furlongs of flat grass and high fences; Moss Leigh to Waterhead is eight miles and one furlong of wild winter valley. In the dark. With magick. It is not for the faint-hearted.

The parade at Waterhead is especially important because the jockeys have to show they can plane-shift to a certain standard – part of the course involves shifting to a higher plane, and this is the Union's minimalist approach to safety. After that, the horses are loaded up and driven under Glamour up Great Langdale to the start. We timed our arrival to coincide with the parade, and I went to have a look at the runners and riders; Mina went in search of a brazier.

The first night of the Waterhead festival is the Skelwith Novice Chase, and they do half of the full course. I took a good look at the pairings, both the beasts and the jockeys as they flickered out of mundane sight. This was not because I fancied placing a bet (that would be foolish), but because I wanted to test out my ability to use the threshold stones. There's no point having a race where the spectators can't see, and the threshold stones allowed even the minimally magickal to see the action on the higher plane.

There was a spare stone at the back (spare because no one else could see over the crowd from it), and I planted my feet. I summoned my magick and stared at the empty quadrant of the paddock. Well, I'll be. It worked. The horses were a little muddy around the edges, and the jockeys' silks a little washed out, but I could see them and distinguish them. I still had a slightly silly grin on my face when a voice said, 'There's a working one free over there, sir.'

It was a young lad (human) with a Marshal's jacket. 'Sorry?' I said.

'There's a working threshold stone free over there, sir. Next to the green trailer.'

'Working?'

He looked at me as if I were mad. 'That stone's discharged, sir.'

I stared at the rock under my boots. Discharged, eh? 'Thank you,' I said to the lad, as if I knew what I was talking about, then I wandered casually over to the other stone.

I felt a jolt of Lux straight away, and now the paddock came alive in glorious colour. It was much brighter, too. I stepped off the stone and stepped away from the enclosure, rubbing my chin as I did so. A couple of months ago, I doubt I'd have seen anything without the stone. Now, if I made the effort, I got a good glimpse into the higher realm. I hadn't seen any flashes of Lux, but then again, I hadn't been looking. Perhaps there weren't any to be seen. I was still musing on this when a shout from the Senior Marshal sent the field heading towards their transport, and I went in search of Mina.

The finish of all the races is a bit like the marathon at the Olympics – you have to go round the stadium, just so people get a look at you. When the horses returned to Waterhead, they would tear round the outside of the market twice before finishing in front of the School House. Although the race could be won at the end, the key action often took place either higher up Great Langdale or on the flat, just west of Waterhead, and that's where we were headed. I hoped.

A section around the paddock had been roped off – invisibly, with Wards, and that was where the Queen had watched her horses and the competition. Parade over, her party headed for a small convoy of 4x4s, and so did we, once the Queen had left.

A single Mercedes remained, tended by two Squires who bowed at our approach. 'Lord Guardian, welcome. Please…'

I helped Mina get in the back and joined her. We set off and the Squire riding shotgun turned round to talk. 'How are you finding the market, my lord?'

'Very interesting. I hope to have time to see more of it when business is done. Perhaps I'll visit her grace's marquee.'

'You would be most welcome. Do you have your eye on one of the horses for tonight?'

'Not this year.'

Mina gave me a dig in the ribs. 'Or next year, I hope. If you spend all your time looking at horses, you will either be sacked by the Union or divorced.'

'It's a good way to meet people!' I protested. 'I'm going to need confidential informants to do this job properly.' I turned to the Squire. 'Do you fancy being the first name on my list?'

He took it in good part, 'That would be an honour indeed, but I must decline. I know nothing. Perhaps in a few decades. Nearly there.'

We turned off the main road, crawled over a tiny bridge about five millimetres wider than the car, and turned into a field. 'The Clan allow us to pitch our tent on their land. Very generous,' added the Squire. 'Have you been to the Clan's Hall?'

I shook my head. I shook all of me as the car rolled and lurched to a halt; the Squires leapt out and opened our doors. To our right, a cluster of lightsticks marked out a pavilion and a couple of extra tents, one of which sheltered a big gas powered barbecue. From the smell, the cooks had been hard at it for some time.

Rich aromas of seared meat were mixed with fragrances I couldn't place that suggested exotic fruits. 'The Chamberlain has asked us to let you know that all the meat tonight is venison,' said the Squire to Mina. He turned to me and added, 'Caught by the Pack, of course.'

Mina smiled politely and bowed her head in acknowledgement. We've dined on venison a lot lately, most recently on Sunday night at Birk Fell. It's a good job we both like it.

We rounded the pavilion, which opened on to the slope downwards, and the Squires gestured to a large male who stood near the entrance. 'The Chamberlain,' they said, then bowed and withdrew.

The Queen of Derwent's Chamberlain was a man (or Fae Count if you prefer) who clearly enjoyed the food and drink side of his job. He also looked appropriately jovial and boomed out a great, 'Welcome, welcome. An honour to me. Come.' He reached up to the top of the flap sealing the pavilion and unhooked a section of canvas, pulling it aside, he went in and we followed.

The Queen of Derwent was holding a party, as you'd expect on race night, and the pavilion had at least twenty people inside it, the smell of Fae permeating the air like the smell of winter grass outside. Their noise had been suppressed by magick (to stop the locals getting too spooked too early), and the Chamberlain had to raise his voice to be heard. Then again, without the magick suppressing it, they would probably have heard him in Ambleside – his voice was as big as his chest.

'The Lord Guardian is returned, your grace, and may I introduce the Peculier Auditor, Ms Mina Desai.'

The crowd parted and the throne was revealed. 'Well met, Lord Guardian, Ms Desai.'

I've encountered the Queen of Derwent before, on the gallops at Sprint Stables. On that day, she was in Splendour, riding a High Unicorn and projecting all her power. She was no less powerful today, but this was her public face.

The Queens I met in Ireland were very different – to Derwent and to each other. The Noble Queen likes to be seen as a hard-faced mob boss who takes no shit, a deliberate contrast to her late rival, the Fair Queen, who radiated Beauty like a furnace radiates heat.

Seated on a portable throne was the very image of a horsey aristocrat: young, lithe and blonde with a square jaw and legs crossed.

We bowed.

'Your grace is kind,' I replied.

She stood up. 'While we're being formal, there are two people you need to know; the rest you can figure out for yourselves. Lord Guardian, may I present the Prince of Appleby and Countess Bassenthwaite. As you can see, the Countess is my right-hand woman.'

The politics of life in the sídhe can, as Vicky puts it, do your head right in. On the one hand, it is opaque and impenetrable; on the other hand it can get you killed if you upset the wrong person. You may have noticed that although the Queen named the Prince first, it was the Countess she introduced properly. These things are important.

A Queen needs a Consort who is also a Prince – needs them biologically, that is. Until I poked the Borrowdale sídhe with my sword, the Consort was Prince Galleny. He is now demoted to Count and has been exiled to the stables in Longsleddale, leaving the Queen with two Princes: Harprigg and Appleby. Prince Harprigg would be with the pack tonight (it being the first night of the full moon), or more likely, supervising the former Prince with the horses. And that left Appleby.

He is something of a mystery outside the People, and doesn't interact much. In person, he looked the very image of a retired colonel: balding, stout and sporting a moustache. We bowed to each other, and I turned my attention to Countess Bassenthwaite.

If I showed you a picture of the Queen and her Countess, you'd assume that the Countess was the older sister, because the resemblance was striking. I assumed there was a point to it, but it's best not to speculate.

Honour complete, the Queen clapped her hands. 'At my parties, it's first names only, if you don't mind. So this is Gerrard and Megan, and I'm Charley. Gustav, you've already met.'

When the Chamberlain heard his "name", he turned and bowed. I could not imagine him referring to his Queen as *Charley* under any circumstances. Me neither, come to that.

'Gustav, we have not just empty glasses but no glasses at all here.' The Queen turned and put her arm round Mina. 'Megs will look after you while I steal your man for a little chat outside.'

With choreography that the Royal Opera House would be proud of, the guests parted, the tent was opened and a hand appeared holding a bright orange padded jacket. The Queen grabbed it and shrugged it on while a Squire held out a tray with three steaming tankards, one large and two small. I grabbed the large one and followed *Charley* outside. As I left, I looked at Mina and raised my eyebrows. She just grinned and lifted a small tankard to her lips. Here we go again.

The Queen stopped at a lightstick about ten metres from the pavilion and waited for me. Out here in the night, steam rose from our breath and from the drinks. I gave it a sniff: hot, spiced red wine. Perfect.

When I was close to her, the Queen touched the lightstick and I got a frisson of magick, edged with brown. Had we really just plane-shifted? I looked around and the tent was gone. We had. Now that was good.

'More secure than a Silence,' she said, 'and I hear that you have a terrible nicotine habit.' Hearing the voice of a rich landowner's daughter come from a creature that can drag someone on to a higher plane with a gesture is one of the contradictions of magick that I will always struggle with. Give me a talking mole any day.

She raised her tankard. 'To new beginnings.'

We clinked and drank. The mulled wine fulfilled the promise of its smell and had a silky finish. I must ask Gustav for the recipe. Yeah. Right.

'Well, Conrad, now we're alone you can drop the act and tell me what's really going on.'

The only possible answer to that question was to take out my cigarettes and light one. 'We all wear masks, your grace.'

'Come off it. I've never met a mortal so tied up with the Sons of Mother Earth, and treated almost as one of them. Now Saul wants you to be his pet policeman. What's he up to? What does he want you for?'

'What do Gnomes ever want?' I countered.

When I didn't expand on my question, she frowned and waved her tankard. 'Go on. You tell me.'

'Like all good capitalists, they want peace, free trade and the rule of law. Saul thinks I can help provide the first of those, that's why I will be Commissioner of the Peace. After all, Harry Eldridge may not have been of the People, but his loss hurt you.'

'A good point. You left out the fact that all good capitalists like a monopoly, too, if they can get one. Do you really believe that rubbish?'

'I'm just a tradesman, your grace, and I try to make the world safe for other tradesmen.'

She considered this for a second, then shook her head. 'After three hundred years, I should be used to bullshit.'

'Perhaps it's good that you aren't. Life's always better when it's full of surprises.'

'Like a Dwarf in the grotto. That's a surprise I can do without. Before I let you off the leash, Mister Tradesman, tell me how you did it. And don't say, "Did what?" Tell me how you smuggled a Dwarf into the Fair Queen's bower.'

'I didn't smuggle Niði anywhere. He'd been plotting his revenge for generations, and he was quite capable of getting in on his own. All I did was give the Fair Queen a chance to make a fair deal to put things right, and when she tried to fob me off, I just made sure that she was on her own and, shall we say, a little distracted.'

She was silent for a moment. Her breath seemed to warm up and get thicker, judging from the small fog gathering around her head. She drained her tankard and looked out across the water meadows, across the River Brathay towards the invisible fells. In my limited experience, I'm not sure I know what a *troubled* Queen looks like. Perhaps this.

It only lasted a few seconds. 'And yet you have the favour of Galway, and Princess Birkdale in your contacts list. Perhaps it's a sign. Very well, I shall consent. Megan will cast her vote for you on the morrow.'

I bowed. 'Your grace is kind. Could I possibly ask a short question and crave a boon?'

She smiled. 'You are very forward, Conrad, given that we've only just met. Ask away.'

'I got quite used to *Fair Queen* and *Noble Queen* in Ireland. Why does that not happen over here?'

'It does, but not in public. Doesn't sound quite the same in brutal English, somehow. And there are fashions. For fifty years, I was the Red Queen, and then Dodgson published *Alice through the Looking Glass* and I didn't fancy it any more. Besides, people would expect me to use red, and red doesn't suit me. Mozart did the same for the Queen of Oxford.'

'Your grace?'

'The Magic Flute. *Queen of the Night*. Do not call the Queen of Oxford by that name if you value your balls, Conrad. We must go now. What was the boon?'

'You've heard about the second Fair Queen?'

She spat out the words. 'Lussa? She was no Queen. Yes, I've heard.'

'I think it might amuse you greatly to send one of your People to improve my swordcraft.'

'You're right. It *would* amuse me. But it stays between us, yah?'

'Thank you.'

She touched the lightstick and we were back, just as a rocket went up in the distance. The race had begun.

The pavilion had already emptied, and I soon found Mina (she was as close as she could get to the barbecue without becoming a samosa). 'We're good,' I said. 'Do you want the binoculars?'

'I want some of that fennel and cumin marinaded venison, that's what I want, but the chef says not until the race is run. What did you two talk about? You were gone for ages.'

'We talked about the principles of political economy, of course. How did you get on in the tent?'

'How do you think? I was passed round like a new toy until they got bored of me. I used to have a doll which spoke when you pulled on a cord. Apparently they didn't like my answers. You should talk to that one, there, with the red hat, if you want to watch the racing. Her name is Florence and she seems human. I am not moving from here. Those horses have twenty minutes and then I am going to offer my body to the chef.'

The last line was delivered loud enough for the chef to look very alarmed, and suddenly he found something to do inside the tent. A Squire supplied me with more wine, and I sauntered up to the well-insulated woman and said hello. Now that we were outside the smell of Fae was dispersed, and when I got close to her I realised that she didn't just seem human, she actually was human.

'How d'you do? I'm Florence, also known as Lady Appleby. Did Mina tell you I'm Andrew's bastard?'

At some point, Prince Appleby must have had a human wife, and this was their child. She called herself a *bastard* because in Fae law, all children with humans are bastards.

Under the red knitted hat, her hair was going grey, and the lines on her face put her in her forties. We shook hands, and she said, 'We'll talk later. The field will be here soon.'

I drank my wine and looked left, towards Skelwith Bridge. Half way between here and there, a temporary crossing of the river had been thrown up, and that's where we'd see them appear.

My first contact with the Chases had been via Diarmuid Driscoll, an Irish trainer of dubious morality. He'd spun me a line about the riders being "masked" so that he couldn't tell me who they were. Hah. Load of rubbish. He was trying to flannel me, and I'd have been back to have another word with him if someone hadn't shot him first.

The reality is that the jockeys' silks don't just identify the owner of the horse, they act as beacons. Can't miss 'em.

One of the party with binoculars shouted that they were in sight, and soon enough, a trio of lights crossed the river and turned left. I was on the lookout for either an orange star on a yellow background (the Queen) or red and green quarters (the Greenings). There was a groan when none of the front runners showed for the Queen. It would have been even bigger if there had been a Greening horse there, but tonight's honours would go outside the Particular, it seemed.

The three leaders were almost past us when the rest of the field came into view. The Queen's horse started to open its stride on the flat, but it was never going to catch the others, and soon it was all over.

'She's young. She'll learn,' announced the Queen loudly. 'Not bad for a first run out. Time to eat, I think.'

We didn't stay much longer, and I didn't learn much more. I found out that the chef was excellent and that Florence was a single parent with a son who wanted to be a vet, and that she had returned from a life in Manchester to become her father's land agent in the Eden valley. She was quite willing to talk about anything except her father, and that in itself told me a lot.

The party was going to go on for some time, and a Squire was ordered to take us back to Waterhead. By the time we got there, all the horse transporters were gone, too, and only scattered knots of hardened racing aficionados were clustered round a couple of booths.

When we got out of the car, Saul came over. 'You're still alive, then. That's always a good start. Is she in?'

'She is.'

He nodded. 'If the Ripleys really do abstain, that gives us a minimum of four votes to three, so you're guaranteed to pass. I'd still prefer it if we could get Eskdale on board, so I've arranged a breakfast meeting with Morgan Torver. Half past seven in the School House dining room.'

'Right. Is it okay if I summon my partner for tomorrow? I'd rather she were in at the beginning.'

'Of course. Good idea.' He paused and nodded his head slowly. 'Well done, Conrad. In all my years I've never once been invited to one of her Chase parties. See you tomorrow. Good night.'

'Shall we find a nice warm pub?' I suggested. 'I need to message Cordelia.'

'Good idea, and I have two missed calls from Myfanwy already. I have a bad feeling about this.'

9 — A New Commission

Cordelia was wearing a thermal base layer tonight, under an oversized jumper and thermal leggings; Evie Mason had gone for a thick down gilet. Middlebarrow Haven wasn't getting any warmer, even with the extra resident.

The new arrival was Saffron Hawkins, and she'd just got back from a trip to the Marches. Cordy tried to suppress a smile as Saffron stood, still in her outdoor coat, staring covetously at the two chairs nearest the Aga. They didn't actually have Cordy's and Evie's names on the back but were very much *their* seats.

Evie turned and stared at the counter-top wine rack. 'It's like déjà vu all over again,' she observed. 'Wine or tea, Saff?'

Saffron looked over. 'Déjà vu? What are you on about?'

'Waiting and waiting while Conrad has a close encounter with a Fae Queen, like women waiting for their husbands and fathers to come back from the sea. Or from the Trojan War.'

Cordelia was stirring the supper, and turned to look at Saffron with a grin and a shake of the head. They each knew what the other was thinking: *Yes, Evie really is like this.* Since Saffron had come up to stay at Middlebarrow, things had certainly become a lot livelier.

Cordy spoke up. 'Make tea, Evie. If Conrad gets the gig, I might have to travel up there tonight, and get a grip: men are just as likely to be waiting for women these days. Or men waiting for other men.'

Evie filled the kettle. 'Except the men would go down the pub while they were waiting, wouldn't they?'

'Stand by your bed, Kennedy!'

Cordy nearly jumped out of her skin and dropped the spoon. She wheeled round to see where the fuck Conrad had sprung from.

Nowhere was the answer. He wasn't here at all. What she saw instead was Saffron, grinning from ear to ear. Her impressions were getting better, and when she needed to use magick to lower the pitch (like now) there wasn't a trace of it to be sensed.

'You are going to get in serious trouble one day,' said Cordelia, retrieving the spoon and turning away.

'Yes mum,' said Saffron.

There was a pause while the kettle reached its peak, and Evie filled the teapot. 'How d'you get on today, Saff?' she asked.

Saffron decided it was worth taking the risk of disrobing, and hung her coat on the back of the chair. 'Better, thanks. Old Piers certainly kept a lot quiet, didn't he, Cordy?'

Cordelia decided that no further intervention was required and left the dish to simmer on its own. She sat down and looked at Saffron. Young, confident, rich, childless Saffron. With all those advantages, why did Saff keep deferring to her? Cordelia hadn't even left the house today: it had been Saffron down in Shrewsbury, turning over stones to see what crawled out. 'Who did you see?' she asked, gently batting the ball back to Saffron.

'That Enscriber. The one who does the hypnosis cards. By the gods, she can talk for England. In the end, I was tempted to actually pay her for the information. That way I could have shut her up and got on with life.'

'Anything useful?'

'She gave me the up-to-date list of coven members for north Hereford. There's a couple there that we might need to keep our eyes on. And she'd heard something about a ruckus in the Fae. Going to get back to me on that one.' With the confidence of rich youth, Saff sniffed her own armpit. 'I am so going to have to do laundry. Either that or go shopping. Anyone fancy a trip to Chester tomorrow?'

'Cheshire Oaks, more like,' said Evie. 'Some of us can only afford outlet shopping. There's always the Internet?'

Saffron rolled her eyes and the conversation rolled on to other things. The text from Conrad came in while Cordy was loading the dishwasher (which didn't get loaded until bed-time unless she did it for some reason). *Get packing and say your goodbyes. Early start tomorrow. I'll call you later.* And that was him all over. Draw a line, turn the page and start over with a new chapter.

She showed her phone and put on her Mum voice. 'Will you two be alright if I leave you on your own?'

'Has he gone and done it?' said Evie. 'Really?'

'Looks like it. He wants me to travel up tonight.' She paused and smiled. 'And now you've got the perfect excuse to live here and be waited on full time, Saff. Much better than getting your own place in the Marches.'

Why did she bother? It was water off a duck's back to Saffron. 'Too right. Evie needs someone to blame for not getting on with her coursework, and that onerous task falls to me. D'you want a hand packing?'

Saffron was brash, entitled and infuriatingly messy, but Cordy would miss her. 'Yes please. It's a long drive to Ambleside, and the sooner I get going, the better.'

The weather had turned nasty during the evening, and Conrad didn't say much when he called. He could tell from her voice that Cordelia was concentrating on the drive, and said there would be a large brandy waiting for her at Windermere Haven.

There was a whole bottle of brandy waiting for her. And a warm embrace, and a helping hand to get her meagre possessions up to a poky room at the back of the hotel's top floor. At least there was an en-suite shower room. Mina saw her looking at the facilities, and lingered when Conrad clumped off down the stairs.

'This is not permanent. Or even semi-permanent. We will find something better, but the room is complimentary for a few nights at least. And here is a spare key to Lake Cottage. I got it cut this afternoon, and you must treat it as your extension.'

'But...'

'But nothing. We have a *bath*, and it is perfectly designed for perfectly formed people.'

Cordy couldn't help but laugh. 'You mean *short* people.'

'That's what I said: perfectly formed. Like me and you. We also have a microwave and unlimited teabags. It may also end up functioning as an office.'

'But is it *warm*?' said Cordelia, following Mina down the stairs.

'I have told Conrad that log-splitting is a valuable form of exercise until his horse is delivered.'

Cordelia closed the door to her room softly behind her and felt excited again, for the first time in weeks. Whether that was being closer to Raven, having a purpose or simply being around the *perfectly formed* whirlwind of Mina, she couldn't tell. Whatever. It felt good, and that was enough for tonight.

The next morning, excitement was blended with apprehension as they approached the forbidding Gothic façade of the School House. The tents of the market were all closed and Warded, and Gnomes were only just beginning to light the fires in their forges. Off to the left, it was still night, and the sun hadn't yet risen over the eastern fells to the right. When she'd gone to them earlier at Lake Cottage, it had been pitch black under the trees and the smell of rotting leaves had hung around in the still air, mixing with Conrad's early morning tobacco fix and tickling the back of her throat.

Ahead of her, Conrad approached the day like he approached everything: by putting one foot in front of the other and getting on with it. Mina seemed a bit more distracted, and it definitely had something to do with the Kelly Situation. When Saffron had arrived at Middlebarrow, it had been the first thing Evie had asked about, and Saff had been almost tied to her chair until she'd given a blow-by-blow account of the Fire Games. Evie had even taken notes.

A teenage girl was waiting for them at the front door of School House, and Cordelia was instantly reminded of Saffron. It was the confident smile that did it, and Cordy wasn't surprised to learn that they had been greeted by Willow Torver, the Head Girl.

'I saw you yesterday in the Union tent, didn't I?' said Conrad.

'That's right. We all take turns, even though it's not my union. Just taking messages and stuff.'

He took an envelope from his poacher's pocket and sorted out a greetings card. Cordy recognised it as part of the evidence in the Harry Eldridge case. He offered it to Willow and asked, 'Has anyone else taken over the poker school?'

She took the card and stared at it for a second, running her fingers over the script and blinking at the memories it brought back. Then she was all smiles again. 'I don't think anyone would dare. Unless you're offering, sir?'

Conrad had mischief in his eye, a bit like Scout. She missed that dog. The human version offered Willow a card. 'Call me and I'll arrange lessons if you want to take over. Or give the card to Iolanthe.'

'Erm…'

Mina shoved him out of the way. 'Please forgive him, Willow. He is so used to working with cadets that he thinks nothing of giving his card to a schoolgirl. I wouldn't say that his intentions are honourable, but it's not as creepy as it looks.'

Willow had clearly reached her threshold for understanding of grown-up behaviour and looked a little pale. 'Shall I take you to see my dad?'

Of course. The Head Girl wouldn't have an ordinary father, would she?

Cordelia had seen the entrance hall briefly on her last visit, and looked around a bit more now she had the chance. Definitely too dark for her tastes. Willow led them down a side corridor and into a dining room that practically dripped with ingrained odours of boiled cabbage, custard and saturated fats.

Cordelia's stomach informed her that she should definitely have turned down that fourth brandy last night.

The room probably held sixty comfortably, and the sole occupant looked up from his phone when he heard the door. While they crossed the room, he shouted through the open hatch into the kitchen and stood up to greet them.

Morgan Torver clearly had Viking ancestry, judging by the sandy hair and pale skin, and while she could see his eyes in Willow, Cordy felt glad on the girl's behalf that she must take after her mother.

The Head Girl left them to it, and Cordelia took a seat where she could watch Torver without staring, because today was Conrad's show, and she was there to observe, just like she'd observed for Raven. The difference was that she'd pass on her observations when she lay in Raven's arms. She jerked for a second and flushed bright red. It was a good job no one was watching her, because her imagination had, for half a second, replaced Raven with Conrad, and that was just *so* wrong that there were no words for its wrongness. She took a deep breath and told herself to get a grip and focus.

She'd tried to remember the names from his briefing last night, and from their earlier mission, but until she met the Greenings, Brathays, Gibsons, Calverts, Prestons and their Uncle Tom Cobley for herself, the negotiations didn't make much sense. The one name already seared into her brain was *Derwent, Queen of.* As usual, the conversation steered around the Fae, because the instinct to avoid talking about them in public was as ingrained in Mages as was the smell of cabbage in the dining room.

After half an hour, a deal was done. There was no assessor for either Eskdale nor its southern neighbour, Duddon/Furness, and Torver's union would only offer support if the new Commissioner had a plan. He did, and hands were shaken just as other senior Mages started to filter in for breakfast.

The food, by the way, had been exactly what Cordy expected. On the way out, she said to Mina, 'You must have been hungry. I couldn't face most of it.'

Mina lifted her hood carefully over her hair. 'You keep forgetting that I have been in prison. By HMP standards, that was acceptable. Conrad needs to see a Gnome about a staff, so I want you to meet someone. They should be at the anvil.'

As they strode out, Mina glanced at her from under the hood. 'I may need to go to Elvenham tomorrow afternoon. It was all very well getting Tamsin out of Earth House and away from the pain, but there's only so much that Myfanwy can cope with.'

Cordy set her face to neutral. 'If you're asking *Can I look after Conrad,* then you should know that he's a big boy now.'

Mina didn't break stride. 'I know he's a big boy, and that's why he needs a minder, so I'll take that as a *yes*. Have a look at this.'

She thrust a printout into Cordy's hands, and stopped to wait while Cordelia read it. Yet again, Cordy had to hold it slightly away from her. Reading glasses were just around the corner, it seemed.

She studied the paper, then stared at Mina, outraged. 'What! They have got to be joking. Who can pay this sort of money?'

'Certainly not nurses, teachers or binmen. The lack of affordable housing in the Lakes is a problem that is only going to get worse. No wonder Charlotte Mason College has its own accommodation.'

Cordelia scanned the cost of renting even a broom cupboard in the surrounding area and swallowed hard. Could she actually afford to take this job?

Mina waited a second, then started walking again. 'I am seeing Lucy Berardi tomorrow about the Cairndale coffee shop and I may carry on south. Do you think Lucy could run a takeout van here?'

They had arrived at the heart of the market, and Cordelia eyed up the options. 'I think she'd make an even bigger fortune. Mulled ale is all very well, but…'

'Precisely. Aah, there he is.'

Mina headed towards Matt Eldridge, who looked older but more at peace than when Cordy had last seen him. He smiled at them both and came to shake Cordy's hand. 'I didn't have you down as a glutton for punishment, Cordelia.'

'I just can't stay away. It's the freezing weather and aura of impending doom that draws me back.'

Mina slipped in smoothly with, 'And talking of staying, I'm afraid that Cordelia has been given a most unsatisfactory room, but it's all that can be afforded.'

Matt frowned with sympathy, and also with puzzlement as to why he was being told this.

'Matt, meet your new lodger; Cordy meet your new landlord. It is a perfect arrangement, and Tom Morton tells me that Matt is house-trained, too. If you don't mind a lot of muddy boots.'

'How…? What?' Cordelia didn't know what to think, and she could feel her cheeks glowing in the frosty air.

'Are you really struggling?' asked Matt. 'Or is it another of your windups, Mina?'

'I'll be fine,' said Cordelia.

Matt raised his eyebrows. 'In other words, you *are* struggling. Look, my apprentice has just left. Her room is vacant, and you can have it for a contribution to bills and your share of the chores. At least until the summer, anyway. It's a serious offer.'

He looked down at the printout, still clutched in her hand, then back at her face. His expression didn't give much away, but he didn't look excited. That would have been very worrying. 'That's very kind of you, Matt. I'll take it.'

'Good,' said Mina. 'Let's go for a look at the lake, then they should be ready for us.'

The School Hall of School House had been placed deliberately at the back of the building. There were windows only on the north side, and they were high and full of stained glass. This was a room that cared nothing about the outside world. This was a room that knew its own importance. Cordelia was fairly certain that it had been designed by a man. Or a Gnome.

The meeting place for the Daughters in Glastonbury was completely open to the elements, and yes, they had met when snow lay on the ground. Actually, that was quite romantic (if you remembered your gloves). It was the rain that got to you. The Mages of Lakeland could do with some rain in here to wash away the gloom, and she suspected that the only reason they didn't is that there would be nothing left.

The panelling gave her the creeps, and that was saying something. Every time she looked at it, the shapes appeared to have moved in a flux of arabesque twisting lines. That was when you could see it, of course. Most of the time you felt that it was lurking in the shadows, watching you. And this was supposed to be a place for young minds. For learning. If Rick fell under a bus tomorrow and she became full-time mother again, she would move back to Glastonbury rather than run the risk of exposing her children to this nightmare.

Chairs had been placed around the Hall, but no one was sitting in them. There was also a ring of larger chairs in the centre with what looked suspiciously like a throne at the North point. As yet, no one was sitting in these chairs either, and so they crowded in the gaps and corners. Within seconds of walking through the door, the back of Cordelia's neck had told her where their enemies were: over there, to the corner of the stage.

She turned slowly to look, and Mina turned with her. 'Would it be offensive to call them the Three Witches?' whispered Mina.

In the middle of the three women was Philippa Grayling, the current Chief Assessor, and she was flanked by Stella Newborn/Ripley on one side and what must be the Housemaster, Dr Judith Yearsley, on the other.

'Yes, it would be offensive, but they deserve to be offended. All three of them.'

Mina whispered back. 'Stella and Philippa, yes, but what has Judith Yearsley done other than be rude to Conrad? If that were a crime, I would be going back to jail myself.'

'She makes her students work in this room. That is most definitely a crime. Is that Saul Brathay over there?'

'Who else.'

Mina did a round of pointing and naming, and a few more of them stuck in Cordelia's memory. Did she need the mental equivalent of reading glasses, because she was sure this used to be much easier?

At eight forty-five on the dot, the woman identified as Victoria Preston moved and stood to the side of the chair of honour. 'Langdale Leven, we're back in session.'

Half a dozen Mages and two Gnomes stood to form a circle inside the ring of chairs, and Victoria continued. 'This is a resumption of the adjourned meeting from Monday with one item left. George?'

One of the Gnomes stepped forwards. 'I propose admission to the Union under Article Nineteen for Conrad Clarke and Cordelia Kennedy.' Cordy nearly jumped out of her skin. What? Why had no one mentioned this? The Gnome continued, 'Both are resident in the Union and Mages in good standing. I propose that we waive the landowning restriction and grant one year's registration at the Union's expense.'

'Seconded,' said an unnamed woman.

From the corner, Judith Yearsley's voice rang out. 'Do you think the Trojans had a vote before they decided to drag the horse in? Because that's what's about to happen.'

Victoria didn't flinch and her eyes didn't leave the circle around her. 'Any comments?' There were none. 'All in favour?'

It was unanimous, and Victoria smiled at Cordelia, then Conrad. 'Welcome to Langdale-Leven. Would you care to sign the register?'

Cordy's memory brought back the Annex of Westphalia from the well room under Merlyn's Tower, when she'd pricked her finger and signed in blood. This was a bit less intimidating – a loose-leaf page in a folder and a pen stamped with *Skelwith Construction*.

From beyond the immediate circle, Saul Brathay led a round of applause, and Cordy didn't need to look at the stage to know that the three witches were all standing with their arms folded and lips pursed.

'Meeting closed,' announced Victoria. 'Over to you, Mister President.'

The members of the Langdale-Leven Union moved away and others took their places, this time standing in front of the chairs, ready to sit down. This was the Council of the Grand Union, and the throne was ready to accept Saul Brathay's backside, but he had something else on his mind first.

The Gnome went straight up to Philippa Grayling, and when Cordelia returned to Mina, she took a detour and used a little magick to focus her hearing.

Saul kept his voice calm. 'Your choice, Philippa. You can resign with our thanks or I'll table this as an emergency motion.' He offered the Chief Assessor a piece of paper and stood impassively in front of her.

'What is it?' said Judith Yearsley.

Philippa slowly put on her reading glasses and examined the paper. She offered it to her friends and said, 'It's a motion to suspend me and initiate an enquiry into the Harry Eldridge affair, specifically my supervision of Kian.'

'I can vote on that,' said Judith. 'So can you. He won't have a majority then. Not if Stella supports you.'

Stella was looking at her feet. 'My union has mandated me to abstain on all matters concerning the assessors.'

'It's time,' said Philippa. 'Time I went.' She turned to Stella. 'I won't put you through an enquiry. You deserve the chance to move on.' She passed the paper back to Saul. 'Give me a minute to draft my resignation. I'll keep it short.'

'Of course,' he said. 'We'll start with the other business.'

The three women went through a door marked *Housemaster* and closed it behind them. Saul took his seat and opened the meeting, moving briskly through the items until the women returned and took their seats.

Ten minutes later, Philippa Grayling had resigned with the Union's best wishes, and Conrad had been appointed to the new post of Commissioner of the Peace for the Lakeland Particular. There was no debate, no amendments and no votes against. Stella abstained, as did two other unions.

Saul shook Conrad's hand, and spoke up. 'I am now adjourning the meeting for the installation, which will of course take place at the lake. I'll see you there in ten minutes.'

'What installation?' said Cordelia to Mina. 'Why am I hearing about this now?'

'Because it has the potential to go badly wrong,' said Mina. 'He didn't want to give you the chance to pull out.'

'Am I...?'

Mina interrupted. 'Don't worry. It is all down to him. He didn't want you to pull out, because then there would be no one to hold my hand and look after me if he dies. He's very thoughtful like that.'

Mina was already on her way out of the hall before Cordy could process that. Mina's definition of *very thoughtful* was rather different from hers.

10 — You Can't Get the Staff

I was quite glad to get outside. The number of layers I'd put on this morning under a relatively smart shirt had meant that I was in danger of overheating in School House. When the wind off the lake hit me, the feeling didn't last long.

The ten minutes that Saul had allocated was spent as you'd expect – having a crafty smoke by one of the forges, and that's where Mina and Cordelia found me. I was going to put my arm round Mina, but Cordy had other ideas.

'What the fuck are you doing and why didn't you tell me?'

There was no answer to that. I hadn't known until this morning that one of Saul's last minute compromises had been to insist that the Commissioner had a staff of office to show that she (or in my case *he*) was authorised by the Particular and not the Watch. And that meant a short conversation with Nimue in front of an audience. Nice. I'd had to run around making sure that I could access the magick in the oak rod, and I'd left it to Mina to explain what was going on. She must have been busy.

'Because I didn't know for certain until the vote,' I told Cordelia. It wasn't a complete lie. 'And it still might not happen today. It depends if they've finished the riveting.' I saw movement behind them. 'Here comes George. Looks like we're on.' I made eye contact. 'Sorry, Cordelia. I really didn't mean to keep you out of the loop.'

Mina gave me a hug, and we had a quick kiss before George Gibson arrived and offered me a three foot long rod of seasoned oak that had been lying around in someone's workshop for generations, soaking up magick and waiting for some idiot like me to bring it alive. Two copper bands had been added, twelve inches from each end. They were blank for now, and inscriptions would be added later, as would a case to carry the bloody thing around.

He presented the staff formally but not ceremonially. In other words, he held it out with a respectful face rather than getting on one knee. If I ever had a successor, I suspect that kneeling would definitely be a part of the installation. 'Thank you,' I said, and grasped the wood.

The magick would really flow when I grasped *both* copper bands. I wasn't going to do that near Mina, though. I wasn't going to do that near anyone. I strode up to the beginning of the jetty and looked around. The whole of the market had come to watch, joining the VIPs from the School House. It was time to assert my authority.

I raised my voice. 'Could all the assessors gather round Matthew, please.' And then I waited.

Of course the existing assessors had been consulted before their unions voted. Some were in favour and some were against, as you'd expect. Now that the Grand Union had given me the job, they were in my command whether they liked it or not, and they could bloody well stand together and watch.

I knew their names from the files, of course, but they'd either avoided me before now or simply not been around, and I wasn't surprised who was the first to show. I'd seen the Greendale Trust at the races last night, and one face who'd been talking to James separated herself and stood next to Matt. That would be Natalie Greening, a cousin, who served as Assessor for Patterdale. She was joined by two other women and one man, making a total of five. There were four vacancies, so all were present and correct. 'I'll talk to you all after the ceremony,' I announced to them, then turned away before I could see their reactions.

The jetty sticking out into Windermere was long. Long enough to accommodate Harry Eldridge's houseboat with a bit to spare, and I went right to the end. I think they expected me to do this bit on the shore or something. Sod that. I like privacy when I'm communing with the Guardian of Albion. I held the staff at shoulder height with my left hand on one copper band, then brought my right up to touch the other. It was a good job no one could see the look on my face or hear the whimper I emitted. Ouch.

I hope they took my gentle rocking back and forth as me balancing in the wind rather than me trying not to scream with pain as Lux coursed around my body in an uncontrolled torrent. I had about a second to either get a grip or lose my grip. I focused on the gap between my hands, on the resistance of the wood and the transistor effect varying the flow of Lux.

Shit. It wasn't working. If anything, the circle was turning into a cyclone as it rushed up my left arm and down my right. Ooooh, hang on. Cyclone. Anti-cyclone. The power was going the wrong way, and I could see only one way to stop it.

I braced my feet and let go with my left hand. Just for a second. The flow of Lux stopped, and a headache lanced me between the eyes. I pooled Lux in my left arm and grasped the copper once more. The Lux in my arm met the

Lux in the rod, and I pushed as hard as I could. Better. A trickle of power, compared to the previous flood, but a controlled trickle. It ran out of my left arm and up my right. I summoned the memory of water meadows and sweet grass, of springtime and blossom, and I used the rod to amplify it across the water.

With an enormous *Whoooosh*, she appeared before me, the memory of flowers turning into actual odours. Urrgh. What was that? Mixed in with the smell was something like the tinny mouthful of metal you get when aluminium foil hits your teeth. She looked different, too. Obviously a Nymph made of water isn't going to be on anyone's facial recognition database, but this manifestation of Nimue had, shall we say, greater assets? Oh, and a fringe.

The former Watch Captain Piers Wetherill had warned me that the Nimue in Windermere was … different to other Nimues. Same Nymph, different composition, and no, I don't understand it. I don't think he does either. I'd asked Saul about that, and he'd told me that the staff would help her focus. Time to find out.

I bowed low, keeping the circuit going, and straightened up. 'My lady honours me.'

'Lord Guardian. How fares the realm?'

'Troubled, my lady, as it ever was, and in need of peace. Would you assist that cause by making your mark on this staff.'

She bobbed up and down as water formed and re-formed to bring her to life. She lost interest in me, and her blank eyes moved along the shore, taking in the audience. Whether or not she found it pleasing, she didn't say.

She turned back to me and stretched out a watery arm towards my right shoulder, dripping on to the jetty as her limb extended well beyond the length of human bones. I kept still as the liquid fingers reached past my ear and touched the pommel of Great Fang, the sword on my back.

A jolt of Lux flared through my body, and I nearly dropped the staff. On top of the smell of Nimue, the iron-rich burnt smell of the First Daughter wafted over the lake. Nimue had touched the badge of Caledfwlch and invoked its magick.

'You have the mark of the sword, Lord Guardian. You need no other. Take care.'

She flopped back into Windermere with barely a ripple and was gone. This was not going to go down well. I sighed and turned to face the future, and the future was wearing a big frown.

Chairman Mao said that all political power comes out of the barrel of a gun, and he had a point. But what about the basis for the rule of law? It's pretty settled in the mundane world, but it's very much up for grabs in the magickal one, both in theory and in reality. I'll give it to you in a nutshell.

Does Hannah wield Excalibur to show that she has the authority of the crown, or does the authority of the crown derive from the fact that Nimue has given Hannah the sword? Answers on a postcard to the Windermere Haven Hotel, Ambleside Road, Westmorland.

The unions wanted me to have a separate badge, to show that they weren't subject to the King's Watch, but Nimue had other ideas. I walked back up the jetty and plastered a smile on my face. Some of the crowd smiled back, and not just because they were engaged to me. I take my positives where I can.

Saul Brathay was not smiling, but then he is a Gnome. When I got to the concrete apron, he managed to lose the frown at least, and turned to the crowd. 'Our lady has confirmed the Commissioner in his office. Would you like to say a few words, Conrad? After all, your words are binding...'

There was the faintest ripple of laughter, which is what he deserved. At least I'd prepared for this bit.

'Someone who I admire and respect told me this: Be part of the solution, not part of the problem. I shall work hard to achieve that, and you should judge me on what I do, not on what I say. Thank you for making me welcome. I look forward to repaying the trust that the Grand Union, and Nimue, have placed in me.'

Saul led a round of applause that ranked about Polite+ on the reception scale. Sufficient unto the day.

I turned and went to Mina for an embrace, giving the crowd a chance to disperse. Cordelia had retreated to give us some room, and kisses over, she came up to congratulate me, followed by Liz and Barney.

'Do you want this back?' said Liz, offering me a sealed box covered in red cross logos.

'What's that?' said Mina.

'A field transfusion kit,' I told her. 'In case Nimue was hungry. We're too far from a hospital out here for major blood loss to end well.'

I took the kit off Liz, and Mina shook her head. 'The fact that it was a good idea makes a sad commentary on my life.'

Liz shoved her hands in her coat and shivered. 'We need to get back to work, and I've bad news on that front. Commander Ross has heard that you've been fired. Sheriff Morton told him that you were on the sick, but I wouldn't leave it too long before you make your peace.' She looked at Mina, then back at me. 'Why do I get the feeling that I'm being used as a messenger? I thought that you and Tom got on these days, Conrad.'

I'm afraid that she's right – Lucy and Mina have refused to get involved, and Tom Morton feels he's owed an explanation for Ireland. He probably is.

'I'll see them both soon,' I told Liz. 'Thanks.'

Liz and Barney exited right, and we headed for the group of assessors. I nearly stopped in my tracks when I saw that Philippa Grayling was standing with them. What?

She saw us coming and moved to intercept me. 'I can't offer my congratulations, Mister Clarke, because I fought tooth and nail to stop this happening, but happen it did. On Friday, I shall go to the travel agent and take the first ticket they have to a sunshine cruise. I have also told your team that the peace of the Particular is more important than any individual. I hope they listen to me.'

'And I hope that you take your phone on holiday,' I replied. 'I'm sure the assessors all have your number, and no one knows the secrets of the Particular like you do. As you say, peace is more important than any individual.'

She pursed her lips and gave a micro-nod. She didn't wish me luck, and I didn't wish her a happy holiday. On the whole, it was a better outcome than I'd expected. Behind me, the first hammer of the day struck an anvil, and Philippa Grayling walked off, back to her waiting friends.

Matt Eldridge made the introductions – Mina, Cordy and me to the other assessors, and the four of them to me. He stood back to join his peers, and I got to make my second speech of the day.

I was still holding the staff, and I started by passing it to Cordelia. 'Ms Kennedy has come with me because it was her choice. That wasn't the case for you. You all know what the new orders mean: I now have the power to assign you anywhere instead of just your old home union. To function at all, I will have to do that. If you want to bail out, I'm giving you twenty-four hours to think about it. If you want to stay as assessors, then I'll be having my first briefing in the School House at eighteen hundred tomorrow, just before the Borrowdale Crown purse. I hope to see you there.'

Natalie Greening was the youngest of them, and she'd been nodding while I spoke. 'I'll be there. Just one thing. Do we have to call you *sir?*'

I considered that for a moment. It was a very good question. 'Do you want the good news or the bad news, Natalie?'

'Oh, the good. Always the good first.'

'You don't have to salute.'

It took a second to sink in. 'Oh. Right. Yes, sir.' She paused. '*All* the time?'

'No. And definitely not when there is alcohol involved, such as now. I need a drink, if you'll excuse me.'

The four assessors said goodbye and left. Matthew stayed with us.

'What in the name of the Goddess do you expect me to do with this *thing?*' asked Cordelia, holding up the staff.

'Sorry about that,' I said. 'And I was lying about the drink. I will have one, but not just now. I need to take Mina down to the station at Windermere town. Could you make sure the staff gets back to Saul? He's got someone working on the case. Perhaps you might want a look around the market after that?'

Matt offered his hand. 'I'll take that, shall I? And I'm on duty, so I can show you round if you like.'

Cordy handed over the staff. 'Thanks. That would be great.'

On the way down to Windermere town, Mina informed me that she might not come back. 'The last thing I want to do is take a train to Cheltenham, but Tamsin really needs someone who understands and who will stand up for her. Myfanwy is a great listener, but... I'll be honest, Conrad. I'm seriously worried about Tammy's state of mind.'

'Oh.'

She didn't need to spell it out. Tammy's complicated neurological history made her vulnerable, to say the least. A mother shamed and cast out, with three young children. *If I can't have him, he can't have the kids.* It has happened before.

I dropped her at the station and turned round to head north again. To be honest, the market didn't hold much appeal any more, and I had two jobs to do. The first was to get some serious cold weather gear in the winter sales, and the second was to find the Executive Officer of the Grand Union, Heather Calvert. Becoming Commissioner involved a lot more than just collecting a staff of office. The paperwork was going to be horrendous.

11 — On the Chase

Cordelia knocked on the cottage door at four o'clock. She had paperwork, too, and after that the Clan minibus would collect us for the night ahead. I poured tea, and she said, 'I'm going to move into Matt's place at the weekend.'

I remembered to stop pouring before I looked up, astonished. 'That was quick.'

She made a sour face. 'You didn't have to sleep in that bed last night. After lunch, he took me to see Blackburn House. It's lovely.' She shrugged. 'We're not going to be making many friends in the short term, are we? It's good to share with someone who understands.'

On the surface, she meant someone who understands our job, but it was obvious that it went a lot deeper. Cordelia is a very private person, as is Matt. I left it unspoken and slid over her tea. 'Have you got your bank details handy?'

'Yeah. Hang on.'

It didn't take long to sort out, and soon we were putting on our heavy duty outer wear. When the minibus dropped us at Waterhead, we could hear the buzz of activity even with the restrictive magick in place. When we got through the trees and on to the School House grounds, we stopped and stared.

'Is *every* Mage in the Particular here?' she asked in wonder.

'I think you're right, and it's not just humans. I'm smelling a *lot* more Fae than last night.'

'How are we going to see anything of the race through that lot?'

'I don't know. Let's find out, shall we?'

As we got closer, the crowd resolved itself into smaller groups. A lot of the human spectators had no magick themselves, but even so, there aren't *that* many Mages around – they just have loud voices when the hot wine is flowing. I grabbed us a couple of mugs from Liz's cousin and we started wandering towards the paddock.

Lightsticks had been placed to stop people straying off the paths and tripping over guy ropes, and the Greendale Trust animals had been taken away for the night, allowing more room for the horses to be shown off. As we walked around, a lot of people stared at us. A few even pointed from a distance. I paused near the paddock, and Cordelia touched my arm, making a small Silence.

'Did you hear them?'

'Who? No. What?'

'I thought not. Ignorance is bliss with your hearing isn't it?'

'That's why I've got you. What were they saying?'

'At least two said, "No, not her. The other one. The Indian one." One Witch called you a Pale Horseman and her friend said no, you loved Gnomes too much to be like that. And most just said, "It's true about him not being much of a Mage."'

'It could have been worse. You know that Hannah will take you back in a heartbeat if you're not happy.'

She let go, offended. 'I like it here. Everyone was so friendly this afternoon. It's just you they don't like.'

Charming. 'You can stand over there if you want.'

She actively considered it for a few seconds. 'No. Mina wouldn't forgive me if I did that. And if I have much more of this wine, I'll never find my way back to the hotel without you.'

'Good to know I have my uses. Do you want any tips?'

'Tips? On what?'

The first of the horses were being saddled. 'The Chase. They've finally found a new bookmaker.'

'On my wages? You must be joking.'

I opened my mouth to respond, then snapped it shut.

'By the Goddess,' said Cordelia. 'Look at that!'

You couldn't miss it. The front of School House had disappeared behind a curtain of magick, and on the curtain was a projection. Not a physical curtain, but a Skyway, a window into somewhere else. It was showing the paddock, but it was *huge*. This was visible magick on a scale I'd not seen before. And that wasn't all.

'Good evening my lords and ladies! Welcome to the two hundred and eighty seventh Waterhead Chase, supported by Clan Skelwith.'

The voice had boomed out from some Work of sound magick on the turrets at the corners of School House. How the hell was this not visible and audible from Bowness, five miles away?

'Did you have this at Glastonbury?' I asked. 'It's … epic.'

She was lost in wonder. 'No. Nothing like this. Not on this scale anyway. We sometimes used one to show rituals to people outside the Grove, but nothing like this. Was that George's voice?'

'I think it was.'

She considered the giant display, which showed a young girl being helped on to an enormous horse. The girl looked petrified, and I don't blame her.

This was the Queen's third horse in the race and the jockey's first time in the Waterhead. She hadn't done brilliantly last night, and I just hoped she made it back in one piece.

'On the screen is High Peak Explorer,' intoned George. 'I'm reliably informed that you can get forty to one on him right now.'

A woman's voice was amplified, muttering something, then George clarified. 'Make that fifty to one. Next to enter the ring is…'

There were only eighteen horses in the race. I was surprised that with the local limits there were even a dozen riders willing to risk it, and I wondered if, down in Cornwall, Morwenna Mowbray was thinking of the scene in front of me. When Morwenna was made a Vessel for Lara Dent, she was expected to win this race. And the one tomorrow. Now it was a bit more open.

Two minutes later, I nudged Cordelia and pointed down the paddock to something that hadn't been shown on the Skyway yet. 'There's that girl from Sprint Stables. Persephone. Does she remind you of someone we've met?'

Cordy thought about it. 'The first time we met, no, but since then … it's more like I've seen someone since who reminds me of Persephone. Weird.'

We were standing not far from a lightstick, and when Perci saw us, she turned the horse away before mounting, and when she was on the big screen, she practised putting on a Glamour. The horse was called *Scipio*, and she appeared as a classical Amazon of some sort, and she got a got a huge cheer for it. She was avoiding me for some reason, a point I made to Cordelia.

'Really?' she replied. 'If I get close enough at some point, I'll say hello and ask how the other grooms from Sprint Stables are getting along. There were rather a lot in hospital after we visited them.'

There was no answer to that. When Perci had gone past whatever they were using as a camera for the Skyway, Perci reverted to her normal self and the orange star of the Red Queen shone out from her silks. I looked at who was next and muttered, 'Here's trouble.'

'Rowan Sexton, I presume. She wasn't there when I visited Linbeck Hall.'

'No. Full time with the Greenings, now.'

The Sextons had been at the heart of my first trip to the Particular. Rowan was being groomed to take over as Guardian of a Dryad in their woods, until her mother and her uncle did something really stupid. Both Diana and Guy are now in prison, and Rowan was cut out of the succession for the grove and the mill. Rowan hadn't really wanted all that, I don't think. What she really wanted was what she'd got now: horses and the chance to ride them. If sporting the Greening colours was the price to pay, she looked happy enough paying it.

Her horse was another stallion – *Star Trek*. Not to be outdone, Rowan's features morphed into what I presume was a character from the show, and her silks became some sort of uniform with a red chest and a black yoke.

'Let's find the bookmaker,' I said. 'And get a refill.'

Harry Eldridge had made a part-time career as a magickal bookmaker, and he'd been underwritten by the Fae. Nature abhors a vacuum, and his place had been filled by a young woman with short hair and a snub nose. 'Why am I not surprised?' I said when we got closer to her.

'By what?'

I pointed to the large blackboard with her branding at the top. 'You can read that in this light?'

'No.'

'The new bookie is Jewel Gibson, and with a name like that, she must be George and Sapphire's daughter. Can't be more than nineteen, I'd have thought, and yet another Daughter of the Earth.'

'And there was me thinking you liked Gnomes. There's a queue, and it's my round. I'll see you in a minute.'

I joined the queue, and sure enough, there was Sapphire, camera in hand. She was taking pictures of what she could, but I recognise that look: she wasn't going to move more than six feet from her child, whether the child liked it or not, and I don't blame her one bit.

Closer still, and another familiar face popped up: Leo Sexton, Rowan's cousin. He was chalking the odds, writing slips and running around like an idiot. He could only be doing this because he loved Jewel, because he didn't look like he had a clue.

Jewel wasn't doing much better, hence the queue, and I got the feeling that her dad was slowing down the parade to give her a chance to keep up, judging by the looks he was giving her from his spot on a small podium. When I got to the front, Sapphire gave me the one hundred watt smile. And her eyes really did glow. How the hell did she do *that*?

'Conrad! Lovely to see you again. Where's Mina?'

'Domestic emergency in Clerkswell. I'm with Cordelia Kennedy tonight. I wasn't expecting your daughter to be making the book.'

Sapphire looked at her proudly. 'Neither did we, which is why I didn't say anything on Monday. This came as a surprise for us at last night's Novice Chase.'

Jewel looked at her mother, then at me. She swallowed hard and tried to smile. 'Can I help you, Lord Guardian?'

'You're doing a brilliant job here,' I replied. 'Congratulations. And it's Conrad.'

'Thanks.' She glanced at the board. 'It's up to date. Star Trek is 6-4 on and Scipio is Evens. Monstrance is at 12-1 if you fancy an each-way bet.'

'You think Star Trek is going to win?' I said. Bookmakers shouldn't be thinking about that sort of thing at this stage, and I wanted to test something.

Her glance at Leo gave it away. She thought that just because her boyfriend rated his cousin, she should, too. 'If it was Lara on Scipio, definitely not,' she replied. 'Perci's too young.'

I took out a wad of notes. 'I'll take a grand on Scipio.' It was tonight's limit, given that this was her first big Chase.

She opened her mouth, thought about saying something, then closed it and wrote me a ticket. 'Good luck, Conrad.' She couldn't resist it. 'Do you know something?'

'I read Harry's form book when it was in evidence. Did no one give you a copy?'

'Yeah, but... Leo, move Scipio to 7-4 on. Mum...?'

'Don't worry,' said Sapphire. 'You're doing great. Don't give up now.'

Jewel handed me the ticket, and when our hands touched, there was a blinding flash of light.

'Perfect,' said Sapphire from behind her camera. 'That's going to work a treat.'

Engines were starting to fire up around the paddock, and soon the mounts were being led away. There would be a lull now, and I told Cordy that we were going to plant ourselves in an obvious place and see who came to say hello.

Quite a few, was the answer, including Erin and Barney. 'I've taken the night off,' said Erin. Another Lakeland connection: not only is Erin a friend and the Guardian of my Mannwolves, she is now tutoring the girl who edged Rowan out of the succession at Linbeck Hall: Pihla Sexton.

'Night off from what?' I asked. 'Shouldn't you be at Birk Fell for the full moon?'

She looked slightly guilty. 'I told you. In that message.'

I folded my arms. 'What message?'

Barney whispered something, and Erin went from *slightly guilty* to *very guilty*, with an additional sprinkling of *embarrassed*. 'Oh. Right. I think I may have sent it when I was in a blind spot and it didn't go. Then I forgot to re-send it.' Erin never feels guilty for long. 'But I did write it! Anyway, Pihla got her head upside down trying to do a Reverse Instantiation, and I had to dash over and help because it's for a client and … And you've stopped listening, haven't you.'

'That's because I'm waiting for the bit where you tell me that it's all in hand and that I shouldn't worry about Karina being left alone in charge of the Pack.'

'Oh. Okay. Look, Conrad, don't worry. It's all in hand. Karina knows what to do. She's totally on top of this.'

I looked down to my left. 'Are you buying this, Cordy?'

'Hey!' said Erin. 'You can't ask her. And besides, everything was okay last night, so what could go wrong. Don't forget, you hired Karina, not me.'

'I think you should send Erin over to Ullswater right now,' said Cordelia. 'I'll look after Barney for her.'

'I … You're not good for him,' said Erin with a dark look at Cordelia. 'I mean, you're not good for Conrad. You're too good at keeping a straight face, you are.' She ran out of steam and looked at me. I *could* send her over there. She would go if I told her to. She would also resign as Guardian before the next full moon.

'If you're sure…?' I said to Erin.

'Yeah. Course. Oh, and congratulations, Commissioner. Tarja was full of this morning's carry-on when she got back.'

Among the others visitors was the bursar of Waterhead College, Martin Hoggart; his wife is one of the Daughters of the Earth who's making Mina's wedding head-dress. He was with an older woman tonight, his aunt Sabrina, and Sabrina had abstained this morning when the unions voted on my appointment. I smiled nicely at her, and was about to say something boring when she turned to Cordelia instead.

'Ms Kennedy, on behalf of the Sisters of the Water, welcome to the Particular. I had the pleasure of being at the Glastonbury Ecumenical two years ago. Please accept my condolences for your loss. Raven was … simply inspiring. Reached into your soul, she did.'

They were shaking hands when Sabrina spoke, and I saw Cordelia's arm flinch with an involuntary spasm. When she relinquished Sabrina's fingers, she looked down and said, 'Raven is with the Goddess, as I hope to be one day.'

'Where are you staying, dear? If you don't mind me asking.'

I would have minded being called *dear* if I were Cordelia, but it seems that women will take that from other women.

Cordelia looked up. 'I'm going to be lodging near Chapel Stile,' she answered.

Sabrina's eyebrows rose a fraction. She clearly knew who lived *near Chapel Stile*, but said nothing about Cordy's new landlord. 'Then you're only a mile from Elter Water! You would be most welcome to join the Sisters there. We have no problem with *Assessors*.'

But they clearly had problems with the King's Watch, something that didn't escape Cordy's notice, because she flashed me a wry smile.

To Sabrina, she said, 'That would be an honour. I'm afraid that I have to work tomorrow night, though.'

Sabrina laughed. 'The coven is here tonight. Wouldn't miss it for the world. For this full moon, they have sunset prayers only. If you're in the area…'

Cordy glanced at me again, and I gave her a *go for it* smile. 'That would be an honour,' she replied.

'Good. I shall let them know.' Sabrina finally turned to me. 'It was good to meet you properly, Mister Clarke. I shall pray that the Goddess inspires your new enterprise.' She hesitated for a second. 'Did President Brathay show you Judith Yearsley's file? Her file on you?'

What was the Housemaster doing writing a file on me?

'I haven't had the pleasure. I presume this was part of a campaign.'

'It was. Perhaps she only circulated it to those she thought might vote against you.'

'Can I get you a drink?' I replied. I was not going to ask what was in the file.

'No, allow me,' she replied. 'Martin. Would you?'

Her nephew looked at her for a second before agreeing, and something passed between them. 'Right. Hang on,' he said brightly. Being a conscientious steward, he picked up the empties from the ground and set off for refills.

When he was out of earshot, Sabrina made up her mind to speak. 'I showed it to Martin. He told me that there were at least three factual untruths in it. I expected better of Doctor Yearsley, and it wouldn't have made a difference anyway. The Western Waters were always going to abstain on this issue.'

Martin returned with four more mugs of wine, and we toasted new beginnings. When they'd gone, Cordelia watched their retreating backs. 'Interesting,' she observed.

'Which part?'

'That she couldn't wait to dob Yearsley in it. I'll add it to the list.'

The big Skyway had gone dark after the parade. Suddenly, it lit up again, and we were at a rocky level, up in the fells. More lightsticks illuminated the horses, and now there was moonlight, too.

'Surely they're not going to follow the whole course, are they?' said Cordelia in wonder. 'Matt said that half of it was on a higher plane, and that would take *serious* Lux. And skill.'

'We'll see. Looks like they're under orders.'

A shadowy figure at the back was standing by a squat tube. When the horses were more or less facing the course, he waved his arm in a gesture I could now copy: he was making a Silence, and with good reason. He backpedalled to a safe distance and used good old-fashioned electricity to set off a huge firework.

You'd call it a rocket, but it's a shell in a mortar, and there was only a small flash at ground level. Instinctively, I turned to the left, and there it was. A huge rainbow of light burst above the hills that stood between us and the start. By the time I looked back, the screen was empty again. They were off.

We got to see the race three more times before the field left the valley and passed the Red Queen's viewing point, beginning with the view over a crowd of about thirty people who were watching a dry stone wall. This also marked the first transition, and the jockeys had to move to a higher plane at the same time as their horses jumped the wall.

There were scattered cries around Waterhead as the first horse appeared and people recognised the Greenings' second mount, a chestnut mare, this one ridden by a boy I'd not seen before and wouldn't recognise again because he was under a Glamour to look like Robin Hood. I think. His timing was perfect, and the mare rose over the wall – and vanished. A cheer went up, and the rest of the field followed. Star Trek was fourth, and Scipio sixth. The poor girl on High Peak Explorer pulled up as her horse refused. She disappeared off screen, and I wondered if she was going to come back for a second try. The Skyway flickered out before we discovered.

'Does Mina know about the grand you're going to be poorer tonight?' said Cordy.

'How about a side-bet? If Scipio wins, you drive tomorrow night. If he doesn't, I'll take you by Smurf to wherever you want in the UK. Valid six months.'

'You're on … By the Goddess! That's incredible!'

The Skyway was showing a higher plane now, no question. I say that because at no point in Langdale does the Brathay form a shallow lake with a ford running through it. Robin Hood was still leading, and the horse sent up great splashes of what must be freezing water. I really hoped the jockeys had wetsuits on under their silks.

The mare found the water hard going, and another horse started to catch up – and then took a wrong turn, floundering up to her chest and swimming in panic in totally the wrong direction. As they passed through, Star Trek was now third, and Scipio had come up to fourth. The Skyway lingered on an empty lake for a few moments, then High Peak Explorer appeared to another cheer. Mage or not, the British do love an underdog.

When I'd looked around this afternoon, some of the higher fells had snow on them, despite the fact that none had fallen on Ambleside. Quite normal in the Lakes. What was not normal was the third and final view of the race. By the timings, it must have been about level with Chapel Stile, and the course had moved from the low tussocks of the glacial valley to a narrow ravine, the sides covered in snow. And spectators.

The view was set quite high, and the path at the bottom of the defile was narrow and twisty. To overtake here would mean risking the snowdrifts at the sides of the path. And the spectators.

Horses can't gallop over terrain like that for the whole course. We were watching the edited highlights, and when not on the big screen they would be trotting, something that a horse can keep up for hours but is hell for the rider if you can't get the rhythm right, or if you're distracted by trying to use magick.

As Maid Marian (the horse) started to make her way through the defile, I could see that she was starting to tire. She made an easy target when the snowballs started.

The riders all had Anciles, and a snowball is very much a missile, especially when Enchanted to burst in rainbow colours or with a bang. None of them struck the mounts, but there was a lot of dodging and counter-magick going on. Half way through the ravine, Maid Marian had slowed to a walk, and the field was catching her. The second placed horse decided to risk overtaking, and a group surrounding an unnamed Fae Count nearby started shouting, 'Come on Monstrance! Go for it!'

The elegant grey, complete with the image of a nun (? No, me neither), broke into a canter and headed up a raise which would form a shortcut if the horse could raise its gait and step through the snow. Maid Marian tried to canter, too, but slipped and stumbled, and Monstrance was in the lead. The rest of the field would have to try something similar or get stuck behind Robin Hood. None of them did. There were now only twelve horses left, with

Monstrance in the lead, followed by Robin Hood, Star Trek and Scipio. High Peak Explorer was still going, and still last.

'It's all about timing now,' I said. 'And stamina. Talking of which, we've got ten minutes to get a refill before they arrive. My round.'

We heard the cheering first as the horses approached down the track that led north, then one ball of light followed by two more. It was a three horse race to the finish, twice round the market, with Monstrance in the lead. That didn't last long, and Star Trek soon passed the grey, followed by Scipio.

Rowan Sexton didn't do anything wrong. She didn't push Star Trek to his limit until she was certain that he had enough left in the tank, and she got the tight turns just right. The problem for Rowan was that Scipio had a lot more left in him, and Perci gave her horse his head much earlier. She won by a third of a lap.

The party had already started by the time High Peak Explorer crossed the line, and it began with Perci being carried aloft to the steps of School House where Saul Brathay presented the cup. I couldn't tell you whether it was a tradition for the winner to keep up their Glamour or whether Perci didn't want to be seen as herself. After the presentation, she took the cup inside to watch her name being added to the honour board of Academy alumnae who had won the Waterhead Chase.

Jewel Gibson had a satisfied smile on her face when I collected my winnings. I pocketed the cash and stepped aside to talk to her mother. 'Harry didn't make a full-time job of this,' I said. 'Can Jewel?'

'She's having a gap year, Conrad. I know that's not an answer, but she's finding it hard to let go of the world of magick. Unfortunately, she takes after her father.'

I looked from mother to daughter and back again. 'In what way?'

'She doesn't have a creative bone in her body, poor thing, and she wants to study civil engineering, would you believe.' She paused and drew a little closer to me. 'I don't think she can face the thought of leaving all this behind her. Including Leo Sexton. Neither am I sure that she'll be safe going to the away meetings on her own.'

I remembered Leo's strong shoulders lifting bales of flax and great sheets of parchment in the paper mill at Linbeck Hall. He would never walk away from that. There was heartache looming there, and I had nothing to offer on that score. Bookmaking was another matter, though. 'I think you're right about her going away with large bundles of cash on her own. I don't know how, but you need to either put your foot down or find her a partner who isn't tied to a paper mill.'

'Thank you.' She folded her arms. 'I know it's wrong to think like this, and that every girl should be safe everywhere, but we don't live in that world yet. See you around.'

Cordelia had been queueing for the ladies. She tracked me down and we wandered around a bit, looking for a party to gatecrash. We were arguing about whether we should make a political decision (and join the Torvers of Eskdale) or go for a good time (and join the Queen of Derwent), when we suddenly looked at each other and realised that neither of us could really be bothered tonight. 'Let's head home,' I suggested. 'Or what passes for home at the moment. I think I can afford to buy you a drink in the Windermere Haven bar.'

Her shoulders relaxed. 'Thank you. That's a great relief for all sorts of reasons.' She winced. 'One of which is that if you have three layers on your feet, it doesn't half pinch your toes. If we detour via the anvil, we can say goodnight to Matt.'

We did, and I arranged to see him tomorrow afternoon for a special chat. In private.

It was a two mile walk back to the hotel, in temperatures now below zero, and Cordelia was good company all the way. I like Rick James, and not just because he's a good Watch Captain. Why on earth he cheated on Cordelia to the point where she left him is a mystery to me. And talking of cheating, I had a difficult night ahead of me.

12 — It's not You, it's Me

We had the bar to ourselves, pretty much, and Cordy was able to take off two pairs of socks and waggle her toes in her thermal tights in front of the fire. After a large damson gin (who knew *that* was a thing), she pronounced herself ready to face the Mattress of Insomnia and left me to take the short walk to Lake Cottage.

I chucked a couple of logs on the embers and looked around. It was very lonely in here without Mina, and very *very* quiet. Of course I missed her, but I sort-of knew she was there in spirit. What I really missed was having Scout around. His leg is much improved under the care of my Pack, but so is his quality of life up there. I'm not sure I could drag him away from that just because I wanted canine company.

I went back out for a smoke, and by the time I'd finished, the logs were crackling nicely. I set up my laptop, checked my phone and sent a message; my laptop pinged with a video call a few minutes later. I haven't seen or spoken to Eseld since the Fire Games, and it was time to reestablish contact.

She was curled up on a big, overstuffed sofa which had a mostly blue abstract painting hanging on the wall behind it. 'I'm guessing you're in Mowbray House, judging by the art work,' I began. Best keep it neutral.

'I can see why you're the detective,' said. 'Congratulations, Commissioner Clarke.' She raised a glass of red wine, and I'm guessing it was far from her first.

'Thank you. And I'm not the detective, that would be Tom Morton. I'm more the strong arm of the law.'

'Too right you are.' She sat up a bit, and knocked ash off her knitted woollen dress. 'How was the Waterhead Chase?'

'Epic. I'll tell you all about it properly next time. You'd love it.'

'Damn. I wish I'd been there. Dad never quite managed to get tickets for the Waterhead.' She went quiet for a moment. 'Oh shit, Conrad, it wasn't supposed to be like this.'

'Like what?'

She drank some wine and lit a cigarette. Her house, her rules. 'I was hoping that it could be done over the summer. Nice and civilised. By September, we'd have been old news.'

'How was the staff meeting?'

She gave a hollow laugh. 'Last term, I sat with the Sorcerers and Chris sat on his own, because he's a department of one and everyone ignored him. Today, we walked in together and the whole room went quiet. Then he sat on his own and everyone talked about him. Except the Sorcerers. We talked about the weather. Only the British can do that. I'll say one thing.'

'What?'

'No one outside the department wants to ask about what you and I got up to in Ireland, because that would mean them holding a conversation with me.' She grimaced. 'At least Oighrig is being nice, because now I know all about the Ahearns, and she's *very* grateful to me for keeping my trap shut.' She delivered the last bit in her awful Irish accent, then held up her glass. 'I'm drinking this wine because I haven't told you the worst yet.'

Eseld likes to make a splash and be the centre of attention – when she's in role. She is finding it harder to have the spotlight on her when she has to be herself. Having said that, she did look very uncomfortable. 'What happened?'

'Heidi Marston has been sticking her nose in. Evil bitch. Oighrig told me that Heidi has been saying things like, "Which one will have buyer's remorse first?" and, "Does anyone have Tamsin's number so that we can show some solidarity with her?" That woman's got a fucking nerve.'

That sounded like Heidi. I'm sure she carries a pot of salt around with her, looking for wounds to rub it into.

Eseld continued, 'I told Oighrig to say that Heidi was jealous of me. What a fucking mess, Conrad.'

Yet it hadn't stopped Eseld and Chris getting on with their lives, while Tamsin was sitting in Gloucestershire bereft. Just because Heidi Marston was obnoxious, that didn't make her wrong, especially as she agreed with Mina on this subject. I didn't tell Eseld that, though. Instead, I said, 'And Chris?'

'Even quieter than normal. He's worried about the girls, of course.' She leaned even closer to the screen. 'And he won't say this, but he's as fixed as the Dartmoor rocks. Even if we split up – and that is not going to happen, by the way – even if we split up, he's not going back to Tamsin.'

That was a curious thing to say. 'Why not?'

'He says she's changed completely because of what she did.' She gave the exaggerated shrug of someone who's had a glass too many. 'I dunno. I didn't know the old version of Tamsin.' She crushed out her fag and sat back. 'The trouble is, Heidi Marston wouldn't be asking all round Salomon's House for Tamsin's number if anyone actually had it, would she? Tamsin literally doesn't have anyone in the world except Chris and Mina. Poor cow. She's at Elvenham with the kids and the nanny, right?'

I nodded. 'And Mina. Look, Es, I wouldn't have asked you to call me if things weren't bad. I think you know that Chris and Tamsin need to start talking, but he's blocking her calls.'

'Do you blame him? If he takes them, all she does is scream at him.'

'Do you blame her? She was humiliated at the Fire Games.'

'Yeah, I know. And we're back where we started: I didn't want it to happen like this.'

We were both quiet for a while. 'Get him to take her calls from tomorrow. Mina will work on Tamsin to lower the temperature for the girls' sakes.'

'You're right. He's spending tonight at Earth House to look after the Distributor, and I've told him I'm not setting foot in that place until they're divorced properly. I'll talk to him tomorrow lunchtime.'

'Thanks, Es.'

She waved her glass. 'And you and me? We're good, right?'

'Of course. G'night, Es.'

We disconnected, and I sat back for a second, then got up, poured a brandy and went outside. The full moon was visible through the bare branches, and just for a second, I wondered how Karina was getting on at Birk Fell. She'd be fine. Unlike Chris and Tammy.

Something Eseld had said made me think – *in vino veritas*, and all that. This was not a mess I could fix, but what I could do was help them to move on. I needed to speak to some people first, though, and that could wait. I drained the brandy, sent a quick message to Mina and headed for bed.

The next morning, I was just about to enjoy my first coffee when a smart knock on the door caught me by surprise. I was meeting Cordelia for breakfast, and that wasn't her knock. I frowned and hesitated with my hand over the Hammer, then left it. Sometimes, you just have to trust people. Even unknown people on the other side of the door.

A woman was standing away from the cottage, and she was holding the reins of a horse. A breeze blew the smell of the beast's odour towards me, and I don't mean the horse. What was a Fae doing knocking on my door at this time of the day?

She had her back to me, a great mane of fair hair cascading down over her shoulders. No, the Fae do not wear riding hats, and yes, their hair is always perfect after being blown around and rained on. Something we have in common.

I got a sense of her magick, a deep well of Lux that was at odds with what my magickal nose was telling me. I was about to say something when she turned round, and boy was I glad of my poker face.

Something – or someone – had raked and slit her face open from her hairline to her jaw, just missing her right eye, but taking out her right nostril and going through to the bone over her teeth. It had been badly sewn together, each stitch a scar, and the tension had pulled the right side of her face even more out of shape. I managed to cover my reaction with a bow, because this was not some Knight I was dealing with.

'Welcome, my lady. What brings a Princess to my door at this hour?'

You can't taste water or smell the gases in the air, because your senses are made of them, and my magickal nose can't detect humans because I am one. Mostly. The creature in front of me had a lot of human in her, hence the weaker odour of Fae. I've sensed it often enough now to tell the difference. But who the hell was she?

'Well met … What do I call you?' she asked.

'Your Queen would have me call her *Charley*, so we'll go with *Conrad*, shall we? Assuming you're local, of course. If you're only in town for the Borrowdale Purse…?'

There was a tiny spasm through her scar as my words touched some sort of nerve. 'Well met, Conrad. I am Princess Faithful of the Borrowdale People. You could say I'm the Designated Survivor of the sídhe. And you're not supposed to call me *Faith* for short.'

'Why not?'

'It is as Her Grace wishes it.'

'When she recognises my authority as Commissioner, then I'll call my guests as she wishes. Welcome, *Faith*.'

The left side of her mouth made a grimace that was only turned into a smile by her eyes. Of course I thought of Mina, the Mina I'd first met, the Mina whose face was barely held together. She used to smile like that. There was clearly a story here, because Mina had needed the nation's top maxillofacial surgeon and a reconstructive dentist to look as gorgeous as she does today. Faith didn't. All she'd needed was time, Lux and Amrita.

She bowed in return and didn't object to the name. I pointed to the cottage. 'I have coffee…?'

'You honour me, but no, this is a flying visit. Grab your blade and meet me by the lake shore. As well as my womb, Her Grace values my swordsmanship, and she's sent me to show you why humans rarely defeat the Fae in fair combat.'

Already? That was quick.

She led away her horse by the reins, and I went to grab Great Fang. And a coat. It was bloody freezing out there.

The Windermere Haven Hotel only has a small frontage on to the lake, but even the smallest strip of shoreline is worth a million pounds. At least. I found the horse tied with magick to a rowan tree and munching happily, and Princess Faith standing by the jetty, staring at the mist on the water and the fells rising above them on the other side. Easily worth a million on a day like this. What the Princess didn't have was a sword of her own.

'A beautiful spot,' she said, turning to face me. 'Let's have a look, then.'

I unsheathed Great Fang and let the magick flow. One side effect of doing that is that the bloody thing growls slightly when deployed. A nice trick in combat, but a little OTT first thing in the morning. As soon as the light glinted off the runes in the blade, Princess Faith winced and couldn't help taking a step back.

'Well we won't be exercising with that, will we? Do you think the Gnome who made it cursed all the People when he hammered out the tip?'

The blade is one single piece of steel, but the tip and the start of the edges have been cold-forged with magick that makes it deadly to the Fae. 'Lloyd Flint swears a lot, but he bears no ill-will to the People beyond what they earn. For him, it's just business.'

'Yeah, and I'm the new face of l'Oreal Paris. Stand well back and show me your practice drill.'

'I normally loosen up first, but here we go.'

I walked slowly through the drill once, to make sure I didn't strain a muscle, then repeated it a couple of times at normal speed.

'Good,' she said. 'I'll dig out something similar from the armoury. Probably something we've taken as a prize, because none of the People would use anything quite so *agricultural*, with or without the *N'hæval* edge and the doggy noises. Then again, a scythe would be fitting for a Lord of Death.'

I just smiled and put my sword away. I am not going to rise to that one any more.

Her hand moved towards her face, then moved away, like a magnet being repelled by the same polarity. Weird. 'I'll message you in a day or so, shall I?' she said, as if she hadn't even noticed her own hand was moving.

I bowed. 'Thank you, my lady. I look forward to being humiliated and put in my place.'

She returned the bow. 'And I shall enjoy doing it. I don't get out much.' She skipped lightly over the frosted grass and vaulted on to her horse. 'Walk on.' In seconds, she'd disappeared into a mist of her own making, and I shivered as the sweat dried on my back. There was a lot going on here, and it might take me a long time to unpack it.

Cordy had a very polite smile on her face when I joined her at breakfast. She was on her second cup of tea already, and her table faced the lake shore. Her legs were crossed and she was sitting back. Oh dear.

'Enjoy the show?' I asked.

She snorted and covered her mouth with her hand to stop herself laughing. 'What was that? Some sort of courtship ritual? The waitress was most amused, until I told her you were an actor and auditioning for a film. She said you had no chance of getting the part, by the way.'

I slumped into the chair, and she poured me a cuppa. 'I don't know whether to feel creeped out or sorry for her,' I said.

The teapot paused in mid air. 'Why *sorry?*'

I moved my hand to mimic Faith's wound. 'Her face.'

'What was wrong with it? You don't normally go for the pretty-pretty ones.'

Oh. Right. 'Never mind. I ... Hang on, I'd better get that. It's Erin.'

And then the rest of my morning was taken up with the events at Birk Fell, because something had happened last night. Something serious, something that needs to be told on its own, which is why the adventure of the Arrow in the Dark is not related here.

After a sandwich lunch, we donned our thermals, and Cordy drove us up to Waterhead. Well, I had won the bet last night. Hadn't I? Matt Eldridge turned up for our quiet chat, and Cordy left clutching the detailed directions he'd given her to find the sacred grove of the Elter Water Sisters.

Martin Hoggart had kindly let me have a room in the School House to do my planning, and when Cordy had returned, I asked her how it had gone. 'I feel much better, thanks,' she replied. 'Bloody cold, but much better. They have a truly beautiful place there.'

'Good. Matt's given me some ideas, and with your suggestions, I think I've got a plan. What do you think of this?'

We finished just in time to meet the rest of the team, so we moved the desks to make a circle, and I put the kettle on. Cordelia sat on one side, away from my seat near the whiteboard and close to the kettle. She may be my partner, but she's not their boss. As the clock tower on top of the School House rang out the hour, the other assessors filed in, led by Matt.

I've only named one of them so far – the youngest, Natalie Greening. She's only been in post for four months, and has the second easiest union to police: Patterdale. I had inherited five assessors for nine unions, and there were no pending applications. Yet. Philippa Grayling hadn't done much more than fire off angry emails to the four unions demanding that they make appointments, and that was one of the reasons Morgan Torver from Eskdale had turned against her.

As well as my appointment as Commissioner, the Grand Union had voted that their members had to pay the salaries regardless of whether there was an assessor in post. My team could guess what was coming.

I started by getting them to introduce themselves and talk about their recent cases. From there, I got them to help me by adding a few more annotations to the rough map I'd drawn on the whiteboard – telling me where the significant places were, who I needed to know about and what their connections were. The last was particularly important because I couldn't put them in charge of an area where their extended families did business, could I?

Nothing we learnt upset our plans, and I moved on to the important bit. 'The rest of the country often asks why there are nine assessors for Lakeland and poor Rick James covers the whole of Wessex.' That got a smile. 'And then they hear about the salaries. The good news is that you're all going to get a substantial pay rise. The bad news is that you're also going to get more than one union to cover. This is what I'm going to do…'

Cordelia had suggested that we should take one union for ourselves, and that Duddon-Furness would be handy (and fairly quiet). The others got two each, except Natalie and the woman I moved to the Eden Valley (huge). Natalie was now in charge of the Northern Waters, home of the Red Queen, while Matt took on Patterdale as well as his current patch.

I looked round the group and said, 'None of you are looking too pleased or too upset, so I guess I've done a good job. Either Cordelia or I will be on call 24/7 for a while, and I'll be coming to see you all for a tour in due course.'

'Just you?' said the assessor for Kentdale, the only one whose unions didn't join on to each other. He was going to love the A590.

'Probably not, to start with. I'm not ashamed to say that Cordelia knows more magick than I do. She's not the Commissioner, though. Any more questions? No? In that case, the first round is on me, if you're staying for the Borrowdale Crown Purse.'

'It's known as the Royal Purse,' said Natalie Greening. 'And you bet I'm staying.'

'Then I'll see you all by the paddock.'

13 — A Royal Mess

W hen she'd got back from her devotions at Elter Water, Cordelia hadn't lied when she said that she felt better, and that the Sisters had a beautiful grove. All of that was true. What she'd left out was the visitor she'd had *after* the service. In her car, no less. That was a first.

When she'd made her devotions, in the short version so everyone could get to the races, the lake had become still for a moment, and the moon had been perfectly reflected in its waters. The coven was a small one, but vibrant with love. The women had held hands, and Cordelia had felt the comfort and the blessing of shared love for the Goddess who moved among them. She took that as a sign. A sign that the politics of Glastonbury was just that: politics. She had brought her quest to find Raven up here, and the Goddess had welcomed her back to the company of women. It was good. She felt good. Until she saw the light glowing inside her car.

She'd been the last to leave (because she didn't need to go home and get changed), and the light had only winked on when the previous vehicle had driven off. 'Don't tell me you're keeping warm in here,' she said to Lucas when she climbed into the driver's seat.

'If you will park on top of a Node, what do you expect me to do? Manifest on the roof?'

She had chosen the spot at random when she'd driven in. Unlike Conrad, she couldn't sense a buried Node without really looking. The Goddess must have guided her. She relaxed and turned on the engine. Just for a minute. 'Where's Helena?'

'She and Maddy are at Waterhead, keeping an eye on things.'

The urge came over her again, the urge to tell Conrad what was going on. She wasn't going to do that, not after he kept everything to do with Ireland to himself. But the urge was there, and she had made a decision. 'It's wrong, Lucas,' she said. 'I am not going to conspire against anyone without evidence.'

She'd had her epiphany, if you could call it that, when Conrad had taken the Commissioner's staff and repeated Hannah's mantra: *be part of the solution.* He had laid down his Badge to go to Ireland, and Cordelia wouldn't act against anyone while she was here as an assessor. The people (and the People) of the Particular had so far welcomed her, and she would not repay that with treachery.

Lucas didn't look annoyed or angry, he just pursed his lips and smiled. 'Have you done what I suggested? Have you made the Abbey lands yours?'

She flushed red in the darkness of the car, and she turned off the engine to stop the heater making her feel worse. It was another betrayal: getting Conrad to take Duddon-Furness in hand, just so she could drag him there. Lucas didn't need her to spell it out.

'When you've been there, you'll know. Don't take forever, though. We'll be waiting.'

Lucas vanished, and Cordy took deep breaths until she was ready to head back to Waterhead. When the other assessors had arrived for the team meeting, she had calmed down, safe in the knowledge that she was part of the solution again: those Fae lands *should* be investigated, and if there was something there, then so be it. She had left the meeting with a lighter heart, and she was very much looking forward to the race.

She and Conrad left the School House together, and tonight's crowd was *very* different to last night's. For one thing, it was a lot smaller (strictly invitation only), and for another, Conrad wrinkled his nose and announced. 'This smells stronger than a sídhe. There are a *lot* of the People here.'

He wasn't wrong. The field shimmered with Glamours, and the air was filled with shouts and song in the Fae language, something they rarely do on human ground. He led her in a shortcut round the side, and suddenly put his hand on her shoulder.

'Watch out. Nearly lost you there.'

'What?'

He pointed down, to where she'd nearly tripped over a taut rope. She could barely see it, because the lights were masked by a marquee. 'Thanks. You go first.'

He did, and round the corner, there they were: the Unicorns. Her breath caught in her throat and she stopped to touch her chest. *Such beauty, such power...*

'Magnificent, aren't they?' he said.

They were, but they were so much *more* than that. He put his arm through hers and led her across the paddock to where a crowd was standing at a safe distance from tonight's mounts.

The first (and only) time that Cordelia had met a High Unicorn, she had discovered something she never knew about herself: she could *feel* them. She could share their being at a level which meant that they must be linked magickally. Cordelia had never ridden a horse in her life, and she'd briefly wondered if it wasn't too late to become a jockey. It had been a bit like discovering at thirty-seven that you've always been able to kick a football like Beckham, or Messi or Ronaldo or whoever the current god of the Beautiful Game might be. Only now it was too late.

They got to the crowd, and Conrad's height meant that he spotted the assessors, all still together (and not just on the promise of free drinks). He let go of her arm and announced that he'd be back with a tray of mulled wine. She didn't offer to help; instead, she allowed Matt to clear a path so that she could get to the front and have a proper look.

Unlike the mundane parade, the Unicorns were stationary, each one contained within a glowing ring of Lux so that the crowd, the *punters* as Conrad called them, could get a good look at the runners – and the riders. Cordelia was *very* jealous of tonight's jockeys.

There are two species of Unicorn, or one-and-a-half, if you can have half a species, and they wouldn't exist without the Fae. Deep in the past, magick had created a small, horned horse that could only be ridden by small magickal creatures (especially Fae Sprites). Later, the hip-height beasts had been transformed into the huge stallions standing in front of her. High Unicorns: creatures of myth, legend and very solid reality. Right here.

She felt a hand on her shoulder. 'Not too close,' said Matt. She hadn't realised that she had started to walk towards them.

'I don't see why not,' she said, turning to smile up at him. 'There's nothing to be frightened of.'

He'd already taken away his hand from her shoulder. 'If you're sure…'

Matt meant well, of course, but he didn't know what she knew. She smiled again, and stepped closer to the restraining circles. There were seven beasts on show, three local and four from outside the Particular, hence the influx of Fae from around Britain, and the weirdest thing of all (in a field full of *weird shit*, as Saffron called it), was the girls standing next to their mounts. All bar one wore a heavy Glamour that presented them as the Fae Queen who owned the Unicorn, which meant *two* Queens of Derwent for her two entries.

Cordelia headed for the one she'd met before. Keraunós. Thunderbolt. Was it her, or did he know her? The great dark eyes of the Unicorn turned to face her, and he lowered his head. Was he bowing? Did he feel their bond through the circle, or was he showing his horn because she'd come too close?

A real Unicorn's horn is not shaped in a spiral. It starts as a little nub, barely through the skin when the foal is born, and is made of what you'd expect: bone. Not the dead protein of a rhino's horn, but living bone, because without life there is no magick. The horns need to be trimmed, and can be shaped, and the Fae fashion is for a serrated blade that makes a terrible weapon.

'Cheers,' said Conrad, breaking the spell.

'What? Sorry.'

He'd brought her a tankard of mulled apple juice (the only non-alcoholic option), and the smell of ripe fruit took her straight back to Autumn in Glastonbury and gathering windfalls with Raven in their first year together. And doing the same with Rick and the kids on one of his rare weekends at home. She blinked away the tears and wondered if the magick pulsing around the paddock was doing something to her head.

'Thank you,' she said. 'Why are we the only two inside the invisible perimeter?'

'Assessors, or Watch Officers, are not easily put off.' He raised his tankard and drank, then used it to point at the faux Queen of Derwent. 'Let's see, shall we?' He took a step closer, moving round and away from the reach of the horn. 'You must be Persephone. We almost met at Sprint Stables.'

The image of the Queen glanced around in something close to panic, then bowed, and the voice that emerged from the illusion was anything but regal. 'Lord Guardian. I … Yes. Thank you for saving Lara's life. How is she?'

'Morwenna,' he replied. 'I'm afraid that Lara is gone forever, but Morwenna is alive and back with her family. She hasn't forgotten you all, but she's still convalescing.'

'Good.' She took a step forward, and Cordy felt Conrad trying to see through the Glamour. As Persephone was still in the circle, he had no chance. 'Sorry, my lord, but we're not supposed to talk to you.'

'My bad,' he said. 'Good luck, anyway. You rode superbly last night.'

He backed off, and Cordelia reluctantly followed him past the second of the Red Queen's mounts. This time, the rider gave Conrad a big grin, and winked at him salaciously. 'Twice in one day,' she said in a posh, plummy voice.

He bowed to her. 'Faith, can I present Cordelia Kennedy. Cordy, this is Princess Faithful, my fencing master.'

'Pleased to meet you,' said the Princess, nodding her head and reaching a hand to the Unicorn's mane. She was standing a lot closer than Persephone had done, and Cordy got the feeling that the Princess was nowhere nearly as much in control of her mount as Perci had been.

'This is Hipponax,' said the Princess. 'Sixth of his name, if you're counting.' The Fae turned back to Conrad. 'I'm filling in tonight because none of the girls from Sprint can ride a Royal Horse except Perci. I'll be glad to make it to the finish at all, so I wouldn't waste your money on me.'

A man came up to them. A Fae Noble of some level, and Conrad stiffened in the almost imperceptible way of his that told Cordelia he was on alert, and if he was on alert, she was too. Before she could think, she'd taken a step to his right, away from his gun hand. Or sword arm.

'Count,' said Conrad with the barest tilt of his head.

The Fae bowed deeply. 'It would please Her Grace to welcome you to her table – after the race.'

Conrad's hand relaxed, and he looked at her. 'In other words, stop pestering the Unicorns. We'll move on shall we?' He nodded to the Count again. 'Forgive our intrusion. It was not ill intended.'

She touched his arm and made a Silence. 'Was that the Count of Force Ghyll?'

'Formerly Prince Galleny. Yes, it was. Last seen beaten to a pulp and humiliated after kidnapping Saïa Ripley and unleashing the Queen's Hounds without permission. Let's make a quick stop at the Greenings.'

The only Unicorn not being ridden by the replica of a Fae Queen was positively surrounded by humans. She hadn't spoken to any of them yet, but she recognised all of them bar one, and all of them bar two were members of the Greening family. She was surprised that Natalie was still behind the line with the other assessors. Definitely a plus point for her new young comrade.

Cordelia tried to commit the names to memory now that they were in front of her and now that she'd felt the magick in their handshakes. So long as Conrad didn't spring a surprise test on her tomorrow, she'd probably be okay.

He stayed respectfully away from the Unicorn (named Blenheim for some weird reason. Wasn't that a palace or something?), and greeted the jockey without words. It was Rowan Sexton, of course, and now was not the time to be starting a conversation with a young girl whose mother you put in prison. And that left one.

Cordy had barely noticed the girl in the background, the one with no magick except the bulky Artefact around her neck. The one with the shovel (yes, Unicorns do produce as many steaming piles as any other horse).

'Hello Sophie,' said Conrad. 'How are you doing?'

The girl looked absolutely shit-scared of him and utterly in awe at the same time. Cordy struggled to remember who she was and came up blank.

'Thank you, thank you, thank you,' said the girl, then ran out of steam.

'The world of magick takes a bit of getting used to, doesn't it?' said Conrad. 'I know how you feel. I see they've given you the good job.'

Sophie tried to hide the shovel behind her back, then realised he was being kind. 'Oh, no. They've made me a full groom at the hunting stables *and* given me a car to get to Myerscough College. They've been brilliant.' She looked to see if the Greenings were listening, and leaned closer to Conrad. 'Mind you, I think the Sextons are paying my wages for two years. Something about Weregild. I don't understand all the magick stuff. I stick to horses.'

'A wise move. I take it you don't have much to do with Blenheim normally.'

She shook her head. 'No way. Even *being* here tonight is a privilege. I'm very lucky. Thanks to you.'

Sophie looked at Cordelia, then back to Conrad, and Conrad introduced Cordy as his work partner. Sophie flashed a smile, and close to, Cordelia could see that the girl was truly a girl, no more than eighteen.

Blenheim snorted, moved his feet, and made a deposit on the event matting.

'We'd better leave you to your work,' said Conrad with a smile.

Sophie brandished the shovel at the fresh, steaming pile. 'If only I could sell this. Real Unicorn Poo. I'd clean up, wouldn't I? If anyone believed me, that is. Could be an omen. If you know what I mean.'

'Who knows,' said Conrad. 'There's a first time for everything.'

Sophie leaned in again. 'There's going to be a surprise tonight, you wait and see.' She touched her nose with a conspiratorial finger, then realised where her fingers had been and grimaced. 'Sorry. Spoke out of turn. Ignore me, Conrad.'

He withdrew and headed round the crowd with a frown. 'There's something going on,' he said.

'Apart from that kid having a crush on you, you mean?'

He waved away her comment. 'No Greening Unicorn has ever finished more than one place above last. They only put them in to show the world that they're the real thing, then auction them off afterwards.'

'I knew that,' said Cordy, a little miffed. 'Matt explained it to me yesterday: they don't have the right tick-tack for the course.'

'Tack. Saddles and bridles. No, they don't. So why are they so up-beat?'

'Because they're about to be even richer than they already are.'

'No one gets that excited about money. Not if you're already rich.'

'I wouldn't know, would I?'

'And Sophie wouldn't have said there was going to be a surprise if there wasn't.'

'Yes she would. Just to impress you. I'm sorry, Conrad, I can't remember where you met her. Is she in the files?'

'She's a footnote. Apprentice groom to Rod Bristow, who was murdered by Rowan's mother, only I doubt Sophie knows that part. I told the Sextons to look after her, because she was an innocent victim. Looks like Evelyn has more than kept her word. We'd better re-join the team before they think I've only paid lip-service to this *all in it together* business.'

Cordelia looked at the assessors. 'I think the tab on the bar has convinced them of your intentions.'

'Tab! I said the first round was on me, not the whole night! Looks like we've got some catching up to do.'

'You have. There's only so much mulled apple juice a girl can take, you know. Mina was right: Lucy would clean up here with a coffee van.'

The team had got bored watching the Unicorns and had commandeered an upturned barrel near a brazier. While they waited for the Unicorns to be taken away to the start line, Cordelia and Conrad carried on chatting and getting to know their new comrades. Cordy watched him make an instant hit with Tanya Dickinson because she was one of the few smokers at Waterhead. Tanya had a dour face most of the time, and a sarcastic tongue, but Conrad soon had her smiling. Cordelia turned her attention to the others, especially Matt. They looked up to him, alright, but he was semi-detached from the group; she saw it as her mission to reel him back in.

Natalie Greening was good fun, too, and Cordy forgot Lucas of Innerdale until Natalie told her about a secret shortcut to the ladies toilets in School House that would avoid the queue. As they crept round the side of the Gothic monstrosity, Cordy picked up the faintest hint of Spirits, up near the woods. They were still here, then. But why?

'Damn,' said Natalie when she saw a queue almost as big stretching out of her "secret" entrance. 'I keep forgetting that all the other Mages used to go here as well. Never mind. We'll be done before starters orders.'

They were, and there was a tension in the air as they made their way back to the barrel. The whistles and high-pitched keening of the People's Tongue was getting louder as the race approached. Any form of competition or contest was taken seriously by the Fae; when it was amongst themselves, it was more than a matter of life and death: it was a matter of Honour.

Squires raced back and forth from well-stocked 4x4s with drinks and trays of canapés that made Cordy's stomach gurgle in protest at the wait: the team was booked in to an Ambleside curry house later.

The Squires were delivering their cargo to big crowds of the People, each one swarming round their Queen, just like the Aculeata they were related to. It was always good to remember that the Fae were part bee. Or wasp. Not a conversation she wanted to have tonight.

'You not a horsey person?' she asked Natalie.

'Well, I ride, obviously. I just didn't want to dedicate my life to it, you know? And with Char and Ira being older...' She shrugged, and Cordy got the message: Charmian and Iras were James's daughters, and they would always be ahead in the pecking order in the Greendale Trust, as would Alexandra's daughter, Jocasta.

'Where's Conrad?' said Cordy to Matt.

'Um, there. Coming back from a trip to the bookies. Bookie, singular.'

She intercepted him and said, 'I thought you weren't betting tonight?'

'I'm not. I just wanted to see where the action was.' He rubbed his chin. 'It's such a weird race that Jewel is running it as pool, not fixed odds. Sensible girl. Keraunós has most of the money, and almost no one has bet on Blenheim. Come on, let's enjoy the show.'

The course for the Borrowdale Crown Purse was shorter than the Waterhead, but had much more violent transitions between planes, and that was why no one was betting on Blenheim. When a Fae Queen or Princess rides a Unicorn, they do it bareback and without a bridle, known as Royal style. They use their innate plane-shifting ability and their special bond to move seamlessly to the best level with the least Lux.

But Queens don't race. Or not any more: too much risk of humiliation if they lose. The honour goes to humans like Cordelia, Persephone and Rowan Sexton, who can feel the mount they're riding. That makes it possible, but even a master like Rowan needs an Enchanted saddle and bridle to transition, and the Fae keep the good ones out of human hands. The fact that the Greenings had a Unicorn at all was a massive anomaly: they are the only humans known to have the skill to breed them.

They were only given one view of the race on the big Skyway tonight (the course was too challenging), and that was the start. Rowan Sexton had put on a Glamour of a some kind of soldier with a red coat for the actual race, not that Cordelia knew anything about military uniforms. There was a huge roar from the crowd when the rocket went up, and then ... And then everyone got out their phones. Oh. Why am I surprised by that, she wondered.

Matt was back at her side. 'The Fae have spies all along the route. Reception is quite good on higher slopes. I'm in a WhatsApp group as a favour from the Queen.' He placed his phone on the upturned barrel, and everyone crowded round to see. As the shortest person (yet again), Cordelia found herself at the front and with the best view.

'What's that?' said Tanya when the first *ping* came in.

She read out the message. 'Hipponax has taken an early lead.'

'Bound to be a pacemaker,' said Natalie (who actually had family messages, but clearly wanted to be in the group with the others). 'Derwent will have told Faithful to set an early pace and try and get the others tired out.'

Ping. 'Blenheim is not last. LOL.'

She hadn't bothered to learn the names of the other four Unicorns and soon found herself mangling something in Irish and three others that didn't make sense in English. Half way round the course, a beast called *Typhonous* took the lead, and Hipponax dropped back. He was soon last.

There was a lull for thirty seconds, then some groups with better spies burst out with gasps and cries of *What?* And *Must be a mistake!* Five seconds later, Cordelia knew why. 'Blenheim is up to third and gaining ground.' And then, 'Blenheim has caught Keraunós but can't get past. They're crossing the Brathay for the last time now.'

'One more shift, then home,' said Matt. 'Let's get a good look, shall we?'

He scooped up his phone and the group dispersed. She started to follow Matt towards the jetty, where they'd get a moonlit view of the riders, then her blood ran cold.

'With me,' said Conrad from behind her. 'All of you.'

She'd turned round before the others realised he was speaking to them. Matt looked confused, and Cordy grabbed his hand. 'Come on. That was an order.'

Matt raised his eyebrows, but said nothing and allowed her to lead him towards the giant shape limping his way towards the finish line. And they weren't the only ones.

From the biggest group of Fae, a familiar figure emerged. Familiar in looks from her jockeys' Glamours, but altogether different in the flesh: the Queen of Derwent, radiating power and wearing a glowing doublet of orange and yellow stripes. Tasteless, yes, but certainly striking. She was accompanied by Prince Harprigg, her senior noble. The rest of her retinue surged forwards, then stopped when two Gnomes held out their hands to keep them in check.

Conrad strode past the Gnomes without looking back, and took up a position about thirty metres beyond the winning post. He scanned the area and waited for his team. Two were missing, presumed lost in the crowd. 'Matt, help Saul co-ordinate crowd control. If possible, push them back further, because they're bound to surge forwards. Tanya, Natalie: you two go up the steps and watch for trouble breaking out further away. Cordy, with me.'

'What's going on?' said Tanya. She looked slightly the worse for wear, and if not quite unsteady on her feet, she was certainly a bit off the pace.

'I hope nothing is going on, but I'm preparing for a possible confrontation. Hopefully we can be a deterrent.'

'Yeah, like *that's* gonna happen.' She raised her hand to forestall Conrad. 'Gotcha, Chief. We're on it.'

It was the first time anyone had called him that. Was it going to stick? Whatever. Cordelia took up a position one step behind Conrad and to his left. Then she shivered from head to foot: they were totally exposed here. Conrad unzipped his coat and touched his gun, and she felt the magick of his Ancile come into shape. He looked away, across the field. 'Here they come.'

Roars and cheers and cries of dismay worked round the spectators as the Unicorns galloped on to the course, heading for their first pass in front of School House. She stared ahead at the turn in front of them, because she couldn't see over the crowds. Why couldn't she hear the hooves?

In a burst of bright blue, the leader came round the corner with the others in line behind. Typhonous was still at the front, with Keraunós second and Blenheim third, but there was nothing in it. They thundered towards them, and now she *did* hear the pounding of steel shoes on the ground, and cries and jeers. Typhonous' jockey brandished her whip three times and tried to keep the lead along the straight, but Keraunós passed her going into the next turn, and then they were gone from sight.

On the second circuit, the noise got louder and louder. Necks craned to see which bright glow was in front – the orange of Keraunós, the blue of Typhonous or the green of Blenheim.

Green and orange came round the last turn together, with Blenheim on the outside. Keraunós cut across his rival, but Rowan had been ready for him and pushed Blenheim through the gap and down the final straight. The Greenings' mount thundered over the line more than half a length ahead of Keraunós, and the crowd went mad.

'Another win for Churchill,' said Conrad. He held out his left hand to stop Cordy rushing to help Matt and the Gnomes. Matt and Saul looked at each other and did something she'd never seen before. They stepped apart, then in one synchronised sweep, they sent a pulse of sound into the advancing crowd. A high-pitched screech worse than nails on blackboard attacked the racegoers, and all of the Fae tried to cover their ears. Cordy was well out of the line of fire, but even she felt needles stabbing her head.

It was over in a couple of seconds. 'Whatever that was, it certainly worked,' said Conrad.

'Could you not hear it?'

'A bit of a whine, that's all. I ... Here come the others.'

Typhonous had squeezed through the gap when the crowd surged, and now the other riders were coming into Waterhead. If you weren't in the top three, you didn't need to do the extra lap, and they trotted over the line fairly close together. Princess Faithful and Hipponax were last, and the Princess grinned widely at her Queen for having finished with her mount unharmed. When the look wasn't returned, her face faltered, and her Glamour shivered out of focus, leaving the fresh-faced girl that Cordelia had seen by the lake this morning.

There was a roar of approval that could only be human. Rowan Sexton had dismounted and was coming back towards them to claim the crown. Her Glamour had gone, too, and she was almost floating on air, so happy was she. Blenheim was steaming from the water that had been thrown over him, and he was being led by Alex Greening's daughter, Jocasta. Charmian, Iras and the rest of the stable team were around, and even Sophie was there, fetching another bucket of water.

Conrad waited until Blenheim had gone past, then beckoned Cordelia to follow him in the beast's wake. The applause was more sporadic now. Some of the People from outside the Particular were thrilled that Derwent hadn't won, while others were maintaining a diplomatic silence while they digested the implications of a mortal-owned Unicorn winning one of *their* races.

At the top of the steps outside School House, a table had been set up. Cordy caught a glimpse of something sparkling with light and Lux, but before the party got there, their way was barred by the Queen of the Derwent. Her grace held up a palm, and Blenheim bucked, nearly dragging the reins out of Jocasta's hand. Around them, the applause turned to gasps and murmurs.

With a glance at Matt Eldridge, Saul Brathay moved to interpose himself, and Conrad touched Cordelia's arm, making a Silence. 'Go round the back and get to the other side.' He let go, and she hesitated for half a second. He wanted her away from him. To protect her, yes, but also to have her in reserve. It was what he did. She turned on her heel and ran round the party. By the time she got into position with her back to School House, things were about to kick off.

The Fae were on Cordy's left, with Prince Harprigg and Countess Bassenthwaite standing behind the Red Queen. Saul Brathay stood opposite Cordelia, and the Greenings were to her right. Rowan Sexton had got well out of the way, leaving Alexandra Greening to take the lead. Cordelia could just make out Conrad, standing on the other side of the Unicorn. She couldn't be certain, but he seemed to be talking to someone.

There was a moment of hush. The cluster of lightsticks on the steps made as many shadows as they did spots of illumination. For atmosphere two tall oil-burning pedestal torches had been placed at the foot of the steps, and the flickering flames cast a red glow on the Unicorn's flank. It was Saul who spoke first, turning and addressing the Queen. 'Your Grace, it is time for the presentation.'

'I demand to examine the mount,' said the Red Queen. 'It is my right in the rules.'

Alexandrea Greening waited for the surprised murmurs of the crowd to die down. 'What are you accusing us of, precisely? And what are you accusing the stewards of, come to that? Blenheim was thoroughly vetted at the start and hasn't been out of sight.'

'It is my right,' said the Queen.

Saul turned to Alexandra. 'If you want the crown...'

'Very well,' said Alexandra. She gestured for her daughter to lead Blenheim towards the Queen and stood away, next to Saul. When the Unicorn stepped forwards, Cordelia saw what Conrad had been up to. He was standing next to George Gibson, and Gibson was looking at his phone. He put it away and said something to Conrad, then turned and took his place in the line of Gnomes containing the crowd.

Grooms always lead from the horse's left, so Jocasta was on Cordelia's side, blocking her view, and Cordy dodged further left to see what the Queen was up to. Her grace walked slowly up to the Unicorn and raised her right hand cautiously, moving it towards the beast's head and almost certainly making a Charm.

The Queen stood perfectly still for several moments, until Blenheim snorted and pitched his head up. Jocasta had to let out some of the lead rope, and that gave Blenheim enough scope to bring his horn down in a swipe at the Fae Queen.

Derwent dodged back out of the way in a blur of motion, but she'd seen enough. Her face was incandescent with fury, and for a second she showed her teeth with a hiss. She closed her lips and mastered her rage, then lifted a finger and pointed it at Alexandra.

'Thief. Grave Robber. You have defiled the tomb of Urien, and you will pay for that. So will the Ripleys.' She barked out a laugh. 'Galleny was right all along: you and Stella Ripley were grave robbing.'

145

Cordelia put the pieces together in her head. The former Prince Galleny had sent Harry Eldridge to Ullswater to check out what the Ripleys were doing. Harry had been caught and murdered, but by the time they'd figured out what had happened, the Ripleys had cleared the site of all evidence. Whether or not the Greenings had been part of the excavation or had come along later was a moot point.

Before Alexandra Greening could respond, there was a thump of running feet off to the right. A very young Gnome sprinted up to Conrad and handed something over, like an Olympic relay runner. Conrad took it and stepped forwards. When he came into the light, Cordelia saw that he was carrying a sheathed sword.

'Stay out of this, Dragonslayer,' said the Red Queen. 'The quarrel is between the People and this bunch of grave-robbing mortal scum.'

Conrad drew the sword and held it up to the light. The half-dozen Fae closest to him stepped back, and that told Cordelia exactly what the blade was made of. Satisfied, Conrad dropped the sheath by his feet and slowly placed the sword on the ground, making sure that the tip pointed at no one.

He straightened up and looked from Alexandra Greening to the Red Queen. 'I take it that the Lady of the Fountain was of the People.'

'How do you know of her?' hissed the Queen.

He scanned the crowd, looking for someone. When he didn't see who he wanted, he focused on Alexandra. 'Last year, Stella Ripley, calling herself Stella Newborn, paid a king's ransom for a manuscript. *The True Tale of Urien and the Lady of the Fountain*. I have that fact from an unimpeachable authority. I also know that Urien was a Mage-King of Rheged, the old British kingdom of the Lakes. It doesn't take a genius to work out that the manuscript led the Ripleys to Urien's burial chamber. Whether or not that bridle was looted from the grave is not for me to say.' He turned to the Queen. 'Do I have it right, your grace?'

'She was my direct line. Great gifts she gave to her mortal consort, and so bereft was she at his passing that she permitted them to remain with him in death. That is where they should ever be, as it is written. For them to be robbed and traded like common trinkets is an affront to the People that we will not allow.'

A great burst of noise broke out around the field, and the crowd shifted again, pressing more closely against the thin line of Gnomes. From her vantage point close to the steps, Cordy heard a muttered *shit* from Tanya Dickinson, and then, 'Come on.' She glanced left and saw Tanya and Natalie Greening descend the steps and move towards Matt Eldridge. Even in the moment, Cordy couldn't help thinking *Conrad won't like that. Disobeying an order...*

While the security team tried to hold back the line, two more Fae joined the Queen, one from the crowd and one from the paddock. The one from the crowd was a corpulent squire (small 's') who had to be Prince Appleby; from the paddock came Princess Faithful.

'You may be right!' said Conrad in his loudest voice. 'This may be the Bridle of Urien. Or it may not. This is not the place to decide. Let the law take its course.' In a desperate attempt to give the Queen something, he turned to Saul. 'If this *is* a disputed Artefact, I think Blenheim would be disqualified, don't you? I think you should postpone the prize-giving until matters are decided. Without prejudice, of course.'

Cordelia braced herself. It was a fair compromise, and Saul was already nodding in agreement. He turned to Alexandra, ready to make his announcement.

He didn't even get to open his mouth: the Greening Matriarch stared at the Fae Queen and spat out her defiance. 'We. Won. This. Race. *Our* Unicorn and *our* rider came first, and the crown is ours to keep. You just can't accept what's been true for a century: the Greening line is stronger and more powerful than yours. With a level playing field, Blenheim was better. We are taking the crown, and you can waste your money on lawyers all you want. Proprietary right died with the Queen of Grace.'

If only she hadn't said the last bit...

The Queen of Derwent made a minor plane-shift, shimmering in and out, and re-appeared with a nightmare face of huge, insect eyes and great claws for hands. Just like the Count of Force Ghyll when he ripped open Morwenna Mowbray. Cordelia sprang forwards, Conrad bent to retrieve his sword, and somewhere a girl screamed.

Blenheim reared, lifting Jocasta Greening off the ground and swinging her round. The girl held on somehow, and pulled hard on the rope when her feet landed on the floor. Cordelia tried to summon Lux to stop the Queen, and Conrad closed the gap, but they were too late.

The Red Queen struck with her claws, aiming for Blenheim's head and trying to rip off the bridle, but Jocasta got in the way, instinctively raising her left arm to protect the Unicorn. With a sickening crunch and snap, the Fae claws broke the girl's forearm like a stick and carried on, missing the head and scoring great lines down Blenheim's flank, from his crest to his shoulder. And then all hell broke loose.

14 — If not Now, then When?

She didn't know she'd made a decision until she dived for the lead rope. Blenheim swung his head, bringing the horn round towards Cordelia. She felt something inside her chest push out, and when the tiny ripple of magick hit the Unicorn, he flicked his head up and away from her. She grabbed the lead rope where it trailed on the ground, and with it she grabbed a world of pain and fear. And heat. Great heat, burning through every sinew in her body.

Her eyes clouded with red mist and she screamed, or tried to. It was hard to know because there was so, so much noise pouring into to her, coming from outside *and* inside her head. All she could do was hang on.

The first wave of pain washed over her, and she knew there was another one coming. She used a jerk on the rope to get to her knees, and then her feet. She forced herself to focus on Blenheim and meet his eye. In a flash of Lux, he knew that she was there and that she was connected to him, and the next wave of pain and fire wasn't as bad.

She managed to keep her feet, and all she could think of was to get away from the light behind her. She forced herself to stumble forwards, and Blenheim turned to go with her, away from the screaming that she now knew was coming from someone else.

A figure came forwards. A familiar figure. A part of Cordelia felt protected when she recognised Charmian Greening. 'Let me,' said the young woman, reaching for the lead rope.

Cordelia wanted to hang on. To make sure that Blenheim would be safe. To comfort and heal him. Another part of her knew that wasn't her job. She hadn't signed up for that. Reluctantly, she handed over the rope and turned to see what was going on.

Without the bond to the Unicorn, her sight cleared and the sounds resolved themselves. She was just in time to see all-out-war averted – by one of the Fae.

If anyone was ever going to make a heroic portrait of Conrad Bloody Clarke, it would be this moment. His sword was raised in his right hand and levelled at the Red Queen's chest; his left hand was raised, palm out, to stop the Greenings charging through him. Below, his legs straddled the stricken form of Jocasta, who was lying on her right side and trying to stop her left arm falling off. In the darkness around and behind them, shadows surged and the air crackled with Lux.

Princess Faithful tried to push past Saul Brathay, and he struggled to hold her back, allowing Appleby to escape and join his Queen. Instead of standing by her, he put his hand on her shoulder and spoke in the People's Tongue. Then he repeated it in English.

'This is not the place, your Grace. Now is not the time. This is not the battle.'

While he spoke, Cordy jogged the few steps to join the circle. She made a snap judgement: Conrad would lose in combat against the Red Queen, but he could hold off the Greenings. She decided to give him a buffer, and slipped by to stand between him and the Fae. Those eyes. Those horrible eyes...

'You will pay for what you have done,' said the Queen of Derwent. 'One way or another.' And with that she stepped back and span around on the spot like a dancer. When the pirouette was done, her hands were hands again, and her eyes were blue once more. Only a Fae noble could do what the Queen had done tonight and then think that she was the injured party.

Conrad turned his back to the Fae and stepped away from Jocasta Greening. Cordy looked down at the poor girl. Big mistake.

There was an extra elbow in the middle of her forearm. A ninety degree bend that shouldn't be there. And bone. And blood. Acid apple juice rose in Cordy's throat. While she tried to swallow it back down, Alexandra Greening rushed to her daughter. As did Princess Faithful.

James Greening and Saul Brathay moved to intercept the Fae, but she stopped and spoke to Alexandra. 'Let me heal her. Let me intervene. I have the skills. I can help.'

'Get out!' screamed Alexandra. 'Conrad! Get your helicopter here NOW!'

'Not an option,' he said grimly. 'Matt! If you're not on the phone already, get dialling. Martin! Someone! Get the School House First Aid Kit.' He chucked down his sword, and with a crack of the knees he dropped to Alex's level, both of their heads over Jocasta. 'I give you my word, Alexandra. Faith could make a difference, if you let her. If you don't, we could easily sever the radial artery. That bone is very sharp. As the Allfather is my witness, Faith will not harm your daughter tonight.'

Alexandra had her hands on her daughter's shoulders, doing what she could as a Mage and a mother to make things better. It wasn't going to be enough, especially when Jocasta muttered, '... leg. Leg.'

Under Jo's right leg, the dark matting had gone darker, and a white flash on her leggings had turned red. 'Pin down her shoulders,' said Conrad. He put his hand under the girl's buttock and knee, then twisted and saw something that made his eyes bulge. 'Martin!'

'Here,' said the Bursar.

'Get out a pad and a bandage.'

'Let me,' said the Princess to Alexandra. 'Before it's too late.'

More in shock than acquiescence, Alexandra let go her daughter's shoulders, and the Fae took over. She massaged Jo's collar bones for a second, then in a burst of supernatural strength, she ripped open the girl's top and dug her blood-red nails into flesh. Jocasta jerked off the matting, then fell back, closing her eyes.

Conrad took the offered medical pad and shoved it against the side of the girl's thigh, just down from the hip. He lifted her knee right off the ground and said, 'Cordy, get winding. I don't want to let this pad go.'

Cordelia grabbed the stretchy bandage from Martin Hoggart and got close to Jocasta. The pad was already showing a little red under Conrad's fingers. Cordy took a deep breath and put one end of the bandage on the girl's groin. Round she went, and her small fingers and shoulders meant she could squeeze in and get the pressure tight. Round once, and again, and again. Then she stopped, because her fingers had brushed Conrad's at the moment she looked up at Princess Faithful.

The acid that nearly come from her stomach before surged back when she saw Faith's face. What was left of it.

'Keep going,' said Conrad quietly. 'You're doing great.'

She started winding again and said, 'I know I am, thanks.' It was uncalled for, but she couldn't help it. Round and round, and round again.

'That should be enough,' said Conrad.

Faith bent down and stared closely at Jocasta's ruined arm. Now that she'd seen the Princess's face, Cordelia couldn't un-see it, and the proximity of that terrible open wound with the blood-soaked, bone-speared mess of Jo's arm was too much. Under the pretence of getting out of the way, Cordelia rolled to one side and stood up, facing away from the stricken girl.

She couldn't see the crowd, because they couldn't see her. Or hear. Saul and Matt had created a blurred wall of distortion and Silence around the incident, and anything could be going on out there. Right here, right now, no one expected Cordelia to do anything, and that was good because she had nothing left to give. Not yet. She closed her eyes and tried to relax every muscle except her braced knees and ankles. She took a few breaths and relished the quiet. She felt the sweat in her base layers start to chill, and she knew that she'd come close to overheating when she was bonded with Blenheim: her metabolism had gone from zero to marathon in a heartbeat, and only now was it stabilising. Even knowing that helped, and she was getting ready to open her eyes when Faith spoke and forced her into action.

'Cordelia, could you run and get a clean towel. Soak it in *cold* water and bring it as quick as you can.'

'On it.' Her feet were half way to the steps before her brain caught up. 'Need a clean towel!' she shouted.

'Shit,' said Natalie Greening. 'With me. This way.'

Cordy followed her new comrade through the open doors and into the hall. Instead of heading for the showers and toilets, Natalie took the stairs three-at-a-time, breaking two Wards and a Diversion Charm on the way. She swerved left at the top, charged down a short corridor and stopped in front of a door marked *Linen*. She placed her fingertips on the wood and concentrated. 'Bugger. I still can't work this fucking Charm.'

'Let me.'

Cordelia didn't even try to work it. She just touched her chest and drew strength from Raven, then channelled the blast magick she'd been practising every day. It blew straight through the lock, punching out mundane and magickal resistance.

'Holy fuck,' said Natalie. 'Good, even. Right.' She threw open the door, dodged in and returned with an armful of towels. 'Bathroom next.' Turn right, two more doors and they were in a half-Victorian, half-Ideal Home communal bathroom, chucking the towels in a giant relic of a bath and running the cold tap.

'Why all the Wards for a linen cupboard?' asked Cordelia. It was an easier question to ask than *Has there been a riot?*

'You wouldn't believe some of the stuff that goes on here, I'm telling you. How is she?'

The look on Natalie's face reminded Cordy that the victim outside wasn't just a victim: she was Nat's cousin. Easy to forget. 'If she carries on getting treatment, she'll live. They look wet enough.'

They grabbed two of the soaking, heavy towels each and ran dripping downstairs, through the big doors and out into the night. On the way, Cordy couldn't help notice an empty velvet cushion on the table, along with one medal and three bunches of flowers. They burst through the distortion Glamour and offered up their towels.

Faith had rocked back on her heels, keeping one hand on Jocasta's left collarbone and one on her left elbow. She spoke without looking up. 'Conrad is going to lift the hand, me the elbow. When we do, put a towel underneath. Then wrap it round and tie a knot. Ready.'

'I'm ready,' said Cordelia.

'On three, Conrad. One…'

151

On the count, they raised the arm in a perfectly synchronised lift, and Cordy slid the towel underneath. 'And down,' said Faith. 'Good. Knot, please.'

As Cordelia tied the knot, she felt magick pulse through the towel, chilling her fingers and nearly making her fumble. 'Keep going,' said the Fae. 'I'm lowering the mundane and metabolic temperature and putting a stasis on the arm. So long as they don't un-knot the towel until she's in surgery, nothing will change. No further damage will happen.'

She delivered the last part to Alexandra Greening, and backed it up by looking the woman straight in the eye. 'You must go with her and make sure that's what they do. They'll think they're helping, but they won't be.'

'I understand,' said Alexandra. 'Someone tell me where that ambulance is.'

It was on its way – by air. Ambleside is too far from anywhere for a road ambulance to get there and then drive to Preston. That's what Conrad said, and then he held out his hand to Cordelia. 'Been squatting too long.'

She used all her strength to stop herself falling over as she heaved him upright. He grunted and winced and couldn't help himself hopping on one leg for a second. 'Oooooooh,' he said. 'Right. Natalie, you stay here and liaise with Matt. He's organising the stretcher to get Jo to the Academy playing field. That's where the chopper will land. Faith will tell you what's needed medically. Cordelia, come with me.' He turned and went through the magickal wall, and Cordy followed.

Beyond the barrier, it was more peaceful than she'd expected. On one side, between Jocasta and the paddock, James Greening and some of the family were waiting for news. On the other side, a group of Fae were talking to Saul Brathay and George Gibson. Instead of a riot, the market grounds were almost empty. Saul broke away from the Fae and came to meet them. 'Where is everyone?' she asked.

'When I said that Jocasta would live, most of the People lost interest,' said Saul. 'I asked them to leave in the name of Peace, and in its name they thanked me and departed.' He shook his head. 'Still can't get used to it. It won't surprise you to know that I got rid of the humans by telling them that there would be free drinks – so long as they stayed near the lake.'

Cordy pointed discretely to the Fae. 'And them?'

'Once the ambulance has been and gone, we're going to have a private ceremony to present Typhonous' jockey with her third place medal.'

Cordelia was appalled. 'How come?'

Conrad clicked his lighter and drew in smoke. 'When dealing with the Fae, you need to adjust your priorities. Well done, Saul.'

Cordelia realised she wasn't needed here, and said, 'Do you mind if I check on Blenheim?'

Conrad nodded. 'Of course. Here comes the ambulance.'

It was midnight-quiet out here. 'How can you hear that when you couldn't hear the sonic assault earlier?'

'Because I'm magickally bonded to fixed-wing aircraft.' He paused, then snorted with laughter. 'Because I can see it. There.'

He pointed in to the darkness. The black emptiness over the lake was pierced by stars, but none of them were moving. And then one of the stars turned from white to red, and the quiet was tickled, then destroyed by the thunder of engines. Help was on its way.

'Right. See you in a minute,' she said.

He touched her shoulder. 'Before you go, you should know you did superbly back there. You saved lives, Cordelia. Stopping Blenheim and getting him out of the way like that was absolutely crucial. Without it, I couldn't have stepped in. Well done.'

She nodded and turned away to hide her blushes. As she walked towards the paddock, her insides were torn between pride at what she'd achieved and devastation at what she'd seen done to Blenheim and to Jocasta. She wondered if any of the Borrowdale people would be there, and if they were, would she be able to restrain herself.

Her fists clenched as she emerged from a patch of darkness into the paddock, then she uncurled them. Only two trailers remained, and neither belonged to the Red Queen. On her right, Typhonous was being readied for his "victory" parade by his handlers, and on her left, the Greenings' stable crew were clustered round Blenheim. Her heart swelled when she saw the moonlight flicker off his great horn. He was alright. He was going to be okay.

I stood back and observed while Jocasta was delivered to the ambulance. People thought I was overseeing things, but I was really taking a break and letting them get on with it. Sometimes the role of the CO is to do just that. If I wasn't there, I'd have expected them to cope without me. The inevitable confrontation came when the helicopter lights had disappeared again. I made sure that I was standing near Saul when James Greening came for his showdown.

'What are you going to do about them?' he said, grim faced and furious.

I was tired, very cold, I had a thumping head and my leg ached like a bad tooth. We could get into a discussion about this, or I could cut to the chase. I cut.

'What do you suggest I do, James?'

His fury boiled over, and he turned it on Saul. Why else do you think I was standing next to him?

'Is this why we voted for a fucking *Commissioner?* So he could stand round like broken lamppost waiting for dogs to piss on his leg? Because he's fuck-all use otherwise. And you let this happen, Saul. What were you afraid of? That you'd lose a few contracts with the Queen of Hell?'

Saul flicked a glance at me first. A glance that said *Take it easy*. 'It is as the Commissioner said. There is nothing we can do except encourage the Queen of Derwent to submit to the Cloister Court and answer for what she has done.'

'Get real, Saul. You had her. You should have held her and put her to Judgement.'

Saul waited a moment before replying. 'For half a second, James, I nearly did, but in that half a second, Conrad and Cordelia jumped in and put their lives on the line. They stopped it turning into a bloodbath, and unless my memory deceives me, Conrad saved your niece's life.'

James's mouth worked furiously. 'You keep telling yourself that, Saul Brathay. You keep telling yourself that this was a disaster averted, because you'll be the only one saying it. Everyone else will be saying that you let the Fae walk all over you and then walk away. That's what everyone will be saying. Everyone.'

He turned and stalked away, his back rigid with anger. When he was out of earshot, Saul sighed. 'Unfortunately, he's right. He was even polite about it.'

'I'd hate to see him when he's rude.'

Saul made a sour face. 'What he missed out is that this anonymous "everyone" will also be saying that you can't trust Gnomes to put the Fae in their place.'

'That bad?'

'Oh yes. We're used to it, but we tread a tightrope all the time. There will be voices calling for a chapter of the Pale Horsemen to be formed again. Our job – yours and mine – is to drag both parties into court sooner rather than later. A two-thirds vote of no confidence and I'll be out as President of the Grand Union. Then the fun would really start.'

I was beginning to feel very uneasy. I thought I'd handled the politics of my new job quite well so far. I was now beginning to see that pride could very easily come before a very hard fall. 'What do you suggest?'

'I suggest that we get this show over as quickly as possible and go to bed. We can start thinking in the morning.'

'What needs doing?'

'For you, nothing. Grab Cordelia and get out of here. Matt can help us disperse the others. Once the bar is closed and the fires have gone out, they'll soon be off.' He nodded to himself and shivered. 'I wasn't blowing steam when I said you stopped a bloodbath, Conrad. That's why I pushed to appoint you, and if you hadn't been here tonight… Let's not dwell on it and hope that things calm down, eh? Goodnight.'

We shook hands and parted. I was rather hoping that we had more than *hope* to stop things getting worse. I limped towards the paddock and found Cordelia watching Iras get ready with a needle and thread. Oh dear.

Cordy separated herself and whispered, 'He really needs a vet to stitch that, but there has to be magick, too, and the only Entangled vet is neither Mage nor female.'

'Do you want to stay and make sure he's okay?'

'I … no. Not important. What's happening?'

'Is there any water around? I'm parched.'

'Hang on.'

She grabbed me a metal cup full of freezing water from an outside tap, and I found a bench to collapse on to. I told her that Jocasta had been got safely away, and I told her what James Greening had had to say.

'He's got a point,' she said.

I frowned. 'In what way?'

'That creature could have killed Blenheim and Jocasta. She can't get away with it. She simply can't.' She took a breath and tried to calm down. 'What I mean is that it must stop. All of it. What about your fencing master? I couldn't believe it when I saw her face through your eyes. What in the name of the Goddess is that all about?'

It was a good question. 'I don't know, and I'm not going to ask. If I had to guess, I'd say that the Red Queen was putting her Princess in her place. She can walk around as much as she likes, but every time Faith presents herself to someone new, she has to show what's been done to her.'

Cordelia stiffened. 'You mean that's the *reality*? I thought it was a forced Glamour, but you're telling me she's really like that? How can you tell.'

'Trust me on that one. It's real. She even uses magick to talk properly. That's their problem, not ours.'

Cordelia was getting angry again. 'But their problem *is* our problem, isn't it? There's no Count or Prince to blame for what happened tonight. The Queen herself attacked Blenheim, and she did it in full view of the whole Particular *and* four other Queens. She won't back down.'

'Won't she? It's up to us to make sure she does, and James Greening isn't the only one who's got a point.'

She looked mystified. 'What do you mean?'

'If that bridle, and other things, really were looted from Urien's grave, then her whole line has been profoundly insulted. The Red Queen isn't the only one who will need to back down if we're going to avoid more bloodshed. Anyway, we're done for tonight. Let's go.'

'Oh? Right. I will stay if you don't mind. Just until they've finished with Blenheim.'

'Of course. I'm sure I can scrounge a lift off someone.'

'Aah. I'd forgotten about that. Sorry.'

I was already on my feet. 'I think I saw Faith at a loose end. The rest of her People had gone by the time the ambulance arrived.'

She stood up too and took my hands in hers. I don't know which were colder. 'Are you going to start your peacekeeping campaign tonight? With her?'

'Something like that.'

'Then take care, Chief.'

I gave her a dark look and limped off into the night. I was right about Faith: she wasn't just at a loose end, she was actually waiting to talk to me, and (wonder of wonders), she had a car.

We started walking down the path that would take us out of the magickal zone of the School House and through to the Academy car park. She spoke first. 'Why did you vouch for me like that to the Greenings? You were putting your life on the line based on one day's acquaintance. And no jokes about you being a sucker for a pretty face.'

That was an easy question to answer. 'You were on damage limitation. Just like Prince Appleby, though perhaps for different reasons. I doubt the Red Queen will admit it, but in the morning she'll be grateful to both of you.'

'Yeaaah. You're spot on about the gratitude thing. The most we can hope for is that she pretends it never happened.'

'And now we have to get her down off the ledge. And the same with the Greenings.'

We had arrived at her car. Before she clicked the locks, she stood by the door and hunched her shoulders. Our breaths steamed and merged over the roof. The mundane LEDs did nothing for her disfigured face, and I hoped that none of the budding Mages in the dormitories behind me were peeking out and testing their Sight. They'd have nightmares if they did.

'The Greenings will huff and puff,' she said. 'It's the Queen that worries me.'

I tried to stare into her eyes. 'You don't get it do you, Faith? The law is a two edged sword. It's nice not to be bound by human law. I can see the attractions. But the law protects, too. The Greenings have done it before, and they'll do it again.'

'You know? Who told you?'

'George Gibson told me to read a book, and the Keeper of the Queen's Library is a friend. She let me borrow the original manuscript of *Reflections on the Wild Hunt of Trafalgar.*' I let that sink in. 'Do you want to come in for a brandy? When you've driven me home, of course.'

She looked troubled, and turned her face to the lake for a second, then shook her head and opened the car. 'Not tonight. I'd better get back to Borrowdale.' We both climbed in. It took me so long to bend my frame and adjust the seat that she already had the engine going and screen heaters full blast. When I was settled, she turned to face me. 'But we will start fencing practice. Not tomorrow, but very soon. Did I hear a rumour that you have a horse somewhere?'

'You did. I was going to collect her myself, but I daren't leave the Particular right now. I'll get someone to bring her up tomorrow.'

'Then on behalf of the Red Queen, I offer stabling. Until you get yourself sorted.'

I was about to refuse: no way did I want to have Evenstar in the care of the Count of Force Ghyll. On the other hand, it would be a sign to the Particular that the Fae can be dealt with. Cordy was already well on her way to getting to know the Greenings, too. And I'd get a chance to see the mysterious Persephone. 'Thank you.'

She put the car in gear and we drove off. 'Excellent. If nothing changes, we can ride out and have our first lesson on Sunday. I'm sure Cordelia will be along soon to raid your drinks cupboard.'

'She'll see you're not there and know that I'm on the phone to Mina. Tomorrow is soon enough.'

We bumped on to the main road. 'Of course. Has Mina any idea what's been going on tonight?'

'Yes. Sort of. I got Sapphire Gibson to call her with the headlines. I'm sure that Mina will make allowances for Sapphire's love of the dramatic.'

Cordelia didn't know what to feel when Conrad got up and limped off towards the Fae Princess. She was beginning to think that she'd used up all her feelings for the day and that she was well overdrawn at the Bank of Emotions. And totally forgetting that she was the designated driver was a sure sign of exhaustion: Cordelia Kennedy did not forget things like that.

She was the one who remembered what needed doing and did it. She'd done it for her mother, for Rick, for the kids, and finally for Raven. And the only one who'd noticed and repaid her care before she met Conrad was Raven, and now she'd let Conrad down. He didn't seem to mind, though, and if she knew him, he'd be working an angle with the Fae before long. And he would be expecting her to do the same with the Greenings.

She sighed and pulled up her fur-trimmed hood. It was late now, and wherever water had gathered, ice crystals were forming. The other remaining Unicorn, Typhonous, was led past her by the Eskdale grooms, all of them smiling and joking. That would be the Queen of Eskdale in North Yorkshire, and not to be confused with the Eskdale Union in the Particular. Bloody Northerners. Could they not have come up with a bigger variety of names? There were *three* River Derwents in the north, all of them associated with Fae Queens in one way or another.

When Typhonous had gone past, she saw that the Greenings were having trouble with Blenheim, and she hurried to join in. 'Can I help?'

'Please,' said Iras. 'I'd swear that bitch Queen had some poison on those claws, and Blenheim doesn't want to be stitched.'

'I'll hold the rope,' said Charmian. 'Rowan, you look him in the eye, and Cordelia, if you could put a hand above the wounds, that might do it.'

Cordelia summoned Lux she didn't know she had and placed her hand on Blenheim's shoulder. She shuddered at the contact, the pain and the confusion, but at least the Unicorn's temperature had dropped. With the patient standing quietly, and three Witches using their power to soothe and anaesthetise him, Iras finally had a chance to do her job. Cordy forced herself to watch, and marvelled at how deft the young woman's fingers were as she closed the wounds and used healing magick to start the regeneration process.

'All done. Thanks, everyone.' Iras looked at Cordelia. 'You've got it, haven't you?'

Cordelia returned the thanks with a wry smile. 'So it seems. Too late, though. I can't even ride.'

James Greening made her jump. Where had he come from? 'It's never too late, Ms Kennedy. Drop in next week and we'll show you round. Someone will be glad to give you an introductory lesson.'

A small voice piped up. 'I would,' said Sophie. She'd been standing, distraught, at a safe distance while the Mages did their thing.

Next week. In other words, if there hasn't been an all-out war before then. Cordelia smiled and stepped away from Blenheim. 'That would be nice.'

James shook her hand. 'Thank you. For what you did tonight, we are very grateful. It looks like one of you has their head screwed on and knows right from wrong.'

She wasn't going to have that. Not at all. 'I think you'll find that the Commissioner knows what he's doing, Mr Greening, if you give him a chance.'

Greening *humphed.* 'He'd better. Right, you lot, let's get out of here.'

Cordelia waved to the women and walked off into the night. Something made her glance to the left, up the side of the School House. The glow of Spirits was still there.

No one was watching, and she jogged round towards the woods. As she got closer to the low fence, she felt the magick growing. This was the conduit and boundary for all the Charms protecting the anonymity of the Waterhead campus, and her acquaintances weren't the only Spirits who'd come along tonight. Close up, the woods were full of them. She hadn't seen this many since Last Samhain at Glastonbury.

They were beginning to drift away, now, but Lucas grew brighter. He manifested on the other side of the fence and stared at her for a second. Her mouth had gone dry, and Lucas broke the silence.

'So now you've seen for yourself, eh? Now you know what the Queen of Hell is really like.'

Cordelia couldn't deny it. The assault on Blenheim and Jocasta. The contempt for human lives and values. Even the mockery of Princess Faithful's face was a declaration of Fae arrogance and exceptionalism. There was nothing she could say, so she confined herself to a nod of the head and an agreement. 'Yes, I've seen.'

'She has to be taken down.'

It was there again: the line she would not cross. 'She has to be stopped.'

'But how many will die before then? I thought you wanted to be reunited with Raven in your world, not join her in ours. The next time you or Conrad act as a human shield will likely be the last.'

Cordelia shivered. She couldn't argue with that, either. All she knew was that Conrad deserved her support.

Lucas waited for her response, and when none came he looked off to his right. 'Make it soon. Go and see for yourself.'

'I think wandering round the Furness Peninsula is somewhat low down his list of priorities at the moment. Sorting out the Kellys divorce comes higher than that.'

'We'll arrange an event that demands his attention. Make sure he's near his phone on Monday.'

'How are you going to do that?'

The set of Lucas's jaw, always firm, had become granite. 'You didn't think we were on our own, did you? You are not our only contact in the daylight world.'

'Who?'

'Every one of us is someone whom the Queen from Hell has harmed. That's all you need to know. The clock is ticking, Cordelia. I'll bid you farewell. For now.'

He bowed and vanished before she could react. The illusion of warmth and contact that the Spirit had brought vanished with him, and every part of her was shivering. She turned and started to leave, quickening her pace to try and get her circulation going. She was tempted to head for Lake Cottage and beg Conrad for use of the bath, but that would mean looking him in the eye. And crossing back over to the hotel afterwards. There were many complaints she could make about her room; lack of hot water in the shower was not one of them. Never mind. She was moving in to Blackburn House tomorrow night. Matt had a tub to die for.

15 — *Trafalgar*

'I don't know about you, Cordy, but I'm absolutely starving. Full Westmorland Breakfast with fried eggs, please.'

The waitress made a note and turned to my partner. 'Same, but scrambled eggs and no black pudding, thanks,' said Cordy.

'Great. I'll get your tea and toast.'

'You're looking a bit more human this morning,' said Cordelia. 'And I mean that in a good way. Any lasting effects?'

'It should be me asking you the same question. I didn't bond with a High Unicorn last night. Did you sleep okay?'

'Good, thanks. Now we've got that out of the way, what are we going to do?' She gave me time to lift my knife off the table. 'Yeah, yeah. We're going to have breakfast before we do any critical thinking.'

'Correct. Protein is a great aid to strategy. I can tell you that I won't be able to help you move in to Matt's place tonight. Evenstar – my horse – is arriving this afternoon, and I want to be there.' I paused. 'I'm stabling her at Sprint Stables.'

'That was quick work. I didn't see Princess Faithful's car outside last night, so unless she put a Glamour on it…?'

I waved away the innuendo. Cordy normally rises above such things, so she must be tired. 'Faith is buttering me up. I imagine the Greenings did the same to you.'

She looked away rather than answer, and she had the excuse of smiling at the returning waitress. Toast deposited, she made the obvious joke. 'This is the only buttering up I'm interested in, Conrad. You're not wrong, though. I've been offered riding lessons, and yes, I'm going to take them up on it.'

'Good. It's crucial that we get lines of communication going. We simply haven't got the connections otherwise. I do *not* want things happening behind my back, and the more we can talk to both sides, the better. And talking of talking, Tamsin Kelly is heading back to London today, so Mina is coming up here. I suggested to her that she catch a lift with the horse transporter, but for some reason she declined and is catching the train.'

'Ooh! I wonder why that could be? Is it because a horse transporter is slow, noisy and very smelly? I would have said that Mina is a natural for spending time in close proximity to livestock.'

'Strangely, she's not. Never mind. Pass the butter.'

When we'd finished breakfast, we set up in Lake Cottage with both our phones in the middle of the table in case of sudden crisis. I put the kettle on and leaned against the sink. 'There's only one hard decision to make today: can we still put Natalie Greening in charge of the Northern Waters? After last night, I'm not sure.'

Cordy jumped straight to the defence of our youngest assessor. 'That's not fair. She stood with us last night, not with her family. If you hadn't already announced your decision, then fine, I'd agree with you. But if you take it off her now, you'll be sending a message that you don't trust her.'

The kettle boiled, and I made the first of many pots of tea. We were going to be writing reports soon, but I wanted to get the hard decision over with first. While I waited for the goodness to steep out of the teabags, I said, 'It's not her, it's the Fae. If she's responsible for Borrowdale, I don't want them trying it on just to push her. It wouldn't be fair.'

Cordy crossed her legs and leaned on the table. 'I get that. If the Fae were confined to Borrowdale and Derwentwater, I'd agree: move her. But they're in *every* union. It could happen anywhere.'

'Fair point. I'll make sure that Tanya hangs around and keeps an eye on her.'

I poured and took my seat.

'Is Tanya always grumpy?' said Cordy.

'She's a great laugh. She just takes an instinctively pessimistic view of the world, that's all. We'll put Natalie top of the list for an inspection visit, shall we?'

And so we plodded on. Reports were written, calls were made, and no one launched a pre-emptive attack on their enemies. At lunchtime, Cordy went for a walk in the winter sunshine, and I Facetimed my own little ray of light. I told you I was missing Mina, didn't I?

A quiet corner of Cheltenham Spa station flickered into life. 'How's things?' I asked. 'Trains on time?'

'Fingers crossed. I take it that no news is good news.'

'Fingers also crossed. Or if they're having a pitched battle, no one's told me. Which is also fine.'

'Talking of pitched battles, Tammy is sitting down with Chris about now.'

'Ouch. Well done for getting them in the same place, love. What did you do?'

'I tried to get her focused on the future, not the past. I tried to get her to see that taking Chris to the cleaners in the divorce would be the best form of revenge.'

'So she accepts it's over between them?'

Mina looked around her and came even closer to her phone. 'It was so sad, Conrad. After the first few hours, it became clear that she wasn't really upset that her marriage was over, only that she'd been publicly humiliated and that Eseld Mowbray had been laughing behind her back.' She paused. 'Not that an affair with Chris Kelly would have me laughing.' She paused again, and glanced up at something. Probably the station display board. 'I wasn't going to say anything, but she brought it up. Our wedding. She said, "Of course Amanda must be one of your flower girls. And Chris will have to help me with the twins. He mustn't be distracted."'

'In other words, *If you want me there, Eseld can butt out.*'

'I think I would be less polite, but you're right. And then the part of me that says Tammy shouldn't suffer for what Chris did also says that Eseld shouldn't suffer, either. I think my train is coming. Can't wait to see you.'

'Me too.'

We blew kisses and disconnected. With Mina on her way and Evenstar nearly here, the Lakeland Particular was beginning to feel a lot more like home.

Mina leaned closer to me and whispered right in my ear. 'No wonder he has never married. Have you seen his bookshelves?'

We were squeezed into a couch that had been designed for two people Mina's size, not Mina + me. At least it meant I could stay close to her without it looking too inappropriate. 'You can't miss his bookshelves. They cover the whole wall.'

I hadn't expected to be invited to Blackburn House less than twenty-four hours after Cordelia moved in, but here we were on Saturday night, waiting for drinks and canapés.

'It's not just the size of the shelves,' insisted Mina. 'It's what's in the books.' The door to the kitchen opened, and Mina looked up. 'Aah! How are things, Cordelia? You look relaxed.'

My magickal partner did look relaxed, in an oversized knitted dress and leggings. Mina was already on her feet to give her a hug, and I followed slowly. I was still recovering from Thursday. I wonder if I could get seconded to the Spanish Inquisition for winter.

Cordelia hugged Mina and stepped back. 'What you mean is that I haven't bothered to dress up like you. I told Matt to tell you it was *strictly informal.*'

Mina pulled her hair behind her head. 'This old thing? It was all I brought with me.'

Cordelia glanced at the corridor that led away from the long room, probably wondering if she should go and change. Instead, she smiled and said, 'Matt is so out of practice at hospitality. He didn't ask you what you wanted to drink, did he? Didn't even find out who's driving.'

I raised my hand. 'That would be me. Early morning chopper flight to Longsleddale for a ride and my first fencing lesson.'

'But we're not going to talk about that,' said Mina smoothly. 'At least not until the cheese has arrived.'

'Cheese?' said Cordy with another flick of her eyes – this time towards the kitchen. She lowered her voice. 'Where do you think you are? Elvenham Grange? Matt Eldridge is the only life-long bachelor I've met who has no interest in cooking. None. Nor does he like Prosecco.'

'All the more for you and me, then.' It was Mina's turn to glance at the kitchen. 'Is he safe to be left in there?'

'It's in the slow cooker, and all I have to do is cook the rice. Back in a sec.'

I didn't need to ask for an update on Jocasta Greening, because I'd been getting them fairly regularly from Natalie. Thanks to Princess Faith's magickal towel, there was no swelling associated with the wound, and the trauma surgeons had been able to set to it on Friday morning. The prognosis was good, but it was going to be a long time before she did anything with that arm, and there was a deep cut to her thigh as well.

Now that I had a licence to stand up, I studied the bookshelves more closely. As far as I could tell, they consisted of three things: every book or map on walking in the Particular ever written (including two complete sets of *Wainwright's Pictorial Guides*, one of which must be a first edition), books on Lakeland in general, and the books with nothing on the spine. That would be the magick. It didn't mean that the contents were in the least magickal, just that an Enscriber had bound them and hidden the titles from curious eyes.

Of course I'm exaggerating a bit. There were at least a dozen books on other things. In other words, about two percent.

'Here we are,' said Matt, carrying a steaming tankard. 'Cordelia's revenge. She said I had to serve you mulled apple juice after you made her drink it on Thursday.'

165

'No I did not,' said Cordy. 'It's just that someone gave him half a barrel and there was nothing else to offer. I for one don't need any reminders about Thursday.'

We sat down again, and this time I stopped to look at the big picture over the humongous slate fireplace. Well, everything was slate at Blackburn House: Walls, roof, floor. It was on the other side of the hill from a slate quarry, so full marks for sustainability. Assuming he hadn't imported the slate from Wales, of course. Nah. He wouldn't do that.

I had expected the landscape picture to be his favourite spot in the Lakes, but no. It was somewhere else. A big river, with mountains behind and central European houses tucked into the forest. Danube? Vltava? No. 'Is this the Rhine?' I asked.

'Well spotted. I inherited it. Are you sure there's enough room on that couch for both of you?'

Cordelia swapped places with me, so I got the spare armchair, which was better for my back, but less good for my soul. Matt was in His Chair. I could tell that because it had a side-table with books, pens and an empty whisky glass on it. And it was just the right height for him. If I hadn't met Mina, I might have a chair exactly like that at Elvenham. Only bigger, of course.

Later, when the coffee was served (Cordy hadn't been lying about the lack of cheese), the conversation did turn to matters in the Particular. Matt hadn't exactly been a block of stone during dinner. Far from it. What he rarely did was start a conversation, though. Until I got back from a smoke break and he looked at me. 'This whole Commissioner thing is going to get some getting used to,' he began. 'Not you, Conrad. I'm getting used to you already.'

'You must tell me your secret,' said Cordy. There were already two empty Prosecco bottles in the recycling.

'I think Matt is trying to be serious,' said Mina.

I don't think he got the irony, because he just carried on. 'Saul Brathay was my boss until New Year's Day, and he still thinks he is.'

'Oh?'

'We were clearing up at Waterhead yesterday, and he told me not to get involved between the Greenings and the People of Borrowdale. When I pointed out that it wasn't my decision, it took me a while to realise ...' he paused and looked at Mina, 'To realise that I was being serious.'

Mina looked down at her coffee. For once, she didn't have a comeback. Matt continued with, 'Not that I've got much to offer. You know that the Greenings and the Clan are like that?' He held up and crossed his fingers. 'Have been for generations. Since well before Trafalgar.'

Mina frowned. 'You don't mean Lord Nelson, do you, Matt?'

'Who?' said Cordelia. 'Oh wait, you were banging on about Trafalgar a while back, weren't you, Conrad?'

I glanced at the bookshelves. 'Have you got a copy here?'

'I have.'

'What?' said Mina.

I scanned the blank spines hopefully, trying to engage my Sight. Nothing doing. 'Trafalgar was a battle, yes, but for some reason known only to herself, the late Queen of Esthwaite decided to give the same name to one of her Unicorns. The story of her violent death was written down by Thomas de Quincy, and he called it *Reflections on the Wild Hunt of Trafalgar*. The Queen you met on Tuesday is her successor.'

'And you have read this thing?' said Mina, looking slightly worried.

'In the first manuscript copy, yes.'

'Then give me the accountant's version: who won, who lost and what the score was.'

'I'd say that the Greenings won by an innings and two hundred runs, wouldn't you, Matt?'

He paused to let me know what he thought of that metaphor. 'If I understood cricket, I'd probably agree. It certainly changed the Particular for ever.'

'It's connected with the Treaty, isn't it?' said Mina. 'De Quincey had a hand in that, too, didn't he?'

'He did, just before he became part-time editor of the *Wezzy Gezzy* and full-time opium addict,' said Matt.

It was Cordelia's turn to look confused. 'What's the Wezzy Gezzy when it's at home?'

By way of an answer, Matt went to the log basket and took out a newspaper. He showed her the masthead: The Westmorland Gazette. 'All the mundane news in Westmorland is here. There's a lot on traffic schemes and flood relief programmes. Oh, and spot the dog.'

'The kids books? I loved them!' Cordy looked as if she was going to add something, then stopped.

'No,' said Matt. 'Spot the dog is a competition. There's a photo of a field of sheep and you have to put a cross where you think the sheepdog's nose is, then send it in.'

'Tell me you're joking.'

'Welcome to Westmorland, where the winters are long. We make our own entertainment up here.'

167

Mina looked at me, bewildered. 'How did we get from the Fae to spotting missing border collies?'

'Thomas de Quincey,' I replied. 'Friend of Wordsworth, friend of the Fae and opium addict. One probably led to the other. It's like this: before 1809, the Particular had its own laws completely. The Silver Queen pretty much ran the show from her sídhe on the western shore of Windermere, not far from Esthwaite Water. Only she over-reached herself and started running extravagant entertainments, races with huge prizes and generally living beyond her means.' I looked at Matt. 'Like most revolutions, it comes down to taxes, wouldn't you say?'

'I'd say it had more to do with appropriation of children for bonded service, but we'll go with taxation.'

'She taxed the roads,' I continued. 'They used to call the Ley lines *Fairy Roads* up here, and she taxed the supply of Lux throughout the three counties. And other taxes. At the Waterhead Meeting of 1809, she came unstuck.'

'What happened?'

'On the second night – The Waterhead Chase – she had a big, public falling out with her senior Princess – Princess Borrowdale, now the Red Queen of Derwent.' Mina nodded, and I continued. 'On the third night, the Unicorn race, the Princess was absent. She'd been ordered to stay in her sídhe.'

'I take it this was a big mistake.'

'Oh yes. The Silver Queen used to ride her own mounts. On that night it was Trafalgar, her new Unicorn. When she appeared in the paddock, the Greenings and their friends attacked her.'

Mina sat up straight. Cordelia was fully focused, too, and Matt was keeping an eye on me. It should have been him telling this story, not me. Not only was the Particular his home, Langdale and Windermere are his patch as Assessor. I looked at him for a second, to see if he wanted to take over. No, he didn't.

In the pause, Mina had remembered something. 'Didn't the Clan intervene? Did they not have the same role then?'

'Not officially. That came later. On that night, they stood back and let the Greening Alliance get on with it. The Queen's People fought back, and the Queen escaped. They chased her all the way down the shore, on this plane and others. They had their horses ready and waiting; the People didn't.'

'How on earth did they catch her?' said Cordelia. 'A Queen on a High Unicorn is pretty much as fast as you can get. Until you learn how to plane-shift the Smurf.'

That was a frightening thought, and I ignored it. 'They didn't catch her. They just had to make sure she headed to her sídhe. They herded her rather than pursuing her. When she got home, she found that most of the Greenings themselves had laid siege to the sídhe. She couldn't get in.'

At this point, Matt did take over. 'It was clever. A lot of her People were stuck at Waterhead, and the ones in the sídhe had to make a sally to rescue her: she was caught between the Greenings and Windermere. At some point, Nimue was involved, but no one's sure how or why or whether she took sides. At dawn, the Queen was dead, the sídhe broken and the Greenings victorious. It's what happened next that's a bit controversial.'

'Unlike a pitched battle?'

'Nothing controversial about that. The controversial part is that the Greenings not only captured Trafalgar, they also found a mare in foal within the sídhe, along with the magick used to quicken a Unicorn. They took the lot, and that's why the Greendale Trust are the only humans who can breed Unicorns. Princess Borrowdale became the Red Queen of Derwent, but she has always claimed, in private, that the Greenings exceeded their agreement and broke their word.'

'I see,' said Mina. She sat back and frowned, digesting what she'd heard.

Cordelia looked like she'd sobered up a fair bit. 'No wonder things kicked off on Thursday night. Is there any chance this can be resolved without another confrontation?'

'Don't forget part two of de Quincey's work,' I said. 'A large number of mundane citizens died as well on that night. Entangled, yes, but mundane. The fallout was epic, and that's why the Unions were dragged kicking and screaming to the negotiating table. The de Quincey Treaty brought the Cloister Court into the Particular and created the post of Chief Assessor. It also gave the King's Watch responsibility for investigating any deaths of mundane people by magick. That's how my involvement started last year: Rod Bristow was mundane. The grooms at Sprint Stables and in Grizedale Forest are all non-magickal.'

Matt Eldridge was nodding his head grimly: we'd first met at the smoking ruin of Fellside Farm which contained poor Rod Bristow's body. He leaned over the table and laced his fingers together, then extended his index fingers to make a triangle that pointed to me. 'And you won't hesitate to bring the Watch in again, will you?' He suddenly sat back. 'That's the real reason Cordy's here, isn't it? Why she's on the Reserve list? One phone call and she's a Watch Captain again. Sneaky.'

I was shaking my head strongly. 'You're giving me too much credit, Matt. I know and trust Cordelia, and she was available. That's all. No malice aforethought. I do not want this situation to get out of hand. If any of those grooms, or any of the Daughters of the Earth, or any civilian is hurt, then I've failed.'

Cordelia looked uncomfortable, and didn't say anything. I hadn't expected her to be in the spotlight like that. Matt saw the look on her face, and half reached out a hand to her, then withdrew it. 'Of course,' he said. 'I didn't mean to suggest that Cordelia was in on this. Far from it. And if you say you've got no hidden agenda, then I have to take you at your word.'

I hadn't said that at all. I do have an agenda, and Saul Brathay knows that I want the Commissioner to answer to the Peculier Constable. I didn't enlighten Matt about that, though. Not tonight. What I said instead was this: 'It won't hurt to remind both parties about the Treaty. Peace is also in their interests.'

'Let's hope they see it that way. What is it you're doing tomorrow…?'

16 — En Garde

If you drove out of the Occluded compound that surrounds the Borrowdale sídhe and set your Satnav for Longsleddale, it would say that you faced a journey of over an hour. On a good day. Naturally, the Queen does not want to spend two hours in her car every time she fancies a ride out on her favourite Unicorn, which is why the royal stables used to be near Keswick. They moved when the Queen discovered both helicopters and field-effect Silences.

If I fired up the Smurf at eight o'clock on a Sunday morning, not only would I wake the whole of Ambleside, I'd have the CAA on my back wanting to know what the f**k I was up to. I've put the asterisks in to show that's how civil servants swear.

To avoid having my licence endorsed, I slipped out of Lake Cottage at half-past seven, leaving Mina to sleep off her hangover, and took a fresh flask of coffee to Princess Faithful, who was already hard at work under the pre-dawn stars.

'Morning, Conrad. Couldn't you have found a parking spot nearer to a Ley line? I can do this as a one-off, but to make it permanent, I need more Lux.'

I poured her some coffee. 'Is there any chance I could do this myself?'

She burst out laughing. 'You are funny, you know. Oh. You were being serious? Sorry.' She blew steam off the cup and tried not to let me see the way her face looked like a total nightmare when she grinned. In return I tried not to feel offended, and I also tried not to shudder. I'm afraid that I failed on the shudder.

'Bit nippy this morning. Going to snow on Tuesday. Proper snow, they say. I'm doing some taxi duty for Chris Kelly next week, so I might stop off here and see if he can show me how to hook a spur off the Spine Road.'

I left the comment there to see if she'd have another go at me. She blew on her coffee again and said, 'Good idea. Shall we get going before the Charm disperses?'

I unlocked the Smurf and chucked in our gear. She declined my offer of flying up front and made herself comfortable in the leather seats. Just before I started the ignition, she looked up and said, 'What on earth are you doing?'

'Breathalyser. It won't start without a zero reading.'

'Oh. No wonder you couldn't fly Jocasta to hospital the other night.' She thought for a second, and then put on the headphones when I engaged the startup routine. 'Couldn't you fake it?'

'Of course I could, but I wouldn't have flown. I'd rather live with Alexandra Greening's anger than have my Spirit torn apart by the ghosts of the family whose house I landed on, killing all the occupants. It'll soon warm up in here.'

It did, and I had to remember my dark glasses, too, because a beautiful sunrise was waiting for us only a few hundred feet above the valley. I took the scenic route to Longsleddale because all routes are scenic in the Lake District, especially from 1,500 feet.

'Shit, Conrad, that was a bit close wasn't it?'

'Optical illusion. We had loads of room, really.'

Silence. With a small 's'.

The last time I'd taken the Smurf to Sprint Stables, I'd landed in the pasture next door, and the wheels had sunk during my absence. I'd probably be okay today, given that the ground was frozen, but now I knew about the Royal Flight, I also knew that part of the grounds at the stable had an LZ built into them and covered by a Glamour that I'd missed last time. In my defence, I did have other things on my mind. The cabin had barely warmed through before I was touching down again, and the sun was just beginning to crest the fells to the south east.

On Friday night, the Count of Force Ghyll had been conspicuous by his absence when I rocked up with Evenstar, and he'd left a young groom called Flora to welcome us. He didn't have much option but turn out this morning, given my passenger and her mount, and he was waiting in the yard with an expression of subservient humility on his face which must have been completely at odds with what he was feeling.

To be demoted from Prince consort to Count and exiled to the stables was deeply humiliating for him, and that humiliation had been compounded because he'd been fought to a standstill by a mortal. Me.

He bowed low. 'Good morning, my lady, and welcome back to Sprint Stables, Lord Dragonslayer. Did you have a good journey?'

Faith nodded in return and started fiddling with the long holdall she'd brought, so I answered. 'Yes, thank you. Is everything ready?'

'Of course. Flora!'

The girl brought Evenstar out of the mundane stalls and hitched her to a post near a mounting block, then went to the roundhouse where the two High Unicorns lived.

Flora and the other grooms had staged a mass walkout last year when the Count's sidekick had been appointed as their boss. On Friday night, Flora had told me that they'd all been given a pay rise and improved benefits to lure them back. Knowing their love of horses, I'm not surprised they couldn't resist.

I had also hoped to have a word with Persephone today, but Hipponax had been bridled, allowing mundane Flora to lead him on a very long rope. She smiled at me and gave me a little wave, then retreated to the side until called for. Hipponax, magnificent beast that he is, started stomping around looking for something to eat.

Princess Faith had finished fiddling, and laid out four swords on the concrete. 'Take your pick. They're all Gnomish work, so the magick should be familiar. That one's the closest in size and weight to Great Fang, but it's pretty rubbish. I'd go for that one: bit heavier, but it has an Ancile built in.'

'Thank you. I'll have a proper look when we get up top.' I was about to do something Eseld had wanted me to try for months: use the Enchanted saddle and bridle that came with Evenstar to plane-shift, like the jockeys had done on the races last week. I've been here before, of course, on the day of reckoning with the now demoted Fae (who was still watching us like a particularly attentive butler). On that day, unknown Spirits had helped me shift from Mittelgard to the Spirit Realm. This time I had to do it on my own. 'Right. Let's go.'

I slung the sword over my back and went to mount up. I can do it from the ground, but my secondary motto is *always take help when offered*, and my bad leg does not like reaching up to stirrups. Before climbing the block, I made friends with Evenstar again, then I was up and we were off, out of the yard, across the grass and into the unknown.

The saddle was well made, and I already had Lux flowing in a loop, completing the circuit between the metal stirrups and making Evenstar and me perform micro-shifts between this world and the one where a large hill appeared in front of us instead of a narrow valley. Surely this was too easy?

Yep. I tried to make the shift permanent, but I'd got something wrong, and Evenstar pulled me back to the lower plane. I made a circuit round the field and stopped. What the hell do I do now?

The grass shimmered, and Faith reappeared. 'What happened?'

'Wish I knew. I thought I had it, but clearly not. I followed you up the path then ...' I shrugged.

'Idiot. The path is a decoy. Just ... I don't know. Just try to make the hill real.'

'Make the hill real. Right.'

Faith looped Hipponax round the field, and I followed. This time, I decided to trust my horse. She was quite capable of finding her own way over the ground; my job was to change the ground we rode over. Hipponax and Faith shimmered out of existence, and I focused on the most real thing on the hill: the trees. Why were they more real than the rocks? Because those trees, Fae trees, are what captures the Lux that allows the Spirit Realm to exist at all. Trees, Lux, stirrups, all in one big loop. Here we go…

And I tipped back as Evenstar began going up the hill. We were there. Cue the silly grin. I made sure it was gone from my face when we caught up with Faith. She was waiting at the top of the slope, at the beginning of the equine obstacle course they use to train the horses and unicorns, both large and small.

In front of us was a variety of walls, ruins, hedges and ditches, all designed to simulate the obstacles the jockeys would face on the Chases. 'Fancy a gallop?' said Faith. 'Not a race, obviously, but a gallop through the long course up to the defile. From what Flora tells me, Evenstar could do with a bit of conditioning.'

'Lead the way.'

She turned Hipponax and spurred him into a trot along the crest of the hill, then she upped it to a canter and turned to tackle the first obstacle, a low wall.

'Come on, girl, here we go.' Evenstar had no trouble, and took the first two walls and a ditch in her stride. Next up was a big hedge that Hipponax soared over with consummate grace. I'd already seen the path to the side, and I'd swear Evenstar rippled with gratitude as we gave the hedge a miss. Unfortunately, the next obstacle had no bypass. Not only that, it was on an even higher plane, and if we didn't make the transition, someone was going to get hurt. Badly.

I don't know why, but reflex made me grip the riding crop that Eseld had given me for Christmas. When I did, a surge of magick flowed through me, and the dilapidated five-bar gate that stood in our way started to go all Picasso – chunks of the image separated and moved in squares. I nearly pulled up and aborted, but Evenstar was in full flow, and there were only a few strides left.

I fixed my eyes on the sundered image of the gate and tried to force the fractured sections back together, and at the same time I used the whip, not to urge her on but to send some magick through. When her feet were in the air, and I was about to close my eyes in terror, the image realigned and we sailed over the gate. This time I didn't bother to hide my delight.

'Nice toy,' said Faith when we'd slowed down and come to her side. 'Where on earth did you get that?'

I breathed heavily for a few seconds. 'A good friend gave it to me. How much more of this is there?'

'I think that's enough for today. We might try the Gauntlet next time, but there's plenty of space here.'

That suited me fine. The Gauntlet is six furlongs of alien landscape, beginning with a narrow defile and ending with a rocky bowl where the topography is flexible, to say the least. I wonder if the rocks are still stained with my blood. The Gauntlet could wait.

Faith dismounted and tied Hipponax to a tree that hung over a small pond. I was also glad that we were missing out the woods. They did not look inviting. 'The water's fresh,' said Faith. I secured Evenstar, and we headed into the open area between the course and the woods.

It was sunny up here, but still cold. Very cold. I was not in a hurry to take my coat or gloves off, but you can't bond with a blade unless you touch the hilt with your flesh. I drew the sword and felt the magick pulse through it, waiting for me to direct it.

Before that, I took a long look at the edge (sharp) and the maker's mark on the ricasso (the unsharpened bit next to the hilt). 'Sterling?'

'Yep. Captured during a raid in the 1720s.' You notice that Faith left it open as to who was raiding whom. The Gnomish clan based in Sterling are still going, but in much reduced circumstances. It was time to try the Works.

I've told you about combat using Enchanted a blades few times, but I haven't gone into much detail about either the swords or the magick in them. Most of the Works created are passive: they just do their job requiring only Lux from the wielder. They all have Eversharp blades, for example, and most can also act as Lightsticks. What really makes a sword magickal, though, is the counter-measures and the *Lift*. By the time you get up-close and personal with a sword, you need to move fast. Very fast. Stopping to perform a complicated Work of magick when your opponent is at arm's length is the quickest known way to become a pincushion.

For that reason, every sword I've handled in combat has its main focus on disrupting the enemy's magick rather than creating my own. Glamours, for example, simply won't work in close combat. Those are the counter-measures, and that leaves the Lift.

No amount of magick can make you a better sword fighter. There is no Work that will help you anticipate an opponent or execute a more convincing feint. What they can do is make you faster, stronger and slower to tire. That's the Lift. The trouble is that when both of you have an Enchanted blade, you both get a similar benefit. As with all forms of magickal combat, there's always an arms race going on in the background.

'Ready?' said Faith. I slipped off my coat and got ready to face my opponent.

Who didn't have a sword.

'I thought we'd start with improving your practice. Use me and get yourself warmed up.'

When practising on your own, you're trying to improve your targeting, figuration and lunges, and you do it with or without a target. Today's target was very much alive, so avoiding actual contact would be good. Here we go…

'Elbow! Too bent! … Right knee. Lower it. Lower … Turn. Turn more … Go closer. Much closer … Left leg! Your left leg is like a fucking tree trunk. Move it! … Okay.'

I stood back, sweating, and lowered my blade.

'Well, I don't think Her Grace will be losing any sleep over you, Conrad. What's up with your leg?'

'I thought everyone knew that. Souvenir of Afghanistan. Don't tell me you actually want to see it?'

'No thanks. I see enough of that when I look in the mirror.' She frowned. 'I thought you were exaggerating when you limped around the market the other night.'

'It's worse in the cold, and most of the time I ignore it.'

'But it's affecting your whole stance and response. You spend a *lot* of energy compensating for the lack of mobility, and it's not efficient. I'll have to give it some thought.' She drew her blade, a beautifully slim rapier. Exactly what you'd expect her to use.

The world of magick is the only one where creatures regularly have at each other with lethal intent. It changes things. When the opponent's thrust might actually go through your heart, or her cut might sever your carotid artery, things are very different. She fitted a plastic button to the point of her blade and chucked over one large enough for my much more substantial weapon.

'En garde.' And we were off.

'Halt!'

I'd lasted about three minutes, and I'd been prodded twice, one of which would have been fatal. She wasn't even out of breath.

'I've heard rumours that you held off Princess Lussa for quite a while. How the fuck did you manage that?'

'Honestly? Because I was actually trying to cut her, and I suppose I'm actively avoiding taking a slice out of you.'

176

She frowned. 'I keep forgetting you're mortal. Must be the aura of inevitable doom you carry round with you.' Her right eye bulged and her Fae teeth showed. 'Only joking.'

That was a joke?

'Have you done much practice against a rapier?'

I shook my head. 'Don't do much practice against anyone except Lloyd Flint, and he prefers an axe.'

'It shows. Try again, and try to use your advantage this time.'

She meant my sword. Her weapon was lighter and faster, which meant lightning thrusts and slashes, but made her much weaker in defence. Time to draw on some more of that Lift.

'En Garde.'

This time I lasted five minutes, got stabbed only once and actually managed to inflict a downward cut that would have taken her leg off if she hadn't thrown herself to the ground to avoid it. Unfortunately, on the last pass she sliced through my gilet and drew blood.

She dropped her rapier and stepped towards me. 'Sorry, Conrad. Do you want me to heal that?'

She was standing very close to me, and I could see the veins pulsing in her open scar. What I did next was entirely a matter of trust.

'Please.'

She ran her fingers either side of my wound, drawing the skin together and sending a surge of Lux through my body's repair system, accelerating its natural healing mechanism. In a few seconds, the work of several days had been done, and there was a fresh scab on top. I wouldn't even have a scar.

Job done, she couldn't help herself, could she? She licked my blood off her fingers.

'Eurgh. Ochh. Eeuw.' She spat a great gob, and the last lingering bit of Glamour she had on her face disappeared. Because a chunk of her lip is actually missing, she either dribbles or has to suck constantly through her teeth. It was the sound that she'd been suppressing.

'You actually taste of Dwarf. Did you know that?'

'I can't say I've ever licked a Dwarf, so I wouldn't know. No one else has ever complained. Not even the Fair Queen.'

She raised her palm. 'I'm going to stop you right there. I do not want to know. Let's have a break. And I'm going to bum a cigarette off you to take the taste away.'

We sat on a wall and relaxed for a moment. 'Tell me about Princess Lussa,' she said. 'For obvious reasons, we haven't heard the full story.'

I told her about the attack on Birk Fell and the single combat I'd been engaged in when the Princess's People turned on her. 'What I want to know,' I concluded, 'is how the arrows got through her Ancile. It's a good trick.'

'Trick is right. You know that we don't use true Anciles?' I frowned, and not just at that gap in my knowledge. I could now hear the constant sucking, and when she spoke, saliva started to run down her face. I hadn't notice how often she wiped it away before – the turn of the head, the gesture, all to cover the deployment of a well concealed tissue. 'We could use Artefacts, but it's much easier to …' She waved her hand. 'This doesn't translate well. It's much easier to *ink* them. I can't explain it, but someone close to Lussa must have copied her ink into the arrowheads. Someone went to Birk Fell ready to strike. Naughty.'

She stood up, ready to start again when I'd have preferred another ten minutes enjoying my coffee. 'You're alive, so I doubt you've fought a shifting blade.'

'As in plane-shifting? Once, yes. And before you ask, I had a temporary gift to help me see.'

She nodded thoughtfully. 'Good to know. If you can do it at all, there's a way of recreating the trick with the …' More hand waving. 'Groovy-thing-in-the-blade. I must get out more.' She sighed and wiped her face. 'But that's for another day. Today, we will focus on the basics.'

And we did. Until I pitched forward and fainted, having used up every drop of Lux in my system. She called it a day then.

I didn't ask about the Red Queen until we were almost back at the stables. Faith gave a big suck on her teeth and said, 'She's not discussing it with anyone. Won't allow us to mention it in her presence. At the same time, she's let it be known that she's booked a conference call with Prince Sherston.' Her eyes flicked to mine. 'Also known as Lord Justice Graveney. But don't tell anyone.'

'I don't need to: his name's on our list. Not that most have a clue who Graveney is, so it wouldn't matter anyway.'

She looked genuinely surprised. 'How did you know that? And whose list is he on?'

'Sorry. I should have said the *King's Watch* list. Not mine any more. Still got a copy, though, and you know I'm not going to give our sources away. Why has he never appeared in the Cloister Court?'

'He has. Anonymously. I shall try to listen in when Her Grace calls him.'

'Thank you. And thank you even more for today. I think. I may regret it later.'

'No, Conrad, it's me who should thank you.'

'For trying to keep the peace? That's my job, Faith.'

'Yeah. I know that. Thank you for letting me out. It's been a while. And if you hadn't spirited Lara Dent away, I wouldn't have had my chance with old Hipponax here, would I boy?'

After I'd flown us back to the Windermere Haven Hotel, and when I'd waved her off, I shouted at the back of her retreating vehicle. 'Morwenna. Her name's *Morwenna*, not Lara.' Maybe next time I'll say it to her face.

'How did it go?' asked Mina. 'Should I prepare for a Greening-Fae apocalypse?'

'You should always be ready for the apocalypse, but this particular one has been postponed. Any chance of you waiting on me hand and foot for an hour? I'm knackered.'

She took a good look at me before quietly nodding and moving off the couch. When she'd brought a mug of tea and a packet of Jaffa cakes, she asked how it had gone. When I'd told her, she said, 'Poor woman.'

'Creature,' I responded. 'You can't afford to think of them as human, though I'll grant you, Tara Doyle comes close.'

'There is something going on, isn't there?'

'Of course there is. I have no idea what, though. If the Greenings go to law, then either side or both could be spinning us along while they gather their forces. If Cordelia gets in with the Greenings, she'll make friends with the grooms.' I shrugged. 'Cordy can be quite sneaky when she wants to be. I think.'

'So do I. And I also think that I need to come with you for your next practice session.'

'I know you love taking me down a peg sometimes, but hang on. Coming along to watch me sweaty and humiliated by a slip of a woman is a bit gratuitous.'

'Creature. You said it yourself, Conrad. She is a creature, not a woman, and we both know that women are the cleverest species on the planet.'

17 — Square Pegs

The second phone call on Monday morning declared itself to be *Barrow Police*. Odd. The first phone call had been from the police, too, but I'd been expecting that one.

'Conrad Clarke,' I announced.

'Good morning, Mister Clarke. Good morning, Commissioner! And congratulations,' said a woman with a firm, local voice. 'I'm Inspector Gibson of Barrow. I expect you've heard of me.'

'Always a pleasure to talk to a Daughter of the Earth. Don't worry, your cousin George said that he trusts you implicitly, and Barney Rubble speaks nothing but praise for your command.'

What I was leaving out of that statement is that Sapphire Gibson hates her and that Barney was terrified of her when he was a PC at Barrow nick. Always best to edit these things.

She chose to ignore what I'd said and moved straight on. 'I've got a funny one here. There were a shedload of UFO reports this morning, and one report of theft of livestock. Twenty ewes in lamb, to be precise.'

'Ouch.'

'Precisely. I've had a good look at the map, and the reports of lights were away from the field with the sheep. I'm not privy to all the details, but I think our UFOs may have been landing on property associated with the Fae. I don't believe in coincidences, Mister Clarke, and I'm sure you don't either.'

I was rubbing my chin, safe in the knowledge that she couldn't see me. Mina could, though, and she was giving me raised eyebrows while she held aloft a slotted spoon. My domestic goddess.

'No, I don't believe in coincidences. I shall send Cordelia Kennedy down to have a look.'

There was a moment's frosty silence. 'Are you not coming yourself?'

'I have been summoned to Commander Ross's office at ten. If you want me to cancel...'

There was a sharp intake of breath. If Inspector Gibson is considered scary, Commander Allister Ross is the boss that the Four Horsemen answer to. 'Better not, Mister Clarke.'

'Thank you. I'll get Cordy to rendezvous with Barney at Newby Bridge, shall I?'

The temperature dropped even further. 'An incident like this would normally be handled by assessors alone. I don't have jurisdiction over DC Smith.'

'I get that, but they know each other, and if this really is a case of sheep rustling, you're going to need an *actual* police officer, aren't you? I'm happy to call Liz Swindlehurst if you want.'

She paused. 'It hasn't taken you long to get your feet under the table, has it?'

'I have a lot of friends in agriculture, Inspector, and those lambs could be the farmer's only income for months. He or she deserves a proper investigation, whoever leads it. Now I presume that there will be information on the system for Barney to access?'

'Of course. Thank you.'

'I look forward to meeting you properly.'

'And I look forward to meeting you, Mister Clarke. And when we do, please don't refer to me as a Daughter of the Earth. I am not defined by my father.'

Ouch. 'Of course. We'll be in touch.'

Mina had come over during the last part, serving the breakfast omelette she'd been making and listening to Inspector Gibson. 'Hmm,' she said. 'This *woman* does not wish to be defined by her father's identity, yet she takes his name instead of her mother's. I am not defined by my father's crimes, but I am proud to be a Desai. Tomato ketchup?'

'Please. Thanks for this. I'd better make a few calls.'

Cordy picked up straight away. She probably had her phone next to her plate. 'Morning. Is Matt cooking you breakfast?'

'What? No chance. What's up, Chief?'

Now I know how Hannah felt when I started calling her *ma'am*. Maybe I'd get used to it. 'Got a job for you in Furness. Strange lights and missing sheep.'

'For me? What about you?'

'Been summoned to Cairndale. This could easily be mundane, so I'm going to get Barney to join you.'

'I … He … Right. Yes, sir. Is he coming here?'

'No idea where he is, so best to take two cars and meet at Newby Bridge. If he was in Barrow last night, I'm sure he'll choose another rendezvous. Keep me posted.'

'Will do.'

Liz Swindlehurst was a little more cautious. She knew exactly what had happened at Waterhead on Thursday, and she wanted to make sure that Barney wasn't heading into a trap of some description.

'I can't promise that, Liz, but why would they? Barney isn't a target, and if someone wants to get at me, all they have to do is drive up to the cottage. Everyone knows where I am. And Cordelia is very careful.'

She grumbled a bit, then said, 'If it really is nothing but theft of sheep, that's going to the rural crime unit. We have a whole nest of drug-dealing vipers to deal with.'

'Fine. Let me know if I can help. One good turn and all that…'

'Yeah. Right. I'll message Barney and tell him to turn off at Bretargh Holt instead of coming here.'

'Thanks. I'll see you later.'

'What for?'

'Ross.'

'Good luck. I'll send flowers.'

She disconnected and left me with only a cup of coffee as an excuse to avoid the day. I'd have to get moving soon if I wanted to be in Cairndale on time, because not only did I have Ross at ten, I also had DCI Tom Morton at nine thirty. For once, Tom was going to be the scarier encounter. Coffee finished, I kissed Mina goodbye and left her to write her report for Napier College.

I only just made it to Cairndale in time, and Elaine Fraser was waiting for me at the back entrance to the police station. I may be a special constable, but I don't have a pass to get in.

'Shame about the weekend,' I said. 'All that way for nothing.'

'No need to gloat, Conrad. And since when have you stuck up for the Scots?'

'I'm just trying to be sympathetic.'

'Yeah, well don't bother. It doesn't suit you.'

Elaine is married to Rob Fraser, starting centre for the Scottish Rugby team, and on Saturday they had been somewhat overwhelmed in Dublin. Not the best start to the Six Nations.

Instead of leading me upstairs to the CID office, she pointed down a back corridor. 'We're in the Secure Suite again.'

It was where we'd started the investigation into the Harry Eldridge case, well away from prying mundane eyes, and where Tom and Elaine had devilled away on Project Talpa, the search for the Codex Defanatus. On my last visit here, they'd told me that all roads led to Ireland, and I'd followed them. It seemed fitting that the post script would happen in the bomb-proof windowless bunker that's normally reserved for Counter-Terrorism.

I'd seen Tom briefly, before Christmas, and he had not been happy that I'd taken his and Elaine's hard work and used it to settle a private score. He hadn't said much then, but I'd known that there would be a reckoning one day, and that day is today.

Elaine used her thumbprint and a key-card to open the door. She waved me in and gave me the sort of smile that Roman guards must have given to the Christians before they sent them to convert the lions.

The door clicked and locked behind me, and I looked around. The room was stripped and ready for its next case, apart from a small pile of paper on one table and Sheriff Morton. He had his back to me, and wonder of wonders, he was pouring two mugs of tea. A last meal?

'Morning, Tom. Did you have a good weekend?'

'Mmm. Take a seat.'

There were only two seats to take, and one had his jacket on it. I sat and stretched out my legs.

Tom brought the tea, his own in a mug with sheriff's star on the side (to show he can take a joke), and a new looking one that he placed carefully in front of me. I could see a city skyline creeping round the mug. An old city, with low buildings and water in front of it. I turned the mug round, and on the front was one word. *Galway*. Oh.

'A souvenir of my weekend,' he said, pulling up the creases on his impeccable three-piece suit and making himself comfortable on the other chair. 'I watched the rugby with Elaine, then went on an adventure. Not as exciting as yours, but an adventure nonetheless.'

I sat up straight. 'You went to Galway? What the fuck for? It's the wild west out there, Tom.'

He does a nice line in wintry smiles. 'Where else would a sheriff go?'

I sat back, bewildered. I had a thousand questions, of course, which is what he wanted. I drank some of the tea and smiled.

When he didn't get a rise out of me, he smiled back. 'My granny has a saying: you'd get in where a draught wouldn't. The more I see you, Conrad, the more I feel under siege.' He leaned forwards. 'Your fiancée, who is lovely but also a felon' He paused. 'Your fiancée is working as my girlfriend's finance director. A Fae Princess, also known as Tara Doyle, regularly visits Lucy's coffee shop in Southport and gets photographed outside it. Takings have rocketed. You have a hold over one of my DSes and one of my DCs. You've even sent him on a wild sheep-chase this morning.' The smile was positively Arctic now. 'And above all, you take months of Elaine's hard work and use it for your own ends.'

He had a point. In his shoes, I'd probably feel the same. I didn't think there was anything I could say that would make a difference, so I opened my hands in a silent admission of guilt and drank some more tea.

He drew the pile of paper towards him. 'Which is why I was surprised when Hannah Rothman got in touch with me.'

This time, I didn't just sit up straight, I blurted out my surprise. 'Say again, Tom? Hannah?'

'The same. She had a proposition for me. She said it would help her cause politically, and she said it would help me walk in your shoes.'

Walk in your shoes. Weird. I swear that man can read minds, sometimes.

He started spreading out the papers, just too far away for me to see anything but the Lancashire & Westmorland Constabulary logo and the heading on each one: *Witness Statement.*

'Hannah wanted corroboration of your version of events, so I've been a busy little detective. Over the last week, as well as trying to get to grips with a completely new job in a new area, I've been interviewing people. Some by phone, and some in person.' He held his left index finger over the first statement and tapped them in turn as he sounded out the names. 'So, here we have Eseld Mowbray, Oighrig Ahearn, Fiadh Ahearn, Lloyd Flint, Olivia Bentley – now that one *was* awkward, Rachael Clarke and Lucia Berardi.' He stopped and looked up. 'If you're wondering why Lucy's in there, it's because Mina told her everything, and Mina was the only one I knew I'd never cajole into silence.'

I didn't know whether to feel angry, to feel betrayed or to admit a sneaking admiration for the man. 'How on earth did you get Rachael and Lloyd on board? Especially Lloyd.'

He held up Lloyd's statement, the bottom of which had been covered by Fiadh Ahearn's. The signature box was blank. 'He used disappearing ink. I can see why you're friends.' He gathered the documents together and straightened the edges. 'You're right, though. Both Lloyd and Rachael would only talk to me after Hannah made a personal appeal and said that I'd fill you in. And there's this.'

He twisted in his seat to get at his jacket pocket and extracted a heavy envelope. 'A letter from the United Inquisition of Ireland. That was the hardest thing to get of all. You should read it.'

'Impressive stationery,' I said. 'I love the crest, even if it is a bit modernist for my taste. Never been a fan of Art Deco.' I scanned the document …*Not policy to comment on internal affairs … private matter amongst the People … No record of the Deputy Constable in Ireland.* What? I read it again. 'They're saying that I never went there? How come?'

'I don't understand the magickal politics of Albion, let alone the Emerald Isle. I asked, and this is what they gave me. I'd take a picture of it if I were you. It's going into the Constable's safe.'

I whipped out my phone and took the snap before returning the letter. 'Why, Tom? Just *why?*'

'I've just told you: I don't understand the magickal politics. I think Hannah wants you back in the tent, but not just yet. I'll Airdrop this to you.'

I unlocked my phone again and he sent me a screenshot. It was of a Message conversation between Tom and Hannah:

Tom: *What about feedback to Conrad?*

Hannah: *Show him everything. Tell him I'm hanging on to it and waiting for the right moment.*

I stared at the screen. Why hadn't she told me all this? Why did she send my former Nemesis to Galway on what could have been a very dangerous and rather pointless mission?

Tom interrupted my thoughts. 'I had to know. I had to know for sure that you hadn't put anyone at risk except yourself.' He sighed and put everything into a folder, and put the folder in his case. 'I still think you could have found a better way. Emphasis on *you*. What you did was beyond me, and that was the point where walking in your shoes became a yoke I couldn't carry.' He stood up, and so did I. 'Before we go and face the music with Ross, there's one more thing to say: if you want my help again, ever, then it has to be on the level. No need to promise, just tell me you understand.'

'I understand.'

'Good.'

'I shall start now, in fact,' I declared.

'What?' said Tom, immediately on his guard. He knows me too well, that man.

'You work for Ross now. He trusts you. Should I try and keep my status as a Special or retire gracefully.'

He laughed and went to open the door. 'That's a no brainer, Conrad. The pain he will inflict on you as a Special cannot be overstated.' He held the door open and pointed the finger at me. 'You are going to keep that warrant card and take your punishment.'

'Lucy is wrong about you, Tom. She thinks you're kind and generous, but really you're a sadist.'

'Only when it comes to you, Conrad, only when it comes to you. You have a lot of suffering ahead of you.'

He wasn't wrong. I have never, ever been torn off a strip like that before. I'll give you the edited highlights:

Duplicitous and untrustworthy Sassenach ... Worse than Macavity the bloody cat ... Like making Sweeney Todd a public health inspector ... Latter-day Typhoid Mary ... Not fit to lace DCI Morton's boots ... And my very favourite: *Going to tie you up and leave you on the ninth green, where the golf club members will beat you senseless with sand wedges, am I clear?*

'Crystal, sir.'

By this point, my armpits were sweating like rivers and what little hair I had on my head was standing on end and saluting.

'Good. So prove it. Tell me who the fifth columnists are in my force.'

It was crunch time. Did I put the law first, or my friends in the Particular? As Tom said, it was a no-brainer. But for a different reason. 'There are three, sir. DS Swindlehurst, Police Inspector Gibson and one more, but she's in Preston now.'

He grunted. 'Exactly what I thought. Good. What about young Barney Rubble?'

'His new girlfriend is one of my lot, but when it comes to police work, there is no question where Barney's loyalties lie. And if Erin Slater ever gets in trouble, DCI Morton will be the first to know about it.'

'Hmmph.' He was silent for a long moment. I hadn't stood to attention this long since before my crash, and it was only willpower that held me upright – my left leg had surrendered five minutes ago.

'Right,' he concluded. 'If you cannot bring the Particular to heel in one year, you're dead to me.' He looked at Tom. 'Is that the right expression? My daughters use it all the time.'

'I couldn't possibly comment, sir.'

'Ach, take him away. He's giving me a bad neck.'

Exit Commissioner, stage left. I managed to make it to the corridor before needing to lean on the wall. 'You enjoyed that far too much, Tom.'

'It's one of the few pleasures in my life where you're concerned. I must admit I was holding my breath when he asked you about *fifth columnists*. I hadn't told him about Liz, so he must have worked it out for himself.'

I levered myself off the wall and started to put some distance between me and the Commander's office. 'She gave you the briefing on Thursday's incident?'

He looked around to see if the walls had ears. I think the whole station may be an extension of Commander Ross's subconscious. Except the bunker. Tom lowered his voice to a whisper. 'Not here. Let's nip outside.'

'Or we could go to Lucy's. I'm paying.'

This time he looked uncomfortable on a personal level. 'I have to ration my visits during working hours. Unless I'm with one of the team.' He thought for a moment. 'Actually, I really need to contact South Lancs Organised Crime and shake them up a bit. Take Elaine and brief her. I'll send her to meet you there.'

He offered his hand, and we both knew that this was to draw a line under my Irish adventure and start again. We shook, and I limped off towards the exit.

I'd switched my phone off when I went into the bunker. Even the apocalypse has to wait for Commander Ross. I switched it back on and headed for the Market Square, home to Lucy's café. When it had powered up, not a single message appeared. Or voicemail. Maybe I'm not so indispensable as I thought. Either that or Cordelia is in trouble. I hovered my finger over the *Call* button, then locked the screen instead. She knew what she was doing.

I stopped and stared at the coffee shop before going in. Lucy took it over before Christmas, and she's only just started to make her mark. Literally. If you want to change the signage on your business in this country, you need to dive into the swamp of Planning Regulations. So far, all I could see was that *Cairndale Coffee* had been replaced by *Caffè Milano in Cairndale*. I still thought that was a mouthful, but Mina assured me that it was better for the global brand.

Inside, there was much more evidence of Lucy's impact, and both parts were staring me in the face. Only one of them blinked.

The huge, bright red, front-facing espresso machine declared that coffee was a serious business here, and the figure behind it was no less imposing. 'Oh, it's you,' she said. Full marks for observation skills.

I've seen photos of Bridget Gorrigan off duty. She's a fully-fledged, Whitby grade Goth. But not at work. At work, she's just as unmissable, but the purple uniform shirt and black half-apron are a moderating factor. Bridget is Lucy's operations manager and had come up from Southport to lick the new base into shape. Cairndale is Lucy's third venture, and I suppose that makes it a chain. There will be more.

'Good morning, Bridget. Is Lucy not about?'

'Garstang.'

Lucy is very protective of Bridget, and won't have a word said against her. It's not my place to tell their stories here, but that loyalty goes both ways. Bridget does not like anything that threatens Lucy's happiness, and I do that simply by existing. In her opinion.

'Medium cappuccino, extra shot, and a croissant, please. What does Elaine Fraser normally drink?'

'She sups on the blood of angels. When we're out of that, she likes a double espresso.'

'Then put one on the slate for when she gets here. I wouldn't want it to get cold.'

'This is not the police canteen, despite what some people think. We've lost ten per cent of our business since *certain families* discovered that the bizzies hang out here. I'm gonna put a blue light on that table, you know.'

I leaned forwards, and was tempted to put my hands on the immaculately polished counter, just to make her clean it again. I resisted that temptation and went for, 'Are you sure they just don't like Scousers?'

'Sod off. I suppose you're gonna take this outside and pollute the atmosphere. I'll bring it out, then I won't have to look at you while you wait.'

'You're most gracious, Bridget. Keep the change.' I put a ten pound note on the counter and left her to make my drink.

I was busy annoying Mina when Elaine appeared from up the old road down to the Old Bridge. 'I am not allowed to pester you when you are at work, so go away,' said Mina. She left a pause. 'But I am glad that you have squared things with Tom and Commander Ross. See you later.'

Elaine Fraser has a very distinctive walk. I think it comes from her years of climbing huge cliffs with no ropes and having a BMI that is close to negative. When she takes a step, her foot becomes almost vertical before her toes leave the ground. I wasn't in the least envious. Honest.

'You've answered my first question,' I said when she arrived. 'Your leg appears fully recovered.'

'Yeah. It is, thanks. I'm not in a hurry to get shot again, though. Just make sure your pet psycho's got the message. And your other pets, too.'

I smiled and nodded. Elaine had every right to call out Karina for what she'd done. And I could understand her being reluctant to engage with Mannwolves again. Let's move on, shall we?

We went inside, and Elaine went straight to the blue light table, ignoring Bridget. By the time I'd gone up the counter, a double espresso was waiting for me. It may be Service with a Scowl in here, but it's definitely efficient. Oh, and the coffee is marvellous.

'Thanks. Why am I here?' said Elaine.

'The Waterhead Incident. Tom wanted my version of events. And to know what I'm doing.'

She put sugar in her espresso and stirred vigorously. 'You mean he doesn't trust Liz Swindlehurst.'

I shook my head. 'I'm sure he does trust her. I would. She's not the Commissioner, though.'

'Why should I care about this? It's got nothing to do with us, has it? Not really. It's not our world, and if it was, there's fuck all we could do about it.' She showed me her extendible police baton (which she is never without). 'This isn't a magic wand, is it? We don't get issued with them.'

'Fair point. It's not as though you're short of crime to investigate. It's just that there are some of us who think that magickal and mundane law enforcement should work more closely.' She shrugged and slurped half of her coffee. I shuffled on my seat to get a little closer. 'There's another reason. I'm out on a limb here. If something happens to me, Mina will be on to it. If something happens to *both* of us, Tom can act as witness.'

She signalled her acceptance of the idea by taking out her notebook and drawing a very neat Valknut at the top of a blank page. 'Tell me.'

I'd finished telling her, and had taken another coffee outside for a smoke when Cordelia finally checked in.

18 — Rustling

Cordelia stared at her phone as if it were toxic. Maybe even radioactive. Was the Goddess sending her a message? Had She inspired Commander Ross to summon Conrad this morning so that Cordelia would be tested alone?

'You look like you've heard a really tasteless joke,' said Matt from the other end of the kitchen. 'You're horrified and laughing at the same time.'

'Sorry, Matt. Just thinking about whether the Goddess could move Commander Ross.'

He had a tea towel in his hands while he administered a thorough polishing to *his* Denby mug (the blue one), and he paused to consider the idea. 'So long as She moved through Mrs Ross, I think that's entirely possible. What's up?'

'Our first case has come in, but Conrad's been summoned to Cairndale.'

He didn't hesitate. 'Do you want me to come?'

She smiled at him. 'That's really kind, but I've been given a man already. Barney Smith is going to take care of me.'

Matt snorted and put his mug away. 'Other way around, more like.'

Cordelia had already got up and was looking for the dishwasher, until she remembered that she'd been looking at him. Matt Eldridge did not believe in labour saving devices. 'Can I dump this? I need to get moving.'

He stepped back from the sink. 'I told you: breakfast washing up is mine to do. What's come up?'

She put her crockery in the sink. 'UFO lights and missing sheep in Furness.' She was about to head out when he frowned, lost in thought. Matt took a lot of getting used to, and one (of many) annoying character traits was that he made her forget he was an experienced assessor because he never talked about it. She decided to push him. 'Any thoughts?'

'Have you got a location?'

'Not yet.'

'If it's just east of Barrow and west of Urswick, then it could be the site of an old sídhe. And I'm talking *really* old. The Radiant Queen was gone well before the Black Death. I used to cover Furness when Petra was on holiday, but I never went there.'

Matt had mentioned the late Petra Leigh a few times. Enough to make her wonder. 'Were you and Petra ever an item?'

He looked alarmed at the question. The file on Petra's murder included a marginal note from Conrad: *M.Eld. Says not in rltnshp*. Fine, but that was the present. The past is another matter.

'You've got a case, Cordy. I don't want to hold you up. But call me if you need me. Please.'

'Thanks, Matt. See you later.'

When she'd finished loading her car, she checked her phone. An unknown number had messaged: *Best to meet at the Swan. I'll be there at nine. How do you take your coffee? B.*

She added *Barney* to her contacts and replied, *Strong and black. No sugar.*

She had no idea where he'd got the takeout coffees from when she finally found the Swan Hotel. It certainly wasn't from the extensive upmarket hotel by the River Leven, the top half of which was glistening white in the sun. At ground level, they were still in damp and freezing shadows. 'Erin does something to change her number plate when she leaves,' he began. 'Shall we take my car?'

He was looking dubiously at her vehicle, and with good reason: Barney Smith might not be as tall as Conrad, but he was a lot wider. And younger. 'Yes please. Conrad's mileage allowance is really stingy.'

'Hop in. Have you been down England's longest cul-de-sac before?'

She got in out of the cold and clutched her coffee. The car was nicely warm, too. 'What do you mean? Cul-de-sac?'

'The A590 to Barrow. One road in and one road out. Unless you've got a boat, of course. Or a helicopter. There's a tablet computer on the floor with the map loaded and the reports flagged. Is there anything coming left?'

Cordelia drank some of her coffee to get the level down before retrieving the device. She did *not* want spillage on her first case. Barney supplied the pass code for the tablet, and she stared at a mostly white screen with a couple of roads and a couple of blobs that must be buildings. There were two red pushpins on the map, both in the middle of blank space. Where was Google Earth when you needed it? 'Can I zoom out.'

'Course.'

She shrank the scale until she could see that Barrow was at the end of a long peninsula. She had to shrink it even further to find where a flashing spot identified their current location. What a strange place to have a large town.

She zoomed back in and saw that the reported incidents were south of a village called Newton in Furness, and due east of Furness Abbey. She recognised that alright. It had once been a famous centre of magick and had lent its name to a few Charms. Now she could definitely see that as a good location for the Art.

'Tap the pins for details,' said Barney.

Her finger hesitated. 'Do you mind if I don't? I've never been good at reading on the move.'

He gave her a sideways glance and a grin. 'I thought that was what multi-tasking was all about.' Point made, he focused on the road again. He needed to – it switched from dual carriageway to single without warning, and the level of hustle and tailgating from some of the drivers wouldn't be out of place in Italy. Then again, if you had to use this road regularly, it would drive you mad.

'I only had a quick look,' he continued. 'I have no idea what the flashing lights are all about. That's your department. What I can tell you is that the rustling was a professional job. Farmer says that he heard nothing despite his wife being a light sleeper. They were rounded up from four fields, so matey was there for a long time. And they made sure to eradicate their tyre tracks from the gateway. Shall we do the farm first? You can read up on the woo-woo stuff before we go anywhere else.'

'Is that what you call it when you're with your Master Enscriber? *Woo-woo stuff?*'

He chuckled. 'Oh no. I wouldn't dare.'

By the time they wound down a country lane towards the farm, she was feeling slightly jealous. Of Erin. Every time she saw Barney, she knew immediately why Erin Slater had set her cap at him (as her grandmother would say), and now she had an idea of why Erin wanted to move in with him. Had already moved in with him, in fact. Perhaps by the end of the day she'd find out why no one had tied him down before. Or maybe they had. Or maybe he preferred being tied *up*. Stop it, Cordy.

'Here we are.'

She unclipped her seatbelt and got ready to get out.

'I thought you weren't coming.'

'Why not? I thought we were a team.'

'We are. A team in wellingtons. You can't wear those shoes in the car if you've been on a farm, and you didn't bring your wellies. I haven't got Erin's with me, either.'

She looked around the car. It was spotless, but she hadn't noticed, having other things on her mind. Why is it that men are perfectly capable of keeping their vehicles clean, but have a blind spot for the laundry basket?

Her phone rang, and she clung on to it. 'Better get this. Might catch you inside.'

He nodded and gently took the tablet off her lap.

Her call was another Unknown Number. 'Hello?'

'Is that Cordelia Kennedy? Sorry to bother you, but I've tried the new Commissioner, and he's not answering his phone, so the Witch of Elter Water gave me your number. I hope you don't mind.'

It was the voice of an older woman, with a gentle Northern accent that reminded her of Barney. Could be his mum. 'Of course not. How can I help?'

'I'm the leader of Bardsea Coven, near Ulverston.' They'd passed through Ulverston on the way to Barrow, but she hadn't noticed Bardsea. 'One of our Sisters felt a distinct presence at the Radiant Queen's old sídhe last night. We thought the assessors would want to know. Petra would have looked into it.'

This was definitely the work of the Goddess. If the woman had left Conrad a voicemail, he might not check it for hours. 'I'm very close to there now, sister. I'm on the case, or I will be soon. What can you tell me about it?'

'About the presence? Nothing, dear. It was definitely there, though. A real disturbance in the Echo.'

'Thank you. I was wondering about the sídhe as well.'

'Don't you know?'

'I know that the Radiant Queen lived there a long time ago.'

'You're not driving, are you? I don't like that.'

'Not at all. I'm sitting in a nice warm car near a farm while my partner looks into some missing sheep, which may or may not be connected.'

'Sheep? Never mind. The Radiant Queen died suddenly in the night, so they say. Almost unheard of. The first thing her People knew was when the sídhe started collapsing into the mortal realm. They ran for their lives. For generations, the place was considered cursed, then forgotten. After the Abbey was dissolved, one of the families claimed to have dug into it, and they were rich for a year and a day. Or they lied. Either way, they all died horribly. I used to love scaring the apprentices with that story. Especially the one about the wild boar.'

Cordy's head was spinning. What had she got herself into. 'Anything more recent than that?'

'Every Mage in the south goes there at some point. Usually in the daytime, then they pretend they went at night to impress their friends. The Fae definitely go there, and it was probably them there last night. Not that you'd get an answer out of them.'

'Thanks. I'll be very careful.'

'You do that, and I shall pray that the Goddess walks by your side. It's good to have a Sister in high places again. I'm sure you'll have that great lump of a Commissioner wrapped round your finger soon, if you haven't already.'

She laughed. 'I'm a bit late for that. I think I'd be better off trying to recruit Mina for the Sisters: she's the one with Conrad on a spindle.'

'Why not? Goodbye, dear.'

It was only when she'd disconnected that she realised she couldn't look up the police reports, because Barney had the tablet. She allowed herself a smile, though, because the Witch had talked about *every Mage in the south*, as if Barrow-in-Furness was the border to some alien world. Presumably they thought that her own county of Hampshire (next stop the Isle of Wight) was on another planet. It was going to take some getting used to, and she still had no idea exactly where this bloody sídhe might be.

She opened Google Earth on her phone and desperately scanned the area. Nothing. She did find Bardsea, though. And Birkrigg Stone Circle (not to be confused with Birk Fell, where Conrad's Pack lived). If the circle were a node on a Ley line…

She took a screenshot and drew a line between the circle and Furness Abbey, and she was still studying the image when a shadow fell over the car and the boot opened. Barney was back.

He got in and passed her the tablet. 'Any luck?' she asked him.

He pulled a face. 'The old guy was very surprised when an actual detective knocked on his door, and I won't be putting his theory in my report, that's for sure.'

'Why not? Does he think his flock were abducted by aliens or something.'

'Close enough. He blames folk from Yorkshire. Says they come over the Pennines all the time to steal things. I don't want the Sheriff reading that.'

'Is he from Yorkshire?'

Barney gave her his amused look. 'Can't you tell? I had to prod the farmer to show me the crime scene. There's no point in you looking is there?'

She shook her head. 'Not now. Unless there was a lot of magick involved, even an expert Sorcerer wouldn't get anything.'

'Shame. Was your caller any help?'

'A lot, actually.'

'Who was it?'

Oh, the shame of it. She'd been so wrapped up in the woman's story that she hadn't even asked her name. Basic procedure. What the hell was she going to put in the report?

'One of the Sisters of the Water. They saw it too. I'll just cross-reference with the police reports.'

She buried her head in the tablet and found the reports. She held her phone next to the screen and compared the two. 'There. I know most of the reports are to the south, but those two are exactly where I'd expect them to be.'

He started the engine. 'Good. Quicker to go via Dalton in Furness. We can stop for another coffee if you like.'

She could take the coffee or leave it, but a comfort break would be *most* welcome. 'Thanks. And my source told me something else. I think I'd better handle this one on my own.'

Twenty minutes later, he dropped her in a lay-by opposite a tall hedge, much bigger and wilder than the well-trained agricultural hedges dividing the fields on her side of the road. 'I can't wait here,' he said. 'I'll drive into Newton and park up at the Farmers Arms. Only two minutes away.' He paused. 'How long should I wait before I call the cavalry?'

'Honestly, Barney, I don't know. I'll have a quick look, and if I think there's something that needs investigating, I'll message you to leave me. I'll find my own way back.'

'From here? You're joking. It'll take you an hour to find a taxi willing to come out, and the fare to Newby Bridge is way more than Conrad will let you claim. Or should that be Mina? I take it she's appointed herself the Commissioner's finance director.'

'How did you guess? It could take me a couple of hours in there. Or longer, and I don't want to put you out.'

'Tell you what, if I haven't heard from you in ten minutes, I'll head into Barrow and follow up on a few other things. It'll keep Liz happy, that's for certain.'

'Great. Let me get my stuff out of the boot.'

Her *stuff* was mostly extra cold-weather clothing. It wasn't getting any warmer, and there was a bloody cold wind coming off the Irish Sea. Conrad was predicting snow within a day.

Barney drove off, and Cordelia addressed the hedge. She could feel magick straight away, but it was coming from *behind* the hedge, not the hedge itself. Odd. Then again, only someone armed with a bulldozer would try to get through the combination of hawthorn and wild brambles that blocked out all view of the other side. The diesel exhaust had dispersed, and she took a great sniff of cold air. Nothing. Apart from the absence of fumes, the countryside didn't smell of much today. Too cold. Left or right? She hadn't seen anything on the way in, so she turned left and crossed the road.

There was a bend ahead, and she could feel the magick getting closer to the hedge. Further round and they converged at a deep-set farm gate. If she hadn't been following the Charm, she'd have walked straight past it and not noticed. This was definitely the place. She sent Barney a quick message – *Going in. Will call you when I'm done.* And then she set about unlocking the gate. Magickally speaking.

When she dropped down on the other side, she could feel the wind blowing up her new walking trousers, because she'd torn a great gash in them getting over the barbed wire topping to the gate (was that even legal?). It could have been worse. She could have been practising first aid on herself. At least her thermals were intact.

The odd thing about the magick was that it was fairly new. In historical terms. No trace of the old, old Charms that still protected Glastonbury after two thousand years. No. There were even bits that she was sure had the signature of Salomon's House on them, and there were very few Chymists in the Particular. She made a mental note (no way was she taking her gloves off to write anything down), and set off up the slope. Another oddity: there was a big farm gate, but no track on the other side. Whoever put the barbed wire up obviously didn't use the gate for access to anything. The short rise soon ended, and there it was: the Radiant Queen's resting place.

Did that place in Ireland look like this? When Niði felled the Fair Queen, had her palace ended up as a convincing impersonation of one of the grass-covered slag heaps that ringed Barrow, a legacy of the ironworks? If there had ever been any beauty in the sídhe, it was gone now, and only the melancholy of gentle mounds remained.

She shielded her eyes from the low sun and looked around. The shortness of the grass was explained by the sheep grazing a hundred metres away, and there were a few mature trees (oak, rowan and hawthorn), but that was it. No ruins, no buildings and certainly no giant stone sculpture like the Innerdales had shown her in their preview at Middlebarrow. The light show here last night had been put on to give her an excuse to be here, so where was the action? Did she have to criss-cross the whole hilly expanse like Conrad with his dowsing rod?

Surely not. She was a Witch, admitted to the Daughters. She was better than that. She looked again at the only clues she had. Living clues. The trees. Oak, oak, hawthorn … Why were there five hawthorns, all spread out like that, instead of clustered? Because they were the five points of a star, that's why, with each one at a precise seventy-two degrees from its neighbours. Game on.

She did end up criss-crossing the field. Just like Conrad. Bloody Fae: they'd only gone and set up an escalator, hadn't they? To get where the action was, she had to find the right sequence of trees to access the gateway to the higher plane. By the time she'd figured it out, hat, scarf and both pairs of gloves were in her rucksack, and she was sweating cobs (as they say up north). Remembering the weather the other night, she forced herself to stop for a minute, cool down and put her layers back on. Only then did she make the crossing.

And very much wished she hadn't.

19 — Over the Rainbow

It was boiling. Everything was boiling: the pools of water bubbled, the grass seethed and churned like an army of moles were digging under it, and the air moved up and washed over her face with tropical wetness, and she could only see a few feet in front of her, so much did everything shimmer. She'd already pulled her hat off before she'd taken it all in. Gloves were next. What in the name of the Goddess had she let herself in for?

She could feel a further barrier, and she pushed through. Heat seared the back of her throat, and sulphur stung her eyes and nose. The shimmering was worse here, and there was a multi-coloured edge to the air, as if a rainbow had collapsed into this little corner of hell. There were creatures here, too. She could feel them. Intelligent creatures. And that made her feel very, very alone. Alone and scared. This was nothing like the image that Lucas and Helena had shown her. If they'd shown her the truth, would she still have come?

Yes, because when she tried to extend her Sight, she could sense that most of the creatures – Spirits – were trapped underground, and that's why the grass was writhing around.

'Well met, fair Witch.'

She gagged and nearly retched when she tried to speak. She coughed. 'Lucas. Where am I?'

His manifestation had real presence here. In fact, he looked more real than the twisted trees (and were those trees moving? She hoped not), and he, too, coughed before he answered. 'Welcome to the royal pens, where the Radiant Queen used to keep her tame Spirits. It's a Lakeland thing. And a few other places far away. It's how the great-souled Raven was bound. Is bound.'

Her heart leapt. 'Is she here?' She extended her Sight further, and wished she hadn't. Whatever was penned under the ground was not Raven. She recoiled, and had to fight against returning to the lower world.

Lucas looked kindly upon her, and held out a hand to beckon her back. 'Don't worry. You're safe. Do you want to see how it's done? Help us trap our enemy. Yours and mine.'

'What do you mean?'

'You've seen him, haven't you? The great rainbow Spirit that follows us around.' She nodded. 'It's the Warden. The late Warden, to be precise. Sir Roland.'

It was so improbable that it had to be true. She'd know in a second if it were a lie, and the rainbow Spirit had looked a lot like that incredible cloak which the Warden had worn on formal occasions. Like his visit to

Glastonbury, when he'd been greeted in the Strangers Hall and Cordy had served him wine. 'How is he your enemy?' She tried to rally. 'He was a good man, and I can't believe that he could be *my* enemy as well. Not if I follow the will of the Goddess.'

Lucas looked around theatrically. 'And where is She today? Roly Quinn had a secret, Cordelia. A secret he's trying to preserve from beyond the grave, at the expense of a young girl, a girl just becoming a woman. Like your daughter will soon enough. They grow very quickly when you're not there. I should know.'

'Leave my children out of this. They're in a safe place.'

'Didn't sound like it to me. When you were talking to their father last week, it didn't sound like they fancy their new school. Bit strict. How would you feel if Rick decided to take them to London. Handy for Salomon's House.'

'This has nothing to do with why I'm here. Nothing.'

'Oh yes it does. Rick loves his daughter, but if he tried to take her away...' Lucas left the thought hanging long enough for Cordy to know that it was true. If Rick tried to take the children away from the orbit of the Circles of Magick, he would become her enemy overnight. When he'd seen the truth on her face, Lucas continued. 'Roly had a daughter, and his daughter had a daughter. You've met her. She's going to die a horrible, early death because the Queen of Hell has her claws in. Not our problem, you might think, but Roly's descendent is also my descendent. Through Helena.'

Cordelia was stunned. Again, this had to be the truth, because why lie?

Lucas was looking around. He held out his hand like a falconer, and a Spirit formed around his fingers. It grew and grew and became Lucas's wife, Helena. When Cordelia saw the woman's face again, the pieces clicked together.

'Persephone!' she exclaimed. 'Perci is of your line *and* Roland Quinn's!'

'And she is being poisoned, like Maddy was,' spat Helena.

'Help us free Perci, and you will be with Raven,' said Lucas. 'Help us bind the Warden, then go and see for yourself.'

'See what?'

'What I say, Cordelia Kennedy. Persephone is avoiding Conrad like the plague. Next time he goes to the stables, go with him. When he walks one way, you go the other and see her for yourself. Take a very close look at her magick, why don't you?'

'If the Warden knows this, why are you enemies?'

'Because he would free her and no more. So long as the Eden line exists, the Queen of Hell will pick them off, exploit them and toss them aside to die. It must be stopped. For future generations.' He paused and she could see his chest rise a little as he took a breath. If Lucas wasn't completely physical, he was damn close to it. 'I don't want to destroy the Warden. Just trap him here until it's over. You can be the one to make the key.'

Cordy teetered on the balls of her feet. If she went in now, it would be almost impossible to row back on what she'd done. *Almost* but not completely. Binding Spirits wasn't like walking into the Fair Queen's sídhe – it wasn't an absolute commitment. There *was* something odd about Persephone: there must be if even Conrad had spotted it. She would take a look, and then she would decide. There was just one problem…

'I have never performed a Binding or made a key, and certainly not in a place like *this*.'

'Don't sell yourself short, chick,' said Helena. 'You have all the magick you need, and we are here to make the triangle complete. None of us could do this on our own.'

Lucas followed straight on. 'Let me show you how one of them is bound, and you'll see what we mean.'

She nodded and braced herself. Lucas stumped across the grass to a spot about ten yards away. The ground was still moving, humps and tussocks rising and falling. In the way of higher planes, the soil remained undisturbed. There was magick here that went way beyond what Cordelia was used to. Underneath her base layer, she was sweating so much that her underwear had become a sort of fabric soup.

Lucas bent down and laid his hand on the grass. He sprang back as the ground bulged, then broke. A bright red figure surged up and lunged at him, reaching for his Spirit form with its claws. It swiped, missed, then fell to earth. When it reared up again, every muscle in Cordelia's back locked into a spasm. What the hell was that *thing*?

The smell hit her first. Not just sulphur, but the iron tang of blood was in the air now. She gagged and had to force down the bitter taste of cheap coffee coming up her throat. Then she forced herself to look, and she wished she hadn't.

Somewhere inside the shape was a human form, and she hoped that this was a coincidence, because it was half way between having two legs and four. The back legs bent like a beast's, but the front legs had more of arms about them, and … by the Goddess, there were thumbs there, and the terrible claws grew like fingernails, black at the end of pale hands. The body was covered in thick red hair, except for the chest, where in two rows of three, she saw six nipples.

The creature went to wipe its face, and Cordelia finally had to look at the head. Red eyes full of hate, anger and pain stared at her from above a pointed snout with two flat nostrils framed by tusks.

'It's a wild boar,' she whispered.

'If only it were,' said Helena. Cordelia didn't notice at first, but Helena had taken her hand, with warm skin and entirely human feeling. That felt so good.

Lucas had retreated to a safe distance, and the creature made no move to strike out. There was more than a beast behind the horrible shape: there was an intelligence of some sort.

'Don't ask what it is or why it exists, because no one knows. I can tell you that this was not the Queen of Hell's work, my dear. We would not trick you like that, but you might wonder why she keeps it here. Now, look at the hind legs.'

The feel of Helena's hand gave her the courage to look back down, and she saw a filigree silver chain leading down into the earth and up to an ornate silver cuff that fastened above where the ankle should be.

'It's a chain of Lux!' said Cordelia. 'How am I supposed to work with *that*?'

'That's our job. Focus. Look at the binding.'

She risked expanding her Sight, and the visual image of the cuff became a whirling lattice of Lux. It was thin, but it had no end, because it flowed up through the ground, into the lattice and back again. Where the lattice narrowed, it passed through a stable structure that glimmered with blue light. Aah. That made sense: a crystal bar. The bar was pierced with two banks of eight holes, just like the lock on a standard box.

But this creature had huge power, and the air was as full of Lux as it was of sulphur. It also had plenty of time. Why hadn't it simply cycled through the combinations? After all, there were only 65,000 or so. Was it so limited that it couldn't see the way out?

'The web is cursed,' said Helena. 'You were thinking why she hasn't tried to escape, aren't you? It's because the wrong key grows the lattice, lets more power in. Four or five tries and the lattice will smother her.'

Her. Helena had given the creature the distinction of sex. There was compassion in her voice, too. Cordelia took another look at the creature, and its – *her* – chest had started to heave, struggling for breath. With one last heave, she opened her jaws and tried to speak, but only an animal growl that rose into a scream of pain emerged. With a shudder, she shrank back underground.

Cordelia let go of Helena's hand and turned to face her. 'I cannot make a crystal bar. I cannot weave a lattice. What do you need me for?'

Lucas was coming over and heard her. He stopped, braced his feet and closed his eyes. In a second, he was glowing brighter than ever before. He joined his hands, then parted them, and in his right palm was a crystal block, and in his left was a blank key.

'Make it your will,' said Helena. 'Something you can remember, then draw it across the key. Quickly now!'

Cordelia stepped forwards and looked at the key. They clearly thought she had more power than she'd used before. Maybe they were right. It was going to take a lot of effort, though. She shifted slightly, raising her left arm and trying to ease her bra away without putting her hand down her collar. Something was chafing under her top, and if she sweated any more, she'd need to drain her boots. Better get it over with.

It *was* hard, but she did it. She Enscribed the pits and left the lands as they were, then Lucas pressed the key into the crystal block. When he took it out, the key would dissolve, and no one know the sequence except her.

'That was quick,' said Helena. 'Are you sure you can remember it?'

It was a wonderful opportunity to get some air. She turned her back on Lucas and lifted her top. Down her side ran the same sequence as a tattoo: .-. .- ...- . -. -..-

She wafted some air, then lowered her top. While her back had been turned, Lucas had retreated some distance across the grass. 'We must act quickly,' said Helena. 'All you need to do is be the third corner. You've done it before.'

She had. One of the basic rituals of Necromancy was the three-hand tricorn. All she had to do was let the Lux flow in from her right and out of her left while she used her Sight to keep both planes in view. But why that ritual? Surely the Warden was on this plane? Before she could ask, Helena was gone to make the second corner, and Lucas had begun the ritual. Shit. She raised her arms and opened channels for the Lux before it hit her like a wave.

She got her answer in seconds. The fronds of rainbow she'd seen lingering around the field were not fragments of stray magick. They were the Warden, and he had already been trapped, but trapped on an even higher plane than this one. The next level looked even worse: barren and rocky, with no trees that she could see. At the centre was Sir Roland Quinn, or what a statue of Sir Roland would look like if it were made of rainbow light.

He was being held by a simple circle, and she could see where he'd already weakened the flow of Lux, and now that Lucas had made a bridge between the worlds, he would soon be out. Cordelia nearly lost her grip on the flow of Lux as the Warden started to fight against his confinement with renewed energy.

'Both levels!' shouted Lucas. 'I need to see both levels!'

She focused on where the hawthorn trees were standing, and forced the image of Hell onto the barren plain, and there was Lucas, no longer so solid but now he had one end of a silver chain in his outstretched right hand. What he did next caught her breath in her throat.

One image of Lucas stood still, both arms out straight. From this, a second Lucas peeled away, and the second Lucas had the chain. Surely only the gods could do that? To function in two places meant dividing your soul, and that meant…

The Warden lashed out at the second Lucas, and Lucas dodged him. If either of the instances were destroyed, the tricorn would collapse and Cordelia would be caught in the mother of all Lux storms. The Warden's CGI arm lashed out again, and Lucas moved with superhuman speed to throw the chain of light around the rainbow wrist. Got him.

LucasII faded back into LucasI, and Roly Quinn started sinking through the ground. Cordelia focused back on the plane of Hell, and the rainbow was gone. In its place, a normal-looking Spirit image of the Warden struggled with the chain that bound him. He didn't even look up and curse them, he just dropped out of sight and was gone. Gone to the same prison as the wild boar creature and the Goddess only knew what else. Would he even survive down there?

'Well done, lass,' said Helena, suddenly by her side. 'We couldn't have done it without you.'

'Let's get out of here,' said Lucas. 'I know a quick way down, if we use the third hawthorn.'

Cordelia shook her head. She couldn't bring herself to speak after what she'd just done.

'Thank you,' said Helena. 'Seek out Persephone as soon as you're able. Before it's too late.' And with a smile, she faded and floated away.

Lucas was holding her top layers in his hand. He'd now become so solid that he could pick up clothes as if it were nothing. 'Better put these on before we go down. Don't want a cardiac arrest from cold air shock, do we?'

She took the fleece and coat from him as a way of avoiding talking about what she'd just participated in. She struggled into them, wet fabric sticking to dry. 'Never mind cold shock, I'll have heatstroke in a minute.'

'This way.'

He led her across the grass, and every time her foot hit the ground, a whisper or a rumble tickled her ears. For once she was glad of an excuse to run and catch up with a man's longer strides. Lucas touched the flaky, shingle-like bark of the hawthorn. A couple of pieces cracked off as he dug his fingers into the cracks. With no warning, he grabbed her hand and pulled.

Frigid air hit her lungs and a tight fist closed around her chest. 'Easy, Cordelia. Easy.' Lucas's hand wasn't holding hers any more, because he'd become an image again. 'Try to breathe.'

She collapsed on to her backside, and the jolt made her take a short breath. Was she having a heart attack? Adrenalin was coursing through her, and her heart was pounding, not stopping. Panic attack. That's all. She forced cold air into her lungs, followed by a full, slow out-breath. In. Out. Better.

'Shit, Lucas, my arse is soaking.'

'I'd offer you a hand up, lass, but you know how it is.'

She was glad of the extra layers now. She found her gloves in her pocket and put them on, then turned and got up stiffly before her bum froze solid on the wet grass. When she was erect, she noticed that something had changed about the site: the large stone she'd seen in their vision the other night was back, squarely in the middle of the pentagon of hawthorns, and now she could see that it was a stone cross of some description, tall and slender, with a Celtic ring at the top.

'Where did that come from?' she said.

'Where did it go to, you mean.'

She took a step towards it. It was real enough, so why hadn't she seen it when she traipsed about the site before? 'It's a marker of some sort. It must have been put here just after the sídhe collapsed.'

'It was. All the Fairy Roads were marked this way once, but most have been replaced with those Geomancer nodes, which are nowhere near as stable in my opinion. Thing about these crosses is that they only exist if you touch them.'

'Yeah, and that wet grass only came into being when I landed on it. I'm too tired for riddles, Lucas.'

'Chuck a stone at it. Go on.'

It took two goes before she believed him. Both stones flew through the cross as if it weren't there. After that, she had to touch it, and she got a tiny glimpse back into the Hell she'd just left. That and a clear sense of Lux moving east, west and north. She snatched her hand away before it burnt. 'Ow. I wasn't expecting a junction here.'

'The Queens of the Particular like to keep hold of the reins of magick, and the Radiant Queen was no exception. Part of the de Quincey settlement included re-routing the main lines to a new junction near Rydal Water. The Four Roads Cross, they called it. It's where I started my final journey in your world. To Borrowdale and to death.' He paused for a second. It was the first time he'd shown any weakness in her presence, and she liked him for it.

She turned her back on the cross and looked around at the field, at the mounds and at the trees. From one of the rowans, a raven took flight, heading above them and off in the direction of the Abbey. A deeper shiver ran down her back. She knew it wasn't a raven from *Raven*, so who? As the bird passed overhead, she saw that the sunlight had tinged its wing feathers green. *The Morrigan*. What was she doing here, and what did it mean? She turned to ask Lucas, indignation rising rapidly. If he knew about this, all bets were off.

But he was oblivious and hadn't even looked up. 'Do you want a hand with the sheep?' he said.

'What sheep?'

'The ones I borrowed last night. To make absolutely sure you turned up here today. I was surprised you didn't track them here. We should give them back.'

She couldn't believe it. 'You stole twenty sheep.'

He seemed proud of his achievement. 'All that time spent as a sheep dog came in handy. Rounded them up and drove them here. With a little help, of course. Do you want them back in the field or just in the road?'

'I...' She stopped. He was right: she couldn't leave the bloody things in here at the mercy of the Goddess knew what predators. But how the hell was she going to explain their reappearance? Come to that, what the hell was she going to tell Conrad?

20 — Networking

'Hi Cordy. How's things?' I said when I answered the phone.

'Hello? Shut up you stupid bloody thing.'

I guessed she wasn't talking to me, because there was a loud sound of bleating. Well, she'd clearly found *some* sheep. Whether they were the right ones…

'Are you okay, Cordelia?'

'What? Yeah. Move! I thought you had them covered, Barney!'

In the distance, I heard the deep tones of Barney Smith shouting *Gerron with you*. The line went quiet for a second, and I checked to see if we were still connected. We were.

'Finally! Sorry about that, Chief. I was so keen to call you that I jumped the gun. I thought we had all the bloody things safely penned in. They are now.'

'You found them? Well done. Where on earth had they got to?'

'Long story. You're going to get a phone call and an apology from your favourite fencing master in a bit, and I am going round to Barney's house in Barrow. I need a shower so badly you wouldn't believe it.'

'Well done. I think. I will be very careful not to text Erin and tell her that you're getting naked at Barney's place.'

'You haven't heard the worst yet: I'm gonna have to borrow some of her clothes. Or nip to Matalan.' She paused. 'In fact, Matalan is definitely favourite, only they won't serve me looking like this, so tell Erin that her boyfriend's going to buy me some new underwear. I'd better go.'

'You better had,' I responded, but I was talking to dead air. The report on this morning's adventure was going to be interesting.

I put my phone away and got ready to leave the Market Square. On an impulse, I took my empty cup back inside for Bridget, and got a nod of approval for my efforts. She was clearly in love with me.

Back in the cold, I saw Elaine emerge from the side road that led to Booth's supermarket, clutching a carrier bag and checking her phone. I fell into step as best I could and pointed to the bag. 'Tonight's tea?' I asked, using the correct Northern term for one's evening meal.

'Nah. CID sandwich order, seeing as the canteen in Cairndale is a kitchen not a full-service café.' She gave him a sideways glare. 'Of course, this should be Barney's job, seeing as how he's the probationer, but someone sent him out looking for sheep.'

'And he found them. Apparently. You can blame me for all sorts of things, Elaine, especially your leg, but you can't blame me for you being here. How's it going?'

She shrugged, a very economical gesture. 'Better than the alternatives. It was this, stay with Professional Standards (not gonna happen without the Sheriff), or disappear into the overworked, under-resourced pool of detectives in South Lancs. It's good. For now.'

'Where are you staying? You can't be commuting to Manchester, surely?'

'In an old friend's spare room. I used to stop on his sofa occasionally, but he's on the property ladder now, so I get a single bed and sore knees from getting up in the night. There's only a bloody exercise bike in there as well. And a bar from the ceiling you'd hit your head on.'

I didn't dare ask what that was for. Elaine seemed more relaxed than earlier, and she knew she'd be rid of me when we got back to the nick, so I casually threw in the first question of Operation Two Feet. 'You might not know the answer to this, Elaine, but what happens to evidence gathered for a coroner's inquest?'

She was so thrown, she stopped and stared at me. 'You're up to something. I knew it.'

'Of course I'm up to something. It's what I'm paid for. There's a couple of old cases from before my time that have got my nose twitching.'

'Where?'

'Keswick and Penrith.'

'Good. They're in Cumberland, so nothing to do with us.' She started walking again, and said, 'A lot depends on whether there's a legal investigation, and I don't just mean a police investigation. The Health and Safety Executive are often involved. If there is an official investigation, the coroners don't do anything themselves. It's not like it is on the TV, so all the evidence is police or HSE evidence, really.'

'Thank you. That was very useful. And don't worry, if I ever have any questions about goings-on in Westmorland or Lancashire, you'll be the first to know.'

'I can wait. I can wait a long time for that, thanks. See you later.'

I waved goodbye and went to my car. Operation Two Feet is strictly personal, so I don't want to tell you too much about it unless it comes off. Sorry.

Princess Faith called me when I was coming out of the Windermere branch of Booths. It was my turn to cook tonight, and they have some amazing ready meals in the freezer. There were at least half a dozen to try yet.

'Have you recovered from your first lesson?' she asked. Hearing her voice immediately brought back the image of her ruined face. At least over the phone she could suppress the constant sucking. I could cope with it if she could.

'Barely. I am sorely tempted to go back to Hledjolf and get an upgrade to my ammunition. Much less effort.'

'You love it really, and I'll see you again on Thursday if that suits.'

'Weather permitting.'

'You're not going to go all southern on me, are you? Wimp.' She sighed. 'We both know that's not why I've called, though. On behalf of the People of Borrowdale, I would like to apologise for the actions of one of our Knights. They exceeded their authority.'

'Go on, Faith. I'm all ears.'

'Prince Appleby ordered them to arrange for the care of the monument, and they thought that "borrowing" some sheep to keep the grass down was an easy option.'

'In January? The bloody grass isn't growing at the moment. Pull the other one, Faith, it's got a titanium rod in it.'

'What? Oh. Right. Well, the grass *does* grow there. All year. And we often use sheep. Apparently. Not my jurisdiction. The Knight *should* have gone through proper channels, but they thought that with Petra Leigh gone, they'd get away with it. Respect to Cordelia.'

I could see that. It made a weird sense. Some of it did. Some of it didn't. 'If it's not your jurisdiction, why are we having this conversation?'

She sighed again. 'Because Cordelia thought that we could keep it off the books, that's why. If Her Grace gets involved, it will only escalate things. The sheep are back, all unharmed, and Prince Appleby will pay an assessor's fee. With a substantial bonus.'

This also made sense. 'Good idea. The fewer people who know about this the better. If that's what it really was. Despite my reputation, I really am more inclined to believe the cock-up theory of history. "Borrowing" twenty ewes is a much more plausible explanation than Summoning Helen of Troy. For example.'

'I forgot you were tied up in that business. You must tell me about it some time. I'll see you Thursday.'

'Thanks, Faith.'

When I got back to Lake Cottage, I had a suggestion for Mina. 'It's about time I visited the Pack, given what happened last week. I don't want them to forget me. Time Cordelia got to know them, too. Do you fancy coming tomorrow?'

'I don't think there's much chance of them forgetting you, Conrad. If I work late tonight, I should clear this report, and I'd like nothing more than to stand by a freezing lake and inspect chemical toilets.'

'Don't say I never take you to interesting places.'

'Actually, Karina has had a good idea. See if you can source some of these.'

She passed me a piece of paper and left me to it. I glanced at my mission and raised my eyebrows. Fair enough.

Sourcing Karina's idea for the Pack proved quite a challenge, and not one I could sort out overnight, especially as our priorities changed that evening: the Pack Queen gave birth to a healthy baby/cub, and we made a quick trip to Kendal on Tuesday morning to get a suitable gift.

Cordelia was genuinely taken aback by the setup at Birk Fell. 'I had no idea,' seems to be the general reaction, even from Mages and Gnomes. When Karina put on her demonstration of junior archery, Cordy was positively alarmed. She caught me on a smoke break and said, 'If they get any good at archery, they are going to be pretty formidable as humans *and* wolves. You'll have your own private army. Their loyalty to you is … it's almost like the Fae.'

'It's nothing like that. Fae loyalty is biological; the Pack's is religious. In a way. Don't say anything to Karina, but there's been a complaint about the archery.'

'Who from? Who knows?'

'Erin has regular consultations with Omnira, and Protectors are not supposed to arm their Pack. And you're right about the private army thing. It's a huge responsibility.' I showed her my half-smoked cigarette. 'I'm not always good at self-denial, Cordy. I've made myself a promise never, ever to use the Pack except to protect my family. There's a problem with that, though: the only times my word is not binding is when it's under duress or when I make a promise to myself.'

She blinked and took a step back. 'I must get my eyes tested, you know. Sorry, you were a bit out of focus there. The problem is deciding what counts as *family*. I presume that I don't. Does Erin?'

Why did she pick on Erin, and why did she put so much emphasis on her name? I know they have different views on some things, but even so…

'Sorry, Cordy, you don't count as family. Just Mina, Sofía and Rachael. Not even Myfanwy or Eseld. Erin and Karina qualify as Pack officers.'

She put on a mock face of outrage. 'And I thought I was your adopted sister. Shocking.' She grinned an especially impish grin and winked at me. That was a *little* too familiar, but Cordelia is a grown-up. Something caught her eye, and she pointed over my shoulder. 'What in the name of the Goddess are they up to?'

Mina had extracted Maria and her daughter, Lottie, from the Pack, and had taken them round the lee of the cottage, out of sight. While little Lottie stood tall, Mina marked her height against the stones with a knife, and while she did so, she showed Maria what to do for next week.

'Mina wants to establish Lottie's growth rate,' I told Cordelia. 'She wants to know if Lottie is going to be a flower girl or a very small bridesmaid.'

'Tell me you are joking, Conrad. You're going to have Mannwolves at your wedding?'

'Technically, Mina is going to have Maria and Lottie in the bridal party, while Alex and Cara will be my honoured guests.'

'How come Maria gets the special favours?'

'Because Maria saved my life, that's why.'

Cordelia looked again, and waved a little wave at Maria, because Maria was staring at me. She does that a lot when she thinks no one is looking. I waved, too. Maria blushed and looked away.

Cordelia said, 'It's not because Mina wants the most magickally diverse wedding since the gods walked amongst us, is it?'

'I couldn't possibly comment. It does leave a problem, though. Erin is a bridesmaid, of course, but what about Karina? I don't want to leave her here. Doesn't seem fair.'

'Do you think she's bothered? It's your wedding, but I reckon she'd feel so out of place that she'd rather stay behind. And you really should have a Mage with them if you're all off to Elvenham.'

'I know. I'll cross that bridge later.'

'And what about the long term? Do you think Karina will want to spend the rest of her life here? From what she tells me, the only human contact she has is with the staff at the village shop in Pooley Bridge. That can't be healthy. No man is an island, Conrad, not even Karina Kent.'

'I had thought of that, Cordy. She's in a good place at the moment, and there's a lot here that needs doing. I doubt she'll stay long-term, but medium term? It's up to me to do the best for her as I see it. And as she sees it, too. Obviously.'

'Rather you than me. I think we're wanted.'

After the usual feast (of venison. One day Mina will refuse point blank to go unless there's an alternative), I left Cordelia and Karina discussing the Sisters of the Water and went for a walk. With Scout.

He isn't allowed to go far yet, because his leg is still healing. The bone is fully knitted, but border collies are easily distracted, and it wouldn't take much for an enthusiastic run to tear a ligament beyond the healing magick of the pack. When I bent down to put his collar on, I half expected outright rebellion, but no: he was quite happy to be on the lead again. He was just as happy listening to me chunter on, too, and I took an executive decision: he was coming home with me.

Mina thought for a second before saying, 'Good. But not until you've built him a kennel.'

'Does it have to be me?'

'No, of course not, but you're not going to spend money on getting a joiner to come out, are you?'

'No. Alex! I've got a job for you. I'll pay proper money, too. Your Madreb will be very grateful.'

When I'd sent Alex off with a sketch, Mina observed, 'You have no shame, do you?'

'I wonder where I get that from.'

'Your father. Shall we go?'

There was a rather poignant farewell along with the more boisterous general parting. I'd first met Inge, the Pack Elder, only a few months ago. She'd been tied up and held hostage, and she had helped me on a day I'd desperately needed it. The end of her days on this earth had come in the night, and I felt slightly guilty that I hadn't had a chance to thank her before the end. Something she seemed to have sensed, because Karina had a message for me. When she delivered it, I could see the hurt in her eyes, along with doubt.

'Before she passed, Inge said something. She made me repeat it twice. It was, "You have ever treated us as who we are, Lord Protector. When you find who bred and traded Maria like an animal, show no mercy. It's all I ask of you." I told her you wouldn't forget.'

'How could I?'

'She understood. She asked Great Fang to name you in his Pack.'

We looked at the Pack in all their joy. 'I will work hard hard to deserve it. Thank you for everything you've done here, Karina.'

She looked at her boots. 'It's nothing. Thank you for giving me the chance.'

When we got back to Ambleside, Mina headed inside and Cordy went to get in her car. I passed her the piece of paper that Mina had given me. She peered at it, held it at arm's length and finally gave up. 'Sorry, Conrad, it's too bloody dark. I am so going to the opticians on Friday. What does it say? The Pack wants more children?'

'Chickens, Cordy. Chickens. Specifically hens in lay. I thought you could ask around the Sisters. Good money paid, of course.'

'Oh. Right. That explains a lot.'

'It does?'

'Karina was telling Mina – very earnestly – about the Omega 3 content of eggs. Mina had that glazed look she gets when you tell her the weather forecast for the third time in the day. See you tomorrow.'

The last time I went to Grizedale Forest, I was called away by news of the murder of Petra Leigh in the staged accident which also put Matt Eldridge in intensive care. Most of the forest is just that – trees. There is also a big adventure centre with tree-top climbing and an amazing set of zip wires. I can't say I've been. Or plan to.

'You should,' said Eva Trask as we studied the map. 'I thought you were an adrenalin junky, Chief.'

'His favourite sport is cricket,' observed Cordelia.

The fourth person around the table was Ellis Baines, and he doesn't say much.

Today is Tanya's last day as Assessor for the Vale of Coniston. Tomorrow she takes over the Eden Valley, and good luck to her. She'll need it. Ellis is already Assessor for Kentdale and this was the handover session for his additional responsibilities.

The Vale of Coniston is by some distance the smallest union in the Particular, but it has four huge magickal centres: the lair of the Dwarf, Haugstari; the Skelwith Clan's copper works; the Greendale Trust; and our current location, the Cloister Court in Hawkshead, where the assessors have an office. If I didn't believe in separation of powers, I'd have my base here as well. Saul Brathay is working on getting me an audience with Haugstari, and I don't care about the mines, so very shortly we are off to see the Greenings.

Having finished the mundane attractions of Ellis's new patch, Tanya checked something on her phone. 'Do you want me to draw the Ley lines in, Chief?'

This was my map. For some reason, Tanya didn't have one. Buying and prepping a paper map was Ellis's second job. 'Not on here. Just show me.'

'The South Road runs through here, obviously.'

'Not obviously to me, Tanya.'

'Oh. You haven't been to the Four Roads Cross at Rydal Water yet?'

'I'll add it to my to-do list. Carry on.'

'Sorry. The South Road runs straight down from the Four Roads Cross, right through Greendale lands and onwards. There's a junction just *here* and that branch goes off to Haugstari's place, the copper works and then on to Ravenglass.'

'Where does is it end? The South Road?'

'Near Furness Abbey. At the old sídhe.'

I looked at Cordelia and raised my eyebrows. She went red and muttered, 'You know Geomancy isn't my strong point. I was more focused on living magick.'

Fair enough. Why shouldn't she have a blind spot of her own? I have more than enough, even with my slowly opening Third Eye. 'Good. Thanks, everyone. Let's go and face the music.'

Tanya looked nervous. I don't blame her. I would in her shoes. I put her out of her misery by saying, 'Don't worry. I shall face Alexandra and James on my own. You focus on showing Ellis and Cordelia the estate and I'll join you when I can. If I'm still in one piece.'

I folded the map away and we started to get our things together. When we left the modern offices at the back of the Court building, we all looked at the sky. The clouds were starting to build, and it was going to snow sooner or later. Hopefully later.

Cordelia and I followed Tanya's car up Hawkshead Hill towards Coniston and half way down the other side. On a particularly nasty right bend, we turned left across a cattle grid that no one notices because it's the entrance to the Greendale Estate, home of the Greening family since, ooh, the 1500s.

After half a mile of thick woods, Wards and Glamours, we emerged on to a plateau with spectacular views of Consiton Water and a spectacular house to match. 'Nice,' I observed. 'Bit grey for my tastes, but it's not at all showy.

Only one set of pillars. Positively modest by Hawkins or Mowbray standards. And all local stone, too. Very unassuming.'

'I think you're using a different yardstick to me,' observed Cordelia. 'It's still fucking huge and imposing.' She looked around as we drove up to front doors. 'It's also in the middle of nowhere. Makes Glastonbury look positively metropolitan.'

Tanya had pulled up ahead of us, and a woman in an apron came out to have a word, then disappeared back inside, shivering. In seconds, my phone rang. 'We're to go to the stables,' said Tanya. 'They're waiting for us there.'

'Fine.' When I'd disconnected, I said, 'Good job they're not Gnomes. At least they won't be getting ready to feed us to the wild boar.'

'That's the second time you've made that reference about Gnomes, Chief,' said Cordelia. 'Is there a reason?'

I glanced over. 'Because that's what they do to their own if they betray the First Mine. I thought everyone knew.'

She went pale. 'No, I can't say that's common knowledge.' She swallowed and shuddered. 'Remind me never to eat Lloyd's sausages. Are you sure you don't want me to come with you? Be a lightning rod?'

'No. You focus on what they're doing in the woods. And on bonding with the grooms. Here we are. Wish me luck.'

'I … Of course. Good luck, Conrad.'

We got out, having left our car at the end of a busy car park. Apparently the Greenings are a very inclusive family, and there are only a couple of staff cottages out here: all of the Mages and most of the grooms live in the Big House. That still left a lot of buildings, though.

James and Alexandra were waiting outside one of them, and there was the briefest of welcomes before the others were taken away by Charmian and Iras, and I was invited inside the estate office. I took what encouragement I could from that fact that their smiles to Tanya, Ellis and Cordelia seemed genuine.

'Excuse the Glamours,' said James. 'Family business and all that. We can go somewhere else if they're giving you a headache.'

'What Glamours?' I said innocently. Two of the walls were covered with magick, presumably hiding all sorts of information that they didn't want me to see. Either that or images of the Red Queen being burnt at the stake.

'Coffee?'

'Please.'

James poured, and when I'd been supplied, Alexandra finally unfolded her arms and spoke. 'We've heard from the Queen of Derwent's solicitors. Just this morning, in fact. There may be a copy on its way to you, but you can have a look if you want. I'm certainly not reading it out loud.'

'That would be kind.'

James passed me a letter with multiple pages and said, 'The meat is in the third and fourth paragraphs.'

I am not a lawyer, still less a specialist in esoteric law; I would be getting help on this later. As far as I could tell, the Red Queen was directing most of her legal artillery at the Ripleys, because they were the ones who disturbed Urien's tomb. Allegedly.

The Queen wanted total restitution of the tomb and all its Artefacts. Plus damages, of course. They always want damages. Right at the end of the fourth paragraph, she named the Greenings as partners in a joint enterprise unless they could prove otherwise.

'We've just come from the Court,' I said. 'I wondered why it seemed busy.' I passed back the letter. 'More importantly, how is Jocasta?'

'Back home. It's too early to tell how well she'll recover, but she can't go back to school for at least a couple of weeks and it could seriously affect her chances of graduating this year. And if there are long-term complications...'

She left the comment hanging for me to draw my own conclusions.

James took over. 'In an ideal world, of course, the creature would have been put to Judgement at Waterhead. Our claim will be lodged next week. After Jocasta has seen the specialist again. For now, we've given the Court notice of intent.'

'I see. Thank you for keeping me informed.'

'And then there's the Sextons,' said Alexandra.

'Is Rowan okay? Has something happened to her?'

'She's fine, thank the gods. Shaken, obviously, but she had a lucky escape. Her mother has petitioned the Court from inside Esthwaite Rest. She's demanded that the Borrowdale Crown be awarded to her daughter.'

Diana Sexton is in the Particular's magickal jail, the Esthwaite Rest, for conspiracy to murder. I made a note to ask how she was getting along. 'Hmm,' I said. 'A little blue bird has told me that the Sextons also had a lot of money on the race, but I'm sure you knew that.'

Uncle looked at niece, and to me it seemed a genuine surprise to both of them. 'How much?' said James.

'Enough that they'll be in serious trouble if Blenheim is disqualified, but they'll make a killing if the result stands. If the race is voided, they'll get their stake back, of course.'

'Who else knows?' asked Alexandra.

'No one outside this room, and I've told the bookmakers to keep it quiet. I don't want the Red Queen to think she's facing a mortal conspiracy.'

'And you? What's your position, Lord Commissioner?'

'The same as it was on Thursday: in the middle. Mina has had an unofficial word with Judge Bracewell, and it's likely that the case will be heard in the Old Temple, not up here.'

'*And the lawyers will feast on our bones, having first stripped them clean,*' said James as if it were a quotation. Who knows? It may well be. In fact, it probably should be. Good job I'm engaged to an accountant, not a lawyer.

'I'd better see how my team are getting on,' I said. 'I'll finish the coffee outside, if you don't mind.' I stood up, and we shook hands.

'Leave the mug by the door when you're done,' said James. 'And there's an ashtray round the corner.'

While I was finishing my coffee, Sophie the stable groom appeared with a smile on her face.

'Morning, sir. I've been sent to fetch you.'

'Morning, Sophie. How's things? How's Blenheim?'

'Healing nicely, thanks. Will you want to ride today? Ms Kennedy is already getting fitted for a helmet.' She blushed a little, and continued, 'Miss Charmian asked me to take Miss Kennedy's first lesson. None of them are used to working with complete novices. You could help me out, sir.'

'You'll do a great job, Sophie. Don't you worry. I'd better not ride today, thanks. If you could give me a minute, I need to make a call.'

'Sorry. I'll go.'

'No need. It's not private.' I made the call, returned the empty mug and followed Sophie into the complex of stables, sheds, pens and mysterious buildings with no windows that make up the Greendale Estate's business. The visible part, anyway.

I looked round and took in as much as I could without being staring, then focused on the group in the middle. Tanya and Ellis were saying goodbye to Cordelia and Charmian Greening.

'Sophie, could you get Cordy's mount. I need a word with her before I go.'

She jogged away, and I took Cordelia to a quiet corner. She began with an apology. 'Do you mind waiting, Chief? Or coming back? Sorry, but it seemed too good an opportunity to miss.'

'Sorted, Cordy. Matt is down Grange way, and he's going to detour to pick you up.'

'Oh. Thanks. How did it go?'

I made a sour face, letting out what I'd had to suppress in the meeting. 'How would you feel if it were your daughter's arm in pieces?'

She went red. 'That's not fair, sir. I'm here as an assessor, not as a mother. That shouldn't come into it.'

Whoa. Where had that come from? 'I'm just asking you to put yourself in Alexandra's riding boots for a minute, that's all. Do you think she's going to be happy with a lawsuit that costs a fortune and drags on for months, if not years? Especially if Jocasta doesn't recover full use of her arm.'

'I don't know, sir. Do you think the Queen will be happy with a lawsuit that drags on for months?'

It was no more than I deserved. 'Unfortunately, both parties are in the wrong here, but so far they're playing by the rules. Let's hope it lasts, eh? Are you still on for a trip to Sprint Stables tomorrow?'

'I thought you were convinced it was going to snow.'

'It is. So long as we don't get freezing rain, it won't bother the Smurf, and I'm not going to have the locals calling me a Southern Softie. Having said that, Mina won't be coming. She freely admits to being a Southern Softie.'

'Yeah. If I can get down from Blackburn House, I'll be there.'

'Good. Enjoy your ride.'

When Sophie saw that I was leaving, she handed the rope to Cordelia and dashed over to me. 'I'll walk with you to the car,' she muttered, looking down at her boots.

I couldn't help laughing. 'You've been told to keep an eye on me, haven't you? Stop me poking my nose into things that aren't my concern.'

'Sorry.'

'Don't worry, Sophie. I'm used to it. And it shows they trust you not to give any secrets away. I'd take it as a compliment.'

'Yeah, right. It means I don't know anything, that's what it means. Not that I mind. Just having the chance to work with actual *Unicorns*. Wow.'

I paused at the exit to the yard. 'I bet you're sick of old farts like me giving you advice. I know I was at your age.' I hoped desperately that she would say that I wasn't old. No such luck. My ego may never recover. 'So don't take this as advice, just as a statement of fact. You will never be head groom here or at any other magickal stable. And when you're qualified, they will pay you more than you'd get at a mundane yard.'

She frowned. 'And that's a bad thing?'

'If you have any ambition, yes. Now, there is one thing you can tell me: where have I seen her before?'

I pointed to a groom with unmissable red hair. She was slightly older than most of her colleagues, and I'd seen her give a couple of them orders.

'Do you remember Blackthwaite Stables?'

'I tend not to forget places where I've been shot. I've still got a couple of pellets in me from that day.'

She went slightly pale. 'Right. Well, Clara was their head groom, but she came over here when the Greenings took over.'

'They did, did they? What happened?'

'They transferred the bloodstock here. I dunno what's happening to the land and buildings, 'cos Rowan doesn't inherit until she's twenty-one. Something about death duties.'

Of course. The late Diarmuid Driscoll was Rowan's unacknowledged father. Who else would he leave it to?

'Clara must be good,' I said casually.

'She's a Witch. She ran Mr Driscoll's surrogacy operation. Having her here gives Iras more time to focus on the non-horse business.'

Sophie's words had slowed down during her statement as she realised she was giving away far more than she should have. It was time to go.

'Thanks, Sophie. The first time I met, I told you that anything you said would be in confidence. Hasn't changed. Take care of Cordelia.'

She looked a lot happier when she waved me off, and I carried my musings back to the car.

I once heard a scientist answer the old chicken-and-the-egg problem by saying, 'The egg came first, and it came from something that wasn't quite a chicken. That's evolution.'

High Unicorns are all male, so obviously they come from surrogates. I'd already figured that out. The interesting part for me was that Iras had a substantial *non-horse* business to tend to. Another thing to add to Cordelia's list.

21 — Quicksilver

It did snow. It snowed a lot. The morning after her first taste of the saddle, Cordelia found herself staring at a valley full of white, topped by white hills and under a sky of white clouds. There was more on the way.

'Do you really want to go to Longsleddale in a helicopter?' asked Matt. 'In this? You must be mad.'

The phone on the table told her that the trip was still on, and that Princess Faith was already on her way to Ambleside. Matt was right, this was total madness. Almost as mad as entombing the Spirit of the Warden in a magickal Hell-hole.

'I trust Conrad. He's all sorts of things, but he's not suicidal.' She tried to change the tone. 'Do you think you ever met him when he worked the rescue helicopters?'

Matt was a dedicated member of the local mountain rescue volunteers, and had already said that he'd probably be called out over the next few days as the snow and ice claimed more victims.

Matt looked out of the window. 'He doesn't remember me. I went to the pub with him when he came on a visit. Clearly I made no impression. There was no point in trying to remind him when he rocked up here as Watch Captain, and now it's too late.'

Cordelia cringed inside. She could just imagine the (fifteen years younger), dashing RAF officer (with hair!) being the life and soul, encouraging all the old-timers to tell the most outrageous stories. And Matt would have been at the back, unable to top them and with no reason to shove himself to the front. He'd probably lived his whole life like that.

'Doesn't matter,' she said. 'I can't go because I'd crash that little car before I got half way down the hill. The snow must be deeper than the tyres.'

Matt thumped his mug down. 'You *shall* go to the ball,' he declared. 'I've got to stock up anyway, and I'm used to this. Why do you think I've got a four-wheel drive pickup with winter tyres?'

'Oh no, I couldn't.'

He looked at her, and looked right inside her. 'Up to you. Don't use me as an excuse. I'm going out anyway. You do want to eat tonight, don't you? And we might get properly snowed in over the weekend.'

'I'll get changed.'

He paused half a second. 'Will you go riding again today?'

'You must be joking. My arse and thighs need at least two days rest.'

When she emerged from the slate longhouse that had become *home* far quicker than she'd believed possible, the tranquillity of the winter's morning had been shattered by the rattle and roar of the pickup's diesel engine. Matt drove incredibly slowly down the hill, showing way more patience than she could ever do. He sped up on the valley floor, and once they got to the main road from Ambleside to Hawkshead, the Westmorland Council gritters had done enough to stop the worst of the snow from sticking.

They saw no less than three cars in a ditch, crumpled into a wall or (in one spectacular case) astride a demolished lamppost. That would have been her. Definitely.

'I'll wait until you're airborne,' said Matt, cutting the engine. 'And before then, I'm going to make sure he still knows what he's doing.'

She was on the verge of objecting to a man looking after her, as she had so many times in her life, and then she opened her mouth and suddenly realised that she was grateful to him.

'Morning, Matt,' said Conrad cheerfully. 'Come to help?'

Help? Help with what? Princess Faithful, with a scarf covering most of her face, was standing mutinously to one side. Conrad had that *I'm-enjoying-this-you-won't* look on his face.

'There's no point in having two Mages and a Fae Noble on hand and knocking the snow off myself, is there?'

She looked at the Smurf and stifled a laugh. With a coating of snow on the top, it looked like a badly executed cupcake made with way too much food colouring. Her daughter had once made one just like it.

'Is it safe to fly after an overnight with snow and frost?' said Matt.

Cordelia patted him on the back of his waist. 'Of course it is. Come on, Faith, can you do the Notus Charm?'

'We call it the Vey Fire, and I can do it. That's not the point, though.'

'Sod the point,' said Cordy. 'I was warm in the truck, and now I'm freezing. The sooner we do this, the sooner we get going. Corner each? And yes, I mean a square, Chief. You're not shirking this. It'll be good for you.'

The Greek God of the South Wind, hot and dry, had given his name to the Notus Charm, and although it took a fair bit of Lux, there was nothing else that would have got the snow off without running the risk of freezing it to the rotors. They'd only been going ten seconds when Conrad put his hand up.

'You'll have to count me out. If I do much more, I won't be able to fence, let alone fly.'

'Bloody Earth Mages,' muttered Faith. 'Completely useless unless they can charge you for it.'

The snow started to blow off. Cordelia snickered when Faith deliberately sent a blast of meltwater in Conrad's direction, hitting him like a wave. She couldn't resist making a snowball and chucking it at him as well, adding a little magick, just enough to make it a missile. When he had to duck sharply to avoid it, she gasped. *No active Ancile.* Oops. Even Matt cracked a smile when Conrad got up, covered in snow and with water dripping down his face.

'If only Mina could see you now,' she said. 'Hang on, where is Mina?'

'Already gone. I'll tell you later. Round about the time I get you back for that, ladies, because I will have my revenge. Now, why don't you three make a snowman while I start the engines?'

She turned to Matt. 'Shall we?'

'He'd love it if we did,' said Matt. 'Because those rotors are bound to cover us all with snow if we're anywhere near here. If I were you, I'd get in sharpish. Have fun.'

Cordy and Faith looked at each other, then raced to the chopper doors, Faith's longer legs giving her a head start until Cordy tripped her up. Snow: the quickest way to feel like a child again, no matter how old you are.

The same principle applied at Sprint Stables. There were already five snowmen in a horseshoe near the yard, and likely to be more later. Although there was a lot of cold, hard work to be done, all the grooms still looked cheerful. Except Persephone. She was nowhere to be seen.

'What are you going to do while we're out?' asked Faith.

It sounded like an open question, so Cordy gave it an open answer. 'Muck in. Muck out, probably. I've got a lot to learn about horses. I might also check for a cache of hidden weapons. What should I look out for, Chief?'

'Rocket propelled grenades are always a favourite. Grab a couple for me if you find some. Now, do you want to say hello to Evenstar before we go.'

'Yes please.' What a beautiful horse. The mare looked pure white from a distance, but was a faintly buttery cream close to. 'Hello, girl. Aren't you a beauty, eh?' She turned to Conrad. 'You really got her as a present?'

'Because I captured the Witches who killed Eseld's father, yes. On the whole, I'd rather Arthur Mowbray were still around.' He paused. 'Have a look at the saddle. That's the *real* gift.'

It would be a long time before Cordy was allowed anywhere near an Enchanted saddle in her lessons at Greendale. She ran her fingers down the tooled leather, going through the parts in her head, like Sophie had taught her yesterday. *Seat, panel, skirt … keeper???* When she touched the way too big pommel, she felt the contained Charms that would induce the plane shifting.

'You're wrong,' she told him. 'Evenstar will get old, but the memories you'll make with her will last forever. This is just an Artefact. Have fun.'

She waved them off and headed for the second roundhouse before the Count of Force Ghyll could intercept her. She was spot on: there, outside Keraunós's stall, she found the elusive Persephone, who immediately looked over her shoulder for a way out. *Not today, my dear.*

'Hello. It's Perci, isn't it? You must know who I am.'

There was little sun around, so the Count cast no shadow when he came up behind her. 'Can I help, Honoured Witch?'

'Persephone is going to show me Keraunós,' said Cordelia without looking round. 'If it were anything else, obviously I'd ask you, but…'

The Count couldn't go anywhere near the Unicorn without risking a stabbing, and it would serve him right, and to deny Cordy's request was outside his remit. She knew he'd left when Perci's eyes widened with fear.

The girl was eighteen, going on twelve. She was an inch shorter than Cordelia, and a lot thinner in the body. What she was about to do didn't make Cordy feel good about herself, but she wouldn't get a better chance to find out. She drew on the abundance of Lux flowing around, opened her Sight and bore down on the girl like one of Conrad's wolves.

And recoiled back.

'Eurgh. What's *that*? What have you got in you?'

Persephone was shaking with fear. She flicked her eyes to the stall where the Unicorn was watching, almost curiously. 'Not here,' said the girl. 'If you want to know, you'll have to come with me. On Keraunós.'

Could today get any better? 'That would be my pleasure.'

The great beast remembered her from her last visit, as you'd expect from such an intelligent creature, and while Cordy held his head, Perci rushed to get the saddle on, anxious to get away. Out in the yard, Perci baulked when she saw the Count standing watching.

'What are you doing?' said the Fae.

'Leave it to me,' whispered Cordelia. She raised her voice. 'Going for a ride, my lord. Keraunós needs his exercise, especially in real snow.'

Perci mounted the Unicorn, slipped her foot out of the left stirrup and pointed to it for Cordy to use. Cordelia swung herself up with some difficulty, and one of the muscles inside her thigh twanged in protest at renewed abuse. But she was up, and she was on the back of a Unicorn. She felt Keraunós's power, and more than that, she started to see and feel the world through his senses.

'Stop it!' hissed Perci. 'You'll distract him! Please. Just block him out for now or I'll never manage the Transition.'

'Sorry.'

'Walk on.' Keraunós high-stepped round the snowy field until Perci was ready to try the shift to the gallops.

By the Goddess, that was *smooth*. The smoothest plane-shift Cordelia had ever experienced put them on the hill, and then into the course. Now that Keraunós had his head, Perci let him run, and Cordy had to hold on very tightly. When she accidentally lost focus on blocking her Sight, she got the same roiling, foul, metallic stench from Perci that she'd experienced in the stables. Her reflexes kicked in, and she let go, backing instinctively away from the repulsive odour and flying through the air when she bounced *up* instead of *down*. *Oooooh shit…*

Thump. Thank the Goddess for snow.

'Are you okay? What happened?'

Cordelia wiggled her toes and fingers as best she could under all the layers. They all moved and the pain in her back didn't seem too bad. 'Fine. I think.'

Perci brought the Unicorn in a slowing circle while Cordelia fought to get up. No cracked ribs, no bang on the head. 'Shall we talk now?'

Perci nodded and dismounted, tying Keraunós to a gate. Very slowly, the girl walked up to Cordelia, who suddenly had a thought. 'Conrad and Faith aren't nearby, are they?'

'No, ma'am. They're way over there, and half a phase up. They don't even know we're here.'

'Good. Now tell me what they've done to you. What *is* that smell?'

'I'm eighteen,' said Persephone with all the stubbornness of the newly minted adult. 'I can do what I like.'

'You can. The Fae can't, though. What have they done to you?'

'Nothing I didn't ask for.'

'Stop it, Persephone. If you want me to treat you like an adult, behave like one.'

'Then start by calling me *Perci*. You're not my mother.'

'What have you signed up to, Perci? I can get the Lord Commissioner if you'd rather answer his questions. He does a good line in father figures if you'd prefer that.'

'Now you really do sound like my mum.'

'Who clearly has the patience of a Christian saint. I am not a Christian, Perci, and I am most definitely not your mother.'

'Had. My mother *had* the patience of a saint. She died when I was a baby and she'd never named a father.' The girl shrugged. 'I was brought up in the Care of the Union. I did quite well, actually, because I got to live with the Torvers.'

'As in Morgan and Willow Torver?'

'Yeah. She's a year older, but yeah, we were brought up together. She was brilliant when we were little.'

'I see.'

Perci's face had calmed down as she told her story, and Cordy could tell that there were no unhappy memories there, and then the girl's tone changed. 'Of course, there was no question of adoption. I am not a Torver, am I? It doesn't matter, though, because I'm from the Eden line.'

The Spirits had talked about that. 'You'll have to excuse an offcomer,' said Cordelia.

'The first daughter of the Eden line was a female Elf. One of only two ever born.'

Perci had said it with such conviction that she must believe it. Cordy wasn't even sure she believed in male Elves, never mind female ones. According to legend, when the Gnomes first appeared out of the north, their encounters with the Fae were brutal beyond words, with most sources glossing over what happened. These sources were especially coy about how come a certain number of Fae Queens had live births with Gnomes as the male parent. The offspring were Elves, highly magickal but sterile.

This was all rumour because there was yet more bloodshed, and all the Elves either died or disappeared into the forests to become the stuff of legend. Female Elves? 'Go on, Perci.'

'It's simple. With help, we can do Quicksilver magick. I started the course on my eighteenth birthday. It was my present from the Queen.'

Of course. Quicksilver. *Mercury*. That was the smell, and Cordy hadn't recognised it because it's so toxic, and whenever she'd sensed Fae before, it had been buried under other impressions. In Perci, it stood out like a muck heap in a beauty parlour. 'What have you done, Perci!'

'Don't worry, ma'am. It's safe. For me. Princess Faithful says that it's something to do with putting a mercury atom in a special protein, but they can't do the research to find out for certain. Not that they do it with Chymical magick, of course.'

Cordelia's head was reeling. She didn't know which line of questioning to follow until she saw the girl's stoic, determined face. She had to put Perci's welfare first.

'How do they do it safely? Have you *any* idea how toxic that stuff is? When a Fae dies, you're supposed to take proper precautions disposing of the body in case it gets into groundwater. It took long enough to get *them* to do it.'

Perci gave her a monstrous pet lip. 'But it's *safe* for them! It's natural and it's safe. They monitor it constantly to make sure it's all taken up, and when the course is finished, I have their Bonded word I can return for conception and confinement!'

It took a second for the message to get through her overheating brain. When it did, Cordelia got in Perci's face. 'Say that again. About pregnancy.'

'It's nothing.' Perci tried to maintain a stubborn silence. It lasted two seconds. 'It really is nothing. It's just that when the Quicksilver becomes part of me, I have to conceive and remain in the sídhe until confinement. For free. As many times as I like.'

'And how long have you signed yourself up for?'

'Seven years.'

Cordelia felt unclean. All the pleasure in the beautiful, snowy morning had gone. 'What's Faith's part in this?'

'Like a sort of nurse. She only took over after Galleny was demoted. The Queen feeds me, and the Princess looks after me when I'm in the sídhe.'

As Cordelia had pushed Persephone back, they'd got closer to Keraunós, and he came up to them in search of a carrot. His breath steamed in a great cloud as he nudged Perci with infinite delicacy. He knew exactly how dangerous his horn was.

Persephone turned instinctively and comforted the Unicorn. 'Hey you. No carrot yet, I'm afraid. Ooh, you're cold.' She turned to Cordelia. 'We can't stand here for hours arguing about this. Keraunós will get a chill. And you're not going to persuade me to give up if Grandfather couldn't.'

Cordelia had to pretend that she didn't know who that was. 'Grandfather?'

'Yeah. Turns out I'm only descended from the bloody Warden of Salomon's House, aren't I?'

'Sir Roland? But he's...'

'Dead. Yeah. Came up to me before Christmas and tried to stop me. I told him he'd had his chance at life, and why shouldn't I have mine?'

Cordelia held up her hands. 'You're right. I chose to join the Daughters at Glastonbury and my mother barely spoke to me again. You know I'm here if you need me. Let's go.'

'Thanks. Thanks for understanding.' Persephone unhitched Keraunós and mounted the saddle. 'Don't let go this time, yeah?'

'I'll try. I might not have such a soft landing again. Shall we go and see what's happening to Conrad?'

Perci froze, just as she was about to offer Cordelia a hand. Clearly she'd forgotten that Cordy was one half of a partnership. 'You're not gonna tell him, are you?'

Cordy held up her hand, and Perci took it. Cordy had to smooth things over. 'Tell Conrad about the current situation? You must be joking. When he joined the RAF, his parents dropped him off at the gates with their blessing. He wouldn't understand your story.'

She climbed up behind Perci, and they moved off at a trot, taking a big circuit of the course before Keraunós launched himself over a gate and on to the next plane, which featured woods on one side and fresh tracks in the snow on the other. They followed the tracks and soon came across the most bizarre scene.

Hipponax and Evenstar were huddled together for warmth, the other Unicorn watching as Conrad had a swordfight with a tree stump while Princess Faith hit his bad leg with a riding crop. She heard them first, and patted Conrad on the shoulder. When he stopped, he looked like he was going to fall over. His head was glistening, and not with snow. He'd really worked up a sweat. Perci reined in Keraunós, and Conrad turned to see what the fuss was about. When Cordy made her eye appointment, she was going to drag the Chief kicking and screaming to have his hearing tested.

'Looking good, Cordy,' said Conrad. 'What's it like up there?'

Conrad was to their right, and Perci had already bent down to her left so that Keraunós's giant head and neck hid her from view. 'Exhilarating!' said Cordy. 'I can't wait to ride one myself.'

Faith snorted. 'You'll have a long wait, Cordelia.'

There was spittle running out of the wound around the Fae's mouth. Why had she not noticed before? Her disgust for this particular creature turned into hatred. Princess Faithful, whipping girl of the Red Queen, was helping poison an innocent child for sport. For an advantage in *racing*. And she was wrapping Conrad round her little finger. It wasn't just a Glamour that Faith tried to wear in public, it was a complete mask. The Fae would strike at the Greenings sooner or later, and if Cordelia could help protect them, she would. Whether or not Raven was being held prisoner, this could not be allowed to go on.

She took a deep breath and forced a smile. 'You two seem to have found a new game to play.'

'Fencing for the partially immobile,' said Faith. 'We need to find a way for him to fight that focuses on what works rather than expect his leg to miraculously heal. It's why I drink a lot of cocktails, Cordelia: good excuse to drink from a straw. We'll take five, Conrad.'

'Ten. Minimum,' he replied.

'We need to get on,' said Perci. 'Can't stop again.'

'See you later.'

22 — Home Comforts

When they had left Conrad and the Princess behind, Persephone urged Keraunós into a flat-out gallop that had him almost taking off in places, and Cordelia's face was raw from the cold wind. She was sure that tears had frozen on her cheeks by the time they descended to the lower plane and trotted back to the stables.

Her legs were begging for a rest, but Perci carried straight on with cooling, cleaning and caring for their mount, and Cordelia had no choice but to join in. Back in the real world, they put their earlier conversation behind them, and Cordelia had a masterclass in Care of Supernatural Creatures that she might not get again for a long time.

They were about to go for hot chocolate with the other grooms when she heard hoof beats in the yard. Cordelia tried to bolt from the roundhouse, but Faith appeared in the doorway, leading Hipponax.

'My lady,' said Perci. 'We were just off for a break. Do you need me to care for Hipponax now?'

'Off you go,' said Faith. 'Cordelia and I will do it together. To start with.'

Oh. That was not what Cordy wanted to hear. Perci scuttled out, and Faith chucked the lead rope to Cordy. 'I'll open the door. You lead him in.'

It was the one thing Cordy couldn't do herself: open the individual stall doors. They were bound with Fae magick, so no wonder Perci had a lot of responsibility. When Cordelia had led the Unicorn inside his large, well-appointed stall, Faith shut the door and locked it. Oh.

'Right,' said Faith. 'Tell me what all that crap was about on Monday.'

'What do you mean?'

'First, what were you doing in the monument? Second, why did I have to lie about grounds maintenance, and third, who put the fucking sheep in there in the first place?'

There had been a tense negotiation when Cordy had rung Faith on Monday, just before Lucas had herded the sheep into the road. 'I told you. I needed Conrad to think that the Fae were responsible.' Cordelia took a deep breath and got ready to lie through her teeth, something that probably came very easily to the angry Fae in front of her, given how exposed Faith's teeth actually were.

'There was a dead human by the cross,' Cordelia began. 'She had taken the sheep in there as cover and to provide a living donation. Your monument rejected her. We can't afford to be distracted at the moment, and in a couple of weeks, I'll "discover" the body and have a full enquiry. She wasn't local, so no one will be looking for her. Only a kid, poor thing.'

Cordelia hated using the word *donation*. She preferred the real word. *Sacrifice*. It was the one small part of being amongst the Daughters that stuck in her throat. Score one for Salomon's House – strictly against the rules there.

'Why should I believe you?'

'You think I'd make something like that up? How else did twenty sheep get half a mile up the road at night? Go and see for yourself.'

Faith hesitated, taking the chance to wipe her mouth. 'No thanks. Conrad's waiting outside. I'll see to Hipponax.' Faith opened the door and stood aside. 'Don't pull a stunt like that again, okay?'

Cordelia nodded and forced herself to walk normally rather than bolting from the stable. She arrived in the yard sweating again and shaking from exhaustion. She cheered up when Conrad actually looked worse. 'There's hot chocolate inside,' she said.

'And also at Lake Cottage. Won't take us long in the Smurf.'

It didn't, and she was soon lighting the fire while he put the kettle on. Mugs of chocolate steaming, they swapped stories of their day. Conrad said that the Red Queen had been slightly miffed about his training session this morning, because she'd wanted Faith to join her in a hunt through the snow, and that far from plotting revenge, the Queen was entirely focused on spending the whole weekend in the wild.

'Could it be a bluff?' she asked.

'Could be, but I doubt it. Did you get anything interesting from Persephone, such as why she's been avoiding me?'

'I don't really know. She talked a lot about Lara Dent, and she wasn't happy when I corrected her. In her head, Morwenna Mowbray is not a real person. I think she might have been in love, and perhaps she blames you. She knows that we took the amulet away, and I can't show it to her to prove that it was discharged.'

As with all the best lies, there was an element of truth. Perci had hero-worshipped the Vessel that contained Lara Dent, and was quite happy to know that the person underneath was okay.

'And what about yesterday? I know you said that Sophie gave nothing away, but did you get any hints that they're up to something?'

She shook her head. Sophie was not the best teacher in the world. Yet. She had mostly channelled memories of her own lessons as a child, and Cordy had gently pointed out that she was thirty-eight, not eight. All the lessons had taken place within an exclusion zone that all the other grooms avoided.

'If you get a chance, focus on Clara,' said Conrad. 'She's the redhead, and she came from Diarmuid's place, so not born to the Greenings. They've given her a fair bit of responsibility, but like I told Sophie, she'll never be head groom.' He paused. 'Are you okay?'

'That fire's warm. Do you mind if I strip off a few layers?'

It was a good cover story. In minutes yesterday, Conrad had found a chink in the Greenings' armour and wanted her to exploit it. She had flushed red, suddenly conscious of what she was keeping from him herself. Next time she blushed, she could blame an early menopause. Men always fell for that.

She changed the subject by asking about Mina.

He looked out of the window, drummed his fingers on the chair and slapped his thigh. 'She's gone to Elvenham and taken the car. Basically, she didn't fancy being snowed in here for the weekend. If it's okay with you, I'm going to fly down tomorrow afternoon and leave you and Matt in charge for a whole week.'

'What?'

'Yep. Sort of. Chris Kelly says there's some sort of Ley line emergency in Dumfries and wants me to take him on Monday, and on the way there, he's going to make a spur to the field here. The hotel doesn't have planning permission for an LZ, and we need some magick to hide the Smurf. And muffle him.'

'Oh. I don't mind being on call, and Matt can certainly get around, but isn't it risky?'

'Not really. So long as I get a message, I can be back in less than an hour. No different to being here and snowed in. It does mean I'll be on the wagon for a week though. Except Friday night. And then there's next Thursday.'

'Thursday?'

'The Warden Election. I've had Seth on the phone.'

'He's back in charge of the Alchemical Society in Manchester, isn't he?'

'He is. It's a funny situation, because the election is actually run by the Court, not Salomon's House, and the Manchester Society are hosting it. And paying for it. He wants to hire me to help Saffron on the day and then to fly her and the ballot box down to London.'

Cordelia was aching and exhausted in every bone, muscle and sinew. When her mug of chocolate had been drained, she'd started dreaming of Matt's bath. She forced herself to think through what he'd said. 'But you're not in the Watch any more.'

'No need to rub it in. Neither are you, come to that. He said that the Lord Guardian of the North has been appointed to protect the realm by Nimue, and if anyone questions that, they're asking for trouble. It would mean you'll be on your own for ten days, and you've been doing this job for barely a week.'

'What does Saul Brathay think?'

'He wasn't thrilled, but now that both parties have lodged suits at the Court, he's a bit less worried. And you can call on him, too.'

'Then it's no problem, Chief. If I was still upstairs at the hotel, I couldn't do it, but with Matt's help, and Saul on standby, we'll be fine.'

'Thanks.'

'No problem. Now, if you don't mind, I'm going to close my eyes until Matt comes to pick me up.'

'Doze away. Just one question: who started the whole *Chief* thing?'

'That would be telling.'

Matt must have turned up while Conrad was outside for a smoke, because there was no way he'd have heard anything coming. While she was asleep, Matt had agreed to help mind the shop while the Chief was away, and she woke to a gentle shake of the shoulder. 'I hope you have a *lot* of hot water,' was her only comment before she said goodbye.

On Saturday morning, Cordy and Matt woke to the second batch of snow, and this time Matt said that he would only be leaving in a total emergency, and did she fancy a walk?

'Like that's so much safer than a helicopter.'

'It is if you have the right gear. Which I do, including your size crampons.'

And so she had her introduction to the Lakes in Winter: exhilaratingly magical and exhausting in equal measure. Also dangerous. Two of the other mountain rescue teams were called out, but not Matt's, and Cordy would have died of exposure if she hadn't had his firm hand and steady eye guiding her up what she'd thought would be an inaccessible cliff-face.

With night already fallen, the fire lit and the dinner in the slow cooker, they relaxed and Matt poured them a glass of wine. Since last weekend, Matt's bottle of single malt had started gathering dust, and disappeared into the cupboard when they cleaned up on Friday.

'You asked me the other day about Petra Leigh,' he said. She smiled encouragingly. 'You know she was fifteen years older than me, right? Would never admit it, but when they've put your name on the honour board at School House for being Head Girl, there are some things you can't deny.' He smiled. 'She would also never admit that I loved her. She chucked me out the day that little Laura called me *Daddy*.'

'Oh, Matt. I'm so sorry.'

He shrugged. 'It was a long time ago. Tell me about the Daughters. I've never met an apostate before.'

She snorted into her wine. *Apostate*. What a word. She laughed properly and said, 'At least you didn't call me a de-frocked nun. I didn't tell Conrad, but I heard a couple of the crowd call me that the other night.'

He stared at her across the open fire, holding his tongue, and it was her who broke the dam.

'You're quite welcome to de-frock me if you want. If this sweater counts as a frock.'

When they ended up in his bed, she couldn't help wondering if he was thinking of Petra as much as she was thinking about Raven. After dinner, she realised that she hadn't felt as close to Raven as she had when she was in bed with Matt. Weird.

The next morning, it was still true, and afterwards she said, 'Please don't tell anyone about this until the snow melts.'

He had looked puzzled. 'Who would I tell, and why would I tell them what I get up to? You're not about to tell Conrad, are you?'

'When he gets back, yes. I don't want to put him in an awkward position.'

Matt scooped her up and rolled her on top of him. 'Unlike me. You're quite happy to have me in all sorts of awkward positions.' It was the only joke he made the whole time they were together.

I'm fairly sure that Cordelia spotted it. She's way too sensitive not to have noticed that Mina had run off at short notice. I wouldn't call it a row exactly. More of a free and frank exchange of views, hers being that she wasn't going to get snowed in to Lake Cottage if she had an alternative. I think she expressed her opinion quite well when she said, 'If I wanted to be shut away from the world, I would go and hit Tom on the head and get sent back to prison. At least I would have my meals cooked. And this wedding won't plan itself, Conrad. I need to be where I can interview people and get quotations. Myfanwy can only do so much before we run into a big problem. She is Welsh and therefore has … different tastes to me.'

We made up when I joined her on the Friday afternoon. She said that seeing Myfanwy, and knowing that the poor woman still had over two years to go before she could leave the village, had made Mina realise that we were indeed very lucky. She was in no rush to get back to Ambleside, though.

Over the next week, peace reigned in the Lakeland Particular. Maybe I should go away more often. I did drop in, of course, when I put the Smurf down on the Haven's field and then helped Chris to run a spur off the East Road, the main Ley line that runs on the other side of the A591.

I do practise, you know. I don't always write about it, but I've taken several walks from the hotel and practised drawing a flow of Lux. One day, I even brought it across the main road and into the field. It's when I get there that I have no clue what to do.

I repeated the trick for Chris (another Skill ticked off), and then watched in awe as he and Kenver did the next bit. He started by getting out a filigree silver box, positively fizzing with magick. 'I'm going to create the Anchor,' he said. 'This was made by Niðr. Centuries ago, and he called it, "A gift to the Earthmaster, that mortals might do a better job." Typical, eh? Basically, I'm gonna power it up and make the Anchor using this as a template, then let the Anchor drop into the ground. If you could attach that flow of Lux you're holding, that would be great. You'll also have passed that whole module.'

As ever, Kenver had a slightly different view of things. 'Just watch you don't set up a standing wave, Conrad. If it hits the Smurf, it'll fry the electrics completely. And you.' He grinned. 'You're a lot cheaper to replace, though.'

I was sweating again. My leg was throbbing. When Chris gets me to do these things, I'll assume you know that in future. Holding on to the end of a flow of Lux while trying to watch him in action was pushing me to the limit. I mentally prepared myself to let go if I couldn't cope. When Chris started the Work, Kenver moved to a safe distance behind me, closer to the lake.

Chris had the box glowing blue in seconds. I really focused and imagined my Third Eye opening just a little further. The box seemed to get bigger, and I could see loops within loops, and something like a Moebius Strip in the middle.

'Voilà,' said Chris. He took his left hand away, and a perfect copy of the box fell slowly to the wet grass and disappeared. 'You're on, Conrad.'

I made a supreme effort and stared at the ground. The grass went a sort of maroon colour, and underneath the roots, I could see the blue box hanging like a balloon in the air. Way to go, Conrad.

Chris's enthralling chapter on this subject said that I had to hang on to the flow of Lux, and let it fall down until it clicked in place, like a wire in a connector. Then let go.

The Lux dropped okay, but I missed the box and it bounced up. The bounce went higher than my hand, and Kenver's words became reality: the wave flicked down the flow of Lux, through the hedge, over the road, and hit the Ley line. Then it started coming back. Bigger.

'Don't panic,' said Chris evenly. 'You've got one more try. If you miss this time, let go. You can do this.'

The leading peak surged over the snow, and I knew I was going to miss, because the trough behind it was too low. Unless I got the distance right and let the wave do its work. I shifted right half an inch and loosened my grip on the Lux, which promptly started discharging through my arm. In a split second, the wave reared up and almost pulled my arm with it.

Click.

How about that?

'Conrad? Are you okay?'

'I…' Not again. Please no. Oh yes. Thump.

We were only a couple of hours late getting to Dumfries after I woke up.

'How come you get to wear a suit?' said Saffron when the Lakeland party arrived at the Manchester Alchemical Society. 'I thought you were still an officer or something.'

She, of course, was sporting Number One Dress, complete with the red cap of the Royal Military Police. 'I'm in the Reserves,' I replied. 'When I get called up again, I'll put it back on. How's life at Middlebarrow Haven?'

She glanced across the entrance hall to see if the Masons had gone through to the rotunda. 'Mad. Quiet one minute, then I'm suddenly knee deep in bits of paper. Evie's Muse is a very fickle Spirit.' She was clearly enjoying it though.

There was a suitably solemn ceremony at the beginning of polling. After all, it's been forty years since the last Warden election, and there has never been a ballot box up here before. The first person to vote was Meredith Telford, the Society's longest serving officer. I'm sorry to report that her affliction by the Mage's Curse hasn't got any better, and her daughter had to hold the paper still while she marked her preferences.

Seth Holgate, Society President, was second, and he placed his paper in the box with a dramatic gesture that suits his personality, then stood back while the hot favourite, Dr Lois Reynolds, voted. For herself, presumably. I know I would. Vote for myself, that is. Who knows, if I get this Doctorate, I might even get to vote in the next election. If I live that long. I wonder which is less likely.

There were no hitches, lots of tea was drunk, and there was a lot of gossip. Before we knew it, Erin and Saffron were sealing the box, and Mina was putting all the records in a big envelope.

Seth was standing by to drive us to the airport, and on the way he finally asked how things were going in the Particular. 'A couple of our members were at the Waterhead Chase. They said they'd seen you doing your walkabout. Pressing the flesh and all that.' He checked the mirror and continued. 'One of them said, and I quote, "If Lois makes an arse of things, Clarke could be the next Warden." Any comments, Lord Commissioner?'

'Yes,' I replied. 'The only circumstances in which I would stand for Warden would be if the election were held on the first of April, which is not due to happen for some years. And that is my last word on the subject.'

He chortled, a big deep sound from somewhere down by his seatbelt. 'We also had one member at the Crown Purse on Thursday. He said he nearly wet himself when the Queen of Keswick went postal. Can't believe what you and Cordelia did.'

'Derwent, Seth. She's the Queen of Derwent. I was just trying to avoid added paperwork.'

'That's code,' chipped in Saffron. 'When he says *additional paperwork*, he means *unnecessary deaths*. He's right about the paperwork, though.'

'If you're free to do the election, you must be confident that things are in hand,' said Seth.

'Oh, you know me. I'd rather they got on with it while I'm away, then I can arrest the winner. Much safer that way.'

'You're not gonna talk about it, are you?'

'Nope. But Manchester Alchemical Society are cordially invited to visit at any time.'

'He's definitely Warden in Waiting,' said Saffron. 'You've got me going there, you know. What would your slogan be? Leave it with me.'

It was a very tiresome flight to London, because one of the Scottish airports was suddenly closed to snow, and getting to Twickenham was a right royal pain in the arse. I'd have aborted if Saffron hadn't remembered how to talk to Air Traffic Control. She learnt during our time in Cornwall, and I made a mental note to train up Cordelia when we got back.

We landed on the snow-free lawn in front of Earth House. It looks a bit like a bowling green, and it's got a good raise above the surrounding gardens because it's a shallow cover over a huge chamber containing the largest Ley line junction in Albion. And totally private. Double bonus.

Chris was waiting to take us into the City. According to Mina, Tamsin has allowed him to set up camp in the basement under Earth House. It leads directly to the Junction and has a separate outside door, so they can carry on avoiding each other. When the house was empty last weekend, he'd been and cleared most of his stuff from upstairs and moved it to Mowbray House. That had not gone down well.

He dropped us at one of the entrances to the Old Network in town, and we were met by Deputy Bailiff Steph Morgan. In the most bizarre procession of my life, she led the way underground, carrying a great Enchanted axe over her shoulder. Mina followed, then me with the ballot box, and Saffron brought up the rear. There was quite a party waiting for us in the Old Temple.

The London home of the Cloister Court is well below today's ground level, because it's based in an actual temple built by the Romans. There isn't much left of the original building except the colonnade down the sides and the Artefact behind the judge's bench, which is just visible during Court sessions. It's the original London Palladium: the London Stone, magickal heart of the City. Tonight was a big night, and it was standing room only in the body of the court.

The whole Inner Council of Salomon's House was there, ready to have an emergency meeting after the votes were counted and to install the new Warden with immediate effect. They weren't grouped together, because the room was pretty much divided into the supporting camps of the three candidates: Dr Reynolds (who'd made her own way down by train after lunch), Lady Selena Bannister and Heidi Marston. Those not affiliated clustered at the margins or around the bench, where the Hon. Mrs Justice Bracewell was waiting.

Perched on top of the bench was the original ballot box – older, more battered and much larger than the one we'd brought down from Manchester, and the box was being protected by Bailiff Morgan and the King's Watch.

Hannah gave our group a professional smile, and her eyes lingered on mine for a second longer than the others, the corners creasing with an extra measure of welcome. Or annoyance. It's always hard to tell. There was no doubt about Vicky's emotions: the big grin and the thumbs up were a bit of a giveaway. Iain Drummond and the others just looked pleased that the day was about to be over.

A woman detached herself from Heidi's group and moved to intercept us. It was Augusta Faulkner, legal nemesis of the King's Watch, mother of my first enemy, Keira, and most recently (believe it or not), my own personal brief. That, however, was a one-off. At least it meant that she didn't send daggers of loathing at me when we made eye contact. I even got a respectful nod of the head, which I returned. Steph Morgan had her back to me, so I don't know what the look was in her eyes. I do know that she took the axe off her shoulder and said a very pointed, 'Excuse me.'

'Sorry, Ms Morgan,' replied Augusta. 'I have a motion here to exclude the ballots from Manchester.' She held up three scrolls tied with pink ribbon. 'This is the formal presentation, but I'll leave them on the bench. I can see that your hands are full.'

'On what grounds!' boomed Michael Oldcastle, Deputy Warden and Chief Slimeball. I noticed that this was very much a surprise to everyone in the room, and Seth's words came back to me: *If anyone opposes this, they're asking for trouble.* Heidi Marston was grinning from ear to ear. I shouldn't have been surprised.

Augusta deposited the briefs on the bench and turned back to continue blocking our way. I was going to give them one minute before I put the box down. 'Our suit is simple: the ballots and the ballot box were not at all times under guard from the King's Watch, and therefore invalid.'

Iain Drummond must have had a really bad day, because he spoke way too loudly when he said, 'Of all the stupid half-arsed nonsense I've ever heard, this takes the biscuit.'

Judge Bracewell was formally dressed, but not in her robes. She's too good at her job to show any reaction to what Drummond said, but she certainly doesn't take any nonsense. She pointed to the briefs and said, 'The Court is not in session, nor do I plan to make it so. You can lodge those in the morning, Ms Faulkner. Meanwhile, both boxes have been received into the keeping of the Court, and the Bailiff will lock them up overnight. See you at ten. Now go away, all of you.' With that, she turned and stalked off round the back to her chambers.

Augusta stepped aside and allowed Stephanie to continue her progress to the bench. I followed and used my height to deposit the Manchester box next to its big brother. Job done, I turned round and shook Stephanie's hand. 'Over to you.'

'Clear the Court!' said Septimus. 'And that's not a polite request.'

'Come on,' said Hannah. 'There's a large scotch with my name on it waiting at the Savoy.'

'Not me,' said Iain. 'It looks like I've got a brief to prepare for tomorrow.'

Hannah put her hand on his arm as we queued up to get out. 'No you haven't, Iain. Go and watch the fun, but this is not our quarrel. Let them get on with it. And that's an order.' She turned to me. 'See? I did learn something from having you around.'

I didn't think that Augusta's intervention could be topped as surprise of the day, but Hannah managed it superbly when we were ensconced in a corner of the Savoy's most discreet bar. 'That worked out nicely,' she grinned. 'Here's to Conrad Bloody Clarke, who can get sacked and still cause havoc.'

'To Conrad!'

'I'm flattered, but what do you mean?'

She gave me the most wicked of her smiles. 'Who do you think suggested that you help out in Manchester?'

'You didn't!'

'I did. Not only did it get the ballot box here quickly and safely, it will force the Court to consider whether the Lord Guardian of the North is a *suitably warranted person.*'

'Well I'll be,' said Vicky. 'I thought you were enjoying yourself way too much.'

'If I have to do that again, I want overtime,' said Saffron.

'And I am most amused, too,' said Mina. 'Except for the part where I have to be on hand to count the votes.'

'Sorry about that,' said Hannah. 'It never crossed my mind. Ah well, you're staying in town for a few days, aren't you? Right, Conrad, go and grab the waiter. We've got some catching up to do.'

When I got back to the table, Saffron was in full flow. '*Vote Clarke, and all your problems will be incinerated,*' she declared. 'Kinda catchy, that one.'

'I know,' added Vicky. '*Vote for Conrad or he'll set Mina on youse.*'

And believe me, there were a lot more where they came from. Matters were about to descend below the belt when I got a text. Given the volatile nature of my new territory, I was not going to be putting my phone on mute for anyone's benefit. Anyone except the Hon. Mrs Justice Bracewell, of course. I never want to be locked in a Limbo Chamber again. Ever.

And talking of Court, the message was from an unregistered French pay-as-you-go mobile. In other words, Keira Faulkner, and it was cryptic enough to be meaningless to anyone else: *A little bird has told me you should have a lie-in tomorrow. Mum's the word.*

Why on earth was Augusta telling me to stay at home? I have no idea, and if it had come from someone else, I'd have been worried that it was a tip-off about an impending attack somewhere. Augusta Faulkner does not work like that. To have sent it via Keira meant that it was personal, so she clearly thought that my presence before the bench might harm her daughter in the future. There was no way that I was keeping this one to myself, so I showed it round.

The consensus suggested that I was (yet again) a lucky bastard. I looked around the group, finishing with Mina. 'Does anyone need me to come into Town tomorrow?'

Mina hesitated, then shook her head. Hannah took that as a cue to go, and the rest of us followed. By the time the taxi got us to Earth House, Tamsin was in her pyjamas – we'd messaged her with the non-result of the election as soon as we'd left the Old Network.

'Well that was the biggest anticlimax since my second wedding night,' she declared. 'I knew I should have given you a key and shown you the Wards. See you both in the morning.'

23 — A Little Light Larceny

Breakfast was total chaos, as you might expect with three children under five, two adults who had to go to work and a guest who doesn't have much experience with small people (i.e. me). Thank heavens for Siona.

Tamsin only got a nanny when she started studying with the Fae Queen of Richmond; before that, she was a full-time mother. After the chaos had subsided, and when Tammy and Mina had headed off, I volunteered to help get the girls to nursery. Siona gave me a dark look – she is very much on Tamsin's side, and sees me as a spy in the camp for Chris. Which just goes to show how little she knows about adult relationships in general and about Chris Kelly in particular.

'Good,' she declared. 'Your mission, should you choose to accept it, is to make sure that Amanda gets there with a clean oversuit and wellingtons.'

Amanda is the oldest: four going on forty. Unless she sees a muddy puddle, of course, in which case she channels Peppa Pig and goes for it big-time. I do love a challenge. I also love to cheat.

Just before we were ready to leave, I went and stood by the Smurf. Amanda came out to see, and immediately asked if I could fly them to nursery. 'Ah, no, I'm sorry, but the Smurf is tired today.'

'That's not a Smurf.'

Which floored me.

'It *belongs* to the Smurfs. You can get a lot of Smurfs in there. Would you like to fly on my shoulders instead?'

'*All* the way to nursery? Not just to the end of the road?'

'All the way, kid.'

'I'm not a kid. A kid is a young goat.'

I was losing 2-0 to a four-year-old.

'I bet you don't know what a lady goat is called.'

'I bet I do.'

'How much do you bet?'

'If I know what a lady goat is called, I get to go on your shoulders *all* the way to nursery.'

I held out my hand. 'Deal.' We shook, and I folded my arms. 'Go on then.'

'A *nanny*!'

'Very good.' I looked up, and Siona was locking the back door. 'Who is Siona?' I asked.

'She's our nanny.'

'Which makes you her kid. Now, are you going to get on my shoulders, or what?'

'Isn't the nursery down this way?' I asked, five minutes later.

'You're having a laugh, aren't you?' said Siona. 'If we go that way, there's two bakeries with fresh doughnuts. And a set of steps. This way is flatter and has no distractions.'

It was also ten minutes longer. No wonder Amanda thought she was getting a treat.

The doughnut-free accessible route also led along the river at one point. The Thames was in full winter mode, lapping against the flood defences and getting ready to give the riverside dwellers some anxious nights if it rained again.

When she saw the boats bobbing and rocking, Amanda announced, 'This is like a ship. Why are you walking funny?'

'It's because I'm a pirate.'

'Have you got a wooden leg?'

'No. A metal one. I'm a *modern* pirate. Would you like to walk the plank?'

'What do you mean?'

'Would you like to walk along the top of the wall? If I hold your hand, of course?'

'Noooooo! Daddy never lets me do that.'

'For good reason,' said Siona.

I gripped Amanda's wrist and swung her off my shoulders and on to the wall. It was only a ten foot drop to the swiftly flowing, freezing river below us.

'Jesus Mary and Joseph!' hissed Siona. 'Get her down from there, or I swear I'll have your balls on toast.'

Did I mention that Siona is Irish? Well, she is. From Dublin.

'What did Siona say?' asked Amanda.

'She thinks that I won't hold you tightly enough to stop you falling over the wall.'

Amanda looked down. And started swaying. Oops. I had her back on my shoulders in 1.5 seconds. Ah well, at least I got a minute's rest. Onwards.

The nursery was nearly in sight (and my back was sending alarm signals to my brain) when Amanda got bored enough to pull my woolly hat off. 'The top of your head is shiny like Daddy's.'

And with that, my humiliation was complete.

Before I could respond, she added, 'But at least you've got *some* hair. Mummy says that Daddy is a *total* slaphead.'

'Does she?'

'Ooh, look, there's Hedge!' said Siona.

All I could see was walls and railings. 'Where?'

'The one with the camouflage coat.'

'The child?'

'No, the fecking invisible dog she has with her.'

'Siona said a naughty word! That means we have doughnuts for tea!'

'I don't think she did,' I said innocently. 'Siona wouldn't do that. She said *flaky*. I'm sure she did.'

'Can I get down and say hello to Hedge?'

I surveyed the last fifty metres before the nursery gates. Too many puddles. 'Today, you're a princess, so today you ride all the way in your carriage.'

'Have you really got a metal leg?'

'Yes. The metal is inside, though. I'll show you tonight. Here we are.'

Our precious cargo safely delivered, I had to rub my back for a full minute before we set off again. As soon as the playground was safely out of earshot, Siona announced, 'You're a fecking gobshite, you are.'

'Don't you mean a *flaky* gobshite?'

'Don't, okay? Just don't.'

I just grinned. We went back the quicker way, and I offered to buy her a coffee to take home. She accepted by saying, 'Just point to me through the window. They'll know what I want.'

I did, and I'm glad they knew. Something to do with vanilla, almond and ewe's milk. Confection purchased, I asked her if she had much to do this morning.

'You know I only do the kids, right?'

'Nanny, not housekeeper. I got that memo.'

'Sure, and I wish Tamsin had and all. So long as all the kids' clothes are washed and put away, and their rooms are clean and tidy, I can knock off until seven. Why? Are you planning on bugging the place?'

'Already done. HD cameras, too.'

'Ha bloody ha.'

'I've got homework to do.' I took an Artefact out of my pocket. 'This is the key to the Wards around the Junction. Chris said you'd show me where the spare key for the actual cellars is.' I didn't give her a chance to answer, and continued by saying, 'So how did a Sorcerer's child from Dublin end up nannying at Earth House?'

'Because I can earn more in a year working for Tamsin than six years in Dublin. I'll be spending next Christmas in Bali, you mark my words.' She paused. 'Chris hasn't really bugged the house, has he?'

'Do you really think he's capable of that?'

'He's capable of having a tart on the side, so why not? You haven't answered the question, Mr Honest as the Day is Long.'

'Earth House has no surveillance devices that I know of. Happy?'

'Hmph.'

And that's how I got the key to the Earth House cellars. When Tamsin got home tonight, the wall-walking and surveillance devices would be all that anyone remembered.

I descended the broad staircase and unlocked the heavy door to the cellars. When I'd found the lights, I had a choice: lock the door and risk raising Siona's suspicions, or leave it unlocked and risk being interrupted. Given my less than acute hearing, I opted to lock the door. I could always say it was for her own safety.

Safely inside, I surveyed the target. The steps were at the back, or river side of the house, and on my right was the Enchanted iron gates which protected the world from the power of the Junction. I could feel the heat of Lux, so I looked closely, and it glowed red via my Third Eye. I really did have homework to do, but that could wait. First, I had to burgle my friend's house.

I snapped on some latex gloves and sorted out what I needed from my toolkit, then went to check out the domestic cellars. 'Impressive. Seriously impressive,' I said to myself when I found the wine store. Earthmasters have been adding to the stock for decades, and although it's not a written rule, it's considered very bad form to leave the wine cellar with fewer bottles than you found it. I took a snap of the Bordeaux section for Alain Dupont to evaluate, then moved on.

I quickly found the lumber room and cast my eye over the pieces: nothing that Dad would be interested in. Ooh. Those chairs maybe? Mid-century modern is trending like no one's business. I peered over the Victorian sideboard and shone my torch deep into the space. Damn. The legs were completely rusty. Never mind.

One room was actually empty, and who can say that about their house these days? One door was locked, the next door led to a modern shower room with WC (for those sweaty days maintaining the Ley lines), and finally I found the old coal cellar. It had been thoroughly cleaned and whitewashed, and the chute converted to a ramped entrance. It was Chris's lair.

I didn't linger. I took his electric shaver out of the plastic bag in my pocket, put it on the upturned tea chest next to the inflatable mattress, took a photograph and left. When I'd volunteered to unload the Smurf in Dumfries, Kenver had been happy to leave me to it, and Chris had already been inside the hotel checking us in. The next morning, he'd moaned a lot and asked me to look for his shaver in Earth House. I was happy to oblige.

I was taking a huge gamble with the locked door, though. I did my absolute best to check for Wards and found nothing. That didn't mean they weren't there, of course. There could be a totally passive Ward on the lock. I weighed the set of keys in my hand and double checked. Yes, there was an unmarked Stamp and only this door that might fit it. Well, I'd come this far. I grasped the stamp (a Level Three), and put all my magick in to working the combination. I got in at the second attempt, and I frowned. Has my magick actually improved? Should I be worried? Vicky says not, so I pushed the door open and felt for the light switch.

When Tamsin Kelly's bicycle was mown down by an oncoming HGV, her body perished and her Spirit rushed away to Merge and Erase the newly deceased Melody Richardson, a client of Tamsin's who had taken her own life. That event had many consequences – Tammy's banishment from Salomon's House, Chris's alienation from his mother, the undying hatred of the late Melody's parents. All of those were consequences that worked themselves out in the foreground, consequences that are still very much with us. Unlike the mortal remains of Tamsin Kelly.

The full truth of what Tamsin had done only came out after I stuck my nose in, and was revealed at the end of Mina's quest for the Nagin, Pramiti. You can read about it in the story of Mina's Ring of Troth.

I turned on the lights and found what I'd been looking for: the first Tamsin Kelly's effects. I waved the musty, mouldy smell away from my nose and left the door wide open for ventilation. I took a good look around and immediately discounted the four suitcases. They would be clothes. Ditto the two packing boxes next to them (shoes and toiletries). It was obvious from the start, really. It was the filing cabinet. The one pulsating with magick.

The first version of Tamsin Kelly was an Imprint Healer. They're rare, apparently, and they mostly work with young Mages just coming into their magick. Mages like Melody Richardson. Tamsin worked in private practice, and here were her client files. I did what I needed to and locked the door behind me. When I got back upstairs, Siona was about to have lunch, and she asked me if I were hungry.

'Cheese and tomato would be lovely, thanks. Kind of you to offer. What time is Tammy picking up the kids?'

'She normally goes for a run after lessons and finishes at the nursery for two o'clock. Why?'

'I thought I might meet her there. The more they get used to me, the less chance of tantrums this afternoon. Are you off soon?'

'One more load in the tumble dryer, then I'm off to get me hair done. Big night out tomorrow.'

'I'll put the kettle on, shall I?'

Chris messaged me during lunch: *Thanks for finding the shaver. Just leave it there.* Now if anyone asked why I hadn't gone into the Junction from the garden (to which I had the key), I had my excuse: looking for Chris's shaver. It takes years of practice to become this devious. Tamsin, I think, was a relative novice. Well, we'd soon find out.

I'd also had a couple of messages from Mina, along the lines that I was well out of things in the Old Temple. I'll spare you the legal arguments, but Judge Bracewell had adjourned for lunch and would be handing down her decision in the afternoon. I think she was as keen for the early weekend as everyone, and I got a call from Mina as I was heading back to the nursery.

'Are you secretly in league with Augusta Faulkner?' she asked.

'No. I'm openly in league with her. What's happened?'

'Something to do with Proof and something to do with Sir Lancelot. I have no idea what they were on about in the end. At half past one, all the lawyers went into chambers, and when they came out, Heidi withdrew her petition. The count will go ahead on Monday morning.'

'Not today?'

'The judge is not available. You should have seen the looks on their faces. I shall have to stay in London over the weekend and into next week.'

'Shame.'

'I must go. We're getting an Uber to Vicky's place.'

Several well muffled infants were running round the nursery playground when I arrived, and the assistant recognised me immediately. It's one of the reasons I have to do all my sneaky work when no one's around.

'You came with Siona this morning didn't you?' she asked.

'I did.'

She looked uncomfortable. 'If you've come for the girls, I'm afraid that I can only release them to a designated person.'

'Quite right, too. Glad to hear it. I'm waiting for their mother. She should be here soon, shouldn't she?'

When she realised I wasn't about to swoop for the children, she relaxed. 'In theory, yeah. She sometimes gets carried away and does an extra mile. Makes me feel guilty every time I see her.' She started to go red again when she remembered something. 'Oh, sorry. I forgot. Mandi said you had a metal leg. I didn't mean…'

'I'm used to it. I think I'll stroll up towards the park and intercept her. See you soon, I hope.'

Tammy didn't add anything to her run today. Maybe she'd had a premonition that something was up, and she was irritated when she saw me and had to abort her sprint finish.

'What are you doing here?' she panted.

'I'll give you a minute to stretch, then I have something to show you, Tamsin.'

I could see why the nursery assistant was jealous: Tamsin Kelly is young, athletic, has three lovely children and can afford a nanny. Makes you wonder why Chris has taken up with Eseld.

Stretching done, she turned to me. 'What?'

I passed her my phone. 'Have a look at these.'

She flicked through half a dozen images, going backwards and forwards and lingering on the last one. She couldn't go any redder than she was already, but she could get very angry. 'You bastards. I'm going to kill Chris for this, then I'm going to come looking for you.'

'Chris knows nothing about it. At all. Neither do Mina or Siona. The van came when Siona left for her hair appointment. This was all my own work, Tamsin.'

The pictures had shown the store room with filing cabinet, without cabinet, and then the cabinet being loaded on to a removal van.

She glanced back down at the last picture, then enlarged it. I'd made sure the name of the company was clearly visible, especially the subheading: *Part of the 8H Group*.

'Gnomes. You've handed my private papers over to the fucking Gnomes, you bastard!'

'Who have no idea what it is. And have put it into a safe place, and will only release it to me personally, or to the Constable in the event of my death. So don't get any ideas.'

She was fuming, full of adrenalin and itching to lash out. I held out my hand for my phone, and she didn't want to let go, as if having the pictures meant she still had possession of the goods. Her mouth pursed, she gritted her teeth and she slapped the phone into my palm. 'What are you up to?'

'Shall we walk? The girls will be looking for you.'

'No, we won't walk. You will tell me what you want here and now.'

'Two things, Tamsin. The first is for your own good.'

'And you would know exactly what is in my best interests, would you? Fuck off.'

'Yes, I would actually. I had to start over after the RAF. I had no friends, no colleagues and no real idea what to do. If it wasn't for the Allfather's intervention, I'd have struggled. You have a good friend in Mina. You've got a whole new set of skills.'

'You're not my counsellor.'

We had to pause to let a brace of nannies come past. I think they were Polish, and they didn't even notice we were there.

'I don't expect you to like me for this, Tamsin,' I continued, 'but think about it. You need a start away from the shadow of Salomon's House. Scotland, Ireland, the USA. Perhaps not the States. Don't want a custody battle, do we?'

'Why should I? He should be the one who runs away. With his tail between his legs. I haven't done anything wrong. I know, maybe he should move to Cornwall.'

I held up my hands in defeat. 'I hear you. Perhaps when you're sitting alone one night, you might hear me, too. But that was only advice. Here's the deal if you want your filing cabinet back.'

She was starting to shiver in the wind blowing up from the river. It was nowhere near as cold down here as it was in the Particular, but it was the middle of January, and Tamsin had just worked up a healthy sweat. She folded her arms, as much to keep warm as to ward me off.

I spoke quickly. 'I'm going to tell Mina that we had a heart-to-heart, and when you get to the restaurant tonight, you're going to tell her that you've reconsidered. That you don't care about Eseld being at the wedding so long as she doesn't sit with Chris. If you do that, and if you behave at the wedding, then you'll get your dirty secrets back, and I won't have to ask Clan Octavius to deliver it to Clan Salz. Lloyd loves a challenge.'

She flinched right back when I mentioned Lloyd. The reason she hadn't tried to kill me in the street is that, in its current state, her tin box is more secure than the Bank of England. The magick surrounding it has two special properties – it would destroy the contents if tampered with, and it was keyed to the caster's full Imprint. Which is why it was still there in the cellar: when Tamsin Merged with Melody, her Imprint changed. Hugely.

'We'd better hurry up,' I said, leaving her to follow or bolt.

She didn't bolt, but she did jog past me and get to the nursery first. I stood back and got ready to walk to Earth House on my own, until Amanda saw me and went wild. Tamsin was faced with a dilemma. Should she have a meltdown in front of the nursery staff, or should she let her firstborn ride on the Pirate's shoulders? There was a muscle in my back that desperately wanted her to have the meltdown, but no, I was summoned.

I'd like to say that things got *worse* when Amanda told her mother that I'd let her walk all along the wall by the river (little liar), but some situations can't actually get *worse*.

I had been booked to give the little girls their tea while Tamsin got ready for the big girls' night out. Once Amanda had climbed off my shoulders, I made myself scarce for an hour while Tamsin spent some quality time with her children and hopefully calmed down.

I did prepare the ground by calling Mina, though. 'You what?' she said.

'I talked to Tammy. I told her that Eseld was both Rachael's BFF and someone who had saved my life.'

'You had no right to do that! Tammy is in a very vulnerable state.'

'I know. That's why I took one for the team, love.'

'How on earth can this be about you?'

'Because I pointed out that everyone except you would blame the victim if the Mowbrays were excluded from the wedding.'

There was an ominous silence. 'I hope for your sake that all she does is hate you more than she did before.'

'So do I. If nothing else, I've salvaged your night out. I've a strong suspicion that if Tamsin doesn't turn up with an olive branch, Rachael would have a go at her sooner or later. Probably while you waited for the taxi to the club.'

'She wouldn't. Not on my night.'

'You keep forgetting, love. Rachael is a Clarke, too.'

'Hah! I wish I could forget. I shall go and pray to Ganesh while Vicky is in the shower.'

When I reappeared in the downstairs playroom, Tamsin had calmed down. A little. She was also shattered after her morning's work with the Fae and sticky from her run. She stood up and stood close to me. 'I am going to do this for Mina, not you. Understand?'

I nodded.

'Good. And I want you to amend your instruction to Henry Octavius: death in the line of duty does not count. Far too much risk of you dying before the wedding.'

She had a point. On the other hand, if that bloody filing cabinet contained what I thought it did...

'I shall leave instructions on Monday for it to be released to Mina.'

She worked her lips from side to side. 'Deal. Right, no biscuits until they've eaten all their tea, and do not, no matter how much you are provoked, show Amanda your leg. I do not want her having nightmares.'

'Message received and understood.'

'And I will get you back for this at some point.'

I let her have the last word, and waited until she'd gone upstairs before I said, 'Who wants to look inside the helicopter before it gets dark?'

I had to drive Tamsin into town later, and she'd clearly decided that now we shared a secret, I was fair game for a third degree on Chris and Eseld. I spent most of the journey saying things like, 'No. Not that I saw,' and, 'No. Not to my knowledge.' The only questions I flat-out refused to answer were related to the filing cabinet – other than to say that it was in a very safe place and that I trusted Clan Octavius implicitly.

Mina leaned in to the driver's window to kiss me when I dropped Tamsin off, and then I heard nothing from her until Mina crawled in to bed at half past four in the morning. Her only comment? 'Oh good, you're warm.'

I stayed long enough in the morning to upset the older females by being bright and cheerful when they were both nursing epic hangovers. I even did breakfast for the kids – complete with my impersonation of an Afghan goat. Very popular with some of the audience.

Mina wrapped up warm enough to join me outside for a moment. 'Do you have to go now?' she asked.

'I've got to go today, and the forecast for later is diabolical. I've left Cordelia on her own way too long, and would you want to be snowed in with Matt Eldridge?'

She shuddered. 'Poor Cordy. Technically, I suppose he counts as company, but not by much.'

'Apart from drinking the club dry last night, how did it go?'

'Which part? The part where Sofía had to produce a fake ID to get in, the part where this man hit on Vicky, then told her that he didn't date Russians, the part where Saffron did impersonations of the bouncers and got barred, the part where Tamsin plane-shifted to avoid the queue for the ladies or the part where Rachael left us for half an hour for some mysterious reason.'

'But you had a good time?' I asked hopefully.

'Yes. We did. No sooner had we sat down in the restaurant than Tamsin says in a very loud voice, "I hear Cornish pasties are back on the menu for the wedding. There's no accounting for taste, so put me on one of the tables having curry."'

'How did Rachael take that?'

'She rolled her eyes and whispered something to Sofía. Then it was forgotten. They even helped each other climb up the stairs to get out of the club.' She snuggled into the gap under my arm and turned me round to become a human windshield. 'I would have talked her round without you getting involved. In the end. I'll leave you to sort out the proper invitations with Erin. Give you something to keep you occupied.'

'I hope that wedding invitations are the most stressful thing on my agenda for some time. I doubt it, though.'

'If I have to come and wave you off, I am going back in first.'

Tamsin didn't come to wave me off, leaving Siona and Mina to pen the children back. The Smurf in take-off mode was too overwhelming for the little twins, but Amanda lapped it up. If she doesn't have a magickal gift, I shall try and convince her to join the RAF.

I can't wait to see the look on Tamsin's face when I do.

24 — Fresh Starts

The snow that had fallen on the Particular last week had pretty much gone by Monday morning, leaving only a few white patches on the highest fells. The reason? Rain. Lots of rain. With more forecast. There was a slight gap in the downpours today, and Cordelia didn't bother to put up her hood for the walk down to Lake Cottage when Matt dropped her by the hotel's front door.

I saw all this because I was outside, finishing my coffee. It wasn't all I saw, either. There was no mistaking the way she had leaned over and given him a kiss before she got out.

'Morning, Cordy,' I said with a smile.

She stopped in her tracks when she realised I was huddled under the overhang to keep the drizzle off. She looked over her shoulder and frowned. 'Just how good *is* your eyesight, Conrad?'

'Good enough.'

'Well, that saves me an awkward conversation. Matt said it was none of your business, but I said you should know.'

'You're both right: I have no problem with you hooking up with Matt in theory. In practice, I need to know if there's a potential conflict of interest. And you do know that anything you tell me you have effectively told Mina as well.'

She flicked her braid over her shoulder. 'Yeah, well, I guessed that.' She blew out her cheeks. 'I doubt it'll last, but it's good. For now.'

'Which is all I need to know. Do you want ten minutes, or shall we head off to Penrith?'

'I could do with going through these reports first, if you don't mind. Just in case they're not up to scratch. Then I'll know for next time.'

'Fair enough.'

It took us half an hour in the end to sort out two inspection reports that she'd done (one with Matt as her driver), and then the bewildering paperwork for a case of false representation she had investigated in Cockermouth.

When it comes to relationships, you shouldn't jump to conclusions. Cordelia seemed a lot more relaxed today – a lot less distracted, a lot more focused. Was that because Matt was good for her? Because she was settled in a proper house? Because she was getting used to her new life? All of the above? You tell me. There was one other possibility, of course.

'Have you been riding again?'

Her face lit up. 'Oh yes. Three times, including all day Saturday.'

I raised my eyebrows. 'Did you go on your own?'

'Too bloody right. Matt hates horses, if he's honest, and as much as I love the fells, they're best appreciated from a distance. I went riding, and he went to explore a new route up Coniston Old Man. Then we stayed at Lakeside. I so needed a massage after a day in the saddle.'

'You get used to it.'

She laughed. *You get used to it* was what Saffron had said about working with me. Cordelia has taken it as something of a personal motto since she left the Homewood in Glastonbury. I'd just put the kettle on again when my phone rang: Mina wanted to Facetime.

'Hello, love. Cordy's here.' I looked at Cordelia and pointed to the kettle. She gave me a thumbs up.

'Say hi,' said Mina. She was calling from the small but perfectly formed garden that sits above the Old Temple. It being London, the snowdrops were in full bloom and the daffs were well above ground. Not like up here.

'Well, my duty is done, and Salomon's House has a new Warden,' she announced. I heard the sound of water landing on teabags and felt Cordelia come up to my shoulder. Mina noticed her, too, and carried on. 'It was closer than I thought it would be, but Lois won on second preferences. The Inner Council have voted to accept the result, and they have all left for the formal installation.'

'Who came second?' I asked.

'Selena. If Heidi hadn't stood, I think Selena might have edged it. She certainly won on first preferences. Hannah, the Judge, and I are the only ones who know this, but the support from Manchester for Lois was nowhere near unanimous.'

'How do you know that?'

She grinned. 'The ballot papers were thoroughly mixed up by Septimus and Stephanie, but I stamped the ballots in a slightly different place to the Clerk in London.'

'What now?'

She looked slightly guilty. 'There is a banquet tonight. Marcia insisted that I be invited.' Marcia is the Judge's nickname. It may even be her real name. No one has the courage to ask.

Cordelia put her hand on my shoulder and leaned forwards to be more visible. Feeling the contact was a shock. I wouldn't describe it as *intimate* by any means, but it was certainly *familiar*. 'Have you got anything to wear?' she asked.

'No, but that's not the problem.' Mina stared at the screen, trying to make eye contact with me. 'It will be my first trip to Salomon's House. I was hoping that you would be there to take me, Conrad. I am sorry.'

I shook my head and smiled. 'Not my territory. I took you to Merlyn's Tower, and that's the one that counts. Vicky will look after you.'

Mina was peeved. 'I'm sure she would, but she is not invited. Hannah is going to be my escort tonight.' She winced. 'And Chris will be there with Eseld. As a couple.'

Ouch. Mina is still staying at Earth House, and this would not go down well. I stood up and moved to pour the tea. 'And talking of couples, love, Cordelia has something to tell you. I'm going to nip outside.'

They were still talking when I came back in, ten minutes later.

'I'd better let you go,' said Cordelia to Mina. 'You look frozen.'

Cordy handed me the phone, and she was right: Mina was shivering. Her eyes were also as big as saucers. I switched to voice only, and put the phone to my ear. 'This is so not fair,' she said. 'I am dying to tell everyone, but Cordelia has sworn me to secrecy.'

We said goodbye, and I turned to face Cordy. She was trying to frown and trying not to laugh at the same time. 'I am so going to get you back for that, Conrad.' The laughter won out. 'You do *not* want to know some of the questions she asked me. Actually, you probably do want to know. And I'm not going to tell you. We'd better get going if we're going to smash this ring of schoolgirl Tarot smugglers.'

'Do you think I need to take both guns?'

'Better had. Just in case.'

'Could you pass them over?'

I could have kicked myself as soon as the words were out of my mouth. Idiot. 'Sorry, I didn't think. I'm really sorry. No, leave them.'

With grim determination, Cordelia reached into the open case and lifted out the weapon that had killed Raven. Her death wasn't an accident, either, it was … It was just fate, I suppose. The Hammer has a work designed to stop it being used by anyone but me, and because a Dwarf designed it, there's a terrible payback.

When you pick up the gun, it heats up, it broadcasts waves of antagonism and almost screams *Leave me alone!* If, after that, you're stupid enough to try and fire it, the Disruption Work in the bullet discharges itself into you. Instant, painful death. A quick way to commit suicide, certainly, but that wasn't what happened to Raven.

Cordelia doesn't know this, but the Allfather told me that someone tried to create a Valkyrie. They tried, they failed, and the bodged result was Raven. At a deep and elemental magickal level, Raven couldn't see herself, and she couldn't hear the Hammer protesting when she used it, trying to save me. Whether or not that had anything to do with the prophecy that she would die if she left the Daughters is a moot point.

Cordelia held the gun for a second, wincing with pain, and then she leaned forwards to drop it on the couch. It bounced, and she gasped in horror as it slid off the cushion and clattered on to the flagstones.

'Internal safety catch,' I said. 'Designed for precisely those moments.'

'I had to know,' she said, and wiped away a tear. 'I had to know what she felt. Or didn't feel. That thing is brutal, Conrad. How could she not have felt it?'

I retrieved the gun and stowed it in the holster. 'I don't know, Cordy, and I'm sorry you had to. I don't know why I carry it any more, other than to access the Ancile. I must get one I can wear round my neck. Let's get going.'

'Yeah. I'll just nip to the loo.'

I was looking forward to receiving a running commentary on the Warden's Banquet, complete with pictures. I got the selfie that went to the group (Mina's new dress was rather understated if you ask me), and then nothing until Hannah's name lit up on the call screen.

'Boss? Everything okay?'

'Mina's fine, but there's a bit of a problem.'

Hannah wasn't using her emergency voice, so what could it be? 'What's up?'

'Her tattoo. Not the Ancile, the one on her arm that registers magick. When we walked through the door into the Receiving Room, it went off like a fire alarm inside her head. Stupid me, I should have thought.'

'Is she okay?'

'I didn't know Eseld could move that fast. She caught her before her head hit the table.'

I was now, of course, sitting up and panicking. 'She fainted!'

'My mother would have called it a *swoon* rather than a *faint*. Eseld caught her, picked her up and rushed her outside. Mina is now wearing three coats to keep off the cold while we wait for Vicky to turn up in a taxi. Won't be long. I'm sure she'll call you when she's safely ensconced and all that, but Lesley is on her way down … in fact, Lesley has just shot past me.'

I had to consult my mental index file: *Lesley Harper, Occult Physician.* 'Good. What's happening *right now.*'

'*Tsk.* Mina said not to ring you because you'd overreact. I thought you should know, so there you go.'

'I am not overreacting. The Works could have triggered a reaction.'

'This is Salomon's House, not Merlyn's Tower. She'll be fine. Hang on ... Lesley has stood up and is looking relieved. No she's not. She's looking angry. Oh, panic over, she's ripped her dress. Serves her right for wearing something so tight. Here's the taxi. I'd better go.'

I got a message from Vicky five minutes later, as I was pacing up and down outside the cottage: *She's fine. She'll call you when we get back to my place. Her fingers are a bit too shaky to text. V. X.*

'So now you know how I feel,' said Mina, when she called me a short while later.

That was harsh but not unwarranted. She's been on the receiving end of those sorts of phone calls rather too often.

'So long as you're okay, that's the main thing.'

'There you are wrong. Eseld saved me from a serious head injury, apparently, and then dumped me on a dirty pavement. My new dress is ruined, I have missed the banquet and I have made a spectacle of myself. All of those are the main thing, and you are no use.' She blew out a deep breath. 'There. That feels better. I ...' There was a crackle, and muffled voices. 'Desi says I must drink this. Here's Vicky.'

Another crackle. 'Hi Conrad. She really is fine. Doctor Harper says she had a Lux Hypo – sudden drain of all Lux. You've had a few.'

'I have. She'll recover?'

'Aye. Massive headache for a bit. Paracetamol and Desi's Mam's special tea should do the trick.'

'Thank you, Vic.'

Panic over. I was kept abreast of Mina's recovery (total), and got into a multi-way conversation with a lot of people. If I ever become Warden (not going to happen), then when I have my inaugural banquet, I will turn off the Salomon's House WiFi and install mobile signal jammers. A lot of the messages were about Mina's health, and here are some of the other highlights:

Eseld: *GG is wearing that dress again. It looks even more out of place. Sorry, Vic, I know she's your friend.*

Vicky: *Aye, but I take no responsibility for her wardrobe.*

Hannah: *The new Warden has just said she's looking forward to working with me, and I agreed. Both of us are lying.*

Francesca: *Shall I upstage her by announcing my retirement?*

Everyone: *NO!!!!!!!!!!!!!! You can't!*

Francesca: *Yes I can. Now the Codex is gone, I suddenly find I'm discounting an interest in knife.*

Everyone: *????*

Francesca: *Damn autocorrect. Discovering an interest in knitting.*

Everyone: *Hahahaha.*

Eseld: *Oldcastle really is an odorous toad.*

Eseld: *Shit. Odourous AND odious.*

Hannnah: *And you're telling me something I don't know? He's finishing…*

Chris: *Is it me, or does the new Warden look like an overpromoted under-secretary of state in the Ministry of Communists and Local Government?*

Vicky: *Are you having fun with Chris, Es? How long was he typing that???*

Eseld: *Don't get me started. She's getting up to speak now.*

At least they all listened to the new Warden's speech, because it went quiet for five minutes at that point.

Eseld: *She's just thanked everyone and said nothing.*

Hannah: *Good job she doesn't have a dog, or she'd have thanked him too.*

Francesca: *Am I allowed to say that our new Warden has no class whatsoever?*

Everyone: *Yes.*

All in all, it made a long night much less lonely – for me. You may have noticed that Tamsin's name was absent from the above. Well, Eseld had just saved Mina from a serious head injury, and Tamsin is barred from Salomon's House, so the composition of the group pretty much chose itself. Sitting on my own in the cottage, I had a lot of sympathy for Tammy. Sometimes you find yourself in an impossible position, and it was only going to get worse for her as time went on.

I was woken up by a pre-dawn phone call and the accompaniment of a thunderous downpour hammering on the cottage roof. The call was from Princess Faithful.

'I am not going up in this,' she began, shouting to be heard over the noise of her car and the rain on its roof. 'And I know you're a good pilot and all that, but I'd rather not be up in the air if I have a choice, and I do.'

'Thank you. It's a day for emergency flying only. Are you still coming anyway?'

'Oh yes. Now that you've got that Ley line spur, I can put a permanent suppression Charm on your … what d'you call it?'

'Landing Zone.'

'That's the one. Let's just hope the lake road doesn't flood.'

'See you soon.' I disconnected, then thought: why is she worried about the lake road?

The answer came an hour later when, thoroughly cold and miserable, I splashed back into the cottage. Faith, of course, was warm and dry. I must practise that umbrella Charm.

'There's a Count who lives down past Bowness,' she announced. 'He has a lovely fencing studio. He's away for now and said we could make ourselves at home.'

It didn't take much effort to make ourselves at home, because he had a staff of six to do that. Over coffee, I stared at the lake through the rain and added a million and a half to the value of the house. Perhaps even two. If I told you the mundane name of the Count, you wouldn't believe me, so I'll just observe that his trophy cabinet had more Oscars than I have gallantry medals.

The fencing / dance studio was awesome, and it was the first time in years that I've had a chance to practise against a proper mannequin. Faith has been as good as her word and come up with a lot of adaptations that take my bad leg into account. The only snag is that I've internalised so much of the craft that I have as much unlearning to do as I have work to pick up the new stuff. I'm getting there.

I spent the afternoon in Kentdale with Cordelia and Ellis Baines, where he's been assessor for three years, and when we got back to the hotel, there was a surprise waiting for me.

'Where do you want this?' said Alex, King of the Birkfell Wolves.

'Arff!' said Scout.

Alex had finished the dog kennel and one of the Skelwith Gnomes had shipped it over from Patterdale in sections, ready to bolt together.

'If Matt chucks me out, I'm moving in there,' said Cordelia. 'It's huge!'

'Nothing but the best for the Lord Protector's mascot,' said Alex proudly.

'Is Matt in danger of chucking you out?' I asked Cordelia.

She waved her hand as if she didn't want to talk about it in front of Gnomes, Mannwolves and berserk border collies. 'See you tomorrow, okay?'

'Cheers, Cordy.'

I turned back to Alex. 'This is a surprise. I had no idea the kennel was ready.'

He pointed to the Gnome, who was taking a tarpaulin off the back of his truck. 'The Iron One said that it was too wet for the digger, so here we are.' He looked at the hotel, and then at the cottage. 'Why aren't you staying in the big house? It's much more fitting.'

I must tell Saul Brathay about that. I'm sure he'll turf his daughter out and let me move in.

'The Madreb can explain,' I said airily. It was way too wet to get into that conversation now. 'Put the kennel round the corner, out of the way. Tea?'

'It should be ready, Lord. We'll start work.'

What? I frowned and looked at the cottage. The bloody door was open! I smiled at Alex and strode into the cottage. Sure enough, there was Cara, making tea.

'Guardian Erin has been teaching us,' she said. 'I don't like it, but she said we should learn.'

'That's excellent,' I said. 'How did you get in? Did I leave the door unlocked.'

She shrugged as if that was nothing to do with her, and said, 'Will the Iron One need tea?'

'Oh yes. Strong and two sugars, probably.'

Cara and I stood and watched the boys erect the kennel in the fast fading light, and Scout disappeared completely, exploring his new home. It didn't take them long, and I took the mugs inside, ready to inspect the finished project. And then I heard the truck start.

I lurched outside as quick as I could, but the truck was already in motion, leaving Alex and Cara behind. They were also naked. I glanced nervously at the hotel, but they were just out of the line of sight. Probably.

'What? Why?' I said, pointing to the disappearing truck.

'We want to explore the route back,' said Cara, as if that were perfectly normal. 'We should know how to find you in an emergency. The Iron One has our clothes and will bring them with him tomorrow.'

I couldn't argue with that logic.

Alex slapped his hand on his head. 'Och, aye, and Karina says to tell you that she's cleared it with Omnira.'

'That's good to know.'

Cara cocked an ear, and sniffed the air. 'I can smell the darkness. Shall we go?'

There was no sensible reason for them to stay, so I said, 'Thank you so much for this. I shall bring gifts for the Pack soon. And I've had an idea. Could you ask Karina to call me when you get back.'

They bowed, and I looked at them properly. It's only been a few months since I first saw Cara, and she has aged visibly. She's pretty much in her prime now, but every time I have their nature rubbed in my face, it hurts.

'You should lock our mascot in the house before we Exchange,' said Cara. She raised her voice and howled. In seconds, Scout was haring up the path. I can't compete with that, and I wondered if I were doing the right thing bringing him back here.

I wondered even harder when I saw how filthy he'd got in less than half an hour. 'In you go, and stay off the sofa,' I told him. Door safely closed, the King and Queen Exchanged into sleek and powerful wolves and had a stretch, as if they'd just woken up. 'Be very careful crossing the road,' I told them. 'It's much busier than any of the ones by Birk Fell.'

Alex glanced at Cara and parted his jaws in a smile. And then he howled, a great noise that would be heard from a long way away. When they'd loped off, heading through the woods to where there was a back gate, I got out my phone and messaged Liz: *Wolves crossing A591@Ambleside. Get ready for some phone calls.*

To which she responded: *FFS!*

By the time I got back inside, Scout had finished exploring. 'Good job I didn't want a quiet night,' I told him. 'Not with all this bloody cleaning to do, you evil hound.' I bent down and he ran up to me. 'Welcome back, you mad mutt.'

'Arff! Arff, Arff.'

'No dogs,' said Grazia next morning. 'No bloody Werewolves, either. I would have kicked his furry Scottish arse out of here yesterday if he hadn't come with my cousin. Do you know what he said? "Are you the Lord Protector's servant?" Bloody cheek. Get out, you stupid dog!'

'Well, there is a vacancy on my staff, Grazia, and Scout *is* the Lord Protector's mascot. I just want to show him round, then I'll take him back. How's Gloria doing?'

'Stop changing the subject. I do not want you bringing Werewolves on to our property again, is that clear?'

I paused. 'Crystal.' Another pause. 'I am concerned about Gloria, though. She didn't look well yesterday, and the Smurf is on standby if you need him.'

'She's a bit better today, thanks, and I'm taking her to Kendal for a scan tomorrow.'

It was the Eden Valley today, and some quality time with Tanya Dickinson, the newly reassigned assessor. I tried to ask Cordelia if everything was okay with Matt, and she frowned. 'Yeah. Great. Mostly. He keeps changing his mind about wanting to go public with our relationship.'

'And how do you feel?'

'I think it's no one's business but ours. And yours, of course.' She turned round. 'You might have a roomie sooner than you think, Scout.'

He had nothing to say to that, so she turned back and said, 'Matthew got in such a mess last night, trying to tiptoe around the fact that Valentine's day is coming up, and did I want to go out. I told him not to bother. What about you two?'

I explained that Valentine's Day is a day of mourning for Mina, and quickly changed the subject.

The Eden Valley Union is huge, and we barely skimmed the surface in one day, especially given that we avoided the Ripleys. I wanted Tanya to build a relationship on her own before I stepped in. Tanya did say that she'd heard nothing to suggest that the family weren't simply preparing to fight the court case.

At six o'clock, we pulled into Penrith North Lakes station and I told Scout to be on his best behaviour. Mina looked tired and drained when she got off the train. And then she saw Scout, and her eyes lit up. When the three of us were curled up as best we could on the Lake Cottage couch that night, she stroked his ears and said, 'This is a good thing, Conrad. In all sorts of ways. Thank you.'

We leaned in for a kiss, and I swear I saw a glint in Scout's eye. When he was bonded with me, he got to feel a lot of things that I did (and vice versa). Whether this included my most intimate moments with Mina is a question we never got a proper answer to. It was one of the many reasons we made him sleep in the stables at Elvenham.

Mina saw him, too, and she said, 'I've been thinking. Playing house here is all very well, but it's getting rather crowded. How about looking for an out of season holiday let for a few months? Until the wedding, at least.'

This couch really wasn't very comfortable for my back. 'Sounds like a good idea. Somewhere with reasonable access to the whole Particular, obviously.'

'I shall start looking. And while you get up to make some tea, perhaps you could explain this?'

I leaned over Scout to look at her laptop. He grumbled and squirmed into the place I'd just vacated.

'Oh, that's just an invoice from Skelwith Construction. Probably for bringing the kennel over.'

'No, Conrad, and I know you can see perfectly well that it's an invoice for two tons of gravel, two wheelbarrows and one hundred square metres of artificial grass. What are you planning to do? Teach the wolves how to play cricket?'

I seized at the chance. 'Yes, actually. Might be better for them than toxophily.'

There was a long pause and a hard stare. 'I was being sarcastic. As well you know.'

I shrugged. 'What can I say? Lucky guess? Lucky sarcastic guess?' After two more seconds of hard stare, I capitulated. 'An LZ for the Smurf. So we can drop in more often.'

'*We????* That is incredible, even by your standards. Where are you going to put it? Their home is not called Birk *Fell* for nothing.'

'On the site of the alleged tomb of Urien. That's flat enough. And it was so badly damaged by the Ripleys that if we don't put some drainage down, it could form a tarn and start eroding the whole slope. And having easy chopper access might be crucial one day.'

She looked at the bill again. It wasn't huge, considering. 'This is nothing. It's the thought that you might get attached to that flying money pit that bothers me.'

'Too late. I'm already attached. And I haven't heard you complaining about the quick access to London and Cheltenham.'

'We are *not* keeping that thing one single day after the Mowbrays stop paying for maintenance and insurance. Is that clear?'

I started to scoop Scout out of the way. 'Yes.'

'Good. I shall … Is that your phone?'

'Yeah. It's Rick. Wonder what he wants?'

I extracted myself from the couch and picked up the phone. 'Hi Rick.'

'Hi Conrad. How's things?'

We chatted for a while, especially about the new Warden and her plans. He asked how it was going in the Particular, and I could tell he was building up to something. We get on well, but this was the first time he's ever called me out of the blue. When he asked whether we were going to Clerkswell at the weekend, I could tell that we were getting there.

'Yes. And given the current situation, we're taking the Smurf in case I need to make a dash for it.'

'Right. Look, mate, I've got something on this weekend, and if you can cover, it would be great if Cordy could come down and spend some time with the kids.'

I looked at the phone, stunned. This could be a minefield of epic proportions. My first loyalty was, of course, to Cordelia. Then again, Rick has never lied to me or been anything other than straight. 'No problem, Rick. In fact, now that we've settled in, we shouldn't need to work weekends on a regular basis. The odd festival, but there should be plenty of notice. Subject to the first rule of the Watch, of course.'

'Yeah. *Shit happens when you least expect it.* Gotcha. Thanks, Conrad.'

Mina picked up on what was going on. 'We can stay here and go house-hunting if you'd rather someone was on duty,' she offered.

'Not necessary. I'm having the team together on Friday morning for a meeting. I'll launch my idea of regular weekend rotations a bit earlier than planned, and we can look forward to stretching out on Friday night.'

'That sounds like the best idea I've heard all week.'

25 — High Pressure is Building

One of the nice things about working with Conrad was that he was a morning person, too. Quite happy to have a serious discussion when most people were still trying to work out whether they could go back to bed. On the other hand, it was a five and a half hour drive to Ambleside. The next time she came down to Wells, Cordelia was definitely going to try and hitch a lift on the Smurf.

She looked at the kitchen clock again: she would have to start kicking the kids out of bed soon, when she really should be on the road. Where the hell was Rick? A flash of light on the wall: headlamps. Here he was. About bloody time.

She opened the back door and went back to get the last of her stuff. She wasn't going to go out into the rain until she absolutely had to. Fast footsteps crunched over the gravel, and Rick bounced into the house. 'Sorry I'm late,' he began. 'The overnight roadworks on the M5 have overrun. You might want to leave it half an hour before you go.'

He hadn't told her where he'd been going, and she hadn't asked. He was entitled to do what he liked, and in return he had refrained from saying that the children were entitled to see their mother in the flesh and not just on a screen. Talking of screens, she put the kettle on and checked her phone: Rick was too good a liar for her taste, a skill he'd demonstrated on many occasions. But not today. There really was no point in leaving now – the local traffic would all avoid the motorway and clog up the alternative routes.

'Good weekend?' she asked. That was a legitimate question.

'Oh yes. And you had good fun with the kids, if that video is anything to go by. Was that Hedda in the background?'

'Yes. She seems quite happy, and the Daughters have got used to the idea of having a non-Mage in the Homewood. She said she'll stay as long as she's not a burden.'

'Good. I'm gonna grab a quick shower. I'll rouse the kids while I'm at it, shall I?'

And in one bound, he was gone, having completely avoided the subject of where he'd been for the weekend. Or who he'd been with. She made some tea for him, and decided to take her reduction now rather than tonight. Less chance of needing to pee on the motorway. The only problem was that she'd forgotten just how quick he could be in the shower.

He returned in his dressing gown, sniffed the air and looked at the bottle next to the kettle. 'I'm pleased for you,' he said. 'I hope he treats you right.'

Shit, shit and double shit. Smelling her contraceptive reduction was not how she'd wanted Rick to find out she was seeing someone. He grabbed his tea and pivoted to go back upstairs.

When he returned, he had two zombies with him, so further discussion of Cordelia's love life was off the agenda. For now. Rick had proven in spades that he would always put their children first, but she'd never been able to shake the feeling that his attitude to women's sexuality had been formed last century and was unlikely to change soon.

There were tears from her daughter when she got ready to go, and a study of heroic indifference from her son. He took after his father way too much when it came to emotions. 'Stay inside or you'll get those nice new uniforms wet,' she told them, then dashed into the rain.

Rick followed her and asked the question when they got to her car. 'When do you think you'll be able to get down again?'

She could feel the water penetrating her fleece already. 'I don't know, Rick. It's a hell of a long way. If Conrad can drop me at Bristol, could you pick me up? It's either that or ask if I can do ten days on and four days off.'

'We'll make it work,' he said. 'Whatever. Take care.'

She dived into her car, and water ran down her fleece on to her jeans. Ugh. She started the engine and waved to Rick and the kids, huddled in the doorway.

Could they make it work? All of it? Well, she had plenty of time to think about it on the journey. She had even longer to think about it when the articulated lorry driver to her left yawned so hard that he swerved into her lane. The first thing she knew about it was when the airbag inflated.

'I've got you. It's okay. Don't panic.'

The voice was calming and soothing, and when he pushed the airbag out of the way, he looked just as calm as he sounded.

'Let's get you out of here. Best not to linger on the carriageway, eh?'

She fumbled the seatbelt open and let him take her arm and guide her out of the wreck of her car. Bloody hell. Damn and blast the bastard lorry driver to eternity in a tumble dryer full of rocks. On High Heat.

Her rescuer let go of her arm, and she could survey the scene. And the damage. Her poor little car was nose-first into the temporary crash barriers of the Staffordshire roadworks. The traffic in the other lane was passing slowly, each driver turning to stare at her. She certainly wouldn't be driving this car again for a long time.

The crash barriers had been displaced, and they squeezed through the gap to stand in the relative calm of the construction zone. As usual, there were no actual construction workers in sight. Not one.

'I've called the police,' said her knight in shining armour.

She started shaking her head. 'No way. It's only an accident.'

'It was a serious accident for which the other driver did not stop. Sorry, what's your name?'

'Cordelia.'

'I'm David. Don't worry, Cordelia. I've got it all on dashcam, including his number. The next time he could kill someone, and you'll need a police report for your insurance company, and if the police are here, you'll get your vehicle recovered much quicker.' He smiled, as if all was going to be right with the world now that he'd taken control. Damn him.

'I really don't think the police are going to be interested in this. I don't want to bother them,' she said.

David frowned. 'You are insured, aren't you?'

Six months ago, she wouldn't have been. Working with Conrad had made her toe the line when it came to Road Traffic Regulations.

'Yeah.' The sound of a siren in the rapidly accumulating traffic ended all hope of avoiding officialdom. It was going to be a long day.

'You're starting to shake,' said David. 'Come over here and sit down before you faint.'

'You poor thing,' said Saskia Mason when she pulled up at Sandbach services. 'You look like an orphan standing there with all your stuff.'

'No room at the inn,' said Cordelia. 'I can't stand inside. Too busy.'

'Let's get you out of here. I'll give you a hand.'

Conrad had been adamant: Cordy was staying at Middlebarrow Haven until she had sorted out a hire car, and yes, of course Saskia would come and pick her up. What was the point of her otherwise?

It was only when the recovery vehicle had dropped her off that she realised what a good idea that was. It was cold, damp and would be dark very soon. Was it today that she'd waved goodbye at the Old Rectory? She seemed to have been living in Motorwayland forever.

'Thank you so much, Saskia. You don't know how good it feels to see a friendly face.'

When she'd been fed and watered, the phone calls started. Conrad offered to come and get her. Matt offered to come and get her. As did Mina. The only one who didn't actually get on the phone and offer their services was Scout.

The matter was settled by the police: they decided that they really would rather like a formal statement, and could Ms Kennedy be available? She could.

She could also have strangled the bloody constable when she finally turned up. Four hours late: too late to go looking for another car and too late to head up to the Particular. On the bright side, it gave her a chance to have unfettered access to Nimue's spring. There was going to be a reckoning tonight.

She looked at the stars as she made her way to the grove. The fact that she could see them at all was confirmation of Conrad's weather forecasting. The grim parade of endless rain storms had finally blown away to the east, and now there was high pressure building. It probably wouldn't freeze tonight, but if that system stuck around, a serious cold snap was on the way. She turned her eyes back to the path and got ready for the encounter.

Before she summoned the Spirits, she prayed to the Goddess. She had felt Her presence in the few ceremonies she'd managed to attend at Elter Water, and she had asked the question every time: *Is Raven alive?* And then, last week, she had been brought hard up against the cold iron reality of the Hammer. How could anyone survive an encounter with *that?*

Every morning, Conrad Clarke got out of bed in the knowledge that he might kill someone that day. Cordelia had got used to the idea that *she* might die, but not to the idea that she might go to bed that night having taken a life and think *job well done.* She tried to see it from Conrad's perspective: *It's not my fault if people keep trying to kill me.* Was that enough to keep her going forwards? No, it wasn't, because the Spirits wanted her to take the offensive.

'It's good to see you safe, little chick,' said Helena.

'Aye, I didn't think our plans would founder on the motorway,' added Lucas. Cordelia couldn't help but smile at the mixed metaphor: worthy of Tom Morton, that one.

'How long before you can return?' said Lucas when she didn't respond. Helena seemed genuinely concerned, but she was under no illusions about Lucas: his value to her consisted only of what she could deliver for him.

'I have to know she's alive,' said Cordelia. 'Before I take part in any attack on the Red Queen, I have to know that Raven is alive.'

'You know we can't guarantee that, dear,' said Helena sadly. 'You've seen what the evil creature is capable of. You've seen the monstrosities she keeps penned up at the old sídhe. You've smelt the poison she's pumping into Persephone. You held Blenheim while they stitched his flesh from the wound she inflicted.' She paused, and lowered her voice. 'You saw what she did to Jocasta's arm. And if that's not enough, you'll see it again the next time you look into Princess Faithful's face. No creature who can do that to her own offspring should be allowed to live. Would you do that to your daughter, no matter how much she upset you?'

'I...'

Lucas interrupted her reply. 'Persephone hasn't got long. She needs help.'

Cordelia took a deep breath and said, 'I agree. And I think Conrad will agree to help us. I need to sound him out.'

'No! He won't have anything to do with it.'

Cordelia was adamant. She'd reached her sticking point. 'You lost your daughter, so what chance have we got with Perci? All she can see in her future is Unicorns and winning posts. If I'd known at her age that I could ride them, I'd have signed up in a heartbeat. She has to have a place to go to, and that place has to be Greendale.'

'Don't talk rot,' said Lucas. 'Rowan Sexton's not going to give up Blenheim.'

'She doesn't need to if the Red Queen gets the Bridle of Urien back and Perci brings Keraunós with her.' She could see the disbelieving looks in their faces, and she pressed on. 'Listen, if the Red Queen has the bridle, her main grievance is satisfied. She won't press for restitution against Perci, because that would mean exposing what she's done to her. She won't want that. She can pursue her case against the Ripleys in court.'

Lucas and Helena looked at each other. 'Alexandra Greening won't give up the bridle. Never.'

'So I'll steal it.'

'And I'll win the next Cumberland Wrestling trophy.'

'Let me try. Let me approach Conrad, gently, and let me have a good look at Greendale. There's time for that, and I've even arranged to stay with them tomorrow night, ready for an early start on Thursday.'

'This is a waste of time,' said Lucas.

'You can talk,' said Cordelia. She folded her arms and set her jaw in case they weren't going to get the message from her voice. 'I've said what I'm going to do. If you really want to convince me, you'll scour *every* one of the Red Queen's lands looking for Raven, and you'll either tell me where she is or give me a list of the places she might be.' She pointed her finger at Lucas. 'You've taken risks before, time to do it again.'

The Spirits shimmered and lost some of their form. They would be talking to each other in their realm. When they became more solid again, it was Helena who spoke. 'Be careful, chick. The Greenings may hate the Red Queen, but they'll gut you and toss you on the midden if you try to steal from them and get caught.'

'Like the Ripleys did with Harry Eldridge, you mean? It's only now that I know Matt properly I've realised just what some of these people can be like. I'll be careful. Until the next time.'

On Thursday morning, Cordelia found a source of joy she'd read about but never believed: galloping over frost-tinged grass with her breath raw in her throat and the wind stinging her face.

Sophie drew level with her. 'Easy now. Slow him down!'

The stone wall ahead was suddenly getting a lot closer, and Cordelia didn't have the first clue about how to get the horse to jump it. She shortened the reins and leaned forwards to press down. Her mount got the message and started to slow and turn away. In a few seconds, they were stationary, abreast the wall. Great clouds of steam were gathering around them, and she wiped the tears away from her eyes, but nothing could wipe the smile off her face.

'Wow. Just wow, Sophie. That was incredible.'

The girl grinned back. 'You were so born for this. You did really well, considering you've only been at it five minutes.'

Cordelia shook her head. 'Doesn't matter how well I did. Just look around you.'

She turned her head to take in the mist on Coniston Water, the white coating on the grass, and ahead of them, the squat turret at the edge of the double-cream coloured Brantwood House. To the left, trees marched up the fell, and more wreaths of mist clung to the pines on the higher slopes. And not a thing could be heard beyond the horses' breathing.

'Nice, isn't it?' said Sophie. 'I brought you down here because I can't use the gallops until after lunch. We'd better go – they'll be arriving at Brantwood soon. The magick stuff in that wall stops them coming in here, but they can still see us.'

Sophie turned her mount to start walking up the field towards the sanctuary of the trees, and Cordelia's horse fell in step of its own accord.

'Have you been?' said Cordelia, pointing to Brantwood.

'No,' replied Sophie as if this were a strange question. 'What was it like in the big house last night?'

'Nice. I didn't get there till late, and everyone was pretty much ready for bed. I even got a room of my own. Why are you out in the cottage?'

If Sophie noticed the abrupt change of topic, she didn't let on. 'Bottom of the food chain. No magick and no diplomas. If I stick at it, I might be promoted to the attic by the time I'm twenty-five.'

The reason Cordy had changed the subject was to conceal the short conversation she'd had when Alexandra Greening had welcomed her to Greendale Lodge. She *was* late (saying goodbye to Matt had taken longer than she had expected), but the lady of the house had been waiting for her, as had her daughter, and Jocasta had not looked well.

'Silly girl tried to mount a horse and damaged a tendon. She thought that just because the bones had knitted, there was no risk,' said Alexandra, casting a disparaging look at her daughter. The cast on Jo's arm was virgin white today, when last week it had been thoroughly annotated by everyone at Greendale (including Cordy). 'Tell me something,' continued the mother. 'Is Conrad still stabling his horse at Sprint and taking classes with Princess Faithful?'

'Yes,' said Cordelia. 'He'll be there tomorrow. He says they don't talk about anything to do with the Red Queen, and that he doesn't think Faith knows much.'

Alexandra shook her head as if Cordelia had missed the point. 'So long as they're still seeing each other. I'm afraid you've missed the main meal. Feel free to scrounge something out of the kitchen – one of the staff should still be there. See you in the morning.'

Cordelia was still turning over what Alexandra had said last night as the horses arrived at the top of the meadow. When they were through the gate, Sophie pointed to a gap in the trees. 'We're going to do the narrow path again. See if you can get to the end without stopping.'

Cordelia laughed. 'Because close control is more important than speed. Right, let's go.'

She didn't manage the path without stopping, but she did do much better than the last time she'd tried. When they dismounted at the end of the lesson, Sophie rubbed her hand over Cordelia's horse. 'He's a good jumper, this one. Next time we'll do more trotting and try a couple of jumps. He can do them in his sleep, so as long as you let him do the work, you'll be fine.' She grinned at Cordelia. 'Better wear a hat, though. Just in case. Don't want the Chief on my case.'

Cordelia smiled back and started to loosen the saddle. It was as good a time as any. One of the senior grooms was heading towards the buildings at the top of the yard, the buildings she'd been kept away from. 'Is that where they keep the Enchanted tack?' she asked casually. 'I'd love to have a look at it.'

Sophie turned away to see to her own horse. 'Dunno. They don't allow me in there.'

Cordelia knew she was lying, because she'd seen Sophie handle Blenheim on her own often enough, and she couldn't do that without access to the proper tack room. Never mind. She'd come up with a better plan for next time.

Her second setback came in the late afternoon, when she finally got to talk to Conrad. Her accident on Monday had come to the attention of some law firm or other, and they'd promised that if she let them handle the case, she could have a proper replacement car. She'd jumped at the opportunity, and after some negotiation they'd promised to deliver a BMW 4x4 to Kendal. When she finally got the keys, it looked a lot bigger than anything she'd driven before. Better not damage this one.

The Satnav was excellent, and she soon tracked Conrad down to a pub near Kirkby Lonsdale, where he was drinking coffee and writing notes on his visit to a Coven of the Sisters near Casterton. When he'd volunteered to go alone (so she could pick up her new car), she'd had a fleeting moment of worry: an unaccompanied man going to an all-female coven didn't always end well. And then she'd decided that he was more than capable of handling women on his own.

After a catch-up on the week so far, she said, 'On Tuesday night, I went through some of the papers at Middlebarrow. They make more sense now I know a bit more.'

He gave his usual self-deprecating smile. 'You don't want to believe everything you read in them.'

'I believe the ones Tom Morton wrote.'

'Ouch! You're supposed to be on my side, Cordy.'

'I didn't look at what he wrote properly the first time,' she lied. She had actually read Tom's reports particularly closely the first time, for exactly the reason that Tom wouldn't lie in writing; this was the first time she'd had to refer to them. 'It was the visit notes and statement from Kirk Liddington.'

'You mean Fae Klass, star of the Fairy Gardens.' He looked longingly into his empty cup before sliding it away. 'One person definitely not in those reports is Stacey.'

Cordelia didn't want to talk about Stacey, whoever she might be, but if she was important to Conrad… 'Oh yes?'

'Mmm. Mina's old friend from HMP Cairndale. Long story short, we got her a job at the Gardens in Housekeeping. Before Christmas, she was promoted to be Fae Klass's PA. That mostly means dresser and driver, but it's a better life than she had.'

'Good. A bit like Sophie at Greendale Stables. I'm glad to hear something good came of it, but you didn't make it a priority to get Kirk Liddington off the Forest Manna, did you?'

The Count of Canal Street had paid for Kirk's feminisation surgery and was giving him Forest Manna, also known as Fae Dust, to allow him to perform with a woman's voice, amongst other things.

'It was hard. Despite everything that's gone on, she's still not Entangled, and she still sees it as some foreign narcotic.' He looked up and smiled, showing her his battered Ganesh Zippo lighter. 'If I can't be convinced to give up the fags, what chance do I stand convincing Fae Klass to give up Forest Manna? It was central to her life, her self-image and her career. Mind you, I'm not sure whether the new Countess is giving her the Rapture or still runs the Well of Desire. Best not to ask that sort of question.'

And with that, he got up, no doubt desperate for his nicotine fix. That made two *better plans* she needed to come up with. On the way out, she asked him if they'd decided what they were doing at the weekend.

'We have. We're going to London – by train – and Mina's spending the weekend with Mister Joshi, her favourite priest. They're sorting out the Hindu part of the wedding, and Sunday being Valentine's day, she's going to visit Miles's grave and pray. Back Monday morning, early.'

'What about you?' she asked. That Mina wanted to remember her first husband was no surprise, but what was he going to do?

'Chris is taking me through the Old Network on Saturday. Reckons he can tick off a couple more modules for my phantom doctorate. And on Sunday, I'm going to the British Museum to play spot the Artefact. I have to hand in my answers by email. Did you ever do that?'

It was a popular game for trainee Mages: go to a decent museum and try to spot which of the artefacts were also Artefacts. 'Yes, but not at the British Museum. That should keep you out of mischief.'

'You're not joking. Nice wheels, by the way.'

271

He had never used an expression like that before, so it must be ironic. She didn't care: it had rear-wheel priority 4x4 transmission and it allowed her to see over hedges, something that didn't usually happen.

She looked at his own BMW, the 5 Series Estate. 'At least mine doesn't smell of fags or wet dog. Where is he, by the way?'

'At the hotel. He ran around so much at Sprint Stables this morning, I thought he'd better rest his leg. I know how he feels, and I'd do the same, but I don't have a kind and generous master to look after me. No peace for the wicked. See you tomorrow.'

26 — The Feast of St Valentine

It was only after she'd accepted the invitation that she remembered she wasn't single. Not really. No one outside Lake Cottage knew about her and Matt, and neither her presence in his house nor his presence in her bed had prompted her to question her right to attend the Greendale Single Ladies Hack and BBQ.

It was a tradition, apparently, for the unattached women of the stables (and the Big House) to go for an afternoon ride and have a small barbecue on Valentine's day. The barbecue was really a bonfire, and more of an excuse to sit around and drink without freezing to death than a source of food. When she told Matt, he seemed relieved and disappointed in equal measure.

Sunday dawned bright and crisp, as had the last five days. Cordelia looked out of the picture windows of Blackburn House and decided that you could actually have too much of this. Days of sub-zero temperatures had leached the heat out of everything, and even a trip to the car needed several layers. She was going to have *very* sore toes by the end of the day. Maybe a night in with Matt and a DVD wasn't such a bad idea.

And when she discovered that she was the oldest of the Single Ladies by a decade, she started to regret it even more. Iras was in charge (Charmian being in a relationship), and Cordy cringed inside when Natalie Greening turned up. The young assessor came over and whispered, 'Don't worry. I won't tell on you. Not that shagging Matt Eldridge doesn't mean you're still single.'

'Who told you?' hissed Cordelia. If it was Matt, then they were over. Totally.

'You've got a great poker face, Cordy. You gave nothing away. It was Matt: he actually looked happy on Friday morning, and he smiled at you in *that* way. Know what I mean? Well, it's good to see that one of you is happy.'

Natalie smirked and moved away, and Cordy had to grin and bear it. Matt was a good man, and it hurt to pretend otherwise.

The Single Ladies gathered in the yard, and Iras started handing out packages to be stowed in rucksacks. Cordy accepted something that weighed a ton and struggled to fit it in, and then she felt a tingle of magick and looked up.

From the top of the yard, Rowan Sexton led Blenheim out of his special stable, and there was no mistaking the saddle and bridle. Cordelia grinned to herself and thanked Fate for her chance.

'Don't worry,' said Sophie from behind her.

'Whoa! You made me jump,' said Cordelia, blushing with guilt.

'Sorry. I was just gonna say that I'll lead. I think you can manage a few of the jumps if you just follow me. Where they're too much, I'll take us round another way.'

'I never thought to ask, Sophie. You're not coupled up?'

'Yeah, right. As if. Do you want me to pass that rucksack when you've mounted?'

'Please.'

Cordelia got on her horse and accepted the heavy pack. When it was secure, Sophie continued her tirade. 'All the boys I knew are knobheads. Total knobheads. And now I'm here, no Mage is gonna look twice at me, are they?'

'Why not? You've got so much going for you.'

Sophie stared at her. 'Have you been in a convent or something?' She reflected on Cordelia's life story for a moment. 'Oh yeah, I suppose you have. Well, if you hadn't noticed before, Male Mages get the pick. Whoever they want, Mage or mundane. And any half-way fit mundane lad is gonna get picked off and picked up by a Mage. Iras calls it *assortative mating*, whatever that means. I call it *being left to scrape the barrel*. And some of the scrapings are *minging*.' Sophie almost vaulted into the saddle as if her own pack were a feather. 'We're off.'

They had to go in single file through the woods, and Cordelia couldn't help thinking about Matt. Was his single status really down to his hopeless unrequited love for the late Petra Leigh? Their own relationship was still like a holiday romance to her: an affair with no responsibilities that provided a little bubble of warmth in a cold world.

Rick was expecting her to go down to Wells again next weekend, and soon enough it would be Spring, and she would face the choice between days on the fells with Matt or trying to get him to develop an interest in something other than work and mountains. She broke into a big grin when she realised she'd answered her own question: she knew exactly why Matt was still single.

The ground opened out and Sophie drew level again. 'What you smiling at?' she asked. 'Are you considering the hopeless state of men in the Particular?'

'You could say that. You know, Sophie, there are other options.'

Sophie grinned. 'Well, the cottage does have a very good washing machine.'

'I was thinking of other girls. I had a long-term partner in my "convent", actually.'

Sophie took this in her stride. 'It's like magick. You're either born a Mage or you're not. I'm not. You either fancy girls or you don't, and I don't, no matter what the alternatives.'

The change in attitude between Cordelia's generation and Sophie's was something Cordy struggled with a lot. Cordelia had been born into a world where same sex relationships were common in the magickal world but frowned on outside it, but now…

'What happened?' asked Sophie. 'Did you leave the convent place because you split up?'

'She died, and when she did, I realised that she was the only thing keeping me there.'

'I'm really sorry. What was she like?'

'She … Look, Iras is picking up speed.'

'Here we go!'

Ninety minutes later, Cordelia was ready for a hot bath, but the rest of the Single Ladies were ready to party.

They were deep within Grizedale Forest, in a large clearing. 'What is this place?' she asked Sophie.

'Greendale Glade. First time I've been invited. It's where they have all the big celebrations – Solstice and stuff like that.'

Everything that could be made of wood without a roof was here: benches, tables, a fire pit, a screened off area for toilets, a stream to water the horses. 'How do they get it here? We're in the middle of nowhere.'

Rowan Sexton was next to them, tying up Blenheim. 'It's deceiving,' she said. 'There's an access road through there. Not quite so romantic, but very practical. Who's got the Tequila?'

'Me,' said Sophie. 'I'll go and get it.'

Cordelia was drawn to Blenheim like the proverbial moth. She went round and looked at his withers, and the mark of the Red Queen was still there: three lines of scar tissue where the pure white hairs would never grow back. Damn the bitch. Damn her.

'He's fine,' said Rowan. 'No soft tissue damage. You were brilliant that night, Cordelia. I'm sorry I haven't thanked you properly, but, well…'

'You'd just won the Borrowdale Crown. I'm surprised you could stand after that. I can't imagine what it must be like.'

Cordelia was still standing close to the Unicorn, and when Rowan found a small apple, Cordy went to grab the reins.

'No!' shouted Rowan.

Cordy jerked back. The alarm in Rowan's voice caused Blenheim to turn his head, looking for a threat, and Cordy nearly got sliced by the Unicorn's horn.

'You can't touch the reins without an isolating lead rope,' she said. 'Thank the Goddess there was one at Waterhead when you saved him.'

The freezing air struck deep through her layers and she felt her bladder contract with shock and fear. 'What do you mean?'

Rowan's coat was half unzipped, and she pulled down her top to show a single, ancient Artefact on a thick gold chain. 'Without this, it's lethal. I'm not supposed to say anything, but you deserve the truth. I know you want to ride him one day, and, well, he's an absolute bastard without the bridle, aren't you?'

Rowan slowly held out the apple on the flattest of flat palms, and Blenheim hungrily snaffled it.

'Thank you,' said Cordelia. 'I realise how difficult it must be for you to talk to me.'

Rowan was only a couple of years older than Sophie, not that you'd know it. Rowan gave Cordelia a sardonic look. 'Difficult to talk to Conrad Bloody Clarke's sidekick? Yeah, you could say that. I don't hold it against him, you know. Well, not most of it.'

Cordelia was alarmed. 'Which part *do* you hold against him?'

'Erin Slater. She's got her feet well under the table at Sprint House. My mother would say that she's a bad influence on Pihla, if my mother wasn't trying to stay sane in the Esthwaite Rest, and I don't hold her being in jail against him. Nor the fact that my uncle is in Strangeways for shooting the father I never knew.'

'It's still not easy, though.'

Rowan sighed. 'Don't be nice. I can't cope with nice. Not today. Let's get drunk instead. And they've got the fire going.'

Cordelia lingered with Blenheim for a second, loving that he looked back when she looked him in the eye, though she resisted the temptation to reach him with magick. When she turned to the fire, she took a look at the group. Out here, it was really obvious why Sophie had invited her: none of the others liked the plain, mundane, working class girl who thought that *Love Island* was sophisticated viewing. They didn't *dislike* her, but they weren't going to sit next to her. Not if they had a choice.

Cordelia had hoped to get some time with Clara, the red-headed refugee from Blackthwaite Stables. It was quite clear that she was being kept completely away from anything remotely interesting on the Greendale estate, and Conrad had been spot on in fingering Clara as a weak spot. Perhaps that was why Clara had been placed firmly next to Iras. Cordelia intercepted Natalie Greening and said, 'Do you want to join me and Sophie?'

'Yeah, great,' said Natalie. 'Saves me being left out. And Sophie's got the bench nearest the fire, too. Result.'

A while later, despite sticking to spirits, Cordelia couldn't stand it any longer. If she didn't go to the toilet *now*, she'd have an accident. 'No one *ever* uses them in the winter,' said Natalie.

'Yeah, well when you've had two children, you have to recalibrate,' observed Cordelia. She weaved through the smoke to the distant wall that protected the earth privies. By the Goddess, that plastic seat actually had *ice* on it. With one superhuman heroic effort, she crossed her legs and used a Charm to heat the air around the seat until the ice melted.

'Here we go,' she muttered. 'You can do this. How bad can it be?'

Very, turned out to be the answer.

She was jumping on the spot, pulling her jodhpurs over her thermal tights when she saw a light in the woods. *What the fuck?*

It was near enough dark now – the girls had told her they were going back by a proper track, and that she was staying over again tonight. No one was paying her any attention, so she put on a Silence and slipped through the woods towards the light, until Lucas of Innerdale took shape behind a yew tree.

He held up his hand to stop her speaking, then made a slight adjustment to the plane they were on that would hide everything from the girls. Was it Cordy's imagination, or was he growing more and more magickally powerful?

'I wasn't spying,' he said quickly. 'No interest in that sort of thing.'

'Good to know. They'll miss me in a minute, so get on with it.'

'I saw you before. With the Sexton girl. She showed you the amulet.'

He left the comment hanging there, and she had to acknowledge it. She couldn't say anything, so she just nodded.

Lucas smiled grimly. 'And how's your campaign to get the Dragonslayer on board with rescuing Persephone?' He waited a second. 'I thought so. Be ready to act at a moment's notice. It will be soon.'

Cordelia had her red lines. 'I will never, ever put Conrad in danger.'

Lucas laughed bitterly. 'Believe me, making sure that Conrad comes to no harm has been the hardest part of this business. Don't worry on that score.'

'And Raven. What about Raven?'

Lucas's face set in a mask. Behind it, she could see boiling fury and pain. 'We've found her. Helena did. That's why I'm on my own today.'

'What happened?'

He shook his head, unwilling or unable to speak.

'Where is she?' said Cordelia urgently. 'I need to know.'

'I'll take you there when it's done. You'll have to trust us. Like we're trusting you.'

She went to speak, but he was gone, and Cordelia had never felt so cold in her life.

She stumbled and ran back to the fire. Natalie held out another glass of Tequila, and Cordy downed it in one.

'How was it?' said Sophie. 'You look terrible.'

'Worst visit to the toilet *ever*,' said Cordelia. 'In fact, I may never recover. Give me more Tequila *now*.'

It's at times like this that you find out who your real friends are.

When I messaged Vicky from the Roman Britain section at the British Museum, she sent back several crying-laughing emojis and this message: *Chris tipped me off. You'll get no help from me, Uncle C.*

Myfanwy, Saffron and Cordelia simply didn't reply, and in desperation I messaged Eseld. I should have known better. *Hahaha. You do know he's sitting next to me, right? He says you're close, but no cigar.*

It being Sunday, Hannah answered at the first ring. 'What? Is everything okay?'

'Yes, ma'am, I…'

'I am *not* your keeper any longer, Baruch Hashem. If you call me that again, I will hang up. What's happened.'

'Nothing. You know Mina's gone to the cemetery?'

She sighed. 'I do. She was in my prayers a lot yesterday. I'm sure Hashem will pass on the message. Is this is a social call?'

She didn't sound busy. She sounded relaxed. Good. 'It could be. I could take you out for a drink, if you help me with my homework.'

'Homework!'

'Artefact Hunt in the British Museum.'

'Oh, you are *so* on your own for that one, and I am not going out for a drink in this weather.' I heard her take a drink of *something*. 'On the other hand, I now see it as a Mitzvah to undermine the Invisible College whenever possible. Where are you?'

I wanted to know what was going on desperately, but my need to get out of this place overwhelmed that completely. 'In a corner outside the Roman Britain section. Using a Silence, obviously.'

'Well, don't linger. They do have Mages on the staff. Right, ignore all the actual Roman stuff and focus on the local material, and have a *good* look at the medical cabinets.'

'Thank you. What's happened?'

'Phthah,' she spat. 'Cora called me the other day. You know what Doctor Loose said? She said, "Cora, you are doing a brilliant job. I want you to carry on doing it while I fuck up the rest of the country." I may be paraphrasing, but that's what she meant. Our new Warden has been on to Tennille to organise a meeting. She has suggested we meet on what amounts to neutral ground.'

'Doctor Loose, eh? Who's idea was that name, and are you going to the meeting?'

'Iain Drummond, and yes, I'm going. It would be stupid and petty not to, and I am not stupid.' She sniffed. 'Naturally, I told Tennille to suggest booking a room at my favourite kosher restaurant, so it won't be *that* neutral.'

'Glad to hear it. I'd better not linger, but I did wonder what had happened to the Dual Natured Commission I was supposed to be leading?'

'Ha. Lost in bureaucratic limbo. You are a very hot potato that not many want to butter, Conrad.'

That was possibly the most alarming metaphor I've heard in a long while. 'Thanks, Hannah.'

'Oh, one more thing. Doctor Loose is going to propose a commission to plan for Salomon's House North, with Seth Holgate in charge. Now that isn't a bad idea. Then again, a stopped clock is right twice a day. Take care up North and don't, whatever you do, miss out the Japanese Collection. Lot of stairs, but worth it.'

Hannah's words were too precise and deliberate for her to have been drinking. Maybe she was letting her hair down. I found the Artefact Hunt App (oh yes, there is one), and went back to work. Hannah was right about the medical items, and I must ask Erin why there is a powerfully magickal calligraphy brush from Japan on display.

I submitted my findings through the App and headed off into the gloom. Today is the second anniversary of Miles Finch's murder at the hands of Joe Croxton, also the day that Mina was arrested. Miles's family (who never approved of Mina) had decided to lay him to rest at a public cemetery in Essex, a fair way out, and when Mina left the hotel this morning, she had taken off her engagement ring.

'Just in case I run into one of them. They won't like me being there, and if they see this ring, they might *kick off* as they say. If I look suitably distraught, they will allow me to place flowers and resist the urge to throw them away until after I have gone. I do not know when I shall come back or how I will feel.'

When she did get back, I asked her how she felt. After a long embrace, of course.

'At peace,' she replied. She put her arms back round me and whispered into my chest, 'His uncle was there. The one who spat at me after the wedding. He was the only member of Miles's family to bother coming today.'

'Did he do anything to you?'

She gave me a squeeze. 'He stood up very, very slowly and told me that he'd been waiting an hour. He said that he wanted to apologise to me, and that there isn't a day that goes by when he doesn't regret what he did. I let him buy me tea and I lied to him about my life. Can we go out, please?'

We did, for a quiet and fairly sober supper with Rachael and Sofía. Rachael being Rachael, she had actually found a table for four on Valentine's night, and we managed not to mention either Chris or Tammy for the whole evening. A result, I'd say.

I did hear from Chris the next morning, though, when we were on the red-eye train to Oxenholme. He sent this message: *I know you had help, but I can't prove it. Doesn't matter, you've passed. Only dynamic switching, load management and flow measurement to go!*

To which I responded: *Thanks. Not sure I can cope with the excitement. And it was Hannah. I caught her on a good day.*

There had also been a voicemail for me, delivered during our meal when my phone was on silent. It was from Cordelia, it featured weird sound effects and lots of shouting. The only thing I picked up for certain was that she was drunk. I waited until we were past Birmingham the next morning before I called her back.

'I got your message.'

'I didn't really call you, did I?'

'You did. Where the hell were you?'

'Ooooh no. I was in the Greendale House hot tub.'

I held the phone away from me and stared at it, confused. I put it back to my ear. 'Did you just say you were in a hot tub?'

'Don't rub it in.'

I heard a voice in the background: *Is that the Chief?*

'You were in the hot tub with Natalie Greening?'

'And others. Please tell me you've deleted it.'

'Oh no, Cordy, I have kept it, and I shall send it to a forensic analyst. When I have the transcript, I shall either put you on a charge or play it at the Solstice Party. Will you still be able to pick us up?'

'Um, yeah. Right. Natalie wants to know if we can do the inspection tomorrow instead of today?'

'You've caught me in a good mood, so yes. See you later.'

And that concludes my report on the Valentine's Day activities of all bar two of the singletons: Karina and Scout. They spent it together.

27 — Airlift

It wasn't Cordelia who picked us up on Monday morning, it was Matt. 'You're a good influence,' he said when we emerged from the tunnel at Oxenholme Station. 'She got one of the Greenings to check, and she was still over the limit.'

'I didn't know you could do that,' said Mina.

'It's not an exact science, but she would definitely have failed a breath test. And more. Have you seen the weather forecast, Conrad?'

I hefted our cases into the back of the pickup and fastened the strap, then nodded grimly. 'I have. Cold front coming.'

Mina rolled her eyes and made steam with her breath. 'Can it get any colder? Is this not front enough for you?'

Matt and I grinned at each other. 'Wet weather on the way,' I explained. 'When it hits the cold air, it's probably going to snow. Or worse.'

She put her hands on her hips. 'And you have brought me back to this? Why did you not leave me in London, where it never snows?'

'I'll start the engine,' said Matt, ducking out of the potential domestic. 'Southbound trains are on Platform One if you want to head back.'

She threw her hands in the air. 'I know exactly where the trains are. That is not the point. Get in.'

We detoured via Kirkstone Pass to meet up with Karina and collect Scout. Okay, not so much of a detour as a totally separate trip. I checked with Karina that the Pack were ready for their second Full Moon under her care, and she said that they were. When we finally made it back, I went straight out to stock up on food, and not just for us.

When I closed the door after getting back from the supermarket, Scout was sitting on the hearth watching Mina sticking lots of printouts to the wall, along with arrows and a map. Poor lad looked most bemused – it wasn't like this at Birk Fell.

'Make tea,' commanded Mina. 'I will explain all shortly.'

I stood, mug in hand, and was given a presentation on our new home-from-home. 'The biggest issue is access to decent roads and trains,' she began. 'And I have narrowed it down to Windermere Town. There are six suitable properties, three here and three here.'

'I'm impressed.'

'So you should be.'

'There's one thing you've missed out, though. Access to the Smurf.'

'Smurf can stay where he is. Windermere is only ten minutes down the road.'

It could be a lot more than that, especially in the summer. On a busy day, it could easily be half an hour. I peered in to look at my options. 'No off-road parking, so those two are out. That one is on the wrong side of the one-way system.' I raised my eyebrows and looked at Scout. 'This one says NO DOGS. Not going to happen. Which leaves this one. Handy for the A591, three bedrooms and a fourth over the garage for when Cordelia splits up with Matt.'

She frowned. 'You are too negative. You have also chosen by far the most expensive.'

'Nothing but the best for Rani.'

'Have another look at the price. Are you sure we can afford it?'

'Oh. Blimey. Do you think they'd do a deal for four months?'

'Three. I asked them. After that, it's full rate.' She slipped her hand round my waist. 'We are very alike. It is the only one I have made an appointment for. Tomorrow morning at ten. You should be finished with Faith by then, shouldn't you?'

I kissed her, and looked back at the property details. 'I will make sure I'm finished. It might be snowed off, anyway.'

She pulled gently away and picked up her tea. 'I must meet her. Soon. How about Thursday, when we test the new landing zone at Birk Fell? And it's about time that Matt met the Pack, too.'

'That sounds rather neat. Have you been organising again?'

'Who me? Yes, after prompting from Cordelia. She messaged while you were out.'

'Sounds like a plan. Weather permitting, of course.'

Weather did permit, and we were shown around our new home while this week's holidaymakers were out. We shook hands on a deal, moving in next Monday. Naturally, Mina had insisted that the professional cleaners did a thorough job first. As we drove back to Lake Cottage, the first snowflakes fell, and next morning was a total winter wonderland. Scout enjoyed it a lot more than the humans. According to Karina (very much human), the Pack had an absolute ball on the first night of the Full Moon – no encounters with ancient creatures, no trespassing on Fae land. All was good.

The weather warmed up a bit overnight into Thursday, and the main roads were pretty much clear, as was the Smurf. Not that this made any difference to Matt. He politely declined the chance to fly with us, saying, 'The bottom of a winch rope is the closest I want to get to a helicopter, if that's all the same to you.' I sent a message to Karina, and she confirmed that his pickup should get to Birk Fell without too much trouble.

We were making a day of it, and Cordelia appeared at around eleven o'clock. I glanced at her car. 'Is that a dent?'

'Don't go there, Conrad. There's a guy who has a little garage in Kendal who's going to come up and look at it in case it can be knocked out without anyone knowing.'

'In this weather? Isn't he rather busy?'

She looked around the front of Lake Cottage and muttered, 'I now owe someone a big favour. I'll leave the keys in Scout's mansion.' As I was locking the cottage door, she glanced at my gear. 'Why are you taking Great Fang? I thought you only practised with the sword you borrowed from Faith?'

I stared at her. 'Great Fang is the sign of my relationship to the Pack. Of course I'm taking it. And I think Scout has found your keys.'

'Grrrr, you stupid dog. Give them here.'

'That's just what he wants to do. He likes this game.'

'By the Goddess, no. They're disgusting. Take him away and let me wipe these in the snow.'

'He's just being a dog, Cordy. C'mon, boy. This way.' We walked down the track, and Mina appeared from the hotel as we passed. She'd nipped in to see Gloria. 'How is she?'

Mina looked uneasily over her shoulder. 'She had a twinge while I was there. Probably nothing, but it really is any day now. No alcohol for you tonight.'

'I'll just stick to a few joints of Sofía's finest grass, shall I?'

'You will shut up and get the engines going while I load the Pack supplies. Where is Cordy?'

'Coming.'

Today was Cordelia's first trip up front. I've given her a few lessons on the basics of being a non-flying co-pilot (if that makes sense), and she set about her duties with the quiet efficiency she brings to all routine tasks. We were airborne in no time.

It was a quiet day in the air, so I didn't have any trouble getting permission to take a very long route to Birk Fell. 'So bleak, and so beautiful,' was the comment that summed it up best.

I came round the south and over Longsleddale on the final approach. 'What are all those cars and vans doing at Sprint Stables?' I wondered aloud.

'What cars?' said Cordelia.

'Maybe we'll have royal company this afternoon,' I said. 'There's High Street. You'd never guess there used to be a Roman Road over that. And the East Road Ley line still goes that way.'

'Where?' said Mina.

'Just passed on the port side.'

'I can only see snow and mountains. Who puts a road through *that*?'

'Romans. Ullswater coming up.'

The Pack had cleared the artificial turf of snow, and I had a nice, bright green target to aim for. Perfect. As soon as the rotors slowed, the whole Pack plus Karina appeared from behind the mound of cleared snow, ready to welcome us and carry the supplies.

'Where's Erin?' I asked.

'Entertaining Matt,' whispered Karina. I don't know why she whispered – even Erin's name can still have that effect on her. 'He was early, and clearly didn't fancy standing around waiting up here.'

What the Pack hadn't done was clear the path down to the Hall. Little Lottie thought it was hilarious that the snow came up to Mina's waist when she took a wrong turn. Mina was less amused.

When we'd extricated her, she forced a smile. 'Now I know why you made me buy integrated waterproof layers. If that happens again, you are carrying me on your shoulders.'

Over a light lunch (for me), it became clear that Matt wasn't entirely comfortable when surrounded by a bunch of kids who could turn into bloodthirsty monsters at a moment's notice. Until they started talking mountains. He was happy then, especially when it came to the exact location of Corin's grove – Matt simply didn't know that area very well, and I think there was an expedition being planned.

After lunch, I had to judge a junior archery contest, a task for which I am supremely unqualified. I asked Karina to tip me off about who I should give the prizes to, and she said, 'But you're the judge. That's your job.' Great.

I gave three prizes to the most enthusiastic and told them that there would be a *proper* contest at the Vernal Equinox, with a trophy. That seemed to go down well enough.

It was going to start getting dark about five this afternoon, and another weather front was picking up speed out in the ocean. When we were about to set off, a strange contraption made of wood and bedsheets appeared with the wolves. 'What in Odin's name is *that?*' I asked Karina.

'They made it after lunch. It's Rani's chariot.'

Mina went bright red and her eyes bulged. For once she was lost for words.

'That's very kind,' I supplied. 'Perhaps if they keep it in reserve. And it will make an excellent stretcher if needed.'

We said goodbye to Matt and Erin (who were discussing the finer points of Particular politics), and Cara howled for Scout to come to heel.

'Sorry, I'll catch you up,' said Cordelia suddenly. 'I was trying to put it off, but I need to go. I *really* need to go. This cold is not good for me.'

We tramped up the snowy slope, and Mina managed to do without her chariot. I was almost ready to start the engines when Cordelia appeared, out of breath and flushed.

'You were saying goodbye to Matt, weren't you?' I whispered.

'Shh! I don't want everyone knowing. Even Scout will have heard you.' I let my eyes do the talking and pressed the starter button.

There was another reception committee at Sprint Stables. A committee of one, this time, but still royal. Instead of the Pack King and Queen, we had Princess Faith in a fetching light blue snowsuit. As we stepped down, I noticed that there weren't any snowmen today. The first time is fun, the second not so much.

I made the formal introduction to Mina, and I noticed that Faith hadn't bothered with any form of Glamour. Barrier cream, yes, but no magick that I could sense.

'There's afternoon tea later,' said Faith to Mina. We can have a proper chat then.'

'I shall look forward to it.'

'And there's a fire in the house while you wait.'

'Good.'

'You know the way, don't you Cordelia?'

Cordy led Mina off and I wandered towards the stables with Faith. 'What were all those vehicles doing here earlier?' I asked. I'm sure there would be a sensible explanation, but any unusual activity around the Red Queen makes me anxious.

Faith glanced towards the house and grimaced, and I tried not to shudder at the effect it had on her face. 'Her Grace has had the legal opinion from Lord Justice Graveney. The plan was always to sell Hipponax, but suddenly she finds herself in need of funds. The traffic was another Queen coming to have a look for herself, which is why I'm relegated to your old friend, Agrippa. I'll get them.'

Scout had been pulling hard at the lead, anxious to get sniffing, and was barking way more than normal. His last visit here had not been a good one. 'Where is everyone?' I asked. 'It's unlike the Count not to keep an eye on things.'

'They're done for the day, and you're not such a novelty any more.' She bent down and gave Scout a good scratch. 'Hello again, you. Aren't you a handsome devil?' She took something out of her snowsuit pocket. 'A present. I've even wrapped it. Won't be long.'

She was gone before I could say anything, and while I struggled to hold Scout with one hand, I peeled apart the Scooby Doo wrapping paper with the other. As soon as I broke the tape seal, magick throbbed gently in my hands.

'What's this, eh boy? An Enchanted dog collar?'

It was brand new, with the stiffness of new leather, but the design looked ancient, and the mixture of tooling and sewn in gems was a work of art in miniature. I looked closer and recognised some of the motifs. When Faith returned with the horses, I said, 'This reminds me of Evenstar's saddle.'

'Got it in one. I had nothing to do this week, so I made it to match. So long as he's alongside or behind and moving, he'll transition with you.'

'You made this?'

'Yeah. Of course. I'm not just a pretty face, you know.' She grinned. 'I'm allowed to say that.'

Scout's new collar was strong, but had no clips to attach a lead. It would be an addition to his regular harness, and he didn't object. After he'd given it a good sniff, of course.

Faith was giving me a funny look when I stood up. 'I've just realised,' she said. 'You've brought that evil thing with you. What for?'

I looked around. 'Sorry?'

'The wolf sword.'

'Oh. Force of habit. It was there, so I strapped it on. Second nature. Don't worry, I'll leave it on Evenstar when we practise.'

'Too bloody right you will.'

Scout took some persuading not to run ahead when we moved to the higher plane, but the collar worked a treat, and we trotted gently to our usual spot. There was no sense in working the horses in this weather: far too much risk of ice. And when we got there, I discovered that there would be snowmen after all.

Or ice-men to be accurate. Six life-size ice sculptures were melting slowly in a circle, each one a stylised opponent, from a Dwarf to an eight foot tall troll. 'Nice work. Also yours?'

'It was the Hlæfdigan. They come up here sometimes.'

I'd forgotten about them. Sprint Stables has a small but perfectly formed sídhe under the larger roundhouse, and it's home to three of the Fae who provide Amrita. It's also home to a tribe of Sprites and a herd of short, natural, miniature Unicorns.

'Thank the Ladies for me. What now?'

'You stand in the middle and practise until I get too cold.' She pulled out an extra thick woolly hat and sat on the fallen log we use as a bench. 'This snowsuit is *very* warm. Off you go. Start with the Gnome, the one on your right.'

I stripped off a couple of layers, released Scout to explore and got ready to have at the ice men. 'Oh no, Scout, did you have to?'

'Arff.'

'We'll leave the Dwarf, I think,' said Faith. 'I wonder why he chose that one to pee against?'

I treated the question as rhetorical and started stretching. Here goes. Cut, thrust, parry, lunge…

There were three dismembered ice corpses around the ring, and I was sweating profusely when I saw that Faith was looking at the woods, not at me, and she was looking with a deep frown. Then she stood up and the frown became alarm. At that point, I heard shouting, neighing and very distressed barking, and it was all heading in our direction.

28 — A Parting of the Ways

There were eight of them.

Six horses and two High Unicorns rode out of the woods and across the snow towards us. Scout's work as an early warning system was finished, and he hared in front, anxious to get to me and let me know that something was really, really wrong. From beside me, Faith whispered to herself. 'No, it wasn't supposed to happen. She gave me her bonded word.'

I looked, and in the late sunshine I could see exactly who was on the backs of the first three mounts. This was so bad that I couldn't take it in at first. Mina? Oh yes. She was there, on the back of Hipponax, sitting behind a child and looking ready to kill someone. If she was that angry, she hadn't been hurt. Yet. They were riding bareback, and Mina's hands were round the rider's middle. No saddle, but there was a bridle in use.

Next to Hipponax was the star of the stables, Scipio, and he carried the Count of Force Ghyll. Behind them was the other Unicorn, Keraunós, and on *his* back were Persephone and Cordelia. Perci looked unhappy and scared, but Cordelia looked guilty. Very guilty. What the fuck?

I stepped back and to the left, and I whipped up my sword, resting the blade on Faith's shoulder, the edge just kissing the skin above her carotid artery. 'Call them off. Now.'

Her head didn't move a millimetre, nor did she raise her voice. 'I can't. They're not here at my command.'

'Then you'll just have to hope I don't cough.'

The horses were advancing slowly. The girl on Hipponax was having great difficulty controlling the huge Unicorn, and when I say girl, I mean child. I think. Her face was covered with a scarf, so I couldn't swear it wasn't a tiny adult of some sort. I've seen stranger things. She was so small that Mina actually looked over her, and as well as anger, her face was full of concentration. She was trying not to hold on so tight that she distracted the rider. Or pulled her off.

Scout arrived, panting, and I said, 'Stay,' without taking my eyes off Faith and the approaching column.

When I was satisfied that they'd hear me, I raised my voice. 'Stop there!'

The Count of Force Ghyll raised his hand. The others stopped, except for Hipponax. He kept going until the girl could impose her will.

The Count raised both hands this time, to show that they were empty. 'We have not come for you, Dragonslayer. Your betrothed is safe and unharmed.'

'Mina?' She nodded briefly, unwilling to scare the Unicorn underneath her or the rider in front. 'Then let her go.'

He had the gall to laugh at me. 'I was going to. When we got closer. To save her the walk. But if you insist.' He turned and shouted at the riders behind. They were clearly Fae, a mix of Knights and Squires probably. The two at the back leapt off their horses and ran through the snow towards Hipponax. They slowed down and approached the Unicorn carefully. The rider put her arms around Hipponax's neck and stroked him. One of the Fae dropped to their knees and offered their hands to help Mina get down. She slid off rather than dismounting, and the Fae had to jump to catch her. I had the satisfaction of seeing them land in the snow, with Mina firmly on top.

She rolled off and stood up, ignoring the Fae and brushing snow off her trousers. With head held high, she crossed the gap towards me. 'Stay, Scout.' I ordered, just in case. 'What happened?' I said to Mina.

It was a bit like flying in a storm through enemy fire. I was trying to watch the invaders, keep an eye on Faith and let Mina know I loved her, all at the same time.

'We had just made ourselves comfortable by the fire,' she said, 'and I asked where the grooms were. Cordelia said she'd go and look, and get tea. When she came back, she was with that Count creature, only now he's calling himself *Prince* again.'

Faith risked instant death by taking a sharp breath. My sword drew blood, and it ran down the blade, dripping into the snow.

Mina watched the red spots melt the white carpet for a second, then carried on. 'He told me that there was a revolution going on, and that his job was to stop you getting involved or tipping anyone off.'

Faith spoke without seeming to breathe. 'That was supposed to be my job. Minus the revolution part.'

Mina looked at Faith for first time. 'So it's true? The Red Queen is attacking the Greenings tonight?'

My arm was getting tired. I'd been practising for a long time before this, and I had a funny feeling I was going to need my strength. 'Faith, I'm going to remove my sword and trust you. I hope I'm not making a mistake.'

'You're not,' she replied, still in an even voice. I slid the blade away and thrust it into the snow. Faith turned to face me. There was drool running down her face, and blood had seeped into the collar of her snow suit. 'Thank you, Lord Protector. This is not a seemly business.'

Not a seemly business. You can say that again. Only the Fae; only the Fae.

Behind her, the column was approaching again, and spreading out. She fished out her handkerchief and wiped her face before shoving the square of linen into her collar. It would stop bleeding soon enough.

'I love you,' I said to Mina. 'Got to get my coat before I freeze.' I jogged the few metres to Evenstar and grabbed my fleece, coat and hat from her saddle. I took the time to throw them on before I moved again, because I wanted something else. When no one was watching me except Mina and Faith, I slipped Great Fang over my back.

I jogged back to Faith. While my back had been turned, Scout had jumped up, and Mina was on the verge of tears as she wrapped her arms around his neck. 'What's going on?' I said to Faith. 'Start with the Greenings.'

She shook her head mutely, pain in her eyes.

My next question had to be phrased carefully. I'd only get one shot. 'Has the Red Queen made a Geas today, and were you kneeling when she placed it?'

Faith nodded. The Queen of the Borrowdale People had placed a deep magickal compulsion on Princess Faithful to stop her talking about what was going on, and there was nothing I could do about it. According to legend, the Geas lasts as long as the bearer is part of the People or until the Morrigan intervenes. I didn't bother looking up to the sky in the hope of divine intervention.

We were being surrounded by all the party except the Unicorns. Time to speed things up. 'Why are you here?' I asked Mina.

'He said his only purpose was to keep you out of action. He said that if you weren't certain I was safe, you'd attempt to escape. I came under protest, but he was right, wasn't he?'

'He was. He's not so daft as I thought. Who's the girl?'

'I have no idea. They call her *Your Grace*, but she has not spoken for some reason.' She glanced at the child on the Unicorn. 'She has brown eyes and brown skin, I can tell you that much.'

'I can tell you *what* she is, but not *who*,' added Faith. 'She's a Princess, newly a Changeling, and they've declared her Queen.'

I hadn't thought today could get worse, but it had. I was stuck on a higher plane with some form of carnage about to happen between the Red Queen and the Greenings at an unknown location, and now I was also at the epicentre of a Fae rebellion. There might also be the small matter of an unauthorised Changeling to deal with, but I'll worry about that later. If I'm still alive.

The Count (or should that be Prince?) dismounted, and the retinue followed suit. The Squire who'd given Mina a soft landing ran to start gathering the horses, and the Count shouted across to the Unicorn contingent. 'Mortal, lead in our Queen!'

Persephone looked utterly terrified, frozen in place and unable to move, her eyes looking everywhere and nowhere. Cordelia poked her in the ribs and said something. Ah yes, Cordelia. Whatever cards she had in her hand, I hoped she played them very carefully. She gripped Persephone by the shoulders and shook her, then leaned round and took the reins from her hands. Persephone seemed to come to her senses, and slipped off Keraunós.

The girl stumbled in the snow and righted herself, then she went to Hipponax and stroked him for a second before taking the reins from the child Queen and starting to lead the Unicorn into the ever contracting circle. She never made it.

Scout let out a furious bark and shot off, through the remaining ice sculptures towards a lone tree, away from the action. It was mad, but everyone, mortal and Fae, turned to watch the daft dog go bananas. And then the Fae started to panic, pointing at empty air and moving their hands in the shape of Charms. Scout stopped running, barked a familiar bark, and in front of him a shape appeared. A human shape.

'Lucas!' I said, blurting out his name. No wonder Scout recognised him.

'Dæmon Spawn!' spat Faith. 'You should be dead.' She raised her voice. 'I killed you! I killed you!'

Lucas lowered his hand for Scout to sniff, and got a nice waggy tailed response. No hard feelings there, then. Satisfied, Lucas pulled back his frock coat and hailed the Count. 'Time for them to go. You've got what you wanted. Dismiss them now or the bargain is forfeit.'

'We have a use for them yet,' said the Count with more contempt than I thought was possible. He's had a lot of practice, I suppose.

'You made a bargain,' said Lucas. 'I'm calling it done.' When he looked at Persephone, there was love, and that love finally joined the dots in my brain: Lucas->Madeleine->Persephone. They were related. 'You know what's going to happen, child,' he told her. 'If you don't move now, you'll die a horrible death.'

When Perci looked around, she surprised me by focusing on Faith. What was going on *there*?

Lucas spoke quickly now, turning away to his right. 'Cordelia! Take her away before this goes down the water. Now's your chance. Your only chance.' How the hell did he know Cordelia?

Before she could react, I spoke up. 'No, Cordy. Hold your position. We're not at risk here. Not yet.'

'Sorry, Chief,' said Cordelia, using magick to project her voice. 'Lives are at stake.'

She dug her heels into Keraunós and urged him forwards. As one Unicorn approached the other, Hipponax took exception and reared away from Persephone. She let go of the reins, and the child Queen was dumped unceremoniously into the snow. Cordy pulled up and held out her hand. With a glance around her, Persephone took the hand and clambered in front of Cordelia. The reins were passed over, and Keraunós broke into a canter, heading off and away, towards the plain, the Defile and one of the many exits from the Gallops that *didn't* lead back to Sprint Stables.

I watched them go for a second, confident of one thing: our ways may have parted for now, but I was going to make damn sure they converged again as soon as possible.

29 — A Question of Judgement

A howl from Scout dragged my attention back to the tree where Lucas had been standing. Not any more: he was gone, too. 'Here, boy. Come here.'

Squires had helped the Queen to her feet, and she made her way to stand by the Count. They were within talking distance of our little group; the other five Fae stood well back.

Faith was to my left, and she pulled out a clean handkerchief to wipe her mouth. She only had eyes for the Queen, and she gave a big sniff. When she opened her mouth, a stream of acid-laden invective poured out. In Fae. Having vented her spleen, she turned to me. 'You won't recognise her, but that little piece of meat next to the traitor is his Gamekeeper.'

Of course I didn't recognise her. When the former Prince Galleny had gone rogue, he'd been aided and abetted by a vicious little gym bunny known as the Gamekeeper. The Red Queen had declared the Gamekeeper anathema and cast her out of the People at the same time as she had demoted the Prince to Count. And then, in front of his People and sundry mortals, the Count had been beaten half to death and humiliated. No wonder he was angry.

The Count took a knee and said, 'Behold the Queen of Grace.' His new leader pulled down her hood. When she slowly unwrapped her scarf, it was Mina's turn to break into a foreign language.

The alleged Queen of Grace was a child of obviously Indian extraction, her skin close to black and her face was a deformed mess on one side, bulbous and sunken in all the wrong places. I don't know, but I'd say it had been like that since birth. She had long hair and from what I could tell couldn't be more than nine or ten. I don't know about the proprieties, but this was no Queen to me. I'll carry on calling her what she was: the Gamekeeper.

Mina switched back to English. 'A Dalit. They used to be called Untouchables, and this poor child was damaged at birth or in the womb.' She raised her voice. 'How much did you pay for her?'

The Gamekeeper's eyes were not the eyes of a child. For one thing, they were sparkling with magick, and for another, they blinked when Mina spoke. She was right: the Gamekeeper had gone out to the streets of India and bought the daughter of a family who would have been glad to sell her and never see her again.

She spoke, using magick to get round the unmoving half of her face. 'I am declared Queen in place of the Red Queen. I regret that I have only one vacancy for a princess, and that will go to Princess Appleby.'

'Hunh?' said Mina. I was inclined to agree. I couldn't see the man she'd described as an overweight retired colonel winning any beauty pageants in the near future.

The Count was relishing this, and had more to add. 'Even now, Gerrard is keeping the Pack penned in. The Red Queen has no horses, no wolves and no idea that all her plans are known.' He turned his focus on to me. 'The Red Queen is outside the law and has no protection from you, Dragonslayer. Nor do her castoffs. This is the business of the People.'

There was silence for a moment. The sun had already started dipping down behind this plane's distant version of Coniston Old Man. I weighed up my options, my position and likely outcomes if I acted and if I did nothing.

'You are not going to do nothing, I hope,' said Mina. It was all the permission I needed.

'There is another choice,' I said to Faith.

She was furious, as you'd expect, but she wasn't afraid. Another wipe of the mouth and she drawled, 'Really? Enlighten me.'

'Submit to me and face Judgement for what you have done, and try to convince the Red Queen to do the same.'

She tipped her head back to roar with laughter. 'That's good, that is. I heard about the skirmish at Six Furlongs. You never faced him, did you?'

She meant the Count, back when he was Prince Galleny. On that day, he had been about to face a combined assault from the Ripleys and me, until the Red Queen had arrived and put a stop to things.

'I remember that he was reluctant to fight me,' I said.

'That's because he doesn't like to lower himself to face mortals. He taught me most of the things I know about the blade. And we are rather outnumbered, in case you hadn't noticed.'

I grabbed her arm and made a Silence. 'I am not suicidal, Faith. Submit and help me. There is hope.' I let go and stepped back. Ahead of me, the Count started to take off his long coat.

'This is going to be fun. I like that.' She took the knee, and I unshipped Great Fang, holding the blade towards her. 'I submit to Conrad Clarke, Lord Protector and Dragonslayer.' She kissed her fingers and touched them to a safe part of the sword, away from the cold-forged iron. 'Now what? This had better be good.'

'Scout! Here boy!'

'You have got to be joking me. That dog is your plan?'

He bounded up, and I grabbed him. 'I need to get an image into his head, Faith. You're good with animals.'

She was still kneeling, and whipped the handkerchief away from her neck. Underneath, blood was still oozing. 'Bend forward and close your eyes,' she said.

I did, and felt the touch of her finger on my forehead, right over my Third Eye. I also felt more than a touch of magick.

'Keep your eyes closed, try to open your Third Eye and give it your best shot.'

I did as she bid, and a murky world of browns and acid greens flickered into life. The strain made me join Faith on my knees, and bizarrely, there was no snow. There was, however, a tiny pulse of red in my hand. Scout. I overlaid an image of Hipponax running towards us and said, 'Fetch the horsey. Good boy. Fetch the horsey.'

I let go and the pulse of red shot off.

'Conrad!' said Mina. 'They're coming!'

I opened my eyes and saw Faith's left hand held out to help me up. I took it, and I got a brief glimmer of carapace and teeth before I shook my head and it cleared. In her other hand, Faith already had her Fae blade out.

'No use,' I said. I pointed to my practice blade. 'Take that one and get ready. I'll hold up the Count.'

I wouldn't say that I staggered towards him, but it took a few strides before I was ready. I swapped hands and quickly unzipped my coat, shrugging it off my right arm to get some freedom of movement. I only swapped my blade back in time to smash his weapon aside and avoid being spitted.

He almost jumped back to avoid my riposte. He knew about Great Fang in theory, but facing up to that much cold-forged edge was different in reality. He feinted right, and his one blade became two, one on this plane and one on another. I've never seen twin blades so clearly, and I was able to parry both. The real blade hit Great Fang close to the hilt, and I knew which was which.

'They're surrounding you!' said Faith.

I lunged, he parried, and I stepped back, risking a glance. There were three of them converging on my back, all with blades drawn. One was guarding the Gamekeeper, and one was cutting off Faith's route to relieve me. I was slightly flattered that the Count was more worried about me, then I realised that he was going to enjoy himself with Faith. I was just the soup course.

I was about to be surrounded and cut down. I desperately needed a distraction. Or something. It was time to put one of Faith's moves into practice. I advanced on the Count again and made a desperate cut that he was forced to parry and avoid, putting his blade right down. I bent my right knee, and instead of pushing off with my outstretched (and trembling) left leg, I put everything I had into launching myself with my right.

It worked. He threw himself backwards to avoid the tip of my sword, but it had already moved on, and I had pivoted away to catch out the nearest of the others. He had no idea what to expect, and went into a defensive stance. I feinted and legged it, breaking out of the circle and gaining a few seconds respite while they decided what to do, and the first thing that happened was the Fae who'd been sent to watch Faith legged it to help protect the Gamekeeper for some reason. What?

It was enough. Mina and Faith turned to look at something, and I risked a glance, too. Enter Unicorn, pursued by border collie. Faith suddenly realised why I'd told her to use my practice sword, and she made a desperate grab for it. Now it was up to her ability to catch and calm a panicked Unicorn before … oh shit. The Count was making a beeline for Mina, and I was fairly certain what would come next.

So was Mina, and she did the only thing that would save her: she ran towards him, putting herself in the path of a galloping Unicorn.

It was tight, but Hipponax acted on instinct, swerving to avoid the woman and heedless of the man. The Count fell down and covered his head with his hands. Hipponax jumped over him and the break in his stride allowed Faith to make a desperate dive for the reins.

The Fae all looked to the Count, and I was able to get one of them on their own for long enough to bludgeon aside his weapon and get a thrust into his body. The Count was getting to his feet, unhurt, and the other two Fae near me separated and got ready to kebab me. Credit to them, because one was guaranteed not to make it.

I'd taken the time to wrap my coat round my left arm. It wouldn't make much of a difference to those blades, but I'd rather lose an arm than my life. Before they could line up properly, something hurt my ears, and the two Fae glanced away. Faith was … singing? Whatever. She was making some sort of noise to a scared Hipponax. At least he was still on the field of battle.

I got ready to face the Fae, only for another interruption. Scout bounded over, barking like mad and coming to my rescue. Oh no, you stupid dog. I had no option but to attack the same one as he did, knowing that the Fae would ignore Scout and go for me instead, which is what happened, leaving me wide open on my left.

I feinted and feinted again while Scout went for the leg, then I swung round to face the other one and put up my left arm. She had gone for a cut, not a thrust, and her blade hit my coat, something inside it and then slid down to my arm. Owww. That hurt like buggery, but my arm was still in one piece, and I brought Great Fang round to make her jump away. Behind me there was a desperate howl, and I span round with a cringe, expecting the worst.

Scout was backing off with a most aggrieved expression on his face. He'd drawn blood, and he really, really didn't like what he could taste. He looked at me as if to say, *Do I really have to, boss?* It didn't matter, though, because behind him, I saw Faith stroking Hipponax's head, and then get ready to mount.

At that point the Count made his only real mistake of the day: he abandoned his pursuit of Mina (who was not making it easy to be caught), and he went for Faith. When I saw her leg go over Hipponax's back, I made a wild slash at the unappetising Fae and started running, turning to run backwards after a few steps.

Scout had had a good mouthful of leg, and the Fae had to limp, which gave me a few metres grace. His friend was okay, though, and she came at me. I tried to raise my blade, but I overbalanced, right on my arse. She dodged right, ready to thrust under my guard, then she looked up, and I saw death in her eyes.

Hipponax sailed over me, and Faith's sword descended, hitting the Fae so hard with a slash that it span her round and knocked her over. Faith nudged the Unicorn with her knees and finished off the one that Scout had started. And talking of Scout...

'Easy, lad. You can stop licking me. I think we're safe now.'

'Arff!'

'Yes, you're the best dog in the world. Official. Now get off.'

I stood up. Or tried to. When I put weight on my left arm, the pain was so bad I fell over. Blood had already soaked through my coat. I grabbed a flapping sleeve, wrapped it tightly round my arm and got up as best I could. When I finally got to my feet, Faith and Hipponax were making a second pass at the group containing the Gamekeeper. There was already one in a bloody pool in the snow, and in a cloud of white powder thrown up by the hooves, Faith cut down the second one.

I looked for the Count, to see if he had resumed his pursuit of Mina, only to find that it was the other way round. Mina had picked up Faith's discarded rapier and had put the Count out of his misery. He'd been hit by Hipponax's razor-sharp horn already, so he didn't put up much of a fight. Good job, too.

And that left the Gamekeeper. Hipponax was keeping his distance, not wishing to charge a female, and the girl who would be Queen was kneeling in the snow her arms outstretched. I limped my way over, and Faith dismounted to join me, with Mina not far behind.

The former child who had become a Princess had not been dealt a good hand by fate and medicine. Whatever had led to her defects was tragic, and whatever circumstances had led to her being sold by her parents were equally tragic. They wouldn't have known what was really going on, I'm sure, but they must have known that whatever line they'd been spun was a lie. That, however, was in the past. The poor Dalit girl was gone, her Identity and her Imprint erased and replaced by the Gamekeeper's.

I opened my Third Eye and looked at the Gamekeeper. Inside the shell of the Dalit girl, the Fae essence was creating something new. I can't say that it sat easily with me, but this was their nature. I switched my focus back to the mundane world and the child in front of me.

'I submit,' said the Fae. 'I submit to the Lord Protector and will serve his Princess as a handmaiden.'

I looked down on her, and my left arm twinged. I raised my right arm and pointed to Mina with my sword. 'Sorry, but the position of Princess is already taken by Rani here, and Faith is *her* handmaiden. For now.'

'Is she?' said Mina.

'Am I?' said Faith.

I reversed my grip on Great Fang and plunged the sword into the snow and through a few inches of frozen ground. The image of Caledfwlch gleamed on the pommel, and I rested my palm on it, summoning the magick.

'In the name of Nimue, I bring you to Judgement.'

'No. No, no, no,' squealed the Gamekeeper, struggling to get to her feet.

Faith moved like lightning to get behind her, and pushed her back down.

'You have broken the peace of the land, and I pronounce Judgement.' I closed my eyes and gripped the pommel harder. I was about to do something that only happens every generation or so. In a few seconds, I might be very, very dead.

'The Judgement is death.'

I spoke the words and waited. Caledfwlch throbbed, and I started to taste sweet flowers and fresh water. And then it stopped, with that tang on my fillings again. Urgh.

What should have happened was that Nimue pronounced which of us was to die, and if I'd overreached myself, I would fall in place of the Gamekeeper. Either Nimue was busy or she just didn't care. I opened my eyes, pulled Great Fang from the ground and administered Judgement anyway. I could always submit myself retrospectively. As the blade bit into the Gamekeeper's neck, I didn't look away from her eyes.

30 — *Loyalty*

'Your arm!' said Mina. 'It's bleeding.'

'Let me,' said Faith.

I stepped back and turned away from the fallen Princess, placing Great Fang on the ground and offering my arm to Faith.

She unwrapped my coat and tossed it aside. There was a six inch gash in my forearm that had gone *very* deep. Faith gripped my arm close to the elbow and I sank to my knees from the pain.

'Won't be long,' she said, trying to be soothing. 'Just need to stop the blood flow and take a look.' She peered into the wound, and I looked away. 'Oh shit. You've lost your extensor. Conrad? Look at me.'

I did, and there was deep concern in her face. 'You won't be able to use your left hand properly unless I fix this, and the only fix is a graft. Do you mind being part Fae?' She said the last part with an attempt at a smile.

'Risks?'

'I might bodge it, but no other risks. It is pretty gross, though.'

I jerked my head in agreement, and she dragged me round with huge strength, pulling me down and dropping my face in the snow next to the dead Gamekeeper.

'This thing was only half a Changeling,' she said, rummaging in her snowsuit. 'Luckily for you. Now I seriously don't want you to watch this. Your subconscious might cause problems. In fact, look away, close your eyes and try to calm your magick. Mina? Cut some cloth for a bandage.'

I did the first two, but calming my magick came a distant second to screaming, which is all I wanted to do after Faith knelt on my biceps and started doing something with her knife. You can guess what happened next.

Could I really smell coffee? I could, and even better, when I opened my eyes I discovered that it was being held by Mina. 'Have I ever told you how beautiful you are?'

'Once or twice, and you weren't lying when you said it, which makes it all the stranger. Ganesh was with us today.'

'You didn't need him to save yourself, love. You did that all on your own.'

'I know I did. It was *you* he saved. Look.'

My new winter coat was laid on the snow, complete with multiple slashes and bloodstains where the Fae blade had sliced through it. Also laid out were my phone, my wallet, my cigarettes, a couple of bits and pieces, and my lighter. Oh.

There was a big dint in the middle, running right through Ganesh's happy smiling face. I looked to the east, where it was already dark. 'Thank you, lord,' I whispered. 'I will make an offering.'

I glanced down and realised that I'd been rolled on to the Count's coat, the one he'd taken off before the fight. It was a long, leather riding coat. I'd need that. I looked at my left forearm, but couldn't see anything because it was bound in the Gamekeeper's scarf, and the binding went all the way down to my fingers. I didn't try to wiggle them. I looked around, and on the other side of my coat was Scout, waiting patiently to come and lick me. Better get it over with before I accepted the mug of coffee. 'Here boy.'

'Arff.'

Faith was standing off, holding on to Hipponax and soothing him still. When she saw that I was awake, she patted the Unicorn and came over. I took the coffee, grabbed my cigarettes and flicked my spare lighter. You didn't think I'd be without one did you?

'How did it go?' I asked. 'And either way, thank you.'

She bowed. 'My lord. Thank you. If you were serious about me going to the Red Queen, then I may not live long, but I thank you for the gift of extra life.' She looked up. 'The graft has taken, and you can ride one-handed, but don't even *think* of flying until you've had it sealed with Amrita, which needs to be soon. We should get you out of here.'

'I agree with one part of that, but not the *we* part.' I paused to smoke and gather my thoughts. 'Now that you are free of the Red Queen, the Geas is gone. Correct.'

'It's all gone. I could even start to heal my face if I wanted to. I won't, though. Not until the next dawn.'

I waved that away. 'Where is the Red Queen?'

'The rendezvous was supposed to be at Hartsop, so that I could bind you here for the night and join them on Hipponax. There is a sídhe there that will hide all the People while they wait, and it's not far as the Unicorn gallops.'

'But a heck of a long way by road.'

'Quite.'

'What time was she supposed to ride out.'

'At midnight.'

'So we probably have a couple of hours before the Greenings attack. I want you to take Mina and get there as quick as you can.'

The women looked at each other, deciding who was going to say *No*. I didn't give them a chance. 'It's the only way the Red Queen can survive this, and I want her alive, tempting though it is to let them wipe her out and for the new Queen to be my vassal.'

Faith laughed. 'Which is why Derwent will kill me out of hand.'

'No she won't. Countess Bassenthwaite won't let her, because that would mean *all* the Princesses and the Queen dying. She won't allow that. And I'm sending Mina because the Red Queen can negotiate with her without losing face.'

'You are not sending me anywhere,' said Mina. She paused to make sure I'd got the point. 'However, it is a good idea. What are your red lines?'

'That the Red Queen submits to me and to Judgement in due course. And that Faith gets to be Queen of ... Where?'

She breathed her answer, scared to think it might happen. 'Staveley in Cartmel, near Fell Foot at the base of Windermere. My sídhe is still there.'

'One day,' I said. 'Not tomorrow, but one day in the future. Now go, both of you.' They stood up and I unlocked my phone. 'Hang on. There's no signal here.'

'Blocked,' said Faith. 'To stop you calling for help. Mine's blocked, too.'

'You'll be out first, so Mina, could you please call Karina and tell her to stop tonight's hunt? Tell her to watch the sky. And neither of you are to call the Red Queen. I don't want her charging off and trying a counter-ambush.'

Faith held out her hand and I staggered to my feet. I took a few experimental steps and didn't fall over. Mina picked up the Count's coat and started stuffing things in pockets.

I tried for a grin. 'And you'd better call Saul,' I announced.

Mina rolled her eyes and nodded; Faith just looked at me blankly. 'Didn't you know?' she said. 'The reason today was chosen is that it's the anniversary of the First Mine. They all went under at sunset.'

I winced. 'What about Matt?' asked Mina. 'Can we trust him?'

'Why shouldn't we?' asked Faith.

'He has it bad for Cordelia,' said Mina. 'Sneaky bitch has probably wrapped him round her delicately crooked little pink finger.'

'Oh.'

'Looks like it's just us three, then.'

'Arff.'

'Four then.'

'Five if you count Hipponax,' said Faith.

'Oh, it'll be more than that. Now go.'

I helped Mina clamber on to our fallen tree, and from there Faith got her on to Hipponax's back. Faith had a parting gift for me. She withdrew the blood-soaked handkerchief from her neck and tossed it to me. 'To the People, this is a mark of my submission. It might help you at the Stables. Good luck.'

With a wave and a kiss they trotted off. I went to put the late Count's coat on, and found that we were very different shapes. To avoid looking like a complete numpty, I hacked off the sleeves. 'What do you think, boy?' I asked my only audience.

'Arff.'

'Quite. You know what? I'm going to have another coffee before I run the gauntlet at Sprint Stables. You can amuse yourself for a few minutes.'

I did, and he did, and I hadn't quite finished when his explorations brought him warily back to the tree where Lucas had appeared. I watched him sniff, then jump back in surprise with a warning bark. He'd been on top form today, so instead of calling him a daft dog, I went over to have a look for myself.

This tree was away from our practice ground, and I'd had no reason to go near it before. It did stand out rather, being on top of a slight slope and on the fringes of the Liminal Margin. You couldn't exit back to Mittelgard this way because you'd appear in mid-air or underground, unless you were a Spirit like Lucas. Or like the creature trapped in the tree.

'Well done boy. Good dog.'

'Arff.' I think he meant *Where's my treat, then, eh?* To which the answer would have been *covered in my blood, so not on the menu.*

I know nothing of Binding save what I've read in a few introductory books, so I didn't have a clue what to do here. On another day I'd have walked away, but today is not another day. Lucas had appeared here, and he is not acting in my best interests, which made this Spirit *very* interesting. I opened my Third Eye and tried to see something.

I did see something: a glowing ball in a cage. Great. It could sense me, and became agitated. If only it could talk, we could wrap this up in no time. I took another look, and tried to see if I could sense the Binding Work. Nope. Not a chance. I stood back and scratched my head. There was very little light left, and the bare branches were starting to disappear into the night.

Bare branches? Hunh? This was one of the few trees in the Fae wood not in leaf, and that was an issue because without leaves, it couldn't make Lux, and without Lux... I focused on the base of the tree, and tried to see down into the roots. Yes, there it was. It was time to pass another of Chris Kelly's modules.

'Here boy, job for you.'

I scratched the frozen ground and pointed to it. I made digging motions, and he got the message, even without Fae help. I didn't need him to get far, just far enough to see a root. 'Good boy! I so owe you a steak.'

I was half way to putting my left hand on the root when I realised that I was going to have to practise right-handed magick today. I gripped the freezing wood and felt the pulse of Lux.

The tree was drawing Lux through all its roots, of course, and although I stopped this one quite easily, that was no use. I took my hand off before I got frostbite, then put it back and remembered that turning Lux into heat may be ludicrously inefficient but is also very easy. And talking of things I've done before, there was only one that might work here.

I stopped the flow, then eased back, stopped, opened... There we go. A nice standing wave, going up the tree, and...

'Run boy!'

I'd got about three steps before there was an explosion of Lux with added ground-up lightning and peal of thunder. I hoped desperately that it was confined to this realm and didn't distract Faith and Mina from their mission. The thunder blew me face down in the snow, and I do mean *face* down: I'd kept my left arm safe, and that meant a wet landing. Good job I'd avoided the patch of yellow snow to my left.

'Conrad! Are you hurt?'

Well stone the crows and dash it all. Not my normal curse, but the far-back voice could only belong to one person: Lucas's daughter, Madeleine, formerly the Spirit in possession of my dowsing rod.

'I'm good, thanks. Give me a moment.'

'Who's a good doggy! You remember me, don't you?'

'Arff.'

He did, and he was wagging his tail at the immaculately be-hatted Edwardian figure of Madeleine of Innerdale. For the umpteenth time today, I got back up and shook myself.

'Good job you were wearing that coat, what?' she said.

'Is it?'

'Deflected some of the Lux. Or didn't you know that?'

'I didn't. Who imprisoned you, Maddy, and what are you doing here?'

'Father. I came to warn you, but he and Mama intercepted me. I must go before it's too late.'

'Wait! What on earth is happening?'

304

'They're going to repeat my first sin. They want to poison the water to save a life, and I must stop them. I know you have other battles to fight. I saw and heard all today, but if you can, before midnight, come to the Four Roads Cross.'

'Wait, Maddy, tell me what Cordelia is up to.'

Madeleine started to fade. 'Making a damned fool of herself, that's what. You have your struggle, and I have mine. I hope we will meet again, Conny.'

I watched her become the ball of light once more, and I watched her streak off in the same direction that Cordelia and Persephone had taken.

'Right, boy, we'd better get a move on.'

It was dark in Longsleddale when I returned to Mittelgard from the higher plane. A very worried looking Fae Knight was keeping watch, and started backpedalling when he saw me and saw that I was alone. I pulled up Evenstar and hoped he wouldn't notice that I hadn't taken the reins in my left hand. I took out Great Fang and shouted, 'Call all of the People to the yard, and do it now or Great Fang will drink Fae blood. Again.'

He got the message. I urged Evenstar forwards with my knees. She didn't need much urging now that she could see a nice, warm, dry stable ahead of her. I took a deep breath and got myself ready for the next step.

There were about a dozen Fae in the yard by the time Evenstar's hooves clattered on to the concrete. The lights were all on, and I looked around. No humans. Good. Hopefully good. They could all be dead in the roundhouse for all I know, but I prefer to accentuate the positive.

There was clearly a leader in front of me, a Countess to judge from the way she held her sword and stared at my chest. Or what was on it. When Evenstar stopped of her own accord, I spoke up.

'The Count of Force Ghyll is dead. You can see that I wear his coat. The Gamekeeper is dead on Nimue's Judgement. You can smell her blood on Great Fang. The Red Queen is betrayed. Princess Faithful has gone on Hipponax to help her, and Persephone is fled. Before she fled, Faith submitted. To me. Those of you who would save the Red Queen know what you need to do.'

'Hold...' began the Countess.

The Fae loyal to the Red Queen did know what to do. The Count's most powerful retainers were dead on the practice ground above us, and his supporters down here were well outnumbered. Two of the Loyalists did for the Countess, and when the last of the rebels fell, six Fae faced me, bewildered and unsure, but full of anger.

I lifted Great Fang, then lowered it and slid it into the scabbard. 'Let there be peace between us, as I wish with your Queen.'

They looked at each other, and inevitably one took the lead. 'What has happened?'

'Peace first, then parley.'

He took the hint, and sheathed his blade. I still wasn't ready to talk, though. Not stuck up here on a horse, I wasn't. 'Where are the grooms?'

'Safe inside. Locked away, but safe.'

'Fetch Flora. Do it now.'

I tugged on Evenstar's reins, turning her towards the mounting block and turning my back on them. It was a calculated risk, and in today's scale of risk, it barely registered. When I turned around, a pale-faced Flora was taking in the decomposing bodies and trying to hold it together. 'A hand, please, Flora. And don't worry, you're all safe now.'

She recognised Evenstar first, then me, and ran over to hold the reins while I dismounted. 'Look after her, and don't worry, the Unicorns and horses are all safe. As is Perci.'

She managed a crooked smile. 'You really think I'd ask after the Unicorns before Perci? Harsh but true.'

She started leading Evenstar away, and I was already marching towards the second roundhouse. 'You, come with me. Open the sídhe and I'll explain everything. Time is of the essence. The rest of you, let out the other grooms and tell one of them to put the kettle on.'

The Fae had no choice but follow me into the roundhouse, and he used his good legs to run past me, taking up a position in front of the doors to the sídhe. 'How can I trust you, Dragonslayer?'

I placed Great Fang carefully on the floor and took out Faith's handkerchief. 'Because I would not take N'hæval into the sídhe, that's why, and because here is the sign of Princess Faithful's submission. I go unarmed. And time is of the essence here.'

He took a closer look, at Great Fang, at the Count's coat, at the handkerchief, and finally at the bandage on my arm. Satisfied, he materialised the doors to the sídhe and pushed them open. I jogged down a ramp into a place that was nothing like the Fair Queen's palace in Galway. Instead of golden halls and secret bowers, this was strictly functional. Same magick, though.

A thump and rush of feet announced the Hlæfdigan, come to see what was happening. Before they could panic, I held up my open hand. 'I come in peace, and in peace I was welcomed.'

There were five of them. A huge number for an out-of-the-way place like this. Very few Counts have even *one* Hlæfdige, so five? The oldest, wearing a tattered summer dress over thermals, bobbed a curtsey. 'We are at your service.'

'Good. I need Amrita on this wound, and I need it fixed.' I turned to the Fae who'd escorted me. 'What's your name?'

'Saerdam Felix. I was made Knight only last week.'

'Congratulations. Well, Saerdam Felix, your first job is to fetch me some of that tea. Nice and strong with two sugars, please. I'm not going anywhere, and I'll talk much better with a drink inside me.'

He ran off, and I was led out of the rough-hewn cavern and into a side-chamber. I stopped at the threshold, astounded. White light flooded out of a well-equipped veterinary surgical room, and the tang of antiseptic hit my nostrils. It hit Scout's too, and he did not like it. He'd clung to my legs since we entered the sídhe and this place was doing his head in. Poor thing. 'Can one of you take him away and feed him?'

The youngest Hlæfdige was delegated, and he reluctantly followed her. The others ran to put a chair next to the operating table and bade me sit. What followed was what you'd expect from a highly skilled group of medical professionals, except for the part where one of them took her top off and expressed Amrita. I looked away at that point.

While they were still prodding and discussing *The knitting*, I said, 'What is it you do here?'

The oldest, who was directing rather than participating, went pale. 'We did not lie, Lord Dragonslayer. We would not. We told your associate everything we know.'

'Associate? Who? When?'

'The little mother. The one with the long Goddess braid.'

'Cordelia?' She nodded. 'When was Cordy here?'

'On the day the last Count died. She came down and demanded to know everything. I think she was looking for something and left unsatisfied. Mind the abductor!'

I went quiet. Cordelia had been inside the sídhe? If I hadn't seen her ride off earlier, I wouldn't have believed it. On the day we'd first faced action together, months ago, she'd already had another agenda. She hadn't said a word about coming in here. Not a thing. Presumably because no one but the Hlæfdigan knew, she thought she'd never be found out. What on earth was she up to? I would swear that her interest in Persephone was recent, and her relationship with Lucas couldn't be that old, either.

Felix arrived, with tea, and I had to put thoughts of Cordelia aside for now. 'We cannot make contact with anyone,' said the Fae. He suddenly looked very worried, and I was no longer the enemy. You could tell that because he had a packet of Jaffa Cakes with him. This boy has a big future.

'We are finished,' announced the Hlæfdige.

'That was quick. Can I use it now?'

'Yes, but be careful. No wrestling of wild boar allowed for a week.'

'I'll try to avoid them. I owe you a debt, and it will be repaid. Thank you. Right, Saerdam Felix, let's find somewhere with a patio heater so that I can smoke, drink this and bring you up to speed.'

31 — Face Off

My message to Felix was simple: hold the line, be patient, and send people to rescue all those horses tied up on the gallops. I did not tell him what my plans were, and he was pleased to have something to do. I had a final thought. 'And put someone on de-icing the Smurf.'

'Would that be the blue helicopter?'

'It would.'

'Then it's a good job we disobeyed the order to disable it.'

'It is, rather.'

Finally, I got the chance to take out my phone. Since the last time I was here, I've switched to a service provider with better coverage in Lakeland. I wasn't going to be streaming movies any time soon, but at least my messages had come through. Hundreds of them, it looked like. Obviously I began with Mina's. Here is a selection:

Matt is innocent. He and Erin's vehicles disabled and blocking access. They are crossing Ullswater by boat when Barney has arrived in police car.

Karina is holding the hunt. She can't do it for long after moonrise.

Matt is co-ordinating other assessors.

Matt has no idea what Cordy's agenda is.

I love you. Take care.

I called Matt, and the man sounded broken to the point where I asked him to put Erin on. 'Where are you now?' I asked her.

'Just got off the boat. Barney's in Patterdale. Here shortly. Matt was on about climbing half way up bloody Helvellyn and trying to roust the Gnomes. I told him to calm down. What should we do?'

'Has he any idea what Cordelia's been interested in?'

'I've asked the same question in fifty different ways. All I can get out of him is that it's his fault for not seeing it. I never did trust her, Conrad. Anyway, all I got was that she was way too interested in old Fae sites, like really old. I think I can see Barney's headlights. What now?'

'Get up to Hartsop and drop Matt off. Then clear out of it.'

'You are joking, aren't you. I'm not gonna clear off and leave Mina in danger. I'd be right off the bridesmaid's list if I did that. On the other hand, unless she sees sense about those dresses, we're all gonna walk.'

I held the phone away and stared at it. Really? Whatever. 'You tell yourself that if you like, Erin. But thanks anyway.'

The next call was to Karina. 'I need a bodyguard of wolves,' I said. 'Purely defensive. I will not be attacking anyone tonight. At least, not at Hartsop.'

'How many?'

'As many as want to come except the nursing mothers, so that's Cara out.'

'And I will lead them,' she stated. It sounded fairly non-negotiable.

'I wouldn't expect anyone else. See you soon.'

One of the most heartening messages was one of the first, and it had come from Natalie Greening. If I'd taken five minutes longer before I was whisked away for fencing practice, things might have turned out very differently. Her first message said: *Have you got a minute, Chief? I think something might be going on at Greendale.* This was followed twenty minutes later by *Something's not right, Chief. Can you call me???* After that, Matt must have taken over.

Word had even reached London. I stubbed out my last cigarette for now and did a few stretches before picking up my belongings and heading for the Smurf. On the way, I called Hannah.

'Who snitched?' I asked her.

'Karina. She was very worried, and had no one else to turn to with you and Mina out of action. I told her I would make some calls, but I was lying. There is literally no one in the Particular who owes me that big a favour. I knew you'd be back in touch soon. I won't keep you, so Hashem guide you.'

'There is one favour. Get hold of Chris Kelly and tell him to stand by his phone. I may need his advice later.'

Horses were returning from the higher plane, and the Smurf positively glowed with magick. It's a good job I've flown at night before. I got to the doors and realised a problem. 'Saerdam Felix! Fetch the youngest Hlæfdige and make it quick. Tell her to wrap up as warm as she can.'

'What for, my lord?'

'I need someone to look after the bloody dog, that's what. I'd leave him here, but he has his uses. Quick.'

We were nearly at ground idle when they got back, and I'd picked the one who'd never flown before, hadn't I? Felix more or less threw her into the cabin and ran off. I didn't bother trying to instruct her on seat-belts and left her to figure it out for herself. Or not. I opened the throttle and started to lift the collective. I don't know whether she screamed or not.

Karina had laid on a nice light show for me at Birk Fell that lit up as soon as I started to cross the lake, and which made landing a cinch. When we were down, I glanced round and found the Hlæfdige sitting on the floor wedged between the seats and cuddling Scout. He didn't seem to mind.

I lowered the throttle and turned round. I pointed at the girl and at the outside. She got the message, though I did have to stop her taking Scout with her. The wolves piled in, led by Alex and with Maria close behind him. There were six in total, and I could feel the magick coming off them in waves. *Please don't Exchange in the air.* It shouldn't be long. I hoped. Karina came last, bow in hand and several quivers of arrows ready.

'Put the headset on!' I shouted.

'No need to shout. I can hear you.'

'Well I can't hear you.'

If she saw the irony in that, she ignored it and put on the headset.

'I've avoided this question, but does anyone know where the actual target is?' I asked her.

'To the west of the village, north of Brothers Water,' she replied crisply. 'There is a Fae bridge over the beck.'

'Flat ground?'

'Just north of the water.'

'Good. Have you flown in a chopper before?'

'No, but that won't be a problem.'

Nothing that Karina could face down is ever a problem. It's the things that won't face her that cause her issues. Unlikely to happen today, though.

'Excellent. Your job is to stop me arriving with more than one four-footed passenger. Got that?'

'I—'

The intercom was off before she could respond.

Flying a helicopter in the dark is very scary. If you aren't scared, you bloody well should be. That doesn't mean it isn't possible, though, and those nice Eurocopter people had done their best to help me out. I let the autopilot take us the few miles to Hartsop village. The night was crisp and clear, and the snow was reflecting all the light in the air. Even so, until the moon came up, I would only be flying manually as a last resort. Which came fairly soon.

Someone had put a marker on the field where I was supposed to land, but there was something going on further down the valley. I disengaged the autopilot and climbed away from the hills that rose on either side of the road.

I slowed down and passed what looked like a major incident. Red and blue lights strobed on the bars above a couple of police cars that appeared to be holding back a convoy of vehicles – 4x4s, a couple of horse transporters and several pickups. This could go very badly wrong very quickly. I did a quick flip and headed back to the marker.

The Smurf has a couple of lights underneath, and I came down very slowly, looking to see who was in the reception committee. When I saw the stoic form of Matt Eldridge getting buffeted around, I dropped faster. By the time I'd finished shutting down, there were half a dozen wolves and one mad dog frolicking in the snow, overseen by Karina.

Matt was burning to apologise and try to put right what Cordelia had done wrong. Was still doing wrong. I went up to him and put my hand on his shoulder. 'Later, Matt. What's going on? Where are they?'

He looked behind him, into the darkness. I could see Lightsticks marking a ghostly bridge, and beyond it a massive bank of trees, black and dense. Within the black curtain, occasional flashes of light told me there was something going on. 'The Queen is holed up in the sídhe, and Princess Faith is being held hostage. Don't worry, Mina is safe, if rather annoyed. She's outside with Countess Bassenthwaite.'

'Good. What the fuck is going on down the road?'

'Barney Smith called up Liz Swindlehurst, and she managed to intercept the Greening convoy. When we got here, Mina sent Erin off to be with Barney.' He tried to smile. 'Mina said that Erin's slot was nailed on, and that she wanted Barney kept safe so that Erin could return the favour. I think that has something to do with weddings.'

'Sounds about right. And the rest of the team?'

He shrugged. 'I didn't know what to do. I told them to head to Ambleside and rendezvous at the School House.'

'You did the right thing. I take it that Liz knows that they can't physically stop the Greenings' hunting party?'

'She does. Alexandra Greening knows that their Plan A has gone up in smoke, so she's waiting to hear what you have to say. I think she might get annoyed if you don't go to her first.'

'Tough. I want you to do the same job as Liz, but do it at the Fae Bridge. If Alex and James Greening turn up in front of you, say that they'll have the Clan to answer to if they cross the bridge.'

'Yes, Chief, but on one condition: you never call me Horatio.'

Was that a joke? I'll say yes, for now. 'Deal.' I turned round. 'Karina, we're going into the woods in search of Mina.'

'What do you want us to do?'

I limped up to her and touched her arm to create a Silence. She flinched at my touch, but didn't break contact. 'You know what to do. I'll follow you.' I broke contact and stood back.

She licked her lips and scanned the area again, looking at it with the eyes of responsibility. 'Alex, guard the Protector. Maria, find Mina. The rest of you scout around.'

Five grey shapes ran lightly over the bridge, their fur starting to glow in the light of the moon that had just crested High Street behind them. I stood aside to let Karina go first, then fell into step behind the Pack's King. A rather bemused Scout was sticking very close to me.

There are Fae Bridges all over the countryside, if you know where to look. Is there a nice looking hill on the other side of a fast flowing beck? Yes? Then you can bet a side of bacon that there will be a convenient bridge in front of it. And if you can see on to higher planes, or if the moon is shining, then you might just spot it. Make sure it's activated before you cross, though.

There was a small gap before the trees hemmed us in, then we were plunged into darkness, and Karina's black outfit almost disappeared. I focused on the wolf in front of her that was tracking Maria, and made no effort to keep quiet. Everyone knew where I was.

After twenty metres of dense undergrowth and twisting around trees, we came to a path, and the wolf broke into a trot for some reason.

'Don't worry,' said Karina. 'That's the *found prey* howl.'

'I'll take your word for it. Good. And that appears to be a Unicorn.'

'Where?'

'Off to the right.'

'Oh. Damn it. I didn't see it.'

'And I couldn't hear the wolf, so that makes us a good team.'

Maria was waiting by a narrower path off the main track that led to a clearing, and in the clearing was a tableau that I desperately wanted to photograph. I also want children at some point, so my camera stayed in my pocket.

Hipponax was happily chewing a bale of hay, and he was being supervised at the end of a lead rope by a most unhappy Mina. Beyond Mina, staying well away from the Unicorn, stood Countess Bassenthwaite. Gone was the country girl look for the Fae Countess, replaced by black armour and a long sword strapped across her back. Guarding the whole scene was the white-banded wolf form of Maria.

'Good. You're here,' said Mina. 'They made me hold this creature because there are no other females around. It smells, and that hay is not helping. Can I give it to someone else?'

I approached gingerly, keeping Mina between me and Hipponax, and gave her a kiss. 'Thank you,' I whispered.

'How is your arm?' she asked.

'Much better. No wrestling wild boar, though.'

'Good.' She stepped away from me, and I stood back to face both her and Bassenthwaite. It was the Fae who spoke first.

'We have a problem. Her Grace is … finding it hard to accept the situation.'

'*Quinctilius Varus, bring me back my legions.*'

That may have been the apposite quotation, but it went down like the only soufflé I've ever cooked. 'Do you think there's any hope of getting inside her head?' I asked.

'Now you're here, probably. If you go inside and talk to her?'

'Not going to happen. I'm not the only one who's here. Karina? Call Erin and tell her to let the convoy up to Hartsop and into the field.'

'Yes, Chief.'

She retreated, and Bassenthwaite did not look happy.

'Here's where we are,' I said. 'My pack will protect me, as will Karina. Matt and Erin will take Mina and Hipponax away, and if I don't see the Queen outside in ten minutes, I'm going back over the bridge to talk tactics with Alexandra Greening. Your Queen has no mounted warriors and no wolves. I'm betting that the Greenings have the Ripleys with them.'

'The sídhe is strong.'

'I'm sure it is. It also contains the only two females of your People. And I control the Hlæfdigan of Sprint Stables. It's up to you to get her out, Megan. I don't want this, I really don't.'

The lupine Alex and Maria turned their heads and stared behind me. After a second, Karina turned, too. 'Engines. The convoy has arrived at the meadow.'

'Go, Megan.'

She ran off through the trees, disappearing into the night.

'I'm glad you are here, Karina,' said Mina with some restraint. 'I'm afraid that I do not know how to tie knots. Would you mind?'

Karina looked at the snow on the ground, and passed me her bow to hold. Hipponax barely looked up as his lead rope was secured – he was one hungry horsey.

I passed back the deadly bow and took Mina's gloved hand. 'Let's go and wait at the front door.' We started walking, our bodyguards before, behind and all around us. I felt deeply protected and also very exposed, a peculiar feeling. Last time I felt like this was when a squad of SAS soldiers escorted a senior officer and me to a Taliban fortress.

'How did the negotiations go?' I asked Mina. 'Any problems?'

Mina looked away, towards where the sídhe must be. 'Time was difficult. She wanted one month, I wanted a year. We compromised on the first full moon after our wedding. Given the circumstances, Megan didn't think any of the other issues would be a problem.' She paused and rearranged her hair inside her hood. 'They were most concerned about Cordelia and Persephone, but as I couldn't add much, they left it.'

'There's more I haven't told you yet. Madeleine was stuck in that tree where Lucas appeared. She's gone to stop them doing something. Or try to.'

'Mmm. About Lucas. They didn't believe it was him. I hope that Faith has convinced them. She should know.'

As we climbed the steep path, lights appeared ahead, and the door to the sídhe manifested in front of us. It was traditional, judging by illustrations I've seen, with great logs framing a simple (but large) pair of wooden doors. They opened as we approached, and a portly male figure appeared, carrying a tray with three golden goblets on it.

'That's Gustav, the Chamberlain,' whispered Mina. 'Only a Queen would take their butler on campaign.'

'You're getting the hang of this magick business, love.'

Gustav approached us and managed the difficult feat of bowing and not spilling a drop. 'Welcome to the ground of the Brotherswater sídhe. Accept this in peace.'

'What does that mean exactly?' said Mina.

'And what's in there?' said Karina. 'I don't want to drink alcohol before a battle.'

'It means we can roam safely and freely outside the doors, but not inside,' I explained.

Gustav had heard all of this and let it pass over him. When I paused, he spoke up. 'I have pleasure in presenting spiced mulled honey. Alcohol free, my lord.'

'Then we are honoured to accept.'

It was as good as it sounded, even if it did leave a sugar coating on my teeth. When I'd finished a cigarette, I looked down into my cup. 'Not much left, Gustav. I'll need to be going soon.'

We were not alone out here. Fae lurked in the woods, and a large Sprite was standing in the open doorway. Gustav looked down at it, and real emotion passed across his face. He barked an order in the Fae language, and the Sprite hopped and flew down the tunnel into the sídhe. 'I am sure she won't be long,' he said to us. 'Or I might need to go and see what the delay is.' He looked into the woods, seeing things I couldn't, and then he spoke to his

People in a voice that Alex Greening could hear across the beck even if she couldn't understand it. Message over, Gustav bowed again. 'We might *all* need to go and see what the delay is.' Around us, the lights grew closer.

Karina had her hand on an arrow. 'Easy,' I said. 'They are no threat to us.'

'I know that,' she replied shortly.

We waited a little more. I took a penultimate drink of my honey and got out my phone. Just before I lifted the golden goblet to my lips for the final time, the Sprite reappeared and gabbled to Gustav.

'My lord and ladies, The Queen of the Borrowdale people approaches,' announced Gustav. He offered us the tray to return the goblets, then he stood aside.

32 — The Matter Before Us

The Red Queen had no trace of red on her, preferring the green and orange of her silks in a cloak that flowed behind her. Her armour was black leather and fizzed with magick, her bearing was regal, and behind her, Knights carried her sword and her helmet. Behind the Knights walked Faith and Megan Bassenthwaite.

The Queen came out and stopped at a respectful distance. 'Well met, Lord Protector.'

'Well met, your grace.' We bowed, and I looked behind her. 'Faith? Would you like to come and check my wound? See if your hard work has paid off?'

I was giving the Red Queen an escape route. If I'd demanded Faith be released, she would have dug her heels in. By way of response, her grace waved a gloved hand, and Faith walked round to join me. I held up my neatly bandaged arm, and she used her Sight to examine the Hlæfdigan's work.

'It is good. I am pleased.'

Faith stepped back behind me. Her blue snowsuit was no longer pristine, but her hair still cascaded down her back in sculpted waves, in stark contrast to the wounds on her face. I had to suppress a smile as a mad idea came to me.

The Red Queen took one more pace forwards. 'It seems that to save the People of Borrowdale, I must submit to a mortal and to a mortal's Judgment. It has happened before, and I have no doubt that it will happen again. It also seems that the future of my People would best be served if they had an extra Queen to look after them. So shall it be.'

'Your grace is wise,' I replied, 'as well as beautiful and magnanimous.'

She acknowledged the praise with an incline of the head. It was time. I took out Great Fang, and the air was filled with the growls of wolves and a collective intake of breath and wonder that whispered through the trees.

The Red Queen of Derwent took the knee and spoke the words. 'I submit to the Lord Protector of the Birkfell Pack, the Dragonslayer Conrad Clarke. All of the Borrowdale People who count me as their Queen also submit, and in due course I will face Nimue's Judgement.' She went one further than Faith had done, and placed her lips on the blade. Mostly I think that this was so that she could taste the Gamekeeper's blood.

When her flesh hit the iron, I was so tempted to twist the blade and inflict on her the damage that had been done to Faith. Even if I become Warden of Salomon's House (not going to happen), I will never has as much power as I do now. This was easy to resist. I'll get my revenge in other ways.

317

'Rise, Red Queen. We have business at the bridge.'

She stood up, and she was different. She had internalised the submission, and it showed in a two millimetre hunch of the shoulders, a five degree pointing in of her feet, a two degree incline of the head and a dozen other micro shifts in her bearing. 'My lord, after Judgement, there will need to be an urgent conversation with the mortals about the Persephone situation. Might I humbly suggest that Princess Faithful bring Hipponax with her?'

'A good idea,' I replied. 'And it's Princess Staveley now. Oh, and Hipponax is hers. A future Queen needs a mount. I'm sure you won't overcharge her on livery bills.'

Faith's eyebrows shot up in wonder. I kept my serious face on for a second, and said, 'Your title is what you deserve, Faith, and Hipponax is yours for services already rendered. Your Judgement, however, is yet to come. Let's go.'

Mina and I led the column down to the Bridge, with Karina and the Red Queen directly behind us. I couldn't see Karina's face, so I don't know how she felt about walking on the same footing as Fae royalty. It will be something to tell her children. If she ever has any. Megan Bassenthwaite led the rest of the People at a suitable distance behind us.

The wolves circled around, sometimes in front, sometimes behind. Except Maria. In her contrary way, she stuck to Mina's side of the track and kept pace with us. As we approached the Fae Bridge, I could see half a dozen figures waiting for us.

The two in Hi-Viz jackets were easy to identify: Barney Smith and Liz Swindlehurst. They were standing aside slightly, and Erin was where you'd expect her to be – next to Barney. A few steps closer, and I could see Matt with his back to us, doing his Horatio impression and keeping Alexandra Greening, James Greening and Stella Ripley at arm's length.

Alex is the leader of the Greening family, even if she shares some of the responsibility with James. Her face was wary around the eyes and otherwise impassive. Matt didn't turn round until he heard footsteps on the bridge.

When I'd crossed over, I turned briefly and said, 'Megan, hold there for now. Send one over with the Queen's blade and helmet, and let Faith pass with Hipponax.' The wolves were already across and had dispersed into the snowy field.

I closed the distance to the others and also beckoned Erin and the mundane law to come closer. 'Erin, put a grade A Silence around us, and if you can haze the visuals, even better.'

'No problem.'

Alexandra Greening decided to get in first. 'Good. You've finally started to earn your outrageous salary. I was quite looking forward digging her out of her bolthole, but now that you've saved us the trouble, let's put her down so that we can all go home and get warm again.'

Matt coughed discreetly and glanced at Erin. 'Yeah,' she said, drawing out the vowel apologetically. 'Sorry, Alex, I may have missed a bit out when I said that Conrad *was going to bring the Fae bitch to Judgement on behalf of the Unions*. I should have added the bit about *and then you*. Sorry.'

Where did *you find her, my lord???*

I almost jumped out of my skin and looked behind me. Had I just received a telepathic message from the Red Queen? Judging by the look on her face, the answer would have to be *yes*. I turned back to face the mortals. James Greening is the politician, and his face gave nothing away except that his brain was working furiously. Alexandra was radiating defiance and Stella Ripley had tipped over into pure hatred. I didn't take the staff of office to be liked, did I?

'James, Alexandra, Stella, you all wanted the Red Queen brought to Judgement in Nimue's name, and so she is. You cannot ask for Judgement for another and not accept it for yourself.'

'The courts will decide,' declared Alex. 'If the plaintiff is still alive.'

I shook my head. 'The bridle is a side issue. You are to face Judgement for your actions tonight.' I lowered my voice and balanced every syllable of what I said next. 'I will not have Pale Horsemen riding on my watch, because that's all you are. You have no more moral right than they did, and you are no less culpable.'

'Defence against the Lawless,' spat Alexandra. 'Allowed and encouraged.'

'Not. On. My. Watch. Period.' I paused. 'You have broken the King's Peace, and you will face Judgement.'

'No.'

'Enough! Either you three submit to Judgement on behalf of both your families and all the mercenaries and vigilantes you've gathered together tonight, or each person here tonight will answer individually.'

She looked at me with incomprehension. 'What do you mean?'

James had twigged. 'You're bluffing,' he told me.

'Mina? Why am I rubbish at bridge?'

'Apart from your mental arithmetic being a continuing disappointment to your mother, you have great difficulty bluffing. And I notice that most of the human forces are still in their vehicles, out of the cold.'

'Do I need to spell it out?' I said.

Stella Ripley spoke for the first time. 'Yes. I want to hear you say it.'

It was time for a shrug. 'As you wish. On my signal, Princess Staveley – she's the one on the Unicorn, by the way – on my signal, she'll charge and cut you three down where you stand. Meanwhile, the Red Queen's people will flood over the bridge and swarm at you. They'll take prisoners where they can. Is that clear enough? You should know, Stella, I promised to burn down your house, and I wasn't bluffing then, was I?'

James and Alexandra looked at Stella, and she shook her head, then lowered her eyes to the ground in defeat. I don't like the woman, and she will now hate me until the day I die, but she is not a psychopath or a narcissist. She wouldn't sentence her family to certain death. Nor would James.

He took his sister's hand. 'The girls are all watching, Alex. They're in the front rank. Jocasta can't even lift a weapon to defend herself.'

'It's come to this?' said Alex. She shook her head, then looked up. 'I accept.'

'As do I,' said James quickly.

'Me also,' added Stella.

'Good. Erin, cancel the Silence. Is Gustav here, Charley?'

'On first name terms, I see,' said Alex. 'Not that this creature has a name.'

I ignored that. A keening cry in Fae echoed over the field, and the portly figure of the Chamberlain rushed over the bridge. I gave him a quick order and stood back to put my fingers in my ears. Mina and Karina did the same.

His chest swelled up like a bullfrog, and like a bullhorn, he addressed the company. 'All parties gather in the centre. The Lord Commissioner will now stand in Judgement.'

His voice was still echoing from the hills when I started to walk towards a suitable spot. I was cold, and tonight was nowhere near finished. This was going to be done, and done right, but I was going to keep the ceremony to a minimum. You could call it genuine field justice.

I planted Great Fang into the snow and stood back. I used a Silence to tell Matt that I wanted the other assessors to come here from Ambleside, then I gave Gustav another order, and he announced who I wanted to join me in the centre. I told Karina how big I wanted the circle around us and left her to organise it, with help from Liz and Barney. They have a fair bit of experience with crowd control. Once Karina had spread the wolves around, most people gave them a wide berth, leaving the interested parties to make their reluctant ways to the middle.

When Jocasta Greening finally got the message that, yes, she really did have to stand with everyone watching her even though she was wearing a pink coat with a bunny on the back, we were ready.

Outside the ring of wolves, the audience had split into the People and the humans, taking a semi-circle each. I couldn't give you numbers, and there were rather more humans and rather fewer Fae than I'd anticipated. Then again, there could be a legion of Fae still hiding in the woods.

The Red Queen was on one side of me, her back to her People, and the three leaders of the humans on the other. Behind them was the mortified Jocasta Greening, and both sides had a Unicorn, Hipponax with Faith and Blenheim with Rowan Sexton. At my back were Matt and Mina. Just before I spoke, Maria sneaked forwards in a crouch and lay down next to Mina. I'd have to have words about that later.

'Tonight, both parties here have conspired to break the King's Peace, as guaranteed by Caledfwlch. We were close to bloodshed on an epic scale. That must not happen again. Here is my Judgement. Both sides will pay a fine of five hundred thousand pounds to the Grand Union before the next full moon. In addition, both sides will each pledge land to the value of ten million pounds to be drawn from all your followers and listed with the Cloister Court as a bond against future behaviour. This bond will expire on the death of the last mortal present. For the personal insult to me, each side will pay fifty thousand pounds.'

I let that sink in for a few seconds and spoke before the murmurs in the crowd could build up. 'Does anyone object to this Judgement?'

'No, my lord,' said the Red Queen. 'Does my portion include Princess Staveley?'

'No. Her Judgement will be pronounced later.'

'As my lord wishes.'

The Greenings and Ripleys didn't have to consent. Now that that they'd submitted to Judgement, their families were safe from attack and could object if they wanted to. Unfortunately for them, and me, the only route of appeal was to Nimue, and she does not like being disturbed: a death sentence awaited the unsuccessful appellant.

There was a whispered conversation under Silence, then James Greening spoke up. 'We accept the Judgement.'

'Good. James and Stella, you may step back. Jocasta, step forwards.' I turned to the Red Queen. 'You attacked an innocent mortal who was living under the King's Peace. You must pay for that.' I turned back to Jocasta and her mother. 'What is your price?'

Jocasta went bright red and looked at her shoes. Her mother's eyebrows shot up. They weren't expecting that. 'The creature can pay our share of the contribution to your wedding fund,' said Alexandra. 'And Keraunós is forfeit if Jo doesn't recover full use of her arm.'

I had expected as much. 'Jocasta? It's you who were hurt. You can name any price, but what your mother has said gives you nothing. No money today and the promise of a Unicorn, but only if you're too hurt to ride it. Are you happy with that?'

Jocasta was beyond *embarrassed* now, and well into *mortified* with a dash of *scared witless*. 'I ... erm, no.'

Her mother finally put her daughter first. 'I will of course put the same amount in trust for her twenty-first birthday, and Keraunós would be sold at auction.'

'Payment with compound interest,' I added.

Alexandra made a lemon face and nodded; Jocasta muttered her agreement.

'Charley? Do you accept?'

'If she allows my People immediate access for healing, then yes. Otherwise, I would be at the mercy of mortal physicians.'

'No,' said Alex.

'Why not, Mum? Faith actually saved my arm! The surgeon said they'd have amputated if it hadn't been preserved "like magic". Why not?'

'Very well.'

'Thank you, Jocasta. I am truly sorry for what you've been through. Go and rest that arm.' As soon as she'd scuttled back to her cousins, I told Stella Ripley and Rowan Sexton plus Blenheim to step forwards. 'Stella Ripley, did you excavate the tomb of the mortal king Urien?'

'Yes.'

The Red Queen couldn't help but make a hiss, and the younger humans flinched at the assault on their ears from a field full of angry Fae.

I nodded slowly. 'Last Sunday, I visited the British Museum. I saw the Parthenon Marbles and I saw the Sutton Hoo treasure. One of those belongs there, and the other does not. How much of Urien's hoard do you still have?'

'About a quarter.'

'Very well. Would the Borrowdale People ruin the house of Ripley by petitioning for the return of every item?'

The Red Queen licked her lips, and we all saw her Fae teeth. The human half flinched back. I saw Karina's hand go to her bow, and she wasn't the only one. The Queen looked from me to Stella and back again. 'Only the sword and the bridle, my lord. And any rings of betrothal.'

'Stella?'

'We have the sword and ring. The bridle you know about.'

'Very well, return those items and sort out the difference with the Greenings. Are you both content?'

'Yes, my lord.'

'Very well, if that will get her off our backs.'

I breathed a huge sigh of relief inside. Because no one was about to die, I didn't have to summon Nimue to get her view on things, and given the issues I'd had earlier, it was a good job. There was one loose end, and then we would be finished.

'Finally, we come to the matter of the Borrowdale Crown Purse.' I looked at Blenheim, and Rowan Sexton stood to attention next to him. 'I am not the race steward, but I will be advising the Clan that the Bridle of Urien was bought in good faith and that the result should stand. Rowan, you did nothing wrong. You deserve the crown. Congratulations.'

Cheering broke out from sections of the human crowd, and Rowan did a tiny little jump for joy. If the Red Queen was bothered, she didn't show it.

'Our business is done,' I announced. 'Alexandra, would you and James do me the honour of a parley with the Red Queen?' I didn't wait for an answer and pressed on. 'All other parties may leave. The Union Assessors will be waiting at the gate to take details, and all other Fae should cross back over the bridge.'

There were a lot of murmurs and mutterings from the human side. They'd get over it. I turned my back on them and limped my way to the bridge. Ahead of me, silver shapes flitted and darted and flowed across the beck.

33 — Towards the Vortex

Gustav was already in position on our side of the Fae Bridge. 'Coffee, my lord? My lady?'

'Can we take you from the Red Queen as part of the final Judgement?' asked Mina.

'If that is what the Lord Protector determines,' replied the ever diplomatic Chamberlain.

'Don't do it, Gustav,' I told him. 'The Red Queen is a much less exacting boss. You wouldn't last five minutes at Elvenham. Thanks for the coffee.'

I took a mug and turned round. Alex Greening was arguing with someone. After a few seconds, she turned her back on him and waved her hand in dismissal. James was already half way to the bridge, and I waited until a smaller circle had formed – Alex, James, the Red Queen, Faith, Mina and me. We didn't bother with a Silence.

'My lord, there is the urgent matter of Persephone and Keraunós to resolve. Not to mention the other assessor,' said the Red Queen.

'Yes, I wondered where Cordelia had got to,' said Alex.

The Red Queen was withering in her response. She might have submitted to *me*, but she was still a Queen of the People. 'I thought you could tell us that, given that you suborned her and allied yourself with enemies of the sídhe.'

'Alex, enough,' I said, to forestall a response. 'We have a situation. Cordelia rode off on Keraunós and took Persephone with her. They were accompanied by the Spirit of Lucas of Innerdale, and...'

Alex had accepted coffee, and immediately choked on it. 'What? Are you mad? Lucas?'

'Yes. He's been lying low, and for a while he was my Familiar. The Familiar Bond was severed violently in Cornwall, and since then he's been wandering freely. Clearly, he's also been in touch with Cordelia. I take you didn't know.'

'I did not! And if I did, I'd have had nothing to do with him. You haven't, have you James?'

He shook his head.

'There's someone else in the picture, too: his daughter.'

It was the Red Queen's turn to be shocked. 'Not possible.'

I took a moment to explain how I'd come to know Maddy, and when I said her full name, I could see dots being joined on their faces, with very different results: concern from the Red Queen and Faith, with complete outrage from James and Alexandra.

It was Alex who spoke first, directing her white hot anger at the Red Queen. 'The Eden Line has come again, and you've latched on to it like the parasite you are! No wonder Persephone won the Waterhead Chase at her age.'

'What do you mean?' I asked.

Alexandra was boiling now. 'The Eden Line are mutants,' she spat. 'Mutants who can take Quicksilver into their blood and turn half-Fae.'

My mind stopped at the first improbability. 'They actually take mercury?'

'Yes. But only if it's fed to them in Fairy Milk. Isn't that right, *Charley*?'

The Red Queen looked serene, which is pretty much the Fae equivalent of *guilty as charged*. 'You just won't accept that we offer things that you mortals cannot, and that we charge a high price for them. What's wrong with that?'

'And if that were the end of the story, it would be a tragedy for Persephone – and her foster family – but that's not the end, is it? We both know what Madeleine did, and if they try to do it again, there could be chaos, and not just in the Particular.'

'It would be unfortunate,' said the Red Queen.

'What would?' I asked, before hostilities could break out again.

Alex answered. 'No one knows exactly, but Madeleine of Innerdale somehow purged herself into the Vortex of Memory at Rydal Water.' She could tell that the only words I understood were *Madeleine* and *Rydal Water*. 'Basically, she poisoned Nimue, and it's taken over a century of collective effort to put it right. Not that this creature lifted a finger to help.'

I held up my hand to forestall the Red Queen. 'How did Maddy end up as a tree at Lunar Hall?'

'You'd have to ask the Sisters that. We assumed she'd run off and lived out her life in secret.'

'You do appear to have a problem, and it would be better if this were stopped before it started,' said the Red Queen as if she were talking about nothing worse than an outbreak of greenfly on her neighbour's roses. 'And don't forget Keraunós. I don't want any harm to come to the Royal Steed.'

Alexandra Greening did not take this at all well.

'*We* have a problem? Let me get this straight: you have been poisoning a young girl. The Commissioner's associate has run off with her. The Commissioner's former Familiar has run off to fix it by poisoning Nimue. The Commissioner's former Chained Spirit has gone with them. I'd say that you are the ones with the problem, and it's not looking good for the

Commissioner right now. He's standing here like a puffed up cockerel because he stopped us doing what's right. All we did was work to bring in new blood, and our allies only wanted...'

She trailed off suddenly, her anger running away. Alexandra Greening had been so focused on the Red Queen and their lifelong mutual hatred that she'd forgotten who was standing on my right. The Greening-Ripley-Gamekeeper alliance had also featured a plot to kill Princess Faith. And Princess Faith was not going to forget that in a hurry.

'How quickly can you get to Rydal Water by Unicorn?' I asked Faith. This had clearly been the Red Queen's plan all along, and it was the best I'd got.

'It's about two leagues by the fastest route. Half an hour now that Hipponax has rested and eaten.'

'Get going and do what you can to hold them up until I get there.'

'Are you going by Smurf?'

I took a deep breath and blew out my cheeks. 'No. Without support on the ground it would be too dangerous, and Lucas knows the Smurf. He flew in it often enough. He could easily lure me into a trap. I'll fly to Windermere Haven and take the car. It's not far.'

'Then I will go with Faith,' said Mina.

What?

'Don't look like that, Conrad,' she said, putting her hand on my arm. 'Faith needs a woman to go with her, and this is not a job for Karina or Erin. And part of this is my fault.'

'Nothing here is your fault.'

'I encouraged you in keeping Lucas secret up here. And Madeleine. You say that Maddy wants to stop them? If you had told Cordelia about Madeleine, would things have got this far? Perhaps I was jealous. I should have seen through Cordelia when you were in Ireland. I should have listened to Erin, who may be as mad as box of frogs but is a good judge of character. I am going with Faith.'

And short of tying her up, I couldn't stop her, so I did what I could. I whistled loudly and shouted, 'Maria!' She wasn't far away, blended into the shadows and the snow. She'd probably heard everything. 'Follow Hipponax. Look after Mina.' The wolf lowered her head slightly in acknowledgement and there was nothing more to be said. I kissed my wife to be and stepped back.

'One question,' said the Red Queen. 'What is Cordelia's interest here? Why has she done this? She must know every door in world of magick will slam closed in her face after tonight. Unless you're going to offer her a job, Alexandra?'

Mina had an idea. 'Your grace, speak truly. Did you have anything to do with the birth of the giant Witch? The one called Raven?'

The Red Queen frowned for a second as the question sank in. She bowed and said, 'My lord, I did not, nor have I ever learnt anything of her origins.'

'This isn't helping,' said Alexandra.

James Greening spoke up for the first time. 'No it isn't. Take me, Conrad. Restoring Nimue has been partly my responsibility. I may be able to help.'

'Too risky,' said Alexandra flatly. 'You're not going to get hurt sorting out the Commissioner's mess.'

'If he dies tonight, we can spit on his grave, Alex, but we'll still have the mess he left behind. I'm going.'

'Then let's go,' I said, pulling out a cigarette for last orders.

The Red Queen had one final request. 'My lord, I crave permission to rescue my Pack. They are still at risk.'

'Of course.'

It was getting dark again in the field. The vehicles had been slowly leaving, taking the Lightsticks with them. I made a couple of final preparations before we left – Karina was to let the Birkfell Pack hunt freely tonight and look after Scout; Erin and Barney would take them back to base. Liz was going to Cairndale to manage the mundane fallout from tonight, and Matt was going to handle the magickal side. Mina, Faith, Hipponax and Maria had already left when I climbed into the Smurf and told James to start talking.

They'd have been alright, if it wasn't for the snow. And for Lucas.

It was exhilarating at first, as Persephone took Keraunós skilfully down into the upper Kent valley, taking one field at a gallop and sailing over the drystone wall at the end. Cordelia barely had to hold on now. Her legs had got stronger and she was able to sense Keraunós's movements almost before they happened and adjust her balance. Her hands were lightly on either side of Perci's waist and the three of them might almost have been one as the Unicorn's hooves dug in for the hard right turn that would parallel the tiny road which led to the tinier hamlet of Kentmere itself. Keraunós took the snow as if it were summer grass, and ahead of them, the last of the daylight glinted off something tall ahead of them. A church spire?

'Why are we slowing down?' said Cordelia.

Perci lifted a hand and pointed at the light. 'That's the Kentmere marker. Old boundary cairn that glows in the first and last rays of sunlight. I've always gone right when I see it and headed back to Sprint Stables.'

They both turned their heads to look at the route they'd have to take. It looked gentle enough to start with, a clear notch in the hills created by one of the Kent's tributaries, but it was featureless with its blanket of snow; the scattered woods, gullies and cairns were getting darker by the second.

The shape of Lucas materialised ahead of them, much fainter than he had been on the practice ground 'What have you stopped for?'

'I've never been that way,' said Perci evenly. 'I was just working out the best route.'

'You've got no choice,' said Lucas. 'Through the village and take the bridges. When you get over the second, keep going and ignore the third. Follow the Old Way into Kirkstone Pass, and keep following the Old Way to Rydal Water. It's a straight line from here.'

Cordy thought that this would be easier said than done. 'What are you going to do? A guide would be really handy right now.'

Lucas was grim. 'We've got away from them for now, but there are many players in this game. Now that we've all shown our hands, they rarely turn out like we expect them.'

'This isn't a game,' said Cordy.

'I know. That's why I'll be waiting for you at the Four Roads Cross. To make sure we don't have company.' He took a moment to stare at Persephone, with love, yes, but also with a hint of triumph in his eyes. 'You'll be human again soon, my girl. We'll get that poison out of you before the longing starts.'

Did he say *we*? Habit of several lifetimes, she supposed.

Lucas raised his hand, wished them luck, and vanished.

'We'll take that gate there and then change,' said Perci, pointing to the right.

'Change?'

'You'll see.'

The Keraunós who landed in the tiny lane was a different beast from the one who took off in the field. Gone was the horn, gone was the gleaming pure white coat. He was still a magnificent stallion, but now he was just a plain grey. He could have been Evenstar's sire. As they trotted into the hamlet,

Cordy wondered if Conrad's horse could actually have been fathered by a Unicorn. She was a little hazy on the specifics, and the experts never spoke about these things.

They had to pull in to someone's property as a tractor came bouncing down the lane, a bale of hay stuck on two prongs and carried at head height – if you were on a horse. The diesel engine roared, and Keraunós backed nervously into a bush. Perci struggled to hold him, and in the tractor's floodlights, the driver passed, open mouthed, then skidded into a ditch. Keraunós's true shape had been momentarily visible. 'Go!' said Cordy, and Perci dug her heels in, urging Keraunós into life.

When he jumped a big hedge into the last field before the trees started, the girls laughed to each other. 'What's he gonna say to his wife, you reckon?' said Perci.

'You think he's got one? Looked a bit gormless to me.'

They shushed each other as they passed a farmhouse, windows aglow and smoke pluming straight into the sky. The wall ahead had broken down, and Keraunós was easily over it. And then they were into the woods, the darkness and the cold. Suddenly it wasn't an adventure any more.

When it took them an hour to find the crest above the Kirkstone Pass, Cordelia had to rally Persephone: the young rider was ready to give up. Perci pulled on the reins and looked into the black trench ahead of them. Two vehicles crawled slowly up the pass, and that was the only light.

'Perhaps the Gamekeeper will become Queen soon, and she can carry on the treatment,' said Perci.

'We are on the greatest Unicorn bred for generations. You won the Waterhead Chase, Perci, and you'd have won the Borrowdale Cup if the Greenings hadn't cheated. We need to shift. We need to find the old ways.' She sighed. 'If he wasn't being held prisoner, Conrad would be useful round about now. He can find Ley lines.'

'Hey, so can Kera, can't you boy? Let's try it.'

He could, and they were soon dropping into the pass. Unfortunately, the Romans had laid the Old Roads with little thought for people following them directly.

At one point, Cordy's phone had started to vibrate in her back pocket. They were going slowly enough for her to get it out without Perci noticing, and she saw several missed calls and messages. From Matt. Shit. It looked like the balloon had gone up, as Conrad might say. From the man himself, there were no messages, but that could just mean he was doing something behind the scenes. She thought of his own personal web and all the strands he could pull on to get little flies like her caught up. She knew the Gnomes were out of the picture until dawn, but that still left him a lot of options. When she thought of Erin, she thought of Barney and of Liz. *Liz, could you organise a trace on Cordy's phone? I'll sort out the paperwork later.* With a stab, Cordelia powered off her phone.

'You're doing great, Perci. We don't have to go over the next one. Let's see if we can follow the sheep round the side. And the moon will be up in a bit. That'll help.'

When they made it around the steep slope above Rydal Water, there were very few parts of Cordelia's body that she could feel any more, and all of those she *could* feel were telling her to jump in a hot bath. Or a snowdrift. One to heal and one to put her out of her misery. She couldn't say that, not to Perci though.

'One more mile and we're there. Just one more mile. Soon be able to speed up.'

'It's icy underfoot here. We'll take it slowly until we get past Rydal Mount.'

And then they could see it glinting in the moonlight: the glassy smoothness of Rydal Water with an extra sheen of magick. Something was already going on down there. Keraunós started to pick up the pace, and Cordelia's heart started pumping again. In the long, slow traverse over the peaks, she'd forgotten what it was like. She held on tight this time, because her legs weren't responding properly any more.

They crossed the empty main road that wound its way north through Grasmere and on to Keswick, and Perci chose a track that looked as if it dead-ended ahead. They were about three-quarters of the way along the water, just by a series of small islands that were starting to pulse with Lux.

'Whoa!' said Perci, suddenly pulling up. Cordelia couldn't cope. In slow motion, she pitched off Keraunós and only managed to cover her head at the last minute. Owww! Bloody rocks.

She was still recovering from the pain in her thigh when the shape in front of her cleared. Keraunós and Perci were moving to a trot, and about to pass on to a higher plane.

'Wait! Where are you...?'

Too late, they were gone from this world, and all that was left behind was Lucas. She waited a second to see if he would offer her a hand up, then she remembered that he was a Spirit. Bugger it. She rolled on to all fours and somehow managed to get herself upright.

'Where in Hell's name have you been?' said Lucas.

'Trying to follow the Old Ways. Where in Hell's name have *you* been? We'd have got here a damn sight quicker if we'd had a proper guide. Where's Perci gone?'

'Out of sight. With a bit of luck, they won't think of looking here. So long as no one's given the game away. You didn't have your phone switched on did you?'

Inside her head, she laughed, but she was too cold and her face was too stiff to laugh out loud. The sight of a Victorian squire talking about mobile phones was so *wrong* that it nearly tipped her into hysterics. The laughter died inside her, and she spoke up. 'I turned it off when Matt messaged me.'

Lucas's shoulders relaxed. 'Well done, girl. I knew I could rely on you to bring my child safely here. And you've earned your reward, right enough.'

'Let me through. I need to know that she's alright.'

'No you don't. She'll be taken care of now she's here. That's all you need to know. Do you want to be reunited with Raven or not? My Helena gave her life for our side of the bargain, and you've delivered yours. The pact is done.'

Cordelia had nothing left. If she didn't get warm soon, she'd need an ambulance. She certainly wasn't about to take on the Spirit of Lucas Innerdale. Raven would warm her, like they'd warmed each other on those long nights keeping vigil at the Homewood. 'Where is she?'

'Hidden in plain sight. As always with the Fae. D'you know the borderlands at Tarn Hows?'

Thanks to Conrad, she'd seen the map, of course. North of the Greenings, south of Clan Skelwith and east of the Sisters' holy places, it was a place of magick, yes, but also of uncertainty. 'I've not been there yet.'

'Then head to Tarn Hows and cast your runes. You'll find her. Perhaps you'll find the Ghost of my Helena, too.'

Lucas's face was set in the grimmest scowl that Cordy had seen on him, and she couldn't think of anything to say any more. 'Right. Thank you, Lucas. I'll … Tell Perci to take care.' It was lame, but it was all she had left.

He nodded. 'Thank you, Cordelia. Take care, and may the Gods walk by your side.'

She turned and walked unsteadily up the track towards the main road. A wide vehicle had been down here since the snow, and there was a shallow tyre track to follow. One foot in front of the other. Up hill. Hwoof. Hard. Nearly there. When she got to the main road, she nearly cried with relief. The tarmac was a godsend after so much fucking snow, even if it was starting to freeze in places.

She steadied her walk, then power-walked, trying to get the blood flowing again. She did, and with the circulation came the pain as nerves thawed out. She had to stop and bend over for a second, just as a lorry thundered through the night towards her. She jumped into the snow at the side of the road and thirty-eight tonnes of Dutch cut flowers roared past. A travesty, yes, but an inspiration, too. She would plant a rose for Raven. An Enchanted rose that existed on all the planes, so that Raven could always see a sign of her love.

She couldn't believe it when the car park appeared in front of her. With a stitch in her side, she limped in to the open space and towards the furthest, darkest corner. Well, that's where she'd have hidden her car if she wanted it to escape attention. And there it was, a little pool of Distraction in the snow. She turned her hand and blew away the magick.

The Fae Knight who'd moved her car had left the keys where she'd asked, behind the driver's side rear wheel, and she took off a glove to press the button. Click. Whirr. Flash. *Please, Goddess, let the door not be frozen shut.* The cabin light came on, she hauled open the door and then she hauled herself into the driving seat, pulling the door closed with her penultimate ounce of strength. The last ounce went on starting the engine and cranking up the heating. She lay back and closed her eyes.

She didn't let go. No matter how much sleep pulled at her, she couldn't drop into the abyss. Not if she wanted to live. She forced herself to look out, and the first thing she saw was the great moon, the eternal feminine. All that would come into her head was *Hey Diddle Diddle, The Cat and the Fiddle,* and she sang it ten times through chattering teeth, then reached into the rucksack waiting for her in the passenger foot well. She grabbed an energy bar and chewed it slowly. Then another. By the time she'd finished that, hot air was starting to emerge from the blowers.

She took off the other glove and flexed her fingers until they could type *Tarn Hows* into the satnav. Now, could she drive? Yes, it seemed she could. She pulled out on to the A591 and gingerly pressed the accelerator, scared of her foot going into spasm and careering her into a wall. She looked right when she passed the lane to Rydal Water. Nothing but blackness. A pair of lights in her mirror told her that one of the local boy racers was on her tail, and she sped up.

She navigated Ambleside successfully, past the entrance to Waterhead Academy, and then she held her breath for no good reason other than that she was entering Gnomish territory. Turn left, follow the road to Hawkshead. Past Skelwith. Breathe out. Out here, there had only been enough traffic to clear one of the lanes, and twice she had to drive into a snowdrift to make enough room for an oncoming vehicle. When she turned off to Tarn Hows, she wondered if *anyone* had been up there.

It seemed they had, and the 4x4 traction just about coped with the climb. Things were going great until she crested the final rise and the tarn appeared in front of her. She unconsciously accelerated and wasn't expecting a sudden bend to the left. The rear wheels finally gave up the ghost, and the car thumped into the side of the road.

Her head hit the side window, but luckily the airbags didn't inflate. The engine had stalled, and it took her ages to get it started – until she realised that the funny noise wasn't a sign of impending breakdown but a gentle hint that she should put her foot on the break before pressing the starter. The ever-helpful satnav said she had less than a quarter of a mile to go, and she gingerly engaged Drive. The onboard computers scratched their heads, shoved power into the wheels, and the car lurched away from the bank with a skid. She tried to correct, and then the wheels got traction and she was on her way again.

The road rose towards a bare-branched wood that shielded the National Trust car park. As good a place as any. She bumped the car over a mound of snow and more or less abandoned it at random. She grabbed her pack, exited and spotted a genuinely open and welcoming ladies toilet. That was going to be a serious relief.

After she'd fastened herself back up, she picked a spot in the lee of a bank where no snow had fallen. She collapsed down to lean against a tree and opened her pack. She felt down to the bottom and took out the box holding the most precious gift she possessed, an Enchanted scarf that Raven had woven herself, and as she'd woven it, Raven had put a little of herself into the weave. It was Cordy's link to Raven's trapped and tortured Spirit.

She must be nearby, somewhere out there in the darkness. Cordy closed her eyes, and this time, she did let her mind empty, getting ready to make the Summoning. She brought alive the magick in the scarf and made a picture of the last time she'd worn it in Raven's company, with the beautiful giant standing behind her as they looked in the mirror.

Soon, Cordelia would no longer be alone. She let her Sight open, then jerked her eyes wide. She wasn't alone. She had company. Four-legged company. Twenty feet in front of her, the yellow eyes of a giant grey wolf stared back.

Where had it come from? The rebel Fae were keeping the Queen's Pack penned in, and it was a physical impossibility for it to have come from Birkfell. The Greening lands began just down the road. Surely they didn't have a Dual Natured Pack? And if they did, why wasn't it with the attack party?

The wolf's big pink tongue emerged and licked its lips. Then the wolf lay down, not once taking its eyes off her.

34 — Inside the Vortex

'You've been damned lucky, is all I'd say.'

James Greening was not impressed by my ability to survive encounters with the Fae, though he saved his real disapproval until after I'd landed the Smurf. Wise man.

It seems that the Fae were at first grateful for human pollution – adding mercury to the countryside during the industrial revolution had made it much easier for them to breed. However, there are limits, and they had (in a rare show of solidarity) declared that they would, henceforth, take out no more mercury than their decomposing bodies put in. Which is why there are rules about what to do when they die. Or are killed by marauding Watch Captains.

James paused in taking me to task for endangering the wildlife. We were about to get in my car, and I'd heard nothing from Mina yet. I probably wouldn't until we got there. He looked over the roof. 'Then again, that's typical of you lot. Leave a trail of destruction with no mind to the world around you. Piers Wetherill was the best of Merlyn's Tower, and you forced him out.'

That was a bit rich coming from a man I'd intercepted at the head of a small army. And as for Piers Wetherill…

I opened the car. 'Get in. And tell me about the Vortex.'

For the ancient creatures, mercury is either essential or fatal. The Nymph of Albion falls into the latter category, and somehow Madeleine had managed to purge the Quicksilver from her body and dump it into Rydal Water, where it had gone straight to the heart of Nimue. Or rather, it had penetrated the Vortex of Memory.

'You lot won't admit it,' he began when the engine had fired. I interrupted him this time.

'Which "lot" would that be, James?'

'Chymists. Salomon's House looks on the Vortices as being the same as Loci Lucis. They're not.'

'I'm only technically a Chymist, but carry on. One sec, something's coming.'

I eased the car on to the road and he continued. 'Nimue is a single being, but she has many centres of power. She's been watching and observing for six thousand years or more, and that's a lot to remember, and one way she does it is by keeping her memories in a Vortex at the bottom of various lakes and rivers. The Vortex for up here is in Rydal Water. One of them, anyway.'

'Right.'

'If you learnt about the essence of magick, you'd understand what a Water Mage does, and why you're an Earth Mage.'

'Do we have time for this? We'll be there in ten minutes, and I need something specific.'

'As far as we can tell, Madeleine walked into Rydal Water and merged herself with Nimue by penetrating the Vortex. It's a risk, but it worked. She walked away free from Quicksilver and left Nimue with what amounts to brain damage. We've been teasing out the mercury ever since. Your Summoning at the Repository did not help matters.'

'So, we need to stop Persephone wading into the lake. Fine. And if she's already started?'

'Then I need time to bring her back and unwind the purge. I may also need industrial quantities of Lux.'

'Who stands to gain from this?' I wondered.

'No one, directly. It's a lose-lose-lose, pretty much. I can only assume that Lucas has a Spirit-sized itch that needs scratching, and that this is the only thing that has kept him going over the last hundred and fifty years. The gods only know how he managed to rope Cordelia into this madness.'

'So, she was already onside with him when you recruited her?'

His response was flat and angry. 'We did not recruit her. That was Lucas. He recruited the Fae, too, and it was them who approached us with the plan for tonight.'

'Tell me about that.'

He pressed his lips together and said nothing. I'd get it out of him later. If we survived.

Neither of us spoke until we were travelling along the side of Rydal Water. 'There's a turn-off ahead, unsignposted. Take it and stop when you're well off the road. Go too far and you'll miss the boundary, and we'll be in the lake.'

I slowed right down and bumped on to the track. This was going to be a bugger to reverse out of. I killed the engine, gloved up and grabbed Great Fang. James was already out and staring at the ground. I joined him, shining a torch over the partly compacted snow.

'Hoofprints,' I said. 'It's a bit of a mess, otherwise.'

'It is.'

I looked further. 'See? There. One or two prints going back the way we came. What does that mean?'

'No idea. I can feel the threshold starting to change. Someone knows we're here. Let's go and see who.'

It was light enough not to need the torch, so I put it away to have both hands free, and we walked down towards the water. After twenty metres, James stopped, and I could feel the magick, too. 'What now?' I asked.

'Can you see *anything* of the magick?'

'Let me open my Third Eye. I'm just getting used to it.'

I did, and the landscape changed dramatically. Instead of murky islands in reed beds, one distinct outcrop shone with Lux. There was a spit of land leading to it, overlaid with the lake water that existed on our level in Mittelgard. And at the centre of the island was a huge cross, easily ten metres high and pulsating like a lighthouse on speed. To get there, we'd have to get past a guardian. A very angry, female guardian who bore a strong resemblance to an older Madeleine.

'Stop there,' said the Spirit.

'In whose name?' said James.

'I am Helena of Innerdale, wife to Lucas, mother of Madeleine and guardian to Persephone of the Eden line.'

I cast my eyes beyond Helena, searching for signs of life on the island. No luck. Too many trees and too much distortion. The guardian worked out what I was up to, and said, 'If you seek your betrothed and your Fae bitch, look elsewhere.'

'That's exactly what I'd expect you to say,' I countered.

'You didn't miss them by more than ten minutes. When I said they could take me on and die trying, or they could get after Cordelia, they soon turned around. And she had a message for you.'

'Oh yes?'

'Said that you had thirty-four stitches in your leg. Said it would mean something.'

'It does. It tells me she's not on the island. You could have sent them on a wild goose chase, of course, but she's not in there.'

'What are you going to do?' James said to me, rather unhelpfully.

'He needs do nothing. It is my turn to act.'

A fourth shape had joined us on the margin of the island. Madeleine was here, and she was closer to manifestation than I'd ever seen her, right down to the muff she was keeping her hands warm in. She looked at me, a knowing look that spoke of shared experiences. 'Mama isn't lying all that much. I saw Father send Cordelia to Tarn Hows, and that's where Mama sent the girls.'

Helena of Innerdale was not pleased to see her daughter. 'Leave it be, Maddy. Persephone is the future now. Your future is all in the past. Isn't that what they say?'

Madeleine glowed even brighter and spoke to me. 'I joined them to protect Persephone. I had no idea they planned another purging. I swear it, Conrad. Persephone will have a good life with the Fae, if we let her. And if you use your influence over the two Queens.'

'He'd be dead in a month if he tried,' declared Helena. 'And then your great-great-grandchild will be mated like one of their mares to preserve their assets. Like they tried to do to you, until we stepped in.'

Madeleine took her hands out of the muff. Her fingers were bare and they'd stopped glowing. She turned to me and lifted her hand. I felt the chill of cold flesh on my face as she stroked my jaw. 'I've been wanting to do that for a long time, Conny. Kiss me.'

She pulled my head down and pressed her lips to mine. I was too shocked at the physicality of her presence to object, and let her lips move against mine as her hand held my head in place. I was about to break it off when she released me and gave me a very private wink. 'Quick!' she said and dashed at the Spirit of her mother, diving into Helena like an Olympic swimmer.

As she moved, she left a trail of sparks behind her, and I followed it. When the two women collided, the trail of sparks became an explosion, and I couldn't see a bloody thing. I put my trust in Maddy and kept going. The surface underneath my feet changed from packed snow to rock, and after a few more paces, I slowed down and stopped, shaking my head to try and get my vision back.

There was no sign of Maddy or Helena behind me, nor of James Greening. Stupid sod had been too slow to react. The bridge was flickering in and out of focus: he might join me or he might not. I turned forwards and realised that Persephone was going to die soon if I didn't do something. She was going to die of exposure.

Almost every muscle of her body was shaking as she approached the water, and I knew that because she was naked. 'Stop! Perci! Stop!' I yelled, and started running towards her.

She appeared not to hear me, and I guessed that the figure of Lucas standing behind her had placed a Silence around them. I needed to get her attention quickly: her skin wasn't turning blue from cold, it was turning silver.

I glanced around the island now that I could see it properly and wondered what the hell to do. The lake shore curved ahead, which meant that Perci was physically close but unless I could walk on water, I wasn't going to get there by running. Away in the woods, the Four Roads Cross stood even taller and glowed even brighter than before, and through the woods were four straight tracks, not at right angles, but slightly askew as the four Old Roads converged and parted, channelling the Lux around the Particular. It would be certain death if I jumped in the lake, so I took the uncertain option, veered right and jumped straight into the Ley line.

Coffee is not a good lining on the stomach, and acid came flooding up my throat as nausea gripped me. All my senses were overloaded from the inside, and I sank to my knees. Out of instinct, I twisted round to put the flow behind me, and wouldn't you know it, that Fae coat deflected a lot of it around me, enough to get my head back.

The only rational thing I could grip on to was the memory of Perci approaching the water. She was over there, to my left. And she needed to know something. I held out my left arm and forced the flood of Lux coming at me to take shape, and the only shape I had in my head was her. I sent it flying out with all the focus I could manage, and then let go. If I blacked out now, it would all be in vain. I lurched up and staggered out of the torrent of power and back into the cold night.

Now *that* was cool. I don't want to try it again, but creating the Glamour of a forty-foot tall Persephone out on the water was quite an achievement. For me. The real Perci was staring at herself and suddenly in no hurry to get her feet wet. I took a breath, forced my clenched muscles to relax, and jogged across the boggy margin to ruin Lucas's party.

'Conrad! You're here!' said Persephone when she saw movement in her peripheral vision.

Lucas had to drop whatever Work he was creating, and turned to face me. All that was now left of the Spirit who had become Scout was willpower and determination, fuelled by hate.

'What's happened?' said Perci. 'How did you escape?'

'I took Faith's submission and we killed them. And then I stopped the war. The Queen and Faith are still alive. You don't have to do this, Persephone.'

'He's lying!' said Lucas. 'Don't listen to him.'

I turned to Persephone. 'How close is he to full physical Manifestation?'

'He hugged me. I felt every muscle,' she replied. That settled it.

I drew my weapon as Lucas drew his, but I didn't draw Great Fang: I drew the other one and shot him. The nervous system he'd just created worked perfectly, and my bullet did its deadly work. Lucas of Innerdale's afterlife of dedication to his wife and his children was over. He wouldn't be coming back from that.

'Conrad!'

I turned, but couldn't bring the gun round in time. The branch in James Greening's hand smashed into my arm, and I dropped the Hammer. It was that or risk discharging it into Perci. He dropped the branch and came at me. After everything I've been through today, my reactions just weren't fast enough, and he knew what he was doing. In a second, I was on my back, and he was reaching into his coat for a weapon.

'Leave him!' screamed Perci. She ran towards us, and James paused to send a blast of magick that sent her sideways into the water. I tried to get my right arm up, but it caught in that bloody coat. The Count would like that: his coat saving me from the Lux, but condemning me to death from the knife in James's hand. He paused and our eyes locked. 'That was a good thing. What you did to Innerdale was a good thing. Thank you. It doesn't make up for siding with the Fae, though. We'll see how long your peace lasts when you're not here to enforce it.'

'You'll regret this,' I said. 'When Mina rips out your eyeballs and serves them to your children on cocktail sticks, you'll remember this moment and regret it.'

'The Clan will deal with her. I'll tell them to make it painless.'

'That will only be the start, James. The M6 will be very busy if anything happens to her.'

'It will be ruled an accident,' he said confidently. 'Now you know why you're going to die, let's get it over with.'

35 — Out of the Centrifuge

Cordelia stared at the wolf, and the wolf stared right back. Cordelia opened her Sight to look at the Dual-Nature creature, and to her shock, it was already looking at her. She had no idea that wolves could have so much magick.

She. The wolf was a she-wolf, and she was blocking Cordelia's attempts to look more closely. Cordy gripped Raven's scarf tightly. So near to her goal, and now she had to deal with a bloody werewolf.

'Over there!' A voice in the distance. A woman's voice. Muffled thuds that Cordy recognised only too well – she'd been listening to them all day, and she knew exactly what sound a Unicorn made when its shoes hit snow. A ripple of speed and the beast emerged from the trees into a patch of moonlight. The rider lifted her head, and the moon picked out the black scar that ran down the face of Princess Faithful. *In the name of the Goddess, how is she here? How is she even alive?*

'I'll tie up Hippo,' said Faith.

Another figure slipped clumsily down from behind the Fae Princess, slipped and fell into the snow with an *Oof*. She got up and dusted herself down, and Cordy didn't need the hood to be lowered to know who it was. The only person who could dress like a penguin and still carry herself like a princess was Mina Desai, and those brown eyes were staring at her, just like the wolf.

Cordelia struggled to get up without dragging Raven's scarf into the muck, but she did it, swaying so much that she needed to lean against the tree to stop from falling down.

Mina picked her way through the deeper piles of snow and stopped at the wolf to squat down and run her fingers through the wolf's fur. Mina looked up. 'In case you didn't recognise her, this is Maria. You met this afternoon. Or was that yesterday? Whatever. It is very rude to speak for the wolf when they cannot, but Maria has given me authority. She is not happy with you, Cordelia. Maria saw you damage Matt's truck, and Erin's. When the panic started, she nearly attacked Matt.'

'What? Why? And is Conrad okay?'

Mina's voice was as dry as the wind coming off the tarn. 'Good of you to ask. No thanks to you, but Conrad was fine when I last saw him. That may have changed, but we'll come back to that.' She ran her tiny fingers (even smaller than Cordy's) through Maria's neck fur again, so delicately that she might have been stroking a baby. 'Maria could not believe that Conrad's partner would betray him, Cordelia. Maria thought that you would only do that to Matt's pickup if Matt was the traitor. When I called to say what was going on, Erin had me on speaker, and Matt was next to her. Maria was on the verge of Exchanging to protect Erin when Erin said, "It's Cordelia. She's trapped us here." Matt had a lucky escape. Or his body did. His heart may be forever broken. Maria doesn't like you for that, either.'

Mina stood up with difficulty and came closer. 'Conrad, with my support, took Faith's submission. We killed your new friends. He took the submission of the Red Queen and he stopped the war. And now he has gone with James to stop the purging.'

'The what?'

'Lucas wants the Persephone child to purge this mercury into Nimue's vortex, or something like that. I leave the magick to the experts. Not that Conrad's an expert. He's just a good man trying to keep a fragile peace that people like you are intent on destroying.'

'The Red Queen deserves it! She's beyond evil. She should be dead.'

Mina opened her arms. 'But she lives. You were a crucial part of all this, Cordelia, but you ran off and left the Greenings and the Innerdales to their business and came here.'

Cordy's mind was as exhausted as her body. Seeing Mina here was almost too much to process, and she hadn't asked the obvious question. 'How did you find me? Is there a tracker on the car?'

She should have checked. She should have bloody checked – she'd seen Conrad do it often enough.

'The Innerdales gave you up to get us away from Rydal Water. Helena fell over herself to sell you down the river.'

'Helena's dead,' said Cordelia flatly.

'Oh no she isn't.' Mina turned her head, and Cordy realised that Faith was standing next to Maria, listening to every word. 'Was that or was that not the Spirit of Helena Innerdale?'

'It was. I should know.'

Like a great ice wall, blocks of Cordelia's life were crashing to the ground and splintering. Soon the darkness would come rushing in. Could she still put everything she had into a Summoning?

'Why, Cordelia? Why did you betray Conrad?'

She knew that she'd run out of road. There was no room for lying or deception any more. And anyway, Mina would understand: in Mina's head, Mina was destined to love Conrad through every reincarnation until they became gods and moved into a bijou celestial mansion, next door but one to Ganesh.

And that reminded Cordelia: she still had a few cards left. If she played them right...

'Raven. I've come for Raven. The Red Queen imprisoned her Spirit. She created her, too, and she called her back to imprison her. Raven is too big for small minds to cope with, and you don't get a smaller mind than a Fae Queen. Raven and I were meant to be together. You understand that. Help me release her. She'll wait. I'll take my punishment, and there are things I can help you with.'

The words had tumbled out of her, and by the end, Mina was looking at Faith with a puzzled expression. Faith raised one eyebrow (the other didn't move because of the scar), and she shrugged helplessly. Cordelia wasn't worried: Faith was so far out of favour at the Red Queen's court that she wouldn't know about Raven.

Mina turned back to Cordelia. 'You think Raven is alive and imprisoned?'

'I know she is. Here. See? This scarf has her Imprint in it, and I'm going to use it to Summon her, then free her.'

Mina shivered in the cold. She had even less fat on her to keep her warm than Cordy did. 'And you have something to offer in exchange?'

'Yes. Roly Quinn's Spirit. Lucas bound it to stop him interfering.'

'The Warden?'

'Yes. Also Persephone's grandfather. He's bound, and the key to unlock him is tattooed on my body. Hidden, of course.'

'Where? The Warden, not the tattoo, I mean.'

They were biting. Good. Cordelia was in with a chance here. 'Oh no. I'll tell you when we find Raven, but I swear on her memory that Roly is penned.'

'What else?'

'I can show you where the secret paths begin in Greendale. I've seen them.'

It was only technically a lie. Cordy knew where the open paths were, so therefore the secret ways must be somewhere else.

Mina sighed and shook her head. 'I'm sorry, Cordelia. So sorry. Raven is dead.'

'No she's not.'

'I have seen far too much death in my life, Cordelia. Raven is gone.'

Cordelia's anger flared. 'You're not a Mage, and you weren't even there. You were back at Pellacombe.'

'Excuse me a moment.'

Cordelia stared in wonder as Mina got out her phone and searched for a number. It didn't take long for the other person to pick up, and a weird robotic voice came over the speaker into the crisp, silent night. 'Ms Desai. Good evening. How may we help you?'

'Hledjolf, thank you. You are on speaker. Could you confirm who you are for Cordelia Kennedy?'

'We are the Dwarf, Hledjolf.'

What on earth was this? Cordelia had never met a Dwarf, but this unnatural creature sounded exactly the way Conrad had described it. And Mina had dealt with the Dwarf on many occasions over the Flint Hoard, so...

'Hledjolf, would you be so kind as to describe the Work in Conrad's bullets in words that a Witch would understand?'

There was a second's pause, then Hledjolf rattled off several combined Charms that made Cordelia's braid lift off the back of her neck. They were *evil*. If anyone but a Watch Captain even had a copy of those, they'd be in trouble. No wonder Conrad's gun felt like that.

Her brain was still processing this when Mina spoke again. 'And could the Witch known as Raven from Glastonbury have survived the discharge?'

Hledjolf didn't hesitate this time. 'With a skin-contact preventive discharge, no human or partly human creature could survive. We have reports on the creature known as Raven, and she was human. Mostly.'

The only sound was the blood rushing in her ears. It couldn't be true. It couldn't.

'It is,' said Mina softly. She was standing next to Cordy now. 'Raven left you twice, Cordelia. Once when she resigned from the Daughters, and again when she picked up the Hammer.'

'What do you mean?'

'She expected you to stay in the Daughters when she resigned. And I think the part of her soul that was hidden from us knew what would happen when she fired the gun. You were right about one thing: she was too big for this world. She's gone. I am so, so sorry.'

It took a few minutes before she realised that Mina had her arm round her, that she had slumped to the ground and that she had let go of Raven's scarf. Mina rocked her like her mother had once done, when she was very, very small. That had stopped soon enough, and Mina stopped, too.

'Which do you want, Cordelia? A public trial and imprisonment in the Esthwaite Rest or permanent self-exile?'

The one was clear enough, but the other? 'Exile?'

'Run away now and leave everything of your old life behind. Including your children. Leave the country and look for peace abroad.'

'Why would you let me do that?'

'Because then Conrad will not have to give evidence. Rick will not have to watch you be sentenced, and your son and your daughter will not have to see what a Limbo Chamber does.'

The shame burned through her. She had to get away from here, that was for certain. Anything to put the humiliation behind her. She knew she'd carry the pain with her everywhere, but if she could get away, the shame at least would fade. 'Exile.'

'We must act quickly. Here. Turn it on.'

Mina had filched her phone from Cordy's pocket while she was comforting her. 'Why?'

'So you can record two quick messages. One for Rick, one for your children. Goodbye, you'll never see me again. That sort of thing. Then unlock the phone and leave it here, along with your Badge of Office. We'll give you a chance to get away, and then we'll "find" them.'

She chose video messages, so they'd see how wretched she'd been. She started with the children. 'Mummy's on the naughty step. I've done something wrong, and I've got to leave. I'm so sorry. Be good for your dad. He's a great dad. You're great kids. I'm sorry.'

To Rick, she said, 'I'll let you decide when to show them the other video. Don't look for me. Just forget me. I'm sorry.'

When she laid down the phone, she realised that of all the betrayals, that one was the worst. Rick had offered her a way back, and she'd rejected it. She didn't even try to stop the tears as she unhooked the filigree raven from her chest and laid it on the ground next to her phone.

She was getting light-headed, and Mina held her hands as she got up again. Held them quite firmly. Faith had come over with a look of concern on her face. 'You look ill, Cordelia,' said the Fae creature. 'Let me give you a hand.'

Faith came up close. Her blue snowsuit was unzipped and she reached inside for something, then put her arm round Cordelia.

'Urgh!'

What was that burning pain in her chest? She looked down and saw the beautifully jewelled handle of a stiletto sticking out from between her ribs. She tried to breathe but couldn't. Faith's superhuman strength was holding her up now, or she'd have collapsed.

Faith leaned in to whisper. 'Won't be long. This was the Red Queen's price for letting me go. I'd have killed you anyway for setting the Gamekeeper on me. That was kind of personal, I'm afraid.'

'And for me too,' added Mina, letting go of her hands. 'But Faith is so much better at these things. I'd rather have seen you die in the Undercroft, actually.'

Cordelia's strength had gone completely, and she saw rather than felt that Faith had lowered her to the ground. The stars were out. She tried to lift her hand to the dagger, but it just flopped a bit. The stars were getting brighter, forming themselves into a tunnel. At the end of the tunnel was a woman, and Cordelia saw the woman turning her back on her. With a spurt of energy, Cordelia gathered her robes and ran after her.

It was quiet everywhere in the woods for a moment. So quiet that the ticking of the cooling engine sounded like a clock. A snort from the Unicorn. Then nothing.

Mina broke the silence. 'She has gone?'

'Gone completely,' replied Faith. 'I wonder if Her Grace will let me keep the dagger when we've finished? Not that I'm planning to steal any more souls, of course, but you never know.'

Mina peered at the body. 'Superb wrist control, Faith. Not a drop of blood. Let's get her in the car.'

'What about the tattoo? Do you think she was telling the truth?'

'We'll look later. Too much risk of getting blood in the car if we strip her here.'

Mina opened the car, and Faith did most of the heavy lifting as they carried the body. Behind them, Maria walked slowly, keeping watch.

When the car and the wolf and the horse creature had all gone, the resident owl stretched her wings and got ready. Now that peace had returned, so would her prey. She waited a moment before flying off into the night. She was annoyed at missing so much good hunting and needed to catch up quickly.

James Greening lifted the dagger and got ready to strike. I opened the virtual valve in my titanium tibia and let the magick flow into my left arm. I am absolutely rubbish at offensive magick. Flies crawling up windows laugh at my attempts to remove them. Now would be a good time for a breakthrough.

I put everything I had into a blast of air to force his arm back, and I amazed myself: he actually noticed. It didn't stop him on its own, but it did make him pause. For a second. Just long enough to dig his right knee harder into my left bicep. And it made him raise his right arm even higher, to get more leverage on the strike. His arm was in the vertical position when icy fingers reached out and grabbed his wrist.

And when I say *icy*, I mean just that. Nimue was standing behind him, and she'd turned her fingers to ice after they clamped on to James Greening. His arm looked like it was going to freeze solid as well.

He cried out with pain as she lifted him, and scrabbled to get on to his feet to relieve the tension. When he was off me, Nimue grabbed his other wrist and spoke. 'Shall I finish him off for you?'

I tried to sit up, and couldn't. Another figure appeared, the naked form of Persephone, and this time she really did look blue. She offered me her hand, and I managed to get to a sitting position. Nimue wouldn't last long like this – a trail of water led back to the lake, and she was already getting blurry round the edges.

'No,' I said. 'Disarm him and hit him over the head. I'll cope. And thank you.'

'Drop it,' she ordered.

'Can't. Arm won't work.'

Nimue relaxed her grip, and the dagger slipped out of his hand. Perci ran to grab it, and threatened him with it. Nimue didn't hit him over the head, she squeezed his left hand so hard he screamed, and she dumped water into his open mouth. He collapsed to the ground, too busy drowning to worry about me any more, and Nimue ran back to the water.

'Perci, we need to get you warm. You'll die if we don't.'

'What about him?'

'I'll deal. Have you any clothes? Quick as you can.'

She chucked the dagger near me and ran off towards the trees. I crawled over to James Greening rather than risk standing. He was busy coughing up water and trying to draw air. I pushed him down on to his front and got out a restraint. Oh. Oh dear. His right hand was a mush of flesh and frozen meat. No point restraining that. I hauled his left hand down and yanked it tight against his left leg, then removed his Artefacts. I patted his pockets for further weapons, and found nothing but his phone. He should be safe for now.

At the edge of the woods, Persephone was struggling into a top layer, and I could see dry base layers underneath. And they were new and clean. Smoke was coming from behind her, and when she twisted to get her arm in a sleeve, I saw a disposable barbecue starting to flare up. There was even a box full of vacuum flasks.

Lucas clearly hadn't brought the stuff here. Probably allies of the Gamekeeper. Just one of many questions. I left Perci to it and returned to the shore, where I bowed low to the figure of Nimue, now fully aquatic and watching me with an amused expression.

'Well met, Lord Guardian,' she said. 'I owe you a personal debt for tonight.'

'I think you've already paid it, my lady.'

'Not in full. I almost didn't bother to help, because I didn't think you could be that stupid.'

'I am capable of all sorts of stupidity when left to my own devices. What did I do wrong?'

'Your left arm was free. You could have reached the Mark.'

'My lady?'

'Touch the Mark of Caledfwlch and bring him forth. You shouldn't have any problems standing next to me.'

Now why didn't I think of that? I touched the pommel of Great Fang and closed my eyes.

'Stop!' shouted the Nymph. 'You need water, foolish mortal.'

When I felt the Mark, this time, I put my hand close to the lake and let my fingers brush the surface. There. There it was. Bloody hell.

I pulled out the sword that has protected Albion for millennia, the blade Caledfwlch, also known as Excalibur. This was the first time I'd touched it in my world, and I knew inside that it only *looked* like a sword made of metal and leather. It was actually a construct of water, air and ice. Still bloody sharp, though. I held it like a dummy for a second, then looked back to where I'd fought James. There was a patch of snow, just where I'd landed. Aah. That would have been enough. Just to make a little blade.

'My lady is gracious.'

'There has been much tonight that I have not seen,' she replied. 'And I am disappointed in James. He worked so hard to free me from the poison. Let this be the last time, Lord Guardian.'

'With Lucas gone, I have hope, my lady.' I breathed in, inhaling Nimue's essence, and that horrible tang setting my teeth on edge had almost completely disappeared. I knew what it was, now: Quicksilver. 'Your Essence has changed, my lady. It no longer savours of Quicksilver. Is the purification complete?'

She was agitated for a second. 'It is not me who has changed, Lord Guardian. It is you. The wound on your arm has inured you to Quicksilver. The purification is not finished.'

Shit. So now I was part Gnome, part Fae and I taste of Dwarf. Why couldn't one of these bloody changes have made my hair grow back? Magick can be a cruel mistress.

I took Caledfwlch and reversed my grip. I plunged it into the shallow water and through to the sand below. 'My lady, today I made a Judgement. I called, but you could not hear.'

Nimue danced on her column of water for a second. 'I heard. She had to die, in confinement or at your hand. You were merciful.'

'Thank you, my lady.'

'Then farewell.'

I limped up to the barbecue and held out my hands to the heat. Perci couldn't, because she'd put gloves on. I closed my eyes and counted to five. Time to move.

There was soup in one flask, still hot after hours out here. And coffee. I poured a mug for Perci and said, 'You did really well there. Thank you. Saved my life.'

'It's me who... who...'

She was starting to shiver badly. I forced her to sit down and put my arm round her shoulder. 'Here's what's going to happen. You're going to get that soup inside you as fast as possible. Then we're going to get help.'

'Soup. Right.'

I only managed half a cigarette and a coffee before the screaming from James got so bad that I wrapped it up. I wondered if Mina had found Cordelia yet, and if there'd be a message waiting for me on the other side of the bridge. I cut the restraint and pushed James ahead, after telling him that he'd either shut up or I'd leave him behind. Perci went first – she was the only one with the magick and the mental capacity to get us over. I left the Unicorn tied to a tree.

My phone was busy receiving messages when it actually rang with a voice call: Grazia Brathay. What?

'Conrad! Thank the Mother. Where are you?'

'Rydal Water. What's up?'

'Gloria's in a bad way. I had to call the paramedics, but she needs surgery, and the M6 is blocked. Bad accident. So bad the air ambulance is there. Can you fly?'

'No, Grazia, but the Smurf can. I should be able to manage a one-way trip to Preston. I've got two more with me, and tell the paramedics not to go anywhere yet.'

Paramedics have strong stomachs. One of the two at the Windermere Haven, however, was only a trainee. He nearly lost his supper when he saw James Greening's hand, or what was left of it. The other one did what he could while a team of hotel guests got Gloria out of the ambulance and into the Smurf. The senior paramedic also told me to leave Persephone in the care of a retired nurse who was on a walking holiday. 'She'll be fine if she has a hot bath now rather than sit in A&E at Preston after a chopper flight.'

Mina *had* messaged: *Still looking. Going to enlist Liz 4 help. We're good.*

I replied: *All done. Flying to Preston. Pray to Ganesh for me. Talk soon and take care.*

I stood by the door and put my arm out to stop Grazia getting in. I summoned a little magick and made a Silence. 'Look, I'm over my hours, I've been in two serious fights and I've done magick that I never thought possible, but I'm sober. Do you still want to risk this?'

'Shut up and fly this fucking thing.'

I took that as a yes.

We beat the official air ambulance to Preston by five minutes, which meant I was told to sling my hook after a hot unload. I got in the air and headed for a nearby airfield that belongs to an aerospace company but is very much part of Britain's defences. I put out a Mayday as I went, and when I emerged from the Smurf, I had my hands held high in the air, as you do when a dozen men and women with assault rifles are pointing them at you.

The sergeant stared, then lifted his weapon and to point it safely at the sky, then shook his head. 'I don't fucking believe it. Conrad Bloody Clarke. What the fuck are you doing here?'

'Long story, Mike.'

He took a good look at me. 'Long story? Tall story more like. Okay, lads. Stand down and escort Squadron Leader Clarke to the interview room.'

'It's reserve Wing Commander now. For when you check me out.'

'Tall story? More like a bleeding fairy story if you're a wing commander.'

36 — Safe Landings

Gloria was safely delivered of a baby boy – Grant. For some reason they decided against naming him after the hero of the hour. There aren't enough Conrads in the world, imho.

Mina was safe, too, but she and Faith were too late to catch Cordelia. She said she'd fill me in when I got back. James Greening was less lucky. They decided to amputate his hand, but he suffered a terrible reaction to the anaesthetic and died from sudden cardiac arrest (which is doctor-speak for "He died but we don't know why yet.").

The RAF regiment were very good to me, as you'd expect. I got food, a shower and a bunk for the night. I also got an early morning call and a polite request to shift myself and my helicopter off their airfield asap.

I had to take a long detour for fuel and a diagnostic test, and it was the middle of the afternoon before I crested the rise and dropped down into the Windermere valley. Mina was waiting for me alone, and I think that was when the reality of Cordelia's betrayal really hit home: I was missing a magickal partner.

Green tufts were sticking through the snow everywhere, and this particular phase of winter was in retreat from an assault by rain and strong winds. In other words, business as usual in the Particular.

We embraced for a long time, squeezing each other to confirm that the kiss we were enjoying wasn't a phantom memory. Drops of rain finally forced us apart, and Mina said, 'I would love to take you to the Cottage and lock the door, but we are expected in the hotel.'

'Who?'

'Gnomes.'

Mina led me to a small lounge with a burning fire and high tea laid out. I recognised some of the cakes from the local bakery, and wasn't surprised to see that Sapphire Gibson was responsible. Very welcome.

'Sapphire is minding the shop,' said George. 'It turns out that Grazia didn't have all the plans in place she thought she did. The guests actually took over last night and again this morning. At least the breakfast cook turned up. Being a nice bunch, they've all left IOUs for their bill.'

Saul had been staring at his phone and his laptop and only grunted when we came in. He typed furiously for a few seconds then closed the lid and put his phone down. 'Well done last night. Both of you. And the rest of your team. The ones that played for our side, anyway.'

He was going to lead with that, was he? It was my fault that Cordelia went psycho on us? I waited until Sapphire had brought the teapot in and left us alone. Not because I didn't want to talk in front of her, but because Saul and George didn't want to. Their problem, not mine.

'Before we get into that, Saul, I wondered if you could explain something James Greening said.'

Saul's eyes narrowed and disappeared into shadows. 'What?'

'When he thought he was about to kill me, he said that you'd look after Mina, and he didn't mean by providing a widow's pension. He meant you'd kill her and make it look like an accident. And then there's the fact that the entire clan was underground last night. Not one member available. I call that turning a blind eye on an industrial scale.'

He thought long and hard before he answered. To his right, George was looking deeply uncomfortable. I'd hit a very raw nerve here. Saul Brathay spread his hands and placed them on his laptop. He was trying to show that he was being open and honest. I would reserve judgement for now.

'We were both played. Lots of people were played. James promised me that you would never be at risk unless you took sides. He promised me that it would be a short, sharp raid to force the Red Queen to come to terms. He never mentioned that Gamekeeper creature or what she'd done. And if you think I'd hurt Mina, you don't know me very well.'

Did I know him? I looked at Mina, and she had her serene face on, the one which says she's above this sort of thing. Which was more likely? That Saul would kill Mina and brush us under the carpet? Or that James thought (wrongly) that Saul would never act against the Greening family? I decided on the latter.

I nodded to show that I accepted the point about Mina. 'Be that as it may, Saul, you still conspired behind my back. Why did you appoint me in that case?'

'My biggest mistake. I'm sorry, Conrad. I'm sorry, Mina. I did it to protect you.' Mina snorted at this point, and I agreed with her. Up on the practice ground, I hadn't felt very protected at all.

Saul lifted his hands in surrender. 'When Alex flaunted the Bridle of Urien in the Derwent's face, and when the Queen attacked Jocasta, it got out of hand. I thought that the Red Queen was the biggest threat to the peace and that we needed direct action to bring her to heel. I didn't think that Alex and James would go for total destruction. They had too much to lose. I was wrong, and I'm sorry. All I wanted was for the situation to be resolved without you taking sides. I was misguided.'

He sat back. It was the biggest *mea culpa* that he'd given in his life, and I wasn't going to get any more than that.

'Good. Thank you for clearing that up, Saul. How do we go forwards?'

George Gibson cleared his throat. 'I don't think it would be in the interests of peace for the Clan's role to become public knowledge. The Unions have to have confidence in Saul's Presidency. For one thing, from what I've heard, the human population is split in two: the majority think you took the Red Queen's side, and only a minority think you acted evenly. A powerful minority, yes – it includes the Sisters of the Water – but a minority nonetheless.'

Saul took over seamlessly. 'Things will really change if that creature actually becomes a new Queen. We haven't had two Queens here since the Middle Ages. Do you think she will?'

'If she doesn't, it won't be because the Red Queen stopped her. I'm confident of that.'

'I wouldn't be, but you know her better than I ever will. What about Cordelia?'

'We should know more later. I'll fill you in.'

'Then we have a basis for the future?' said Saul with a tone of finality.

I looked at Mina. She leaned her elbows on her knees and gave the Indian nod. 'Only if you promise never to go behind the Commissioner's back again.'

'I wouldn't be so stupid,' said Saul.

'Then let us move on,' concluded Mina.

'Good. That tea will be nicely stewed by now. Let's celebrate little Grant with some cake. I wanted to get the other business out of the way before I thanked you for flying Gloria to hospital. It was a very close call, apparently. It would have been the gods' judgement on me if I'd been stuck in the First Mine while my daughter's partner died. For that, I owe you a personal debt. Name your price or bank it.'

Mina spoke quickly. 'I am sure you're expecting a wedding-related request from me. Everyone else seems to, but no. I did not get in that chopper. I do not know what Conrad risked, so it is down to him.' She gave a sly grin. 'After all, the Greenings and the People of Derwent have already made a generous contribution.'

Saul laughed. 'Then I owe you one, Conrad. When you're ready to collect, let me know. So long as it's not that coffee renoir. That's got my name on it.'

When afternoon tea was done, Sapphire caught us as we passed through reception. 'Persephone is awake now, if you want to see her. She's pretty much expecting you.'

'I'll leave you to it,' said Mina. 'Unless…?'

'No, it's fine, love. Won't be long.'

Persephone had the strength of youth and the growing power of Quicksilver magick on her side. She'd make a quick recovery, but she still looked like an undernourished child who's been dumped naked in a freezing lake. Which is what she is.

I asked about her health, and she asked a few questions about the situation, then she turned to the subject she really wanted to avoid: herself.

'Sapphire Gibson's been really good to me,' she began. 'Sort of like, no nonsense but she still really cares? Does that make sense?'

'It does. It's the only way to be when you've got five children under twelve.'

'Wow. She brought her husband in, and he talked me through the magick stuff and what it really meant. Lucas lied and lied to me. He said that the purging was safe and that there was no risk.' She forced herself to look at me. 'You didn't come to save me, did you? You came to protect Nimue.'

'I came to do both, Perci. And you saved me. That warning you shouted saved my life. Thank you.'

'He'd gone mental. You would have put Nimue first, wouldn't you? If you'd been a bit later.'

'Of course not. Nimue can look after herself. She's a big girl. I'm the Commissioner for the living, not the never-alive.' I didn't give her time to wonder whether I was lying (I was), and continued, 'Are you going back to the Torvers to recuperate?'

'Can't. I need to carry on the treatment at Sprint or Borrowdale.'

'Then good luck, Perci. I'm going to want a statement from you about some of the things that have happened. I might get Faith to take it, is that okay?'

'Course. She can still do my treatments, right?'

'She can. For a while, at least.'

She went even quieter for a second. 'I know that Lucas and Helena are gone, and that Cordelia's run off, but what about grandfather?'

'Sorry?'

'The Warden. Roly. He came to see me a few times. He wanted me to go to London and talk to people in Salomon's House. He was dead against what Lucas wanted.'

I was still scratching my head over the first part. 'The Warden was your grandfather?'

'Yes. He hasn't been around recently, though.'

This made sense of something else, but I'll come back to Cordelia's last message later.

I shook my head in wonder. 'It may be a while before you get to see the Warden again, or should I say *The Late Warden* as we've got a new one. But I think I might know a bit more about your ancestry than you do. I think we may be going on a journey soon to meet one of your relatives. I still don't understand how Madeleine fits in to the story.'

'Right. Like that's going to happen. Mum had no relatives. End of.'

'We'll see. Take care.'

After a long shower and some time together, Mina and I got changed to go out. We were swapping the delicate confections of patisserie for the sturdier fare of Ukrainian cuisine tonight.

The taxi dropped us at the Oak Tree, and Zina showed us in to the back half of the restaurant. Matt was already there, and jumped up to abase himself. He looked like a broken man. Again. So soon after losing Harry, this was a huge blow. Erin was trying to comfort him, and Barney was looking on helplessly.

I didn't let Matt speak. I took him in a big hug and said, 'It wasn't your fault, Matt. If anything, it was mine, but mostly it was her. Let's focus on that, eh?'

'And let's focus on the facts,' said Mina, separating Matt from my embrace and guiding him with her hand.

He slumped back into his seat and spoke rapidly. 'I didn't know a thing. Honestly. Nothing.'

Mina sat on one side and Erin on the other. Mina put her hand on Matt's. 'We know. We all know. She fooled me, too, Matt, and for that I may never forgive her, wherever she's got to. We wouldn't even have found her phone and Badge if it hadn't been for Madeleine.'

That was news to me. 'Helena said that it was her who pointed you in that direction.'

'And it was, but we were intercepted by Madeleine before we got there. She said that we should believe her mother, even though Maddy had no idea why they had sent Cordy to Tarn Hows. Probably just to get her out of the way in case she had a change of heart.' She turned to Barney. 'Could you tell us what you and Liz found? We know some of it, but…?'

356

'Erm, right. Yes.' He tried not to go into policeman mode, but couldn't help himself. 'Acting on Mina's information and likely destinations, we discovered the hired BMW in the public car park at Hawkshead. CCTV confirmed that Cordelia abandoned it and disappeared. Shortly afterwards, a van was stolen from a nearby farm. It was recovered from Lancaster Station car park. We didn't bother checking the station CCTV for reasons of Glamour.'

He paused, and I could see him flicking through a mental notebook. 'Analysis of the BMW's satnav showed that it was moved from Lake Cottage when Cordelia was with you at Birk Fell. We looked at the phone she left at Tarn Hows, and there were messages to and from some unknown numbers.'

Erin took over. 'That's right. I had the idea of contacting Countess Bassenthwaite, and they turned out to be the rebels from the Borrowdale People. Including a couple the Red Queen didn't know about.' She went slightly red. 'She's going to pass on any information she learns.'

'After she's tortured them and killed them,' said Matt grimly.

'No torture,' said Mina softly. 'I insisted. Death, I have no control over.'

'And then there's the videos,' said Barney.

'Show me,' said Matt. 'I want to see them.'

'Me too,' I added. 'It's going to be on me to tell Rick what's happened.'

Barney passed me his police issue tablet from under the table. I placed it so that Matt and Mina could see, and ran the clips. We watched a tearful Cordelia, sitting with her back to a tree, telling Rick and her kids that she was sorry and that they would never see her again. No one outside the Particular knew about Cordelia – except Hannah, of course. I was going to fly to Wells on Monday, when the kids were at school, and lay it all out for Rick.

'And then there's the last message,' I said, leaning back and returning Barney's tablet.

When the RAF Regiment had finished with me last night, I'd finally been able to catch up. One of the many messages had been from Cordelia, and she'd sent it straight after recording those videos, according to Barney.

The message said: *I'm sorry, Chief. I hope you get this. I was so wrong. I'm going into exile, but you need to know something. Lucas imprisoned the Spirit of the Warden somewhere. He let me choose the key: RAVENX in Morse code. Don't look for me. Don't blame Matt. Look out for Rick. Cordy.*

I put all of what Barney had told me with what Perci had said this afternoon. The Late Warden needed to be freed, but looking for him was a job for another day, though. Tonight, we had to remind ourselves that we were still alive and to be grateful for that.

When we left, I looked at Matt. It would be a long time, if ever, before he was grateful for anything.

Mina forgave me for flying off to see Rick on Monday. 'I'm sure you didn't come up with this idea just to avoid moving into our new house,' were her grudging words.

She spoke them as I finished loading everything we owned in the Particular into the car. All she had to do was take it out at the other end, all of ten minutes away. I didn't point that out. I kissed her instead, and she waved me off a few minutes later.

The encounter with Rick was as bad as you could imagine, especially as I couldn't answer the main question: *Why????*

The best I could come up with was, 'I think it had something to do with Raven. She'd been asking about her, and she left a scarf behind with her phone. Erin tells me that the scarf had something of Raven's Imprint in it.'

'Such a fucking waste,' was Rick's concluding remark when he dropped me back at the airstrip.

This time there were two figures waiting for me at the Haven, and one of them had four legs. 'Sorry we abandoned you again, lad. And I owe you big time for last week.'

'Arff!'

'That's as maybe,' said Mina. 'He is not dining on steak forever.'

Mina drove us down to Windermere and our rather minimally appointed arts and crafts villa. 'There is so little here because they have problems with hen parties,' she told me. 'But it has a big bath, and for that I will forgive a lot.'

We made ourselves at home on Monday night, and I had a lot planned for Tuesday, including a trip to Cairndale. It seems that Commander Ross believed Liz's explanation for the events of Thursday night, but he wanted me to explain it in person. That was cancelled when I got a message from Hannah in the morning: *Standby for a video call this afternoon. Something's come up.*

We had talked at length over the weekend, and Hannah hadn't hinted that there was anything on the horizon that might concern me. I found out what was going on shortly after we connected on Tuesday afternoon.

'Were your ears burning this morning?' she began.

'It's a lot milder up here today, so no frostbite. And I expect people to talk about me. It befits my station.'

'Ha ha. Your name came up in a private session of the Cloister Court.'

Now I did sit up. 'How come? I thought Marcia hated private sessions.'

Hannah tilted her hand from side to side. 'It was a legal argument, not an open case, so not truly private. Anyway, it started with Saffron.'

'She's not in trouble, is she? I haven't heard anything.'

'Nor has she. Yet. Last week she fined one of Clan Blackrod for misrepresentation in a transaction with the mundane world. The details aren't important, but the Clan decided to appeal the decision, and their point of appeal was to the Lord Guardian of the North.'

That would be me, as appointed by Nimue. For the first time in centuries, however, the Lord Guardian was not also the Deputy Constable. I can see why that would be an issue. It was also at the heart of Heidi Marston's legal action over the election.

'What happened?'

'Judge Bracewell said that it was a crown decision, not a legal matter. And that has caused a big stir. No one wants this to become an issue at the moment. As soon as the decision was announced, I got a call from Doctor Loose. We had lunch together.'

'Weren't you planning that anyway?'

'Next week. This was an emergency. She made me an offer: it seems that Michael Oldcastle has got so far up her northern nostrils that she wants rid of him. In return for my support against Oldcastle, she offered her support to reinstate you as Deputy Constable.'

Wow. I sat back. That was unexpected. 'I can't abandon the Particular.'

'No one wants you to. You had the idea of getting the Commissioner to answer to the Watch. This will make it a lot easier, presuming you can find a replacement Commissioner in the near future.'

'Matt. It has to be a local, and he can do it. Not tomorrow, or next month, but he's the man.'

She nodded. 'You know them. I don't, so whatever you think best. It should be official by the weekend.'

I couldn't resist it. I stood up and saluted. 'It's good to be back, ma'am.'

'Don't start. Oh, who am I kidding? Of course you're going to start.' She returned the salute. 'Now go and tell Mina.'

'She doesn't know?'

I got a dark look in return. 'No. Of course not. I may be her Matron of Honour, but you're my Deputy, and that comes first. Always. Go on, make her day.'

So I did. Mina was one very, very happy fiancée.

There was a huge amount of fallout from "the events of last week". Some are calling it the Peace of Brothers Water, and that's as good a name as any. Not very accurate, especially the *Peace* part, but there you go.

Alexandra Greening made a pilgrimage to Rydal Water and summoned Nimue. Rumour has it that she put her people on standby to, 'Hunt down Conrad Clarke like the rabid dog he is.'

She had then returned from her audience with a grim expression and gone very quiet. I have that on good authority from an eye-witness: Sophie. My spy in the Greening camp had been in the yard when Alexandra came back, hatchet faced and covered in runny mascara (Sophie's words, not mine), and Sophie had watched several important looking people come and go. 'I think they looked relieved,' she told me.

Shortly after, Sophie herself had been summoned to the office, handed a large wadge of cash, told to keep the car, and then been fired on the spot. 'I'd been gonna quit anyway,' Sophie had told me. I didn't ask whether Alex had fixed her makeup before the interview.

On Friday morning, I flew the Smurf down to the tiny hamlet of Staveley in Cartmel, not to be confused with Staveley in Kentdale, the large village between Kendal and Windermere.

The newly re-minted Princess Staveley's sídhe has superb views over Windermere, and most of the mundane infrastructure (road, power etc.) is still in place from when it had been abandoned; it would take a lot longer to rebuild the magickal parts. Faith never told me what her original offence had been, and I never asked. She'd done something to get on the wrong side of the Red Queen and been punished, and now that punishment was over. The Red Queen had returned her lands, and more, and by Friday, Faith had two working lips and very little left of the scar.

We were standing on the old threshold at the top of a path to nowhere. In time it would become the entrance to the sídhe of a new Queen, and the grassy bank behind us would have doors in it. In the meadow that sloped down away from us, a very nervous Sophie was trying to ride Hipponax.

'She'll get there,' said Faith. 'She's good.' Faith whistled and waved, and Sophie dismounted rather than risk riding up the slope.

The young groom brought the Unicorn up to us and grinned from ear to ear. 'He's magnificent. Mega magnificent. Well sick. Are you serious, my lady?'

Faith twitched her lips. The result wasn't what she was aiming for, but like Sophie with the Unicorn, she was getting there. 'Mega serious, Sophie. The position of Head Groom Mundane is yours. It'll mean living at Sprint Stables until this place is up and running, but I wouldn't have anyone else looking after Hippo.'

'Thank you. Thank you so much. And you, Conrad.'

Sophie came to give me a hug, and things could have gone very badly if Faith hadn't grabbed the lead rope from her and steered Hipponax away. Hug finished, Faith handed back the lead rope and told Sophie to take the Unicorn down to the transporter. There were a couple of Squires waiting, the first of Faith's own People, another gift from the Red Queen.

When Sophie was out of earshot, I turned to Faith. 'Right, what's this big confession? Mina said she wouldn't come here, and when I landed there was a message from her saying that you both had something to confess and that it was all true. What's this all about?'

I had a polite, puzzled look on my face, but there was a tiny corner of my heart that was seriously worried. What in Odin's name had they been up to?

Faith was clearly expecting this. 'When we arrived at the Broadwater sídhe – that's the old name for Brothers Water. Did you know?'

'Get on with it.'

The mischievous look was back. 'The Red Queen was a little narked about the situation, obviously, but she soon came round. When she realised that it was only a temporary submission, she started to negotiate. Mostly with me, as it happens. She gave in to Mina's terms fairly quickly.'

'So what was the sticking point?'

'She was very generous, you know, in deed *and* in spirit. All you'd stipulated was that she release me from the People, and why should you be familiar with the terms of separation when a Princess flies the nest? It's not as though there's a course on it at Salomon's House.'

She had a point. New Queens usually come about because the old one has died of natural causes or violently, but a peaceful spawning is not uncommon.

She continued. 'There's a lot to negotiate if we're to live peacefully – land, dowry, spheres of influence and so on. I had to promise not to poach Persephone, for example, and only take Squires, not Knights, into my service. I could have been out on my ear with nothing but a uterus and a Unicorn, you know, but if I wanted the land and the Squires, I had to promise that the First Seed would be yours.'

'Erm. What? Did you just say…?'

'I did. You know what the First Seed is, right?'

'The first sperm donor after you become a Queen, right?'

'*Before.* I can't become a Queen without it. Her Grace thought it was hilarious – I could only complete the change by having sex with a man who famously turned down the Fair Queen of Galway. You'd call that Fae humour, I suppose.'

'I'd call it mean and petty, actually. What happened?'

'I've seen the look in Mina's eyes. I've loved and been loved as a human woman. I knew what she'd say when she found out, and I was right. She said, "Conrad has promised to Faith that she will be Queen. If that means having sex with a Fairy, he will do it, and I'd rather he did it with my blessing. That way, he won't enjoy it."'

I rubbed my chin. No wonder Mina didn't want to talk about it. Pretending it wasn't going to happen was the best way, I suppose. Ah well.

Faith brushed back her hair. 'It's a good job Her Grace taught me patience, Conrad. You've kept me waiting a week to know what the full terms of my submission are.'

'It's about time, then. Shall we?'

We started to walk towards the Smurf, and I remembered a letter from yesterday. 'The Red Queen has submitted a formal proposal for Countess Bassenthwaite and that Count with the mansion on Windermere to seek Changelings. Through official channels, of course.'

'Good. It shows she's completely accepted things. She wouldn't give up Megan's company if there was an alternative. I suppose she'll have to find a new "Megan" now.'

There was still snow on the tops of the fells as we made our way to Ullswater, and if you came from the north, you'd think they were completely covered. As we descended, Faith rudely interrupted my concentration by shouting, 'Oh my god! Is that whatshername? Cathy?'

'Yes, now shut up.'

As well as the whole Pack, Mina, Erin, Karina and Scout were waiting. Plus one. The Hlæfdige I'd stolen from the Sprint Stables sídhe was still here. The Red Queen wouldn't miss her. She had dark brown hair and dark brown eyes, and someone in the People had decided she looked like the character from *Wuthering Heights*. The Hlæfdigen don't get a lot of choices in their life, but I was going to give her one.

When we were down, I said, 'Yours, Faith. If Cathy wants to serve you, that is.'

'She'll jump at the chance,' said Faith confidently. She was right, too.

We were having a feast, to celebrate the Pack's role in the Peace of Brothers Water. And the christening of the new septic tank; the Pack found that more exciting than I did, I'm afraid, but I don't have to live here. Unlike some.

After the fires had been lit and suitable clothing donned, we gathered on the benches. The wolves gave the single-natured a lot of space, but they were there. All listening.

'I've started a new tradition,' I said. 'No more discussing the Pack's future behind closed doors.'

Karina nodded earnestly; naturally I'd asked her first, and she'd agreed. What she didn't know was *why* we were having this discussion.

'I understand you're moving to Kendal, Erin,' I began.

'That's right. Our offer has been accepted. Well, my offer. Barney's going to re-mortgage his house in Barrow as a buy-to-let then buy in, but we needed to move.'

'Congratulations. Cheers.' We lifted the first of many toasts, and I went on. 'Faith, I have a proposal for you. Come what may, I will release you a year and a day after the date of your submission. That is settled.' Faith nodded. 'During that time, I'd like you to take over here, as Madreb, and for Karina to step up to Guardian. Erin's work is done, I think.'

'What...?' said Karina.

'Ooh!' said Erin.

'Go on,' said Faith. 'There's more, isn't there?'

'Yes. You wouldn't be tied here, of course, and Cathy would be here to help and begin your change in due course. Apart from your regular duties, you'd have to find a Mage to take over at the end, and that's a condition. Subject to Karina's agreement, of course.'

'What about me?' said Karina.

She doesn't like change or surprises at the best of times, and I did feel slightly guilty about dropping this on her. I could see the worry and stress descend on her like a cloud coming down on Helvellyn: what would she do? Where would she live? Had she done something wrong?

'Karina, I want to offer you the job of Commissioner's Adjutant. I need a Mage, and you're the one I trust most. You'd be a salaried assessor, of course, and the post is permanent even if something happens to me. For now, there's a small flat over our new rental in Bowness for you.'

'I ... I don't know what to say. You trust me?'

'Actions speak volumes. You faced down the Greenings with me. You would have been in the front line if things had gone pear-shaped.'

'What about the Watch?'

'Mmm. Not up to me, but if you've served as an assessor, how could they say no? In time, of course.'

'Then I'm in.'

Karina is Karina. Having just made a momentous decision, she naturally reverted to what was important in her priorities. 'What about Corin? Did you find anything?'

I gestured to Faith, who answered for me. 'I have spoken to the Red Queen. She knows of Corin, of course, but she gives her word that it was neither her nor any of the Borrowdale People who imprisoned him. It must have happened during an interregnum or during a civil war. There were a few at that time. When she became Queen, Her Grace ignored him. Too much trouble for no reward.' Faith paused and looked closely at Karina. 'If the Lord Protector places you over me, I will serve faithfully as regards the Pack. You can rest assured of that.'

'You'll take the job?' I said, just to confirm it.

'Yes,' said Faith with something approaching a sweet smile. 'And if at the end, some of the Pack want to leave, you won't stop them, will you?'

I pointed to Karina. 'I won't, but she might. Karina will always put the interests of the Pack first. That's why she's Guardian.'

Faith shrugged. 'I understand. Will we be talking in private later, my lord?'

'We will.' I stood up and looked out across the fire. 'Does anyone have anything to say?'

'They've been muttering non-stop,' said Mina.

'Have they?'

Alex and Cara came forwards and knelt down. In front of me. 'You know best, Lord Protector,' said Alex.

Cara nudged him in the ribs and looked up, still on her knees. 'That didn't come out right,' she said. 'What he meant to say was that you have made a wise decision, Lord Protector. That's what you meant, didn't you?'

'Aye. Of course I did. We'll miss the Archer, though.'

'You'll see plenty of me, don't worry,' said Karina. 'For one thing, I imagine that your new Madreb will be needing regular time off.'

'Hey, won't you miss me?' said Erin, half-jokingly.

'Yes, but you'll get a leaving party,' said Alex. 'We'll tell you then whether or not we miss you.'

'Yes. Right. Fine. Carry on, Conrad.'

'I'm done. And very thirsty. I think a lot of toasts are called for.'

At some point after midnight, Mina, Faith, Scout and I wandered up to the Smurf. Partly for privacy and partly because it was here that it all began: we were standing over the spot where Urien had been laid to rest.

'One more thing,' I said to Faith. 'And then the terms are complete.'

'Why is this the first I've heard of it?' said Mina. 'I thought we'd agreed.'

'We did. I kept this one as a surprise. Faith, I was joking about you becoming Mina's handmaiden, and then I had an idea.'

Faith didn't quite believe me. 'I thought I'd just agreed to run a pack of wolves.'

'You did. But for one week in May, I'd like you to be Mina's bodyguard, gofer and hairdresser.'

'Really?' said Faith.

'Really?' said Mina.

'Yes. Especially the bodyguard part.'

'And friend,' said Mina. 'I wouldn't want you to do this out of obligation to Conrad.'

Faith asked a question I should have anticipated. 'What about Princess Birkdale? I don't want to step on her toes.'

Mina waved off the objection. 'She has hundreds of thousands of Instagram followers. She won't see you as competition. So long as you stand behind Chris Kelly for the pictures.'

Faith opened her mouth wide to roar with laughter. 'Thank you, my lord. I accept gladly.'

Faith and I shook on the deal, and she embraced Mina. She also ran her hands through Mina's hair and shook her head. 'I don't know what we're going to do with this.' She grinned and stepped back. 'I'd better go and start learning all those names, hadn't I? Thank you, my lord. You gave me a gift of life, and I find that it is good.' She bowed and jogged off down the track.

'Maria!' I shouted. 'You can come out now!'

A grey shape padded out of the trees.

'How did you know she was there?' said Mina.

'I'm getting better at this magick stuff. And besides, Scout kept looking her way. I'm sure Maria will hide better next time now she knows I can see her.'

Maria came up to Mina, and Mina bent to flick her fingers over Maria's white ruff.

'You two are up to something,' I said. 'You've been giving each other meaningful looks all day.'

Mina carried on stroking. 'Guilty as charged, Conrad. We are planning a wedding surprise, that's all.' She let go of Maria and grinned at me. 'You'll have to wait and see. We might have to change our plans now that Faith is going to be in the picture more. Thank you, Maria. Lottie will wonder where her mother is.'

Maria lowered her head and trotted off, back to the Pack.

Mina and I put our arms round each other, kissed and then looked out towards the lake. The full moon was passed, but enough light filtered down for us to see the water. Right on cue, my phone pinged. He couldn't have timed it better. 'One sec, love,' I said.

I checked to make sure it was him, then opened the link. 'Have a look at this.'

She took the phone, stared and scrolled. 'Why am I interested in a seminar on … Conrad! It can't be, can it? And on the weekend of our wedding!'

She looked at me. 'How did this happen?'

'Stewart McBride thought I might be interested,' I said innocently.

'And I am a six foot tall supermodel. Hah! I shall get to the bottom of this, you mark my words.' Her face turned from wonder to fear. 'But… Will he want to…?'

'You need to talk to your sister in law. I've got her number if you haven't. She'll make him see sense.'

'I have never met her. Or spoken to her.'

'But you will. She wants to come to Clerkswell. She wants to meet her husband's sister. I know that much.'

She passed me back the phone and wiped away some tears.

'A lot's happened since I got back from Ireland,' I said quietly. 'Is this what you imagined when we first kissed, under the mistletoe in prison?'

She squeezed my waist. 'Better than I could ever have dreamed. And this is just the beginning. Imagine what it will be like when we are married.'

***

Conrad and Mina's adventure will continue in Third Eye, due in Spring 2022, and find out what happens next for Karina in the forthcoming novella from Lucy Campbell – Tangled Web.

PAW PRESS

Coming Soon from Paw Press

Third Eye

The Eleventh Book of the King's Watch

By
Mark Hayden

The waiting is over. The day is here. Time to tie the knot. But first...

#TeamConrad is looking forward to the 'Royal Wedding' (as Vicky calls it). Months of preparation have gone into making it something special. 'I want it to be memorable for all the right reasons,' said Mina.

Will she get her wish?
And before the day itself, there is business in Lakeland and London: time to pass on the Commissioner's Baton at Waterhead and see what the new Warden wants at Salomon's House.

There's never a dull moment now that Conrad is back in The King's Watch.

And why not join Conrad's elite group of supporters:

The Merlyn's Tower Irregulars

Visit the Paw Press website and sign up for the Irregulars to receive news of new books, or why not join the Facebook Group? Search FB for *Merlyn's Tower Irregulars.*

Author's Note

Thank you for reading Conrad's latest adventure. I hope that you've enjoyed it. This book is the longest book of the King's Watch so far, mostly because it had to tell both Conrad's story *and* Cordelia's. And I was not happy with Georgina Gibson for blurting out what Chris and Eseld had been up to. If she could have kept her mouth shut a bit longer, there would have been a lot less drama. I am going to ask the players to let me know in advance if there are going to be further revelations.

It gives me great pleasure to finally dedicate one of my books to my niece & my nephew, Jen and Richard. They have had to wait patiently for me to work through their children. A bit like Christmas, really.

If you've followed Conrad through nine books and many novellas, you'll know that sometimes he visits places that are clear for all to see, and sometimes the locations are shrouded by Occulting. Most of the places in this story can be seen from a distance in the Lake District, but you might find it hard to get closer. The Red Queen has put extra warding around Sprint Stables and is not at all happy with the publicity.

There are many reasons for visiting the small but perfectly formed County of Westmorland. If you do, and you buy yourself a copy of the *Wezzy Gezzy*, I'm afraid that you will no longer be able to enter the *Spot the Dog* competition.

Like many local newspapers, the Westmorland Gazette has had its staff slimmed right down, and a competition which requires a human to judge it is too much of an overhead.

If you haven't sampled the novellas that go alongside the King's Watch novels, can I urge you to try Lucy Campbell's stories about Karina. I have thoroughly enjoyed welcoming her into the Paw Press fold and working with her on the first two. There will be at least one more to follow.

Shakespeare said that A good wine deserves a good bush. In other words, a good book deserves a good cover. I'll never be able to prove it, but I strongly believe that The King's Watch would not have been the same without the beautiful covers designed by the Awesome Rachel Lawston.

An additional note of thanks is due to Ian Forsdike for casting his eye over the final draft. Any remaining typos/errors are all mine.

Finally, this book could not have been written without love, support, encouragement and sacrifices from my wife, Anne. It just goes to show how much she loves me that she let me write the first Conrad book even though she hates fantasy novels. She says she now likes them.

Until the next time,
Mark Hayden.

Made in United States
Orlando, FL
15 February 2022

14851174R00225